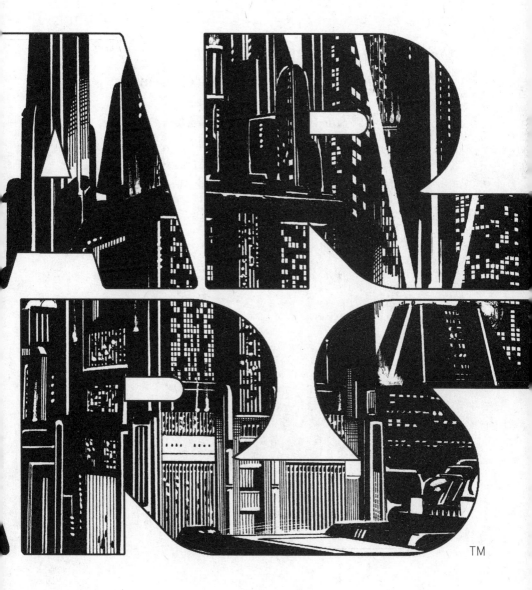

BY ALEXANDER FREED

Star Wars: Battlefront: Twilight Company

Rogue One: A Star Wars Story

Star Wars: Alphabet Squadron

Star Wars: Shadow Fall

Star Wars: Victory's Price

Star Wars: Reign of the Empire: The Mask of Fear

STAR WARS

REIGN
OF THE
EMPIRE
THE MASK OF FEAR

STAR WARS

REIGN OF THE EMPIRE

THE MASK OF FEAR

ALEXANDER FREED

RANDOM HOUSE WORLDS

NEW YORK

Published in the United States by Random House Worlds,
an imprint of Random House,
a division of Penguin Random House LLC, New York.

RANDOM HOUSE is a registered trademark,
and RANDOM HOUSE WORLDS and colophon
are trademarks of Penguin Random House LLC.

Hardback ISBN 978-0-593-72346-3
Ebook ISBN 978-0-593-72347-0

Printed in the United States of America on acid-free paper

randomhousebooks.com

2 4 6 8 9 7 5 3 1

First Edition

Book design by Elizabeth A. D. Eno

To Laura, who gave up Mondays and a road trip to make it happen

THE STAR WARS NOVELS TIMELINE

THE HIGH REPUBLIC

Convergence
The Battle of Jedha
Cataclysm

Light of the Jedi
The Rising Storm
Tempest Runner
The Fallen Star
The Eye of Darkness
Temptation of the Force
Tempest Breaker
Trials of the Jedi

Wayseeker: An Acolyte Novel

Dooku: Jedi Lost
Master and Apprentice
The Living Force

I THE PHANTOM MENACE

Mace Windu: The Glass Abyss

II ATTACK OF THE CLONES

Inquisitor: Rise of the Red Blade
Brotherhood
The Thrawn Ascendancy Trilogy
Dark Disciple: A Clone Wars Novel

III REVENGE OF THE SITH

Reign of the Empire: The Mask of Fear
Catalyst: A Rogue One Novel
Lords of the Sith
Tarkin
Jedi: Battle Scars

SOLO

Thrawn
A New Dawn: A Rebels Novel
Thrawn: Alliances
Thrawn: Treason

ROGUE ONE

IV A NEW HOPE

Battlefront II: Inferno Squad
Heir to the Jedi
Doctor Aphra
Battlefront: Twilight Company

V THE EMPIRE STRIKES BACK

VI RETURN OF THE JEDI

The Princess and the Scoundrel
The Alphabet Squadron Trilogy
The Aftermath Trilogy
Last Shot

Shadow of the Sith
Bloodline
Phasma
Canto Bight

VII THE FORCE AWAKENS

VIII THE LAST JEDI

Resistance Reborn
Galaxy's Edge: Black Spire

IX THE RISE OF SKYWALKER

A long time ago in a galaxy far, far away. . . .

The Jedi rebellion has been foiled. The remaining Jedi will be hunted down and defeated. The attempt on my life has left me scarred and deformed. But I assure you, my resolve has never been stronger. In order to ensure the security and continuing stability, the Republic will be reorganized into the first *Galactic Empire*.

For a safe and secure society . . .

—EMPEROR PALPATINE

So this is how liberty dies, with thunderous applause.

—Padmé Amidala

PART I
DAWN

CHAPTER 1
THE HOLY CITY

The Holy City was chiseled from the stone of the desert, rising into the twilight like an outcast in a wasteland. Its dun walls were coated in the dust of ages, and from afar it had seemed a lifeless place, blessed only in its failure to erode into the sands.

Yet despite the suffocating clinch of antiquity, despite the dying sun that blanched all things on Jedha, the city streets were full of color: red-cloaked shoulders jostled sapphire pauldrons, and jade arms brushed opalescent antennae. Beings of every shape pressed down the cobbled avenues, striding, crawling, marching beneath archways and merchant awnings and listless banners unstirred by the air. The atmosphere was of grief and whispers, but the movement of thousands—the endless footfalls and the rustling of garments—created a susurrus like the harbinger of a storm.

Someone cried, "The Jedi! The Jedi are gone!"

As if it were news. As if they'd vanished from inside their temples that morning and not been slaughtered weeks before in an act of violence and betrayal and cruel vanity.

Dressed in a Ztenortha pilgrim's gray wrappings and stukleather boots, Bail Organa—Bail of House Prestor, Royal Consort to the Queen of Alderaan, father of the crown's heir, once senator of the Galactic Republic and now senator of the Galactic Empire—went unescorted and unrecognized among the mourners, shivering in the winter chill. Deep in the crowd he was mercifully alone, and even the ghosts who pursued him seemed lost in the throng.

The crowd squeezed together. The procession turned a corner and crept down a narrow tunnel. Slits in the primordial brickwork suggested the ruins of a fortress, where hidden soldiers might have once fired upon intruders besieging a keep. Bail kept his head bowed, to keep from stumbling as much as to avoid the prying eyes of hidden cams. The mob was not swift or belligerent, but it possessed the force and inertia of a glacier; to be caught underfoot was to be crushed.

The passage opened into a massive plaza dominated by an upright stone disk on a great dais. In ordinary times, the plaza harbored beggars and criers and would-be prophets, and the structures surrounding it hosted herbal-tea vendors and trinket dealers. It was, Bail had been told, one of eighty-eight such plazas in the Holy City and unremarkable in its sanctity. Only today the beggars and criers and prophets, and the merchants, too, had fled to make room for the endless procession. Of the thousands of mourners in the plaza, perhaps a hundred could squeeze onto the dais, and these crushed together, casting their bodies against the disk and turning it on its axis. Old men pushed on their knees, while a gargantuan Cragmoloid panted and groaned as he leaned onto the disk with his shoulders, eyes cast skyward with a look of profound grief. With every quarter turn, a dozen pilgrims scrambled away and others raced to replace them, ensuring that the grinding of stone went uninterrupted.

Weeping and screaming rose from all quarters, as the mourners were overwhelmed by purpose and ritual. "Master Tiin!" someone called, and another cried, "Sister!" A third began a litany: "Allie! O'ra've! Caladastorous!" But mostly the shouts were wordless and instinctive. Bail was tempted to join the chorus, but his was not a howling grief. Not a grief of helplessness, absent of responsibility. If he called out, his ghosts would hear, and the haunting would resume.

The current carried him inexorably toward the dais. A fainter cry rose in the distance: "Betrayers! Betrayers of the Republic!" Yet no one seemed to notice the protest.

He checked his timepiece and delayed climbing the dais steps as long as he could, but soon he was crammed among the mourners striving to rotate the disk. He found it difficult to gain traction—the dais and the carvings on the disk itself were worn smooth, and only the ubiquitous dust of the Holy City offered any purchase. He began to sweat as he pushed, despite the cold. Yet the disk *was* moving. It seemed that his efforts made no difference, that the larger and stronger mourners were entirely in control, yet he pushed anyway and stone scraped against stone.

To his right was a saffron-skinned Tarsunt in a worker's jacket and rugged pants. The man was broad-shouldered but squat for his kind, and his wedge of a face turned to Bail and nodded slowly. "You should be home," he said, "with your wife and newborn girl."

I should, Bail thought. There was no use denying it. Instead he said, "And you, Admiral, have a fleet to command. But both of us are here."

Each man returned his attention to the disk. It shrieked and moaned, turning another half a meter, before the admiral asked him, "Why?"

"Why am I here?"

"Yes."

Bail tried to shrug, but it was impossible when his arms were straining against the stone. He felt likely to collapse if he unclenched his muscles. "You first," he said.

Bail had never thought of Tarsunts as particularly strong, but the admiral seemed unwearied. It made Bail feel old and feeble—which he supposed he was nowadays. He certainly wasn't *young* anymore.

"I saw the Jedi fight in battle after battle," the admiral said, his body arched against the stone. "Some of their Order I monitored from a distance. Others I dined with, plotted with, shared barracks with in the field. I liked many of them, grew weary of others, but all earned my respect. All were brave and honorable guardians of the Republic.

"I don't suppose that was true of *every* Jedi. No organization is free from corruption, and what the Jedi Council plotted in the end I cannot say. But the actions of the Jedi Knights I met are not darkened by the shadows of their masters. I refuse to believe they were *less* than what they appeared, no matter the Council's treason." He paused a moment, glancing at the crowd. "It seems I am not alone."

"Not alone." Bail had barely enough breath to speak. "But there was no vigil like this on Coruscant."

"Nor on my world," the admiral said, "nor on my brother's, Alsakan. On Corellia, where I was stationed at war's end, crowds in every city burned Jedi in effigy. Some blasted the Order for its betrayal, while others . . . others were merely tired and blamed the Jedi for failing to prevent the war entirely or to win it more swiftly.

"Here on Jedha we appear to be many. A million, perhaps, all visitors to this holy world. But scattered across the galaxy, returned to our home planets, we who remember the Jedi with fondness will be so very few."

A surge of bitterness rose in Bail—directed at the admiral or the Emperor who had ended the Jedi Order or at the people who believed the Emperor's lies. Directed at the stars themselves, for all it really mattered. He put his anger into his arms and pushed. The disk turned another half meter. Someone to Bail's left slipped and fell, and there was a scramble to get the mourner upright.

"Why are you here, Bail?" the admiral asked again. It was not a kind or gentle question. Nor was it impatient, but it brooked no equivocation.

Bail's anger subsided as swiftly as it had risen. What could he tell the admiral? He trusted the man; Bail would never have requested the meeting otherwise. But no single truth seemed sufficient. He could say he'd had Jedi friends, but that seemed trite; say he'd come to honor a woman who'd loved the Jedi dearly and who was now gone; or say it was a way of spitting in the face of the new regime. What he *couldn't* do was admit the horror of what he knew—the secrets that had driven him from home and wife and daughter.

"When I was young," Bail finally said, barely leaning upon the disk as he tried to regain his strength, "I met a Jedi who was involved in a family incident. I didn't know him well—I thought I did, you know how children are—but I looked up to him. I told myself . . ." He remembered the face of his father and his complicated relationship with his grandfather, then hurried to find what mattered for *this* moment. "The Jedi Code meant something more real, more substantial, than any set of rules I'd been taught by the house tutors. I grew up among people who valued outcomes more than methods or people. I told myself that if I couldn't live by Jedi virtues myself, I would assemble my own set to be proud of."

The admiral showed no sign of hearing. Bail returned to pushing. His fingertips clawed at impossibly ancient carvings, dug out microscopic flecks of kyber crystal embedded within the rock, returning glory and power to the universe. The disk, the Stone of First Tears, turned, and as it turned, the spirits of the dead were milled to stardust, changed from restless wraiths into the energy of life, to be reborn in myriad forms. So the legend went.

Bail put no stock in that particular legend, but rituals had potency all the same. He wished he could tap into the power of the stone and feel what the mourners around him seemed to feel, instead of aching and groaning and pitying himself, along with the whole damned galaxy.

Then the full quarter turn was complete, and the admiral pulled Bail away as others rushed to take their places. Bail was part of the procession again, forced to make each step with tired legs.

"What would you ask of me?" the admiral murmured. "Your access to secrets is greater than mine."

Bail shook his head and huddled closer to his companion. He was overheated despite the cold, doubtless stinking of sweat, but they couldn't afford to be heard now. "The intelligence services are stonewalling. I've made demands in public, pleas through back channels, but they aren't listening. The new regime . . ." *Careful, now. Don't scare him off. Don't talk about things he doesn't already know.* "You saw Palpatine's proclamation when he declared himself Emperor. He said the Jedi were corrupt from top to bottom. That was his entire justification for wiping them from existence! But an act like that, to annihilate a whole culture, to put an ancient and respected religion to death—"

"—demands a high bar of proof." The admiral cut him off. "One the

Emperor has not offered, despite his evidence against individual wrong-doers. I concur, but *you* sit on the Senate Intelligence Oversight Committee. I say again, your access—"

"My access *should* be greater than yours. But times are changing, my friend. The intelligence services may accommodate an admiral when they won't give a senator a polite word. I don't expect you to work miracles, but you and I would both like to see the regime's evidence against the Jedi in full. Even if Palpatine's already signed their death warrant."

The admiral grunted and nodded. "Signed the warrant and carried out the sentence." He appeared to consider the request. "You'll promise a full and public hearing?"

"If it's within my power."

"I'll make the inquiries and call in favors owed. We'll see if it does any good—even those who worked alongside the Jedi have become embittered toward the Order. But ask for nothing else, and attach my name to none of it. The military cannot be drawn into political affairs, especially with the peace as tentative as it is."

"More than fair." More than Bail had expected, as well. He hoped his expression conveyed appreciation and not merely surprise.

They shuffled forward and left the Stone of First Tears, departing the dais. The procession's route would continue for a kilometer, though Bail could already see tributaries spilling into side streets as mourners returned to their lodgings or visited the temples and churches of sympathetic sects. Bail believed at first that his conversation with the admiral was over, but the man stuck close to him—closer than even the crowding required—and spoke again: "There is another question I'd like answered. Another truth that the new regime has obscured."

"Tell me."

The admiral was silent awhile, but when he spoke his voice was resolved. "Why did the Jedi Council do what it did? Why did the masters attempt to assassinate Supreme Chancellor Palpatine? Regardless of whether any Jedi *beyond* that inner circle was involved, the question remains, and it troubles me. What did they hope to gain? How could the righteous fall so far, with none outside their ranks suspecting?

"Were I in your position," the admiral went on, "*that* is what would concern me most. I can only serve my superiors. *You* are a senator, and you serve the interests of your people."

He waited for Bail to answer, but Bail did not speak. Then the admiral began to separate himself from Bail, pushing forward meter by meter to overtake the procession's natural pace. Bail did not pursue. It was best if they weren't seen together, and who could say who was watching in the depths of the Holy City?

Still, the admiral's questions had been wise and thoughtful. They were also ones Bail had answered to his own satisfaction the day the Jedi had died. Supreme Chancellor Palpatine—the man who had declared himself Emperor—had committed greater and darker crimes and been possessed of more terrible ambitions than anyone had predicted. The Jedi had learned the truth and, for better or worse, had taken it upon themselves to stop a warmonger, a child slayer, a monster. They had failed.

That had been the end of the Jedi.

Bail *knew* these things. His friends and allies among the Jedi Order had told him, and he had incriminated himself helping them to find safety in the far reaches of the galaxy. But he had no evidence, let alone proof. All he could do to exorcise his ghosts was clear the names of the dead and hope for a better tomorrow.

Perhaps then he could look at his wife and daughter and believe he had done his duty. Even if he had failed to do *enough*.

He walked on, away from the plaza and into narrow streets bordered by crumbling towers, until a rumble of thunder shook him from his reverie. He was puzzled until he saw the crowd shift nervously around him and he heard sharper wails, desperate cries from somewhere in the distance. He looked behind him and saw a shock wave ripple through the throng as those far behind pushed forward faster, away from whatever horror they had encountered.

The crowd began to run.

In an instant there was chaos. Mourners fell, trampled by other mourners. People called out for one another, cried for help from anyone who would hear. Bail was shoved ahead, jostled, and though he tried to catch hold of a hand rising from the cobblestones and aid some poor soul, he was swept away by the tide, and all he could do was fight to stay upright. Something—an elbow, perhaps—boxed him in one ear and left him reeling. He was turned around and battered, tried to ward off the barrage of bodies and shield his face, then somehow turned again and ran with the others. The road channeled them forward. There was nowhere to escape to.

How long it went on he wasn't sure. He had impressions of pain, of his body—weak from the task of rotating the stone—being dashed against flesh and chitin and ancient brickwork. For a while, he wrapped his arm around the shoulders of an elderly woman—whether coaxing her forward or leaning on her for support, he was uncertain. He tried to do what he could. He could do very little.

Later, sitting in the dust of a dead-end alcove too small to be called an alley, he laughed bleakly and wiped the blood from his face. He listened to news feeds about a bomber, someone determined to follow the lead of the Empire and wipe the Jedi and all their supporters from the galaxy, and he tried not to think about the people he'd seen crushed in the stampede. He felt filthy, tainted by death and his own exhilaration at fighting for life. He felt unworthy of his daughter—the last gift of another dead friend. The gift of a woman who'd died along with the Jedi, and who'd known a Jedi's love.

He felt unworthy of the Jedi. Their burden was nonetheless his. It had to be, lest it become Leia's. He was her father, not her mentor or guardian, and he would do anything to carry that weight himself.

CHAPTER 2
REGENERATION

What surprised Soujen most was how quickly the war had ended. That and the Jedi, but the Jedi had never been important in the grand scheme of things.

He'd watched the war's end from a somnolent state, his neural pathways stimulated to induce a so-called "slow sleep" as the pod fed him news feeds and intercepted communiqués. He dreamed of Separatist fleets besieging Republic worlds, mechanical armies landing on planets untouched by conflict for millennia. He imagined workers cheering in the droid factories and freedom fighters in the Rhanipur Belt fluttering in celebration, all of them relieved that the terrible deal the Separatist Confederacy had made—the choice to sell itself to corporate masters in return for a chance at self-determination—had proved wise.

Yet his dreams hadn't ended there. Phantasms had cascaded over his unconscious mind, revealing the Republic's ruthless assassination of Separatist military leadership. He'd watched armies crumble with their commanders gone. In his state of slow sleep, he'd been unsure what was real data and what were his own nightmares. Had a billion or more droids all gone dormant at once? Had the Executive Council surrendered or been slaughtered by the Jedi mystics?

That last one didn't matter. The Jedi were gone now, the Republic's self-proclaimed guardians massacred when they'd sought to overthrow their own government amid the chaos. Thus wounded, the Republic, too, had died, and from its ashes now rose a Galactic Empire. Soujen saw that the war was well and truly over and that nothing could ever be set right.

That it happened at all wasn't surprising. But no one—not Soujen Vak-Nhalis and not his makers—had expected it to happen so *fast*.

⁄⁄⁄

How long had it been since the war's end? Why hadn't someone retrieved him? His cybernetic implants might have told him, but in the slow sleep he found his interest diminished. For Soujen there was peace in dreams and nightmares—a sapping of rage that left him resigned, if not content.

A vague sense of motion reached him inside his pod, along with fever chills and an almost ecstatic exhaustion. He did check his implants then, and the pod's computer reported that his slow sleep was ending. He began to hear noises—actual noises transmitted via eardrum instead of implants—and after a while he recognized them. The sound of screaming was distorted by the fluid barrier, muffled by the pod, but it was familiar. He smiled.

Then he was awake, heaving his body upright. He shivered as a chemical bath poured off his arms, spilled over the pod's sides, and drummed onto a metal floor. He smelled soap and remembered to breathe, vaulted out of the pod, and allowed the stabilizers drilled into his knees' dermal plating to restore his balance and prevent him from toppling. The pod had kept his muscles from atrophying, but it would take him some moments to remember how to stand and walk. He'd been warned of as much.

Someone was shouting in the next room. Soujen surveyed his surroundings, taking in bulkheads and straps and temperature control units, filthy walls and dim lights. He was in a cargo bay, and though the world seemed half a dream, he was confident he was someplace he'd never been before—a fact that was not inherently concerning, though by the oscillations underfoot and the whiff of acrid smoke, he concluded that whatever ship he was aboard was damaged and listing. He wondered whether his pod had been programmed to release him in the event of its imminent destruction.

He narrowed his focus to the open doorway as a flash of crimson light illuminated an outer passage. Blasterfire, along with more screams.

A figure stumbled into view. One of the galaxy's countless humans, but this one was notable for the weeping red blisters covering her face. She looked surprised to see Soujen and coughed wetly before staggering toward Soujen's pod.

His thoughts remained placid even as his dual hearts beat swiftly and his muscles tensed. The immediate threat was reassuring—danger reduced the scope of his decision-making. He did not need to dwell upon where he was. He suspected the woman had been affected by a bioweapon—maybe a nerve agent, noncontagious and slow-acting. What she wanted from his pod was a mystery, but he'd seen enough people dying in pain to know rationality fled with life.

He would've killed her—out of mercy or prudence, he couldn't honestly say—yet her pursuer did the job first, dropping her with a shot to the back. Soujen instinctively stepped out of the newcomer's line of fire, but the man was inside the cargo bay and adjusting his aim before Soujen had shifted more than a meter.

"Stop!" the man called.

As Soujen braced to leap, the man snapped two more bolts from his rifle. The air sizzled with blue light, and Soujen felt heat over his shoulder, watched error codes waterfall over his field of view and obstruct his natural sight as his implants rebooted.

That surprised him—no one had ever damaged his implants before. As his vision cleared, he listened to the man say again, "Stop."

The man held his weapon—a clone-army carbine, its black metal scratched and scarred—with the ease of a trained soldier. He appeared wary but not tense. "You felt it?" the man asked. "Ion output is four times standard. Plays havoc with augs and machine parts."

Soujen looked from the weapon to the man's face. This being, too, was human—dark-haired and dark-skinned, scarred as his blaster. Somewhere beneath the callus of violence might have been a relatively young man, but Soujen couldn't be sure. Among his own kind, among the Alvadorjian clans, Soujen could have judged the weathering of scalp plating or the eyespots on neck and throat—the colorful whorls and dots that spread with age, serving no purpose but to designate wisdom.

"I felt it," Soujen said, because answering bought him time. The deck quaked. He could no longer smell the chemical fires over the char and fluids of the woman, whose body slumped by the pod.

"Do you know?" the man asked. "About the Empire?"

Soujen judged his distance from the man. Six meters. Easy enough to cross, but with Soujen's balance still off and his implants still resetting from the ion blast, he put his odds of living at no better than fifty-fifty.

The man was laughing. "I know that look. You're deciding how to kill me."

"I am," Soujen said. He'd never been much of a liar.

"Then we'll postpone the speeches. I know what you are. I know how you came to be here and why these pirates took you." The man gestured with one hand at the body or the pod. His weapon remained level. "You can come with me, or you can go down with the ship."

Soujen weighed his options. The deck bucked again, and he heard metal tear somewhere above.

"I'll go with you," he said.

The man squinted and smiled as if to say, *I know a rascal like you won't stop trying to kill me.* Soujen's uncle had smiled that way when Soujen had tried to sneak sweets.

They left the cargo hold together, performing a cautious waltz so that neither left the other's sight. Out in the hallway, smoke billowed from side passages while maintenance panels sparked. The passage was broad but low-ceilinged, laid with tracks and rails for ultrawide loading vehicles.

"Old Krezchak's crew has been busy, pillaging every Separatist installation in eight sectors," the man said. "Pity we couldn't cut a deal with him. Pity he wouldn't surrender his ship and cargo. But don't pity the pirate himself." The man gestured toward a corpse splayed out on the deck. *Old Krezchak,* Soujen assumed, though the name meant nothing.

The man kept talking. "Wherever he found you, the Separatists must have left quite the stash. He was taking you to Kafrene—said he planned to sell his plunder at auction, blasters and chemicals and your pod. Pod was priced at a million credits, but I doubt he appreciated what he had."

That fit with what little Soujen knew, and it explained what had happened to the woman contaminated by the bioweapon. He confirmed his databank was functional again and checked his records—there had been nearly a kiloliter of gray Syntox in storage with him, enough poison to putrefy a small moon. If pirates had found him, if they hadn't understood what they were looting when they hauled the pod and the Syntox canisters aboard the ship . . .

It was a waste, Soujen thought. *Such a waste.*

They moved through the vessel as rapidly as caution allowed. The screams and the blasterfire had tapered off, and roaring flames nearly drowned out the distressed whine of the ship's reactor. The two reached a hatch, and Soujen's companion crouched to open it. Chill air rushed out, smelling of sweat and alien beasts instead of murder and catastrophe.

"You don't ask a lot of questions," the man said.

"No."

"You're like one of their droids."

This irked Soujen, but he didn't object. He'd been called far worse.

"You have a name?" the man asked.

"I'm Hress," Soujen said.

The lie was unnecessary. Still, after such a short time awake, he'd barely returned to himself. This man had earned nothing of Soujen's soul or his person—the child of the Nahasta clan, the Alvadorjian, the son of his fathers, the sacrifice in a galaxy of injustice. The truth of Soujen was quiescent while matters of life and death were addressed.

It was not for a doomed stranger to awaken that truth.

The man descended first, dropping over the lip of the hatch in an unbroken motion. Soujen saw his opportunity and half rolled, half dived into the hatch in an effort to land on his adversary's spine. Instead his hands and feet landed hard on another deck. He launched forward, his body low and compact, while his eyes adjusted to the brighter light in a cleaner, utilitarian corridor. Breaking the man's back would've made things simple, but he had other resources ready to deploy.

He felt like a fool when he saw, clamped to the bulkhead beside him, the metal cylinder of an ion mine. He drew breath to curse and attempted to sprint past the device, but he knew he'd been beaten as he saw the flash. His readouts died. As his brain returned to hibernation, he heard, "My name is Saw Gerrera, and you belong in your grave."

CHAPTER 3
THE POLITICS
OF VICTORY

From the proper angle, you couldn't see the wreckage at all. The fires had long since gone cold, and smoke and dust no longer darkened the air. The skyscrapers encircling the impact points obscured any sight lines from outside the zone, as long as you didn't take a flier directly above. There wasn't even much missing from the skyline up close—a spire here, a platform there, but the landmarks were all intact. The endless cityscape dominated Coruscant as it had since time immemorial, with its thousands of stacked levels resting on a rocky core that no one had much thought about in living memory.

Ride a shuttle past the air barricades, though, past the New Neimoidia Hotel and taking a left at the Museum of Contemporary Music (closed until further notice), and the damage became apparent. Coruscant was wounded, and though newly erected skybridges and gravity platforms patched the upper levels, beneath there was only ruin. The sturdier buildings had been sheared in half by falling debris, leaving the innards of offices and apartments and shops clearly visible. Less fortunate structures had been smashed to pieces—their highest stories devastated and their lower stories pulverized as the highest stories crumpled inward. The farther down into Coruscant you went, the more complete the destruction became. Three weeks after the disaster, no one had even cleared the debris from the housing blocks and clinics four hundred levels beneath the apex.

Mon Mothma had seen the HoloNet images. But to be surrounded by the devastation, swallowed by the canyon gouged into the cityscape, was something freshly appalling.

The others felt it, too. "Where are the ships?" someone asked. "I thought there would be ships." But one of their guides from the Engineer Corps answered that the *ships* had broken apart as they'd fallen through the atmosphere. There were no intact hulls littering the surface, but dig far enough into the rubble and one could locate the cockpit of a Republic starfighter or the wings of a Separatist vulture droid. Someone else inquired about torpedo casings and turbolaser fire, and a military representative explained that—conspiracy theories aside—there had been no direct Separatist bombardment. The Siege of Coruscant had left tens of thousands dead and millions without homes, but it hadn't been an attack meant to terrorize and cow the civilian population. The Separatists' focus had been on the capitol and on the capture of the Supreme Chancellor. Everything else, every other horror, was collateral damage.

Surrounded by a dozen fellow senators and three times as many aides, engineers, medics, press officials, and thoroughly vetted refugees, Mon peered over the railing of the airspeeder as it surveyed the rehabilitation zone. Unseen particles stung her eyes as she watched construction droids and rescue workers scuttle among the ruins—no longer urgent and exhausted, but diligent and resigned. She only half listened to the patter around her but made sure to set her expression to something compassionate and somber. She shook her head in disbelief at the proper moments. Her dismay at what she witnessed was genuine, yet she'd learned long ago that what one *felt* was a poor substitute for what one clearly and concisely *expressed*. Being ready for cams and holofeeds at all times was a habit of mind.

The airspeeder let them off at a broken tram station, where another crowd waited. Mon smiled (neither too cheerfully nor too sadly) and ventured forth to clasp hands and listen to stories and offer consolation and, when the opportunity arose, make points to the droid reporter tailing her about the need for galaxy-wide relief efforts. She managed not to laugh, even when a rodent-faced safety inspector made one of the bleakest jokes she'd ever heard, and she managed to say something she hoped wasn't overly trite to the woman begging for help locating her missing child.

Next to the tragedy, the droid's inquiries felt farcical. "I have a question about the Delegation of Two Thousand," the machine said as the group proceeded into the hollowed-out shell of a skyscraper. "Senator Mothma, you were one of the organizers and primary sponsors of the delegation. You signed a petition toward the end of the war—"

That's not a question, Mon thought, not looking at the droid.

"—a petition that called on the Supreme Chancellor to immediately surrender his emergency powers and begin peace talks with the Separatists. Looking back, how do you justify undermining military leadership and requesting concessions for war criminals on the eve of our greatest victory?"

The droid was a freshly programmed agent of the new Imperial news service. Mon found the attack as predictable as it was absurd. She'd grown used to being portrayed as a coward and a turncoat for her efforts to counter the chancellor's power grabs, and her answer was well practiced: "Had the chancellor chosen to keep the Senate fully informed of his military strategy, the delegation might have approached the matter differently. As it was, I had to fulfill my vow to the Republic—as I gladly uphold my vows to the Empire today. Relitigating the past instead of focusing on rebuilding is the last thing we need."

It was a statement that would win no supporters, but it wouldn't lose her any, either. Galaxy-wide, her approval ratings were poor and falling. On Chandrila, where it mattered most, she had middling approval and years to go until she was up for re-election. She had all the wiggle room she needed.

"Is it true you've considered resigning?"

"No," she said.

"Rumor is that you've been approached about speakership of the Chandrilan House of Representatives—"

"No."

Not true, and I wouldn't be tempted if it were. She was hard-pressed, but she'd never been one to surrender when the odds were against her. Or to pursue local planetary politics.

The droid hadn't finished. "About those vows . . . you were *arrested* on charges of disloyalty shortly after Palpatine's ascension to Galactic Emperor. How can the public believe your dedication to the Empire is sincere?"

This attack, too, was predictable, and Mon should have parried it casually, made an unctuous statement about how the Empire represented an evolution of the Republic, argued that the Emperor represented the highest of Republic ideals, so how could her loyalty have changed? She could've quibbled with the use of *arrested,* pointing out that it was officially a *detention* authorized by a mid-level lackey and that no charges had been brought—but the words wouldn't come. Her body resisted, back in the coffin again, and her smile feigned to conceal an irrational panic. "My dedication is what it's always been," she said, hearing the sharpness in her tone.

"Given your sympathy for the Separatist cause, what can the public expect as former Separatist worlds are reintegrated into the Imperial Senate? Many Coruscanti citizens are justifiably concerned about handing power to enemy agents who devastated this world only weeks ago—"

Was she still smiling? Her face was turning numb, and the droid's words were difficult to hear. She started to say something—anything, she'd *find* something to say—when another voice broke in.

"I think that's hardly an appropriate question, given the circumstances. The victims of the Siege of Coruscant deserve our full attention. We can talk about *politics* back at the Senate."

And with that, the droid's attention shifted, and Mon felt a mixture of rage and embarrassment and utter relief. She'd been rescued, which was a miracle. She'd *needed* rescue, which was humiliating.

Her savior—now exchanging niceties with the droid as he gently corralled the machine toward a gaggle of engineers—was Lud Marroi, longtime senator from Cerberon, a broad-faced and dark-haired gen-

tleman who gave off the air of a dignified older statesman despite being
two years younger than Mon. She tried to relax her shoulders and shake
the tension of the moment, watching Lud until a construction worker
approached her. She made herself smile thoughtfully again, turn to the
woman, and shake off memories of her arrest and her coffin cell and her
torture, to focus on someone else's troubles.

///

As usual, their conversation began with sports. That was what they'd
first bonded over a decade ago: Negotiating a tariff overhaul had drained
them to exhaustion, and they'd slipped out of the Senate chambers to a
smashball bar. They'd spent hours watching holos of no-name Expansion Region teams battling it out in the Overring Tournament. They'd
sipped wine, later switched to brandy, and learned to laugh at each
other.

Until that day, Mon had loathed Lud Marroi. She'd openly scorned
his affected parochial speech; his hypocritical protectionism (always
right for his homeworld, never for the rest of the Republic); and, worse,
his willingness to court voters who were isolationist at best and xeno-
phobic at worst. Yet gradually she'd begun to like the man. She'd found
herself looking forward to sharing committee assignments with him
and discussing smashball and ceramics. With some reluctance, she'd
realized they'd become friends.

She'd asked Lud once about his retrograde policies. He'd turned very
serious and told her, "The Cerberon worlds orbit a black hole that will
one day swallow us up. Every time my constituents look at the sky,
they're reminded of our culture's mortality. I like being a senator. I like
talking and I like the attention, same as you. But I take my people seriously, and I don't blame them for their anger or their grief. I represent
them, and they deserve to be heard."

Mon hadn't been persuaded, but she'd begun to recognize a secondary foundation to their friendship: In a Senate full of members appointed by their worlds' leaders, who'd inherited their roles by birthright

or who'd gone through every imaginable trial *except* a democratic election, Mon and Lud understood what it meant to campaign and compromise and await the verdict of their people. They understood who they
spoke for, and they felt the weight of that responsibility.

Now the tour of the wreckage was over, and they'd slipped away from
press and aides and come to a droid-staffed diner on Coruscant's 4643rd
level, where no one seemed likely to recognize them and no one would
care if they did.

"I can't keep up with it," Mon said. She took a bite of orobird eggshells.
The bitterness balanced the sweet goo of the yolks. "Every day, there's
some new edict from the grand vizier citing the Emperor's authority,
judicial appointments no one asked for, an entirely new plan for this regional governor business . . . they're deliberately burying us in changes."

"You're giving them too much credit." Lud gestured with his sausage
before biting off one end. "They're boys given the keys to the store,
making up rules as they go. Once the adults corral them, it'll all settle
down, and half those edicts will end up like . . ." He frowned, bringing
his bushy eyebrows together in a V. It was a look Mon had come to find
charming, though she knew better than to say it. "Law on the records so
absurdly archaic it's become unenforceable."

"On Chandrila, offworlders are technically trespassers if they enter
public property without a parkland visa." She held a hand up, beck-
oned for silence as she took another bite. "You can't tell me you're
comfortable with all this. Forget the 'Galactic Empire' business. The
renaming is symbolism—it's theater. It's absurd and offensive, and it
has absolutely no power without the law to back it up. But this effort to
intimidate senators and steal authority for the executive . . . even you,
Lud—"

"Yes, *even me,* thank you." He shook his head. "I hear you, Mon, I do.
From your vantage—and mine, too—we see an administration riding
the coattails of victory to grab wildly at every level of power. But would
you be half as outraged if you agreed with Palpatine's policies?"

"Which policies? The kleptocratic economics or the populist scare-
mongering?"

Lud grunted. She rarely baited him so, but she was in a mood.

"Then forget the job for a second," he said. "Forget you're obsessed with the inner workings of government and spend your days with people who share your obsession. When you're riding to your office, or—or sitting in a diner eating food that was clearly thawed moments ago—tell me things don't feel more *normal* than they have in ages. Tell me you're not finally catching your breath with the war over."

He was right, in the way Lud occasionally *was* right. For three years, they'd all lived in existential fear. Now Palpatine was Emperor and the galaxy was changing and it was all so *ordinary*. Except when it wasn't.

She considered arguing with him. She could say that just because Palpatine's desire for greater authority wasn't new didn't mean it wasn't a profound threat. He would say that executive authority had always waxed and waned within the Republic. She would call the Emergency Powers Act unprecedented. He would point out that the act was popular and had been in place throughout the war years, and the Senate still functioned just fine. She would say that things were different now, that during wartime the struggle for power had been a secondary concern compared with securing the peace, but now—

But now there *was* peace. And they were back to that.

"I do feel like I'm catching my breath," she finally said. "But only so I can run again."

"The war changed us all," Lud said. "It makes it difficult to trust."

There was nothing teasing in his tone.

They ate awhile in silence, and eventually Mon asked whether he'd seen the latest from the grand vizier. Lud delicately changed the topic, and she took the hint, putting talk of government aside so they could debate trends in neo-revivalist architecture and other rubbish neither of them knew much about. They finished their meals and split the bill and debated sharing a taxi before deciding no, better not—the media had caught them together once today already. *Once* was fine, *once* was a demonstration of nonpartisan fair-mindedness, but *twice* showed an absence of conviction and a willingness to fraternize with the enemy. Politics was a strange game, but they both knew the rules.

They were standing under the diner's awning, watching the first fat drops of rain smack on the boulevard, when Lud—quiet and almost casual—said, "The intelligence services. They're monitoring us. Looking for signs of disloyalty."

The rain smelled like oil. The droplets on the street traced the labyrinthine outlines of the skyscrapers and platforms that blocked the clouds. "'Monitoring' how?"

"*Monitoring.* More than tracking headlines and less than tailing every Senate staffer and tapping every call. I don't know how serious they are or how many senators they really care about or what they're doing with the information they collect. I don't know whether the Imperial Security Bureau or Imperial Intelligence is taking lead. I don't even know what they define as *disloyalty*. But given your involvement with the Delegation of Two Thousand and—"

The arrest, she thought, but he said only, "—the incident after the Emperor's ascension, I imagine you're high on somebody's list."

"That's madness," she said softly. "Who told you this?"

"A friend in the administration. No one directly involved, and if he had the details, he wouldn't tell me, but I trust his sources and I'm not giving you his name. I just want you to be careful what you say and where. No joking about strangling Palpatine or wishing—"

"What are they *thinking*?" she said. Lud had access to the right people, and he'd never been one to spread rumors—Mon had no reason to doubt him. Yet the whole notion was loathsome and baffling. "Is the grand vizier afraid of a revolt inside the Senate? Who's running things over there?"

"I'm not sure even they know. Everyone's vying to become intelligence chief, which is why this is probably some half-baked initiative from an ambitious ladder climber. I genuinely don't believe you're in danger, Mon. But I don't want that to change, either."

"Palpatine wants to be a dictator. He wants to be a dictator, and everyone else wants to prove their loyalty in case he gets his wish." She wasn't really talking to Lud anymore, but she had to say it aloud.

"They'll settle down," Lud said. "Boys with the keys to the store. Just wait it out."

That done, she unlocked a desk drawer and withdrew a datapad. She skimmed over the list displayed. Among the more recent entries were:

Grand Vizier Amedda's "true Imperial citizens" speech

Relief shipments to Cato Neimoidia held up

Replacement of Republic credits with Imperial credits (now with unspecified "safeguards")

Renaming of Parnarosis 3

Chief justice administrator fired after eight days on the job

The war was over. Instead of people dying by the millions every day, there was stability—and surely the price was low enough. What did it matter if ruined sectors of Cato Neimoidia were denied water and medicine because one of Palpatine's rivals publicly mocked the new regime? What did it matter if the memory of the dead Jedi Master Parnarosis was wiped from the galaxy and replaced by a dead warlord? Could Mon say she'd never voted for worse?

Most of it, she imagined, wasn't even Palpatine. It was his damned supporters, imperialist true believers and power-hungry sycophants alike, who were running wild. Who knew what Palpatine wanted— besides loyalty and control—when he'd given his beasts free rein?

She paused and added a new line to the document:

Spying on political enemies

The end of the war was a miracle, but the price of peace was growing. They'd been an Empire for less than a month. How long would they be tallying the cost?

CHAPTER 4
AN AUDACIOUS
REFUGE

"For these reasons and others, I am requesting a full investigation of the circumstances surrounding the attempt on then–Supreme Chancellor Palpatine's life, the directive designating the Jedi Order as a hostile actor, the clone army's tactical protocols for confronting Jedi combatants, and the treatment of juvenile Jedi combatants by our military. This investigation must be carried out by an independent coalition of military and civilian justice workers, or else the Senate will be forced to step in."

Bail barely heard the words as he spoke them. He stood on a supervisor's perch overlooking the factory floor of Eurivos HoloDynamics—one of the last manufacturing companies still operating on Coruscant's upper levels, and a fitting venue for what he'd promised would be a speech on industrial revitalization. The sparse audience shifted uneasily beneath sheets of glittering mirrors and prisms waiting to be laser-cut into holoprojector components. Some present were employees drafted into attendance—mostly nonhuman, working-class, and politically nonaligned. Some were Alderaanian expatriates come to see their homeworld's senator out of enthusiasm or curiosity. A few were fervent imperialists, believers in Palpatine's new order who were bent on chronicling the acts of politicians they deemed opponents of the administration. There were no representatives of the press, but a few cam droids floated listlessly about the floor.

Bail felt frustration, irritation, bitterness at the reception, but no surprise. He tried to keep his tone both dignified and pointed as he went on. "No one can expect perfect understanding amid the fog of war. I imagine the administration"—he lied grudgingly, but there were norms to follow—"acquitted itself admirably in those chaotic final days of the war. But it is important to know exactly *what* our leaders knew and *when,* and to hold them accountable. With the military continuing to hunt any Jedi on the run, we must arm ourselves with the information to judge which tactics are wise and which are"—the prompter hovering in front of him said *irregular*—"savage and cruel. We defeated the likes of General Grievous. Let us not imitate our foes in victory."

He wrapped up with the uncontroversial boilerplate, reiterating the need to improve medical support for clone veterans and thanking Euri-vos HoloDynamics for hosting the gathering. The visiting attendees began drifting away. The floor supervisor was ushering workers back to their stations before Bail even made it to the exit.

He'd given this speech or variations thereof half a dozen times since the end of the war and Palpatine's ascension to Emperor. The first had garnered minor interest from members of the press and public interested in the Alderaanian firebrand's take on the changing status quo; he'd even spotted an intern from the grand vizier's office. But reactions had grown increasingly tepid in the weeks since, as the Jedi had faded from public interest and it had become clear Bail was still what he'd been for the past decade—an irritant to greater powers, not a threat to them. Today was his first appearance since returning from Jedha, and it was the most dispiriting yet.

His staffers clustered around him as they all made their way toward a waiting speeder. Someone passed him a comlink, and he attached the earpiece. Breha's voice came through and immediately his muscles relaxed. He became more aware of his breathing and his pace and his body. His wife, as always, was his salvation.

"How did it go?" she asked. "Your chief of staff says you went off script."

"My chief of staff should complain to me himself instead of dragging you into this. Yes, I slipped. But I told you about Jedha. Palpatine's got people so riled up, they're killing us just for mourning our losses."

"Imperialist supporters still baiting you?"

"They didn't even bother heckling."

"Which offended you—"

"Of course not. Maybe." He sighed. "I'm not trying to make enemies. Truly, I'm not—I don't need *more*. It's just . . ."

He trailed off. Breha waited awhile before asking, "Just what? Your instinct is to fight, but I want to hear you say *how*. Tell me the strategy. Or tell me you're sure and that I should trust you. Either will do."

Bail grunted. She was right, of course, about him acting on instinct. Instinct had led him well in life, and sometimes picking it apart, delving into the plan his subconscious had cobbled together, felt like second-guessing himself. He did his best for her sake. "Yes, part of it is stubbornness, I'll concede that." *To you and no one else.* "Part of it, though . . . we can't let the Jedi slip out of the public eye, and no one else is talking about them. We—I—need to stay on message.

"But most of it"—he didn't know how the sentence would end as he felt his way along its contours—"is about the people who *aren't* at the rallies. Palpatine has turned so many against the Jedi and made the Order into villains, yet I promise you not everyone believes it. For the people who are scared to speak out, who don't want to be tarred by their neighbors as Separatist sympathizers and who can't afford a ticket to Jedha—or who just want to keep their heads down? I have to speak for them. I have the platform, and the administration won't touch me. I have a responsibility."

Breha said nothing. Bail lowered his voice so that not even his staffers could hear. "Besides, everyone will care again once the truth comes out, once they have something concrete to get behind. I need to stand firm until then."

"Is it possible," Breha asked, "that you're overestimating the number of people who are silent and scared? Not everyone loved the Jedi like you—for most people they've always been distant—and Palpatine is very popular."

"No. They're out there, Breha. They are."

She didn't believe him. He knew that and he could live with that, but he didn't intend to argue. They said their goodbyes and promised to see each other at home, and Bail piled into the speeder with his staff and headed off for the next meeting or rally or fundraiser or whatever was on the schedule. As he did, he thought about just how untouchable he was and how he knew the administration wouldn't come after him—not yet.

They'd arrested him already along with Mon Mothma and dozens of other senators in the days after the proclamation of Empire. Most of those taken had been prominent signatories to the Petition of 2,000—the delegation's earlier call to strip Palpatine of his emergency powers had been reinterpreted as an act of treason. Security officers had shut Bail in a comfortable cell, given him access to news feeds and datapads and most anything he'd asked for, and all he'd had to do to secure his release had been to pledge his loyalty to the new regime—to treat the whole affair like politics instead of like the atrocity it was and assure everyone that the Emperor was legitimate. He'd agreed—for his own sake, for the sake of his family, for the sake of the galaxy—and he'd kept within the boundaries of political dialogue since then. He'd kept words like *tyrant* and *massacre* out of his speeches, even when the implication was there.

The Emperor was a monster. But Bail was convinced that the arrests had been a bluff—an attempt to scare the Senate into compliance, because Palpatine still needed them and didn't fear senators the way he feared the Jedi. Palpatine wouldn't come after Bail until Bail demonstrated he was a true danger to the regime.

Which meant Palpatine was unaware that Bail knew the truth. Bail knew how Palpatine had risen to power, and that *was* a danger.

Bail was protected until he wasn't. With every word he spoke, every ripple he made, the Emperor might become more suspicious. A sort of countdown had begun, and Bail could not slow it; he could only accelerate his own exposure.

Which meant he had to work fast.

CHAPTER 5
A MISSION OF
VENGEANCE

Soujen woke amid the odors of stone and soil, his body damp and sore and sprawled across a cot. He identified his surroundings as a cell, whether for a hermit or a prisoner, and opened his eyes with unhurried interest. Particles of dust eddied in the sickly light of overheads, clouding what appeared to be an alcove laser-hewn from a natural cave. A gap like a doorway led to a tunnel beyond, but there was no door, and his limbs were unbound.

If he was a prisoner, his chains were subtle.

He recalled the fight aboard the pirate ship, his meeting with the man called Saw, and his own neglect at being caught in the ion blast. He swallowed his humiliation and ran his implants' diagnostics. His vision shifted through the spectra, and he tasted the grit and bacteria on his tongue with artificial acuity. Notifications blinked onto his retinas as his weapons and muscular enhancements reported full function. His power source—the diatium-baradium cell that sat heavy in his lower abdomen—was undamaged. It might last a dozen more years, though neither Soujen nor those who'd made him had ever planned for him to survive that long.

He confirmed that the trigger mechanism for his self-destruct remained intact, and the normalcy of it all struck him then. He'd adapted well to the implants. He tried to recall his awkwardness after the initial surgery, but those memories were too foggy to grasp. They were like the holes in his databank—a darkness he could worry like a missing tooth, but harmless. His makers had hidden code from him and denied him access to certain files, yet what soldier ever knew everything his commanders intended?

He rose and reviewed his surroundings once more, half expecting to find a cam or laser tripwire. He found none and strolled out of his cell. Whatever his captors had planned, he saw no reason not to meet it directly.

He explored the tunnel and its branches, noting which passages bore lighting strips and which appeared unoccupied. He considered locating and disabling the power generator to take advantage of the resulting darkness, but as he was in no immediate danger, he chose to wander. Soujen was a violent man—his vocation *demanded* violence—yet he wasn't cruel or bloodthirsty. And he wasn't defenseless.

Eventually he heard voices, following them into a natural cavern hung with spiral stalactites stained by calcite and jade. A cord ladder on a jutting crag led down to an improvised mess, where a dozen individuals sat on rocks or supply crates. Most of the cavern's occupants were eating from ration packs, while a few were engaged in conversation. Saw sat among the group, though he seemed to hold no place of honor.

Like Saw, most of the others were human, or close to it. They were filthy and scarred and built like soldiers. Some carried blasters or kept blasters close at hand. One young woman wore a bandolier of knives, in the habit of Primtara-sector mercenaries. Another carried a bulky device Soujen took for a Corporate Sector riot-control cannon.

"You said we'd hit back," the woman with the knives said. She was looking at Saw. "Robbing supply convoys isn't *hitting back*. Wiring tunnels isn't *hitting back*."

"Then tell me," Saw asked, "what would you do in my position?"

The woman shrugged. "Trash a guard post. Shoot some clones."

"Clones are like battle droids. They're not the enemy—they're *weapons* of the enemy, and the enemy can always manufacture more." Saw ran a gloved hand through his hair—a strange, deliberate gesture that struck Soujen as almost scripted. "For now, all we can do is make the cost of pursuing us too high."

"'For now,'" said the woman carrying the cannon. She was older than the knife carrier, with a crown of red hair and a full set of metal teeth that gleamed in the dim light. "How *do* you plan to escalate?"

"Always the same with you, Karama." A muzzle-faced simian with dirty-blond fur produced a hiccoughing laugh. "We agreed to follow his lead."

"I didn't agree to not ask questions," Karama replied.

Soujen crouched in the shadows atop the crag and considered the scene. Saw's band was poorly equipped and ununiformed. Outcasts, clearly, but were they mercenaries? Criminals? They spoke with only the loosest regard for rank or hierarchy. Yet they also spoke like ideologues, like people indoctrinated into a cause they were still grappling with. There was something distantly familiar about their confused zealotry, and Soujen thought of his eldest brother, long dead from drink and unfocused fury.

Right now, however, Soujen needed actionable intelligence on where he was and how to leave. He had a mission and a purpose, one he'd had no chance to consider since his awakening. Even the reason he'd been kept alive was a secondary matter.

"The questions do not offend me," Saw said. His voice was casual, if not friendly. "Karama's more than earned the right. We found her in a Separatist prison camp after she deserted the Republic, and she paid her dues long ago. Vorgorath"—he gestured at the simian—"has medals and ribbons enough to shame us all, but those mean as little as your own crimes." His eyes were on the girl with the knives.

"Then we have Hress," Saw said. His eyes left the girl and rose to focus on Soujen. "He wants answers, so he spies on us instead of introducing himself properly. The man is a Separatist agent lacking any detectable conscience. He was responsible for assassinations on Duro and Nacronis, the trainee barracks bomb on Carida . . . yet I'll feed him, clothe him, even answer *his* questions if he proves useful."

The others were looking at him now. Saw's litany of accusations was fiction—Soujen had rigged a dozen bombs to kill Republic fighters in their sleep, yet not one of them on Carida—but he felt no need to make a correction. He could've fled, but that would gain him nothing. So he descended the ladder and approached the gathering.

Saw remained seated. The others did, too, though several placed their hands upon their weapons.

"*Hress,*" Saw said, pronouncing the name Soujen had given him with a sneer. "*You* ought to meet Nankry, here. She was a guerrilla on the Perithal front . . . no support, no coordination, but she managed to slit the throat of her colony's Separatist governor, waged something of a one-woman war."

Soujen glanced at Nankry, who slid her fingers over her bandolier. She was wiry and nervous. He suspected she was also fast and sloppy.

"If you're looking to test her skills," Soujen said, "find someone else." *I'm not your pet, and I won't be baited.*

Saw squinted at Soujen. Soujen stepped into the band's circle and reached for a ration pack. He heard metal scrape rock as someone to his left lifted their blaster.

Saw only laughed. "Eat," he said. "You've had a long journey."

Soujen tore open the pack and heard foaming as the envelope swelled. Something that smelled of yeast and synthetic meat was bubbling up, and he lifted the pack to his lips to swallow the bitter slurry.

Saw was talking again. "Did your masters ever mention me? Saw Gerrera of Onderon?"

Soujen didn't answer, which Saw seemed to interpret as no.

"My world tried to avoid taking sides in the war," Saw said, "but the Separatists staged a coup in the guise of *legitimate political action*. To buy our freedom, we threw in with the Republic."

Nankry grunted and shuffled off. Soujen finished half the ration pack and forced himself to slow down. He hadn't realized how hungry he'd been. He supposed the implants had numbed the pangs, but he was still an animal, a creature of flesh, and he'd had nothing to eat or drink since waking up in his pod.

Saw continued to speak, his intonation rising and falling with an al-most playful rhythm—the oratory of a man too self-aware for pomposity. Soujen forced himself to pay attention in case something proved useful.

"It was a good pact," Saw said, "and the Republic gave us the support we needed. Not what we wanted—they wouldn't get their hands dirty—but they trained us, armed us, and we overthrew the Separatists' puppet government and kept fighting after.

"The thing of it is, Onderon never made a pact with any *Empire*. And once you've seen one government usurped, one tyrant installed who cracks down on anyone who might threaten him, you recognize the signs. Palpatine's no different from King Rash, the Separatists' man on the throne."

Soujen licked his teeth and swallowed the mouthful of slurry. "You were in the habit of fighting, so you turned on your new masters when an excuse presented itself."

If it was a challenge, it hadn't been a calculated one—it had been a blunt, unsugared assessment. Soujen knew what he was dealing with now. But Saw went silent, and Soujen felt the attention of the others shift—they'd almost begun to relax, yet now they were tense again.

"Believe what you like," Saw said at last. "I tell you this: The Republic's new Emperor has already turned his eye on Onderon. He seeks to disarm us, to register and monitor us, to make us willing cogs in his great machine. He murdered the Jedi who dared to aid us. In return, he asks for our loyalty and seeks to punish those who refuse.

"Not many people see it yet, but they will. The Empire fired the first shot—*we* did not ask for this war. It is the Empire who chased us when we simply tried to survive."

Soujen was only half listening now. What did the justifications of Republic turncoats matter to him? It was his disinterest that allowed him to notice the presence behind him—the shift in sound and airflow as a body approached. When the attack came, he still held the ration pack in his right hand. He reached back with his left and caught the descending wrist, felt a blade slash his forearm—the cut too shallow to cause real damage. In the same movement, he knelt and tugged his attacker forward, throwing her over his shoulders and dropping her at his feet.

It was Nankry, of course, now with a sprained—possibly broken—

wrist and clutching not one but two knives. He hadn't expected the second weapon, and he barely stepped aside as she jabbed at his thigh with her free hand. He maintained his hold and, with a flex of his forearm, activated the shock conductor in his left palm. His muscles spasmed, and he dug his nails into Nankry's skin. She screamed as electricity flowed from his body into hers, and he smelled burning flesh.

She kept fighting anyway, scrabbling upright, admirably feral, slashing wildly. Soujen released her and kicked at her stomach, sending her stumbling onto the rocks. The others had risen to encircle the combatants—Saw, too, though he kept his distance—and Soujen moved to end the fight. He stalked forward and raised one foot to stamp the woman's head into the dirt. One good blow would crush her skull or break her neck. She'd meant to slay him; no reason not to return the favor.

Nankry was too stunned to move, yet Soujen was denied the kill. His sole struck the cave floor as Vorgorath yanked Nankry away. The others were aiming their weapons, but none dared fire—if they missed their shots, they'd likely hit one another instead of Soujen.

Soujen prioritized the threats, his instincts and implants feeding him positions and estimating danger levels from each combatant in the circle. He barely heard Saw's call: "That's enough! That's enough!"

The soldiers backed away. Several tended to Nankry, while others kept their weapons trained on Soujen.

Saw slapped down another man's rifle as he marched forward. "I saved your life," Saw said. "Brought you here as my guest. It would be discourteous to kill my people."

"You let her try to kill me," Soujen said.

"Had to see what you were made of," Saw said. "Besides, she needed humbling. You were never in danger."

Saw had stopped three meters away. Soujen could kill the man if he wanted—Saw would have his own defenses, but he didn't know Soujen's full arsenal. Escaping the rest of the band would be troublesome but manageable. Yet he still had questions.

"Next time, you die," Soujen said.

Next time you use me. Next time you lie to me.

"More than fair," Saw said. His smile didn't reach his eyes. "Why don't we talk in private?"

///

They trekked through the tunnels together. Soon they reached the end of the lights and walked in darkness. Saw seemed to know his way by feel, moving with a shuffling gait that steered him away from stray rocks and through narrow passages. Soujen adjusted the visible spectrum processed by his implants—the caverns seemed to glitter with emerald light, and Saw glowed like a beacon.

When they'd gone half a kilometer in silence and darkness, Saw produced a handlight and used it to navigate more swiftly. Perhaps, Soujen thought, Saw hadn't realized Soujen was unaffected by the gloom. Perhaps he'd been trying to ensure that Soujen couldn't backtrack to the camp. Or perhaps Saw had other enemies he didn't want tracking him.

"Surviving against the Empire will take resources, more than my band can acquire through ordinary means," Saw said, as if they were resuming a conversation begun some time ago. "When the Republic supplied us, we'd go through power cells, blasters, explosives, fast as they would come in. There were always more Separatist targets than we could afford to hit."

The reasoning was familiar. Before his augmentation, Soujen had fought as a mercenary on the front lines with every weapon the Separatists could imagine. The Techno Union, the Trade Federation, the Commerce Guild—the great holders of wealth and material resources in the galaxy had all backed the Separatist cause, quietly purchasing planets' loyalty while loudly proclaiming neutrality. The corporations had lifted up the Separatist movement, and everyone knew it. But they hadn't *created* the desire to escape the Republic's clutches, a wish shared by thousands of neglected worlds that could never have afforded to rebel without patrons. How self-interested those patrons might have been mattered little.

Yet Soujen had also fought behind enemy lines, deep within the Republic. And he'd fought before the war, too, hired into tribal conflicts that meant nothing to outsiders. Saw might tell his troops that skill and will and heart were what mattered, and he might dream of clever ploys and sneak attacks. But Soujen knew what it was like to spend days worrying over every damaged blaster and searching for clean water.

They ascended a steep incline, Saw on his hands and knees while Soujen took on an insectoid crouch. At the top, Saw said, "We have no more backers. The Republic is our enemy, and even if we had the credits, there's no third party that wants to get involved. The Hutt Cartel won't make an enemy of the new regime. The syndicates are reorganizing. Yet the Separatist military had weapons aplenty, and I started to think . . .

"Well, I'd heard rumors toward the war's end—just stories, from prisoners apt to say anything under interrogation. They spoke of Separatist contingency plans, stockpiles of arms and chemicals and precious metals being amassed across the galaxy. These caches would have their own operatives attached, augmented assassins and saboteurs to keep the war going in the event the droid armies were defeated.

"I didn't think much of it—it seemed like the sort of lie the corporations would spread to reassure the Separatist loyalists, let them know they'd never give up the fight. But after the regime change, when my people and I were forced into hiding, the stories seemed worth looking into. And when I heard of a pirate ship that had stumbled upon something precious from the war . . ."

They emerged from a crack barely wider than their shoulders. Something musty and acrid reached Soujen's nostrils, and he saw they were standing on a ledge covered with pastel spatters—the guano of four-winged, two-headed creatures that circled in the gloaming above, leaving a visible wake in the violet clouds that blocked any sun or stars. Below, rose and green and azure rocks descended toward a scrub plain where fleshy grass writhed in the breeze. Soujen had the unpleasant sense of existing at the edge of an ocean abyss.

"The pirates had erased their logs and navigational data by the time we boarded, but I assume the bioweapon that killed them was one of yours. Maybe a booby trap? Or maybe they got sloppy." Saw paused for Soujen to confirm his suspicions, then went on. They stood beside each other, both facing the horizon. "But you *are* the operative. You are the Separatist contingency plan."

Was there a point to denial? Saw knew what he knew.

Soujen shrugged. "Close enough."

"Don't suppose you'll tell me your technical specifications? How many augs? How much of you is metal?"

"Less than you imagine," Soujen said, which was probably true. The implants improved his balance and coordination. They offered enhanced sensory input, a data link, and select onboard weapons. But his blood and bones were real. His mind had been augmented but not replaced.

"You conscripted? Forced into it?"

"No."

Saw scuffed his heel against the ledge, sending grains of dust tumbling toward the scrub plain. "Did they program your mind?"

"You want to control me." It was a statement, not a question.

This time it was Saw who shrugged. "I would if I could. Do they control you?"

"No." Soujen spat over the ledge. The thought alone repulsed him, and that Saw would consider it showed the sort of man Soujen faced. "I volunteered because I wished to serve." Not strictly true but, again, close.

"Serve as a killer. What do the Separatists expect you to do now?"

Soujen scowled. The question was a fair one, and he lacked a complete answer. His directive was open-ended, yet the galaxy Soujen had awakened into was worse off than anything he'd prepared for. He had expected to be revived by Separatist order after years of hibernation, emerging from his pod with up-to-date instructions. Instead, the end had come so swiftly no one had even signaled for his revivification. If the pirates hadn't found him, who knew how long he might have stayed in storage, collecting dust in a forgotten arsenal?

"Enough," Soujen said. "Tell me what you're after."

Saw turned to face Soujen. Soujen remained still.

"Krezchak found your cache, but he and his pirates only scratched the surface," Saw said. "He told me himself before he died—he planned to sell what he'd found, then fund a second expedition to seize everything he left behind. He needed slicers, security experts, explosives to penetrate vaults. I want what he wanted—not just a few blasters, not just your containment pod, but everything the Separatists stockpiled and locked away. Enough resources to fight a war."

Which explains almost everything, Soujen thought. Saw needed Soujen because, with the pirates dead and their ship destroyed, only Soujen could find the cache where he had been in stasis. Saw needed Soujen to lead his crew into the facility and disable the safeguards.

"Your people," Soujen said.

"What about them?"

"Do *they* want to fight a war against the Republic? The *Empire*?"

Soujen wasn't sure whether it mattered, but it bought him time to think.

A year ago, he would have killed Saw without pause. The man was on the wrong side. But Saw was no longer fighting Separatists, because there were too few Separatists to fight.

Part of Soujen found his own thoughts, his hesitation offensive— they suggested a weakness in his determination, as introspection often did—but the obstacles were what they were.

Saw twisted his face into a grimace. "Most of them have been with me for years. Some I picked up recently, and their views of our situation differ. But they have nowhere to run to. The Empire wants us all dead. Sooner or later they'll all accept that when someone hits you, you hit back harder or you let them abuse you forever."

Soujen nodded. It was an oversimplification, but it was good enough.

"You can leave now, if you like," Saw said. "I won't help you, but I won't stop you. If you can find your way off this planet, you can hunt down Imperials, Separatists, abandon the fight for all I care. But if you stay, we can find the wealth of your dead backers."

Soujen paced along the cliff's edge and listened to the braying of the sky beasts. He didn't believe for a moment that Saw would let him walk. Maybe Saw would allow him to descend as far as the scrub plain, or maybe Saw had hidden weapons pointed at Soujen as they spoke. And surely Saw was aware that Soujen was considering turning on him—stealing his ship and making his way from there.

But the fundamental truth was unchanged: Soujen had little to work with. His enemies were many, his friends were few, and he had been tossed haplessly about the galaxy. His purpose felt distant. He felt small, a grain of sand adrift in the abyss.

Returning to the cache would not be simple, but it would provide him with a starting point—information, resources, and clarity. If his handlers in the Separatist Confederacy had left him any guidance on how to handle this new and terrible galaxy, it would be stored there.

Perhaps. Perhaps.

Saw would wait to kill him, in that case. And Soujen could wait to kill Saw, until he could walk the road to the cache alone. Soujen found the notion distasteful, but he had killed better men than Saw with poison and bombs and sniper fire. He had shed innocent blood for the sake of pragmatism and to spread terror to the guilty. He could abide the taste of betrayal.

"I'll work with you," Soujen said.

Saw laughed. He did not speak as he returned to the caves.

Soujen lingered where he was.

CHAPTER 6
A WAR OF MANNERS

"
. . .

Not since Valorum's chancellorship, if that's possible? It's so *good* to see you."

Mon was sparkling company, cycling through the party with such exquisite timing that the entire affair might have been choreographed. She swapped banter and anecdotes with guests who wanted to see the Chandrilan senator at ease and unguarded. She listened thoughtfully to donors who'd spent ten thousand credits for a lukewarm meal and the chance to demand action on certain issues. Mon felt a touch guilty that she didn't care about any of it—that her anecdotes were recycled, that she was paying only enough attention to smile and nod at the right times—but a mentor of hers had once told her that inattention was the payoff of experience. After enough years, you *earned* the right to stop caring.

"You're absolutely right. Our entire system for regulating hyperdrive safety is antiquated, and we *have* to get back to business."

Officially, the dinner was to honor veterans returning from the war. Seven decorated non-clone troopers were in attendance, including an infantry medic who'd lost both legs and a commodore who'd won a stunning victory in the Outer Rim. Yet the truth—known to everyone, except perhaps the poor medic—was that the event was a fundraiser for the upcoming senatorial campaigns. Mon had colleagues who viewed fundraisers and polling as undemocratic, and these colleagues invariably extolled the superior virtues of their homeworlds, where public campaign funding or complex systems of meritocracy or the presence of a species hive mind rendered such things unnecessary. But for the most part, there was a shared understanding that political allies were to be kept in office by whatever means their home governments allowed. The alternative—lost allies and lost votes—was too terrible to contemplate.

"You want to know a secret? We're not even supposed to be here. Renting the Senate building for private events violates the Bentrinus Act, but there's been no enforcement for years."

Six senators from the Colonies would be recipients of the night's windfall. Three of them had been fellow signatories to the Delegation of 2,000 and staunch advocates for peace and reform—for an end to the war and the rollback of the Emergency Powers Act. The others were less steadfast allies, but they'd all caucused together and proved reasonable and reliable when trading votes. *Better to have them retain their seats,* Mon thought, *than see them replaced by imperialist supporters of the new regime.*

Mon searched for her husband, weaving among the marbled columns and holographic artwork of the seventh-floor atrium and waving off catering droids. (There'd been no budget for organic waitstaff.) Even if the romance had faded from their relationship, Perrin had never failed in his role as Senator Mothma's public partner. He was the charming everyman, and Mon was the principled intellectual. And while she'd had no luck yet with the Toydarian wine merchants or the emissary from D'Assem, Perrin might still be her salvation.

A booming voice distracted her from her mission. She turned to the Fountain of Mournful Waters and saw a dozen guests packed around a gesticulating figure. "The chain codes are an absolute violation of Republic principle! Imagine a government—any government—with the ability to track its citizens wherever they go. The grand vizier claims it's for security, but whose security?" And with barely a segue the speaker was excoriating the regime for eliminating oversight boards and privatizing the news feeds and banks.

Senator Bail Organa of Alderaan. Mon sighed and tried not to let her dismay show.

Bail was charismatic and popular—being married to his world's beloved queen made him the darling of Alderaan, and his public intensity attracted press from across the galaxy. He'd once been loathed as a radical reformist, ready to tear down Republic institutions he claimed had become the tools of moneyed interests. But he'd been loved by discontented youths for the same reasons, a hero to those looking to spread the Republic's wealth and resources from the Core Worlds to outlying systems and local planetary governments. The war had muddied his position in the public eye—some of Bail's supporters had seen Palpatine's power grabs as exactly the sort of reforms they'd wanted, while Bail's unwavering support for the Republic military and the clone army had boosted his numbers among moderates—but he'd maintained his image as an irascible truth teller.

Mon admired Bail. She'd called him a friend, and he was. But the man was exhausting at best; at worst, he was insufferable.

Hypocrites were easy to find in the Senate, but their flexible values meant they were also uncommonly willing to negotiate and compromise, so the systems of government never ground to a halt. Bail's advocates pointed out that he was, in the end, a reliable vote—never opposing a bill just because it was imperfect, always falling in line when there was not a more constructive option. But the energy Mon had spent arguing, negotiating, and pleading with him behind closed doors could have powered starships. The capital she had expended to distance herself from his tossed-off statements might have bought her the chancellorship.

They'd stood side by side at the funeral of poor Padmé Amidala. Senator Amidala had shared Mon's views on how to structure legislation and Bail's way of winning the public's heart. Mon's differences with Bail had always seemed lessened in Padmé's presence.

Mon and Bail had barely spoken since the funeral. They hadn't argued, hadn't had a falling out, but where was their common ground now?

Bail was laughing. "Patience? Palpatine was Supreme Chancellor for a decade, senator for twenty years before that. He's not a novice who needs time to learn the ropes. I respect the role of Emperor—"

You do not, Mon thought, *and you're not subtle about it.*

"—but I say we judge him on his actions now, while there's still a chance to change direction."

It was a speech he couldn't make in public nowadays—not without making himself toxic, pilloried by a public wildly supportive of Palpatine and abandoned by colleagues who wished to avoid the stench of his association. Here, in private, he was emboldened. But Lud Marroi had told her the intelligence services were watching, and if that was true, then Bail Organa was surely a target. She had to stop him before he said anything worse and her friend and ally was somehow forced out of the Senate.

She doubted he'd be grateful. She wondered whether she'd be set on his preservation if he were merely an ally or a friend instead of both.

All of which returned her to her initial task: finding her husband. She continued her circuit of the room until she spotted Perrin entertaining two Rodian women, one whom Mon recognized as the mother of Cydek Noorah of the Judicial Review Board. Perrin was gesturing madly with a glass of wine in one hand. The women appeared spellbound, and Mon would have paused to enjoy her husband in his element if she hadn't been in urgent need. He really did have his charms.

"So sorry to interrupt—I need to borrow Perrin, but please keep enjoying yourselves."

There were the usual protests and apologies, but Perrin understood the prompt and he extracted himself on Mon's arm. They were a half dozen paces away when he asked (a bit smug, knowing he was needed), "What's the crisis?"

"Have you spoken to Bail tonight?"

"I thought the Queen's donation was a lock? If you didn't want me branching out—"

"You were perfect. Things have changed."

Perrin watched her, his brow crinkled and his wide, lovely eyes expressing an innocence that had never really existed. Not at fifteen, when they'd wed according to their parents' wishes and ancient tradition. Not in the months after, when they'd carried on as awkward and passionate and spiteful a romance as two teenagers could hope for. Not at twenty, when they'd fallen out and decided that there would be no children, no shared bed, and no questions between them. Not at twenty-four, when the pendulum had swung back—and it had kept swinging over the years, until Mon and Perrin had reached their current equilibrium. Of late, they'd lived separate lives, but they didn't hurt each other or carry on affairs or talk about the rules. She supposed they were both waiting for the day it all changed again.

Mon shook away the memories. She said, "Get Bail talking about something else, *anything* else, please, other than how much he loathes the Empire."

"You figure I'm up to *that* challenge? You really do believe in me."

Mon laughed despite herself. "He likes you. Go!"

They crossed the floor together at first, until Perrin made for Bail and Mon angled away to orbit the group at a distance. She heard Bail call her husband's name, and then their voices overlapped and she could make out none of the words.

Before she could decide how to proceed, she was intercepted by Breha. The Queen of Alderaan was a stately woman, possessed of a comfortable formality that her husband often lacked. Mon had never gotten to know her well—Breha rarely stayed on Coruscant long—but Mon found Breha pleasant enough company. Mon greeted the Queen warmly and asked after her newborn daughter.

They went through the familiar small talk, yet Mon's attention remained on Perrin and Bail, so much so that she barely noticed Breha's segue to more somber subjects: "Alderaan is committed to taking in another twenty million refugees over the next year, but we're coming to a point where the financial strain will be noticed. I don't intend to force anyone out, yet if we can incentivize people to return to their homeworlds, give them the resources to rebuild *and* ensure a lasting peace . . ."

Mon resisted the urge to turn toward Bail and Perrin. Bail's voice was rising again, and he was saying something about suffering, about security—

"You're right, of course," Mon said to Breha. "The less we do to rebuild the Separatist worlds, the more likely we are to see fresh radicalization."

But she wasn't listening to herself. She could hear Bail clearly now.

"They can arrest me again, for all I care. Take a father away from his baby girl! Let the Empire show people how they fear criticism! If senators can't voice the opinions of their people, then the Emperor may as well replace all of us with droids!"

Mon recognized Perrin's tone as he tried to change the subject, but Bail kept going.

Breha smiled softly at Mon and said, "He's not fearless. He's not foolish. But he made a choice that night when they took him away. He wouldn't let them see what it did to him then, and I intend to do the same."

"That's brave of you," Mon said. Was it a critique of Mon's own positioning? She doubted it, but it was hard not to wonder. "If you'll excuse me, I promised my staff I'd make another round before the hour is up."

Cutting short Breha's farewells, Mon left the atrium and listened to the pounding of her heart.

She came to the Senate Rotunda and stood in one of the viewing pods slotted into the walls. She leaned over the pod's edge, peering into the dark below and the dark above—a space vast enough to house a stadium or a small city, lit at night so the pods seemed to spiral ever-upward into the heavens out of a small and simpler world underfoot.

This was her temple and her battleground, a place both sacred and profane where she'd spent half her life working to better the galaxy. Her predecessors had done the same, and their predecessors, stretching back to the founding of the Galactic Republic and the first days of that great and ancient and flawed institution. The pods were a comparatively recent innovation, and several were scarred and damaged from the Jedi coup attempt at the war's end. But the chamber itself was *old*. No being still living had seen its construction.

She loved the Rotunda as she loved few other places. In her youth she'd wanted to be a historian, and she'd given up that hope to follow the path her family had mapped out for her. Yet she walked daily in the footsteps of politicians and philosophers and civic leaders nearly forgotten outside the capitol, and this calmed her when times were trying.

She tapped at the pod's familiar controls and accessed the program meant for tourists and schoolchildren, muting the accompanying recording and letting the pod circle and ascend. She let her mind drift, urging it gently away from her arrest but otherwise letting it wander like the pod. She thought about Breha's hopes for the refugees. She thought about the wreckage of Coruscant's lower levels. Her eyes took in the constellations of machinery, and she thought about how everything had gone so wrong.

The Separatists had felt unheard. Their senators had stood in the Rotunda and called for change, but no one had cared or at least not cared *enough*. Now Mon and Bail and their allies could make their own speeches and, like the Separatists, know that their passion would make no difference. The administration would not act. The Emperor and the grand vizier would ignore them or mock them or arrest them, because Palpatine and his cronies had worked the rules to their benefit—not through bribes and corruption but by earning acclaim for their deeds and playing the long game. For over a decade they'd amassed influence, from Palpatine's rise to the chancellorship to the passage of the Emergency Powers Act to the declaration of Empire, and Mon could respect the strategy, because it had ultimately relied upon Palpatine's administrative competence and the effectiveness of his circle. They'd done the work and earned the votes and ended the war. Who could say that what they'd won weren't the spoils of democracy?

Only now it wasn't about the work. The administration had crossed a threshold with the war's end, accelerating and prioritizing its efforts to consolidate power. Palpatine and his circle no longer needed to pursue military victory or protect Republic worlds. Instead, they had begun their endgame, placing their full focus on entrenching themselves for a lifetime. And as the loyal opposition, as a senator and a student of history, it was Mon's responsibility to answer that challenge, to work the rules to *her* benefit and restore the balance.

Passing the pods for Cerberon and Vardos, she wondered for only a moment whether she'd have felt the same principled outrage if she'd believed in Palpatine's agenda. Lud had asked her that question, and she'd deflected it. Now she decided the question was unfair. Palpatine's program for stability was indistinguishable from his efforts to become a dictator. Whether his advisers' policies had other merits, whether the bloody purge of the Jedi was somehow counterbalanced by the stabilization of interest rates in the Deep Core, and whether Palpatine himself believed in his promises of peace and the betterment of the galaxy were irrelevant. The acquisition of power was the solid thing. All else was shadow.

Mon looked around and imagined the thousands of representatives who could, in a moment, cast out Palpatine and his people and restore the Republic as it had been. Those representatives lacked the motivation, but they had the power, just as the people of the galaxy had the power to be rid of their representatives. Mon mapped the Senate coalitions onto the geography of the Rotunda, imagining the factions and interest groups that aligned their pods in solidarity. As her own pod came to a stop in the center, she peered into the blackness below—the place where, for years, the seats had been left empty in memory of the Separatist worlds.

Since the war's end, no one had spoken for the breakaway systems, but the Emperor had promised this was soon to change. Members of the Separatist Parliament who pledged their loyalty to the Empire—who passed the regime's security checks and who weren't being tried and imprisoned for war crimes—were supposedly coming back soon. They numbered more than ten thousand, dwarfing the delegation she'd built. They would come, cowed or ostentatiously devoted to the administration. But they, too, would possess power.

Mon began to smile, and she began to plan. The history of the Republic was not a history of grand schemes and inspired leadership. No history was. Cultural change was unpredictable, composed of subtle shifts, of eddies turned to tidal waves that the brightest and most capable politicians could ride to their own ends. Palpatine had taken advantage of the discontent that had spurred the war long before the war began. Now the war was over, and there were new opportunities. The balance of power was shifting.

The Separatists had once been her adversaries, but they were returning home.

The Separatists were the key. With their votes, she could reforge the Empire into a cage for its Emperor.

///

Ten minutes later, she'd made her excuses to Perrin and was in the back of a taxi, relaying instructions to Zhuna over a comlink. Mon felt only a moment of guilt—she'd promised her aide she wasn't needed—but Zhuna was blessedly focused, inputting half a dozen names into her datapad without ever looking into the imager. Only when Mon heard a metallic clattering in the call's background did Zhuna's professional mien slip. Zhuna's expression turned ferocious as she muted the call, shouted something to someone out of Mon's view, then apologized repeatedly.

"Is everything all right?" Mon asked.

"Absolutely," Zhuna said.

"Where are you, exactly?"

"My—my mother's apartment. We've got family over. The kids knocked over—it's not important."

Mon wanted to ask so many more questions: *Do you live with your mother? Was that a sibling you were yelling at?* She enjoyed it when her staff acted like people instead of droids, and it was rare for Zhuna, in particular, to let her guard down. Yet if she asked, she expected Zhuna would feel obligated to answer. Mon had no wish to violate the girl's privacy.

"This was your night off," Mon said. "Do you need to go?"

"You called me. Can it wait?"

Mon shook her head and smiled softly. "I suppose it can't."

"Then I don't need to go."

Mon allowed herself a moment to feel smug—*I could have hired anyone, and somehow I found you*—and returned to her instructions: "We're setting up a meeting for Delegation of Two Thousand leadership. I want you to contact the offices of these senators . . ."

CHAPTER 7
INTELLIGENCE CLASSIFICATION

Bail Organa sat in the viewing chamber at his Cantham House estate, reclining in his chair with his fingers steepled. Dimmed windows blocked out the Coruscant cityscape. To his right, on a small control console, sat a stack of datapads brightly stenciled with classification markings.

Like a man settling in for an evening's entertainment, he lifted the first datapad and read:

JEDI TEMPLE ARCHIVES
File JC-G052F9B38 (partial)

MASTER YODA: To war, the Padawans must go. Bond them to their masters, it will.

MASTER SHAAK TI: No doubt. But many are still children. Surely the younglings needn't be asked to fight and kill.

MASTER YODA: Seen, have you, the loyalty of the clones?

MASTER SHAAK TI: They lay down their lives for the Republic without fear and without question.

MASTER YODA: But only to the Senate do they answer. For millennia, the Jedi have protected and guided the Republic. Now the Supreme Chancellor possesses emergency powers and an army dangerous beyond compare.

MASTER SHAAK TI: And we, too, must have absolute loyalty from our Knights and Padawans. So that whatever our Council decides, all will follow. All will do whatever we ask.

MASTER YODA: Hope, we must, that such a need will never come.

Bail shook his head and closed the file. On the front of the datapad was a sunrise crest.

He tapped a button on the console. Without prelude, he asked, "The seals validate?"

"All of them," a man's voice replied through the comm. "Archives are gone, so we can't check that way. But I'm in my workshop now, and they look genuine to me."

"No possibility of forgery, then?"

"Anything's possible," the man said. "I've never seen anyone duplicate a Jedi seal, though. They took their encryption seriously. I can swing by and walk you through the specs—"

"Thank you, Spelter," Bail said. "That won't be necessary." He tapped the button a second time before picking up the next datapad. This one, too, showed the sunrise crest, as well as a time stamp. There was no other text.

Bail seated the pad in an open socket in the console, and the room's holoprojector ignited. Blue fire coalesced into two discrete figures, the first robed and hooded in peasant's attire, shown from behind, and the second a white-haired man in an aristocrat's dark cape. As the aristocrat spoke, the pad displayed a transcript of his words.

"You should not have summoned me," the aristocrat said. His voice was cut with static but deep and resonant nonetheless.

"I bring word from the Jedi Council, good Count," the robed figure replied. This voice was more distorted still. "Master Kenobi sends his regards."

"Kenobi should know better than to waste my time. I have a war to wage and a Confederacy to run—a Confederacy which *your* Order has committed to destroying."

"The Supreme Chancellor sees the Separatist Confederacy as an existential threat," the robed figure said. "As long as he maintains this position, the war can end only through total victory or total defeat."

"And the Jedi Council sees matters differently?"

"The Jedi Council would prefer to keep the Republic intact. However . . . if that should prove impossible, they *are* open to other options, ones the chancellor may be too close-minded to accept."

The aristocrat chuckled, low and brittle. "Then contact me when the Jedi have the fire to finally do what is needed. Until then, we remain enemies."

Here the recording ended with an abrupt flash and a static hiss. Bail's face screwed up, and he slapped his palm against the arm of his chair. He sat still briefly, shook his head a few more times, then lifted a third datapad from the pile.

This one read:

JEDI TEMPLE ARCHIVES
File JC-N091FFC74 (partial)

MASTER KENOBI: If we continue this war, the Republic may not survive. The Supreme Chancellor means well, but his strategies have cost us victory time and again.

MASTER YODA: What the Force shows us, he cannot see. The day we feared may have come.

MASTER KI-ADI-MUNDI: We must not be hasty. Count Dooku was once one of us, and in his passion to cleanse the Republic of corruption, he became the Separatist enemy we now oppose. If we follow the same path he did—

MASTER KENOBI: Count Dooku is *not* our enemy. The atrocities of General Grievous and the droid army are not his. My own master was trained by Dooku. I know he desires peace as much as we.

MASTER WINDU: Then there truly is no choice. We *must* take control from the chancellor. We must command the clone armies ourselves as Master Sifo-Dyas intended. We must fortify the Republic and forge a treaty with Count Dooku that will allow both sides to disarm.

We've trained our Knights for exactly this contingency. Even the youngest Padawan will obey. If we move quickly, with the clones in line, we can complete the operation in less than a day.

MASTER KENOBI: When would we begin?

MASTER YODA: Soon. It must be soon.

Bail remained in his seat, staring for a long moment, and then began to laugh. The sound was powerful and boisterous, loud enough that a moment later it was joined by a wail from the next room—the crying of an infant awakened from deep sleep. Bail looked chagrined but kept on laughing, exiting the room, then returning with the baby girl in his arms.

He sat in the recliner and played the holorecording again while Haki Zeophrine, the gray lady of Imperial Intelligence, observed at her monitor, sipping her tea and wondering what the senator from Alderaan was so excited about.

///

Haki had made her cubicle as cozy as she could, draping a woolen throw over her office chair and keeping teas and sweets in a little tin beside her

monitor, atop the locked cabinet where she stored her sidearm. Officially she wasn't supposed to have any of it—not the blanket, the food,
or the modified Telltrig-X blaster—but if she'd followed every new rule
since the reorganization, she'd have still been waiting for a security
pass.

She was a practical woman, and she was good at her job. If that didn't
buy her a bit of leeway, she could busy herself elsewhere; Imperial Intelligence needed the Heptooinian spy more than Haki needed the work.

She smiled at the image of Bail cradling the newborn, then double-
checked her notes. The senator had received a package from Military
Intelligence approximately two hours earlier. The package included files
officially requested by the Senate well over a month prior. Someone had,
according to Haki's research, recently ushered the request out of limbo
and received appropriate signatures for distribution. Technically, Haki
wasn't cleared to see the file contents herself, so she'd need to be careful
about what exactly she reported. But the fact that Bail Organa had a
burr in his foot about the Jedi was public knowledge, and now he'd finally seen the evidence that proved the Order's corruption.

So why was he so *chipper* about it? What did he see in the recording
and the documents that Haki was missing? She'd been watching him on
and off for weeks, noticed his moodiness and his intensity and his
swings between genuine and affected foolishness. She found him oddly
charming—and the child really was adorable—but this was the most
excited she'd seen him.

She'd keep an eye out. Meanwhile, he was back to reading the Jedi
Council meeting transcripts, and she couldn't be bothered to watch
him slouch in his chair any longer. She flipped through other feeds on
her monitor, peering into the Naboo embassy, the caf stop across the
street from the Senate Rotunda, and the bedroom of Senator Hagran's
mistress. She skimmed through reports from her field agents, which
were by turns mind-numbingly thorough (0813: VEHICLE STOPS TO
PICK UP CHILD FROM SCHOOLYARD, 0815: VEHICLE RESUMES JOURNEY
TO SENATE OFFICES) or ineptly incomplete (0730 TO 1400: SENATOR
JAGRAINASHOD MEETS WITH CONSTITUENTS). She wanted to blame the
agents—they really were green, hired by the bucketful in the past month

with their only qualifications enthusiasm and an ability to pass a loyalty exam—but even skilled operatives couldn't have made the work worthwhile.

They could note down all the signs of disloyalty they wanted, but the fundamental problem was that they had no reason to suspect anyone— not one out of thousands of senators and tens of thousands of senatorial staffers—of being a true threat to Imperial security. The entire apparatus of Imperial Intelligence had been pointed inward while there was still fighting on the fringes of Separatist worlds. They were doing *busywork* while they should have been securing and fortifying the hard-won peace.

Busywork was what the Imperial Security Bureau had been created for—monitoring the home front, running pointless background checks on career civil servants, pretending every dropped satchel or broken-down speeder was a potential bomb threat. Police actions and paranoia, not spycraft. But the bureau was still in its infancy, so the work fell disproportionately on Intelligence.

Haki spotted a notification on her monitor, sighed, and checked her appearance. She pinned back her gray hair (verging on white these days, barely darker than her ashy skin) and adjusted stray strands around her drooping ears, then started the trek through the maze of cubicles and offices that served as the Imperial Intelligence adjunct operations center. She found the door to her superior's office open and slipped inside, where Gerrus Bariovon held up a finger and kept his attention on his monitor, looking at Haki only after a good minute of delay. Haki smiled politely and tried to feign respect. He couldn't have been more than a third her age, and like nearly all the newcomers he was human— ridiculous nose, tiny mouth, the usual. Rumor was he'd been in private industry during the war, safely profiting from it while sacrificing nothing.

"Haki, thank you for coming in," he said at last. "Everything going all right? Any issues with the junior agents?"

"They're still teething, but I can work with them."

"It's why we're assigning them to you. Just don't be afraid to learn from them, too. A number have experience in corporate intelligence, planetary security—"

"*I* started as planetary security," Haki said, though it wasn't really true. Her world had called the Bureau of Border Control a law enforcement agency, but they'd been spies and everyone had known it. They'd spied on non-Republic planets in their sector and on Republic planets when it had seemed useful. The Clone Wars had proved out their techniques at scale.

Bariovon looked displeased by the interruption, and she added, "Believe me, if anyone's developed an innovative stakeout technique, I'd be thrilled to add it to my repertoire."

"I'm glad to hear it. We need to be open to change, even as we hold on to what works." In lieu of a segue, Bariovon simply halted for a few moments, then asked, "What about the signatories of the Delegation of Two Thousand? You've been watching them?"

"The delegation is defunct, but I've been tracking the ringleaders best I can. Bail Organa's been researching the Jedi coup and keeping to himself. Senator Alavar's gone back home, where I imagine her protests will be more welcome—"

"Don't worry about Alavar. What about Mon Mothma?"

Haki shrugged. "Mothma's complaining about the administration in private and grumbling in public, but she hasn't crossed any lines."

"How many people do you have on her?"

You haven't read any of my reports, have you? "Handling her myself right now, with help from a rotation of secondaries. I've got a source close to her office, someone I've been hand-rearing. Plus the electronic taps, of course."

"You don't think she requires more attention?"

Another shrug. "You wanted coverage as wide-ranging as I could manage, and forty agents isn't a lot to track two thousand senators. We've got the priority list, of course, all the folks detained those first few nights, but that's still sixty-three representatives. Include their staff, spouses, associates—"

Bariovon cut her off with a gesture, as if to avoid learning anything that might require action on his part. "I appreciate the challenges you face. All right, no need to watch Mothma more closely until she makes her move. But when she does, be sure to let me know."

Haki doubted whether Mothma's "move" would be dramatic enough to demand anyone's attention. Did Bariovon expect her to attach a bomb to the Emperor's personal speeder? At worst she'd try to leak a classified document or rig a local election. More likely she'd stick to legislation—which was, by its nature, public work and not the purview of spies.

Bariovon was dense, but even he knew that much—which meant all the concern about *security* and *radicals* was a front. What Bariovon or his superior or his superior's superior really wanted was to show that Intelligence could be a political tool, too, and wouldn't the administration like to keep pouring funds into its coffers? Wouldn't a raise and a promotion be in order? Haki could've accepted all that if there weren't urgent tasks to be done.

She promised to keep Bariovon apprised. They transitioned into strained small talk, and when Bariovon offered a rhetorical "Is there anything I can do for you?" Haki took her chance: "One thing, if you don't mind"—one advantage of being an old woman, even a Heptooinian one, was that people rarely admitted they minded—"you may have heard we lost track of quite a few assets in the last days of the war. Our own agents, Separatist informants, moles at every level . . . vanished in the chaos."

Bariovon stared at her blankly.

Haki kept speaking: "If we've got people rotting in Separatist captivity, or just agents afraid to come back into the open, we really do owe it to them to bring them home. Our leads haven't gone cold, but it won't be long, and I wouldn't mind a chance to pursue a few." *That's supposed to be our job, in case no one briefed you.*

Bariovon smiled as if he'd been practicing. "Your concern does you credit. But I'm afraid with the Senate as it is, we can't spare the agents."

"Oh, I'm not asking for an honor guard, and I'm glad to keep tabs on the senators remotely. Like you said, the junior agents have a lot to offer, and I'm sure they can keep watch without someone supervising their every move—"

Bariovon's smile faded. "I understand capital security isn't the most exciting assignment, but we really need you here, Haki. The administration is committed to restoring public confidence in government. It's not just about unrest. It's about showing a united front and not letting disagreements between the Senate and the administration give anyone the wrong idea. We need to prove to Coruscant—and the galaxy at large—that the peace is real and the Emperor is in full control."

Then he adjusted his tone to something vaguely conciliatory. "Things are bound to settle as we staff up. You're very good at what you do. Keep out of trouble, give them what they're asking, and you'll be in line for a chief-of-subsection posting before you know it. Right now, though . . . we have to trust the administration's priorities."

Did Haki perceive a hint of a genuine personality? Some shred of dignity fighting to survive beneath the surface?

It didn't matter. She smiled civilly and shuffled back to her desk. Her tea was cold. One of the large-screen monitors in the corridor was showing interviews with Separatist collaborators—Yadoska Nir of the Commerce Guild, Separatist Parliament backbencher Tychon Nulvolio—at importunately high volume. Haki typed up her resignation letter and ran the sums—as long as the Empire honored her pension, she'd be comfortable in the Mid Rim somewhere, away from Coruscant real estate prices. But it was all playacting. She deleted the letter as soon as she heard one of the junior agents walking past her desk.

She wanted to go. She wanted to get away from the paranoia and the busywork and the lack of regard for common sense, away from bosses who prioritized loyalty to the administration over loyalty to their agents.

But for now, she was still needed. And she had one more visit to take care of before she was done for the day.

///

"Senator Mothma is organizing. She's been in touch with Senator Marjolos, Streamdrinker, Norve-Gloss, all part of the Delegation of Two Thousand."

Haki waved for silence as she fumbled through the cabinets. "I've no doubt," she said. "Where are the Cook'em Cakes?" She pushed aside canisters of quickflour and a bottle of hot sauce, a jar of pickled vegetables and a motion-activated vermin trap, then finally found the little foil packets and seized them with a grunt of triumph. "That's another lesson," she declared as she shuffled back to the balcony and dropped into her chair. A humid breeze tickled her cheek, and she heard the bass of warbat trance playing below. "Stock your safe house for comfort, not just survival. You get stuck waiting for extraction, state of mind matters. Give yourself a little luxury, and you'll have an easier time focusing."

Chemish was cinching their calloused human fingers together and trying to feign patience. "Did you hear me?" they said. "I *have* something. It could be big."

"Could be!" Haki tore open a packet. The little cake rose and sweated jelly, and the artificial berry scent wafted over the table. "But we start at the beginning, child. Always start at the beginning. So tell me: How's the family?"

That was how they passed the next half hour, on the balcony of a run-down apartment overlooking a street where Aqualish gangsters mingled with frozen-treat vendors, and children raced against speeders trapped in traffic. Haki had chosen the safe house because it was half a block from Chemish's own apartment, but she'd grown fond of the neighborhood over the past months. It reminded her of the better days of her youth.

There was a thin line between source and operative, she thought. Agencies always tried to pretend otherwise: Sources were kept off the payroll, never told anything, used and then disposed of, whereas operatives received proper training, enjoyed the perks of employment, and were forever cherished. Snitches were not spies. But when a source stayed loyal for decades, got paid out of operational funds, and risked their life for their handler, whether out of duty or for friendship, it put the lie to the whole affair.

"Aunt Clejo is still out of work, but the medics say the lung damage isn't permanent. She's worried the shop won't hold her position, but really money shouldn't be an issue . . ."

Haki listened—to what Chemish volunteered and to what they shied away from. She wasn't testing the kid, not really, but she needed to understand them. She couldn't afford to make a mistake, because it was Haki who'd deliberately blurred the lines, recognizing an opportunity amid tragedy. Rather than squeezing Chemish for all they were worth, she had decided to make the exchange more equitable—out of guilt as much as duty, she could admit.

"I volunteered to take care of the triplets one night a week, as long as I'm not working. Their mom is involved with the Eighty-Fourth Street Razers again, but she says it's all small-time . . ."

Chemish was perceptive and curious. That was promising—Haki would've never started down this road if they hadn't been. Chemish was also cautious, and that was another reason Haki had decided to treat Chemish as more than a "source." Too many young folks mistook rash decision-making for dedication.

But the longer they spoke, the harder it became to focus on the conversation. Haki studied Chemish's browned skin, the bright-green eyes, the runner's shoulders concealed beneath the gaudy jacket, and all she could see was Homish. She let Chemish finish recounting their cousin Focoult's misadventures and then waved them to silence.

"Still no word from your brother, I'm afraid," Haki said.

"It's all right."

"It's damn well not. If Homish is alive—and he was a good operative, he may well be, but the chances aren't high—we'll bring him home sooner or later."

"It's all right," Chemish repeated.

"He was mine, my responsibility," Haki said.

"I know."

"Whatever happens, I'll take care of you. I owe that to him."

"I know."

She laughed. Chemish had given up all hope of their brother coming home. *Probably for the best. As long as they don't get it into their head to imitate him and become a martyr.*

Haki imagined some people in her position would've kept Chemish far from spy work for fear Chemish would suffer the fate of their brother. But that was the sort of paranoia that led to a life of indecision. Finding

Chemish had been a stroke of fortune. They had Homish's smarts and determination, but unlike their brother, Chemish had been blandly unaware of the complexities of politics and war and spycraft, so they'd had little to unlearn.

One day, Haki would even let her superiors know she'd trained a new agent. Her bosses could figure out for themselves whether Chemish was source or operative.

"Any of the family ask about Homish?" Haki asked. "Any questions about what happened?"

"Everyone believes the official story—Separatist attack on his cargo transport, all that. We talk about him a lot, but I cleaned out his belongings, like you said. Nothing's turned up. No one knows he was Intelligence. No one knows he was a hero but me."

"Not even your cousin Zhuna?"

Chemish shook their head. "She'd tell me if she knew. Or if she didn't tell me, it'd show. She's not a good liar, Zhuna. Just stops talking, like her jaw's been wired."

"Good. Good," Haki said. Not that it would be a disaster if word about Homish got around, but if the family knew, they'd try to turn him into a public hero. Imperial Intelligence would have to confirm the story, and then it would be easy for an ex-Separatist operative or a freelance data broker to connect Homish to the sources he'd cultivated. Chemish's operations would need to be put on hold indefinitely, too. No one would trust the sibling of a spy (and rightly so), and then there was the risk of Mothma making the link, the subsequent scandal . . . It would be a series of manageable troubles. Haki preferred no troubles at all.

Yet for once, things were going well. "Now," Haki began, smiling and waggling her brow, "tell me what you learned about Senator Mothma."

Chemish did—first shifting their seat to recheck for surveillance, facing away from the street so no one could read their lips, explaining how Zhuna had been called up after family dinner and put on task. "I couldn't listen in on the conversation, but she *told* me—she told me the senator had a list of people to contact. I got a glimpse of her notes. I've got it all in my head. I don't know what it means or if it's useful, but I've got it."

Not exactly treason, but it's a start. Bariovon would be thrilled.

"Give me everything," Haki said. "But whatever happens, don't lose Zhuna's trust. Don't push for what she doesn't give."

"I won't."

Haki nodded approvingly, thought over her list of operations, then added, "Still, lots going on right now. Might be good to accelerate your training."

CHAPTER 8
"NO ONE CARES"

The meeting was at Lud Marroi's getaway in the TriOpt District, a chaotic series of capsules and skywalks jutting out from a shopping complex and overlooking a rooftop jungle tended by droids year-round. Mon was confident Lud wouldn't approve of her plans, and Lud had skipped the obvious questions when she'd asked to borrow the chalet. That, she thought, was what made a true friend: an appreciation for plausible deniability.

But the location was what she needed: convenient, secure, and—best of all—neutral territory. This would be the first gathering of Delegation of 2,000 leadership since the Emperor's ascension, and holding it somewhere far from the Senate itself might help keep egos in check. She'd taken pains to arrive just late enough to allow the others to settle in, and she'd dressed and accessorized for a working lunch. She'd made and studied extensive notes about each of the attendees. There was nothing else she could do to prepare.

She found the twelve senators arrayed about Lud's living room, already forming the expected cliques in roughly even numbers. The anti-militarist faction, notably younger than the others, was seated on hoverchairs by the fireplace. The institutionalists, notably older, who prioritized the integrity of the Senate and the Republic above all else, chatted by the window. And the unprincipled opposition, the senators whose disdain of Palpatine himself overrode all else, gathered about the tea table.

Mon was surprised to see Bail Organa among the institutionalists rather than the anti-militarists. It might have been a sign of the changing times or a whim on Bail's part—a desire to swap news with Senator Marjolos, perhaps. Either way, she hoped it meant he was in the mood to listen to reason. She'd been tempted not to invite him at all, but too many of the original delegation had resigned or thrown in with the new regime. And of the fifteen senators she'd approached, three declined to be involved. She couldn't afford to be picky.

She acknowledged the senators closest to her, then waited for the chatter to subside. "Thank you all for coming," she said as everyone gravitated to the center of the room. Most took seats. Mon, Bail, and Senator Streamdrinker of Tynna remained standing. "I know many of you have suffered for your association with the Delegation of Two Thousand, and doubtless you have concerns about being seen here. I don't need to say that there can be no recordings and no leaks if we're to make an honest assessment of where we stand. I *can* assure you no one is listening but us."

"Many of you have suffered for your association" was a sentiment diluted to the point of meaninglessness. Some of the delegation had been unmolested by the administration. Others, like Bail, had emerged from their arrests unscarred. Yet it was the only acknowledgment she was prepared to give, and her boilerplate guarantee of security would suffice for all of them. She didn't need to give them the particulars of Lud's warning or explain the efforts she'd made to sweep for bugs.

"Times are strange and times are difficult," she went on. She had their attention and didn't intend to lose it. "The administration is bombarding us with change even as it tries to convince the public that everything's returned to normal. It's easy to forget how vulnerable the Emperor is, how *frightened* he must be of our democratic institutions."

Streamdrinker looked ready to interject, but Mon spoke over him. She couldn't afford for this to become a discussion yet.

"Palatine ordered many of us arrested, investigated, *intimidated* after the war ended—but he didn't dare charge us. He's proposed appointing governors to oversee whole sectors and increase his control—but he's been careful to frame it as a means of *oversight*, not a challenge to planetary governments. For all his talk about a glorious new Empire, the fundamental systems of governance remain in place. He has changed rhetoric, he has changed tactics, but he has not changed the anatomy, the heart of the Republic. And although he's popular, he can't afford a backlash while he's promising peace and stability. If he overreaches now, the entire Imperial project will collapse.

"Most importantly for today, he knows he needs *us*. I don't doubt his minions dream of abolishing the Senate entirely, yet Palpatine knows that's an impossibility. The Senate is a powerful symbol, and that's valuable—but not as valuable as our ability, our willingness to regulate the workings of tens of thousands of star systems. As long as the Senate is a functioning entity, he can concentrate on consolidating his might and"—she smiled wryly—"continue to blame us for whatever problems he encounters.

"Which brings us to this: Palpatine's plans to reintegrate the Separatist worlds into the Senate are an act of desperation. I believe he originally hoped his governors would manage the Separatist systems, but he underestimated the task. Now, left with few other options, he's being uncharacteristically forgiving—allowing rebel worlds and insurrectionists to rejoin with full representation and surrendering power he'd rather keep for himself. He'll use all his leverage to ensure the rejoining senators are loyal to him, but once they're inaugurated, the ex-Separatists will be a formidable voting bloc."

The others were still listening. Norve-Gloss smirked at "uncharacteristically forgiving," which had been a cheap shot but it had done its work. Zar stared thoughtfully at the carpet. Mon had said nothing revelatory, but by verbal sleight of hand she'd suggested that the power and advantage were theirs. Whether it was strictly true didn't matter. If Mon's plan worked, it would *become* true.

"Now," she continued, "is the time to redraw the boundaries of our coalitions. The Delegation of Two Thousand came together out of a dedication to peace and democracy." *And personal grudges against the Supreme Chancellor.* "That was admirable . . . but ultimately ineffective. We failed because our righteous demands had no constituency. The public saw us asking Palpatine, the one man who could save them, to abandon his power."

Bail was beginning to say something, and Mon raised her voice: "We need a new coalition. One with the simple, unmistakable goal of fortifying political power in the Senate instead of handing it to the Imperial executive. The Emperor's rule is not supreme, and we must not let it *become* supreme, legally or otherwise.

"Think of your colleagues. Think of your rivals. Whatever they may feel about Palpatine, whatever they owe him, they all have egos and opinions. None desire to be rendered impotent. There are allies to be found among the most self-interested of our peers if our goals are kept simple. And when the Separatists rejoin, they, too, will want a voice— one that we can offer them. Together we would have enough votes to throttle the Emperor's powers and move authority back to the legislature."

She had them now, the anti-militarists and unprincipled opposition in particular. She caught Senator Breemu whispering excitedly to Streamdrinker over the arm of the couch. Zar nodded twice to the carpet, still thoughtful. But Bail was fidgety after being shut down, and his discomfort was spreading to the other institutionalists.

Mon raised the datapad she'd brought as a prop. "I've laid out a framework for what I'm calling the Imperial Rebirth Act. My goal is not to create a public stir or incur the ire of Palpatine's supporters. I will argue this bill *clarifies* the new division of powers, that it will streamline decision-making and guide future legislation in this bold new era. In reality, the bill is designed to secure the Senate's position and avert executive overreach while allowing Palpatine to save face.

"We will accept that we are an Empire now, then turn the Emperor into a glorified figurehead while his supporters dismiss the bill as bureaucratic nonsense. Palpatine will of course be furious and use every means possible to stop the act from passing, but he's stretched thin. The Senate still controls the Empire's finances, its trade, its industry . . . and if Palpatine openly defies us, he'll be left with a galaxy spiraling into anarchy."

"What about the military?"

The question came from an unexpected source: Tontra Doroon of Chibias. Doroon had typically conferred with Senator Amidala before making challenges. With Amidala's passing, Doroon had apparently chosen to go it alone.

"Yes? What about them?" Mon asked.

Doroon lifted her chin. "Palpatine had no compunctions using the clones to slaughter the Jedi. We vote to reclaim power, he could have us all arrested. He's ruthless enough."

"But he's not *careless* enough," Mon said. "Arresting thousands of senators? What better way to signal weakness to the Separatist worlds? Why should the Separatist holdouts still entrenched not renew their fight for independence?

"And what of the corporate power at play?" She hurried on. "Why should the corporations tolerate an emperor who would throw his empire into chaos? The mega-conglomerates who backed the Separatists aren't eager for another war, but another financial shock wave could leave them in dire straits. Those companies who stayed loyal want stability. If Palpatine moves against the Senate, every tax break, every incentive, everything we've done to grease the wheels of commerce is potentially lost to them."

"She speaks truth," Streamdrinker said. "Palpatine is cautious by nature. He wants predictability. Like Senator Mothma and Senator Organa, *I* was arrested after his ascension. I, too, was released. I do not believe Palpatine would gamble the entire Empire if he believed the threat to himself was manageable."

"Which is why we mustn't leave him feeling cornered," Mon said. "We leave him his dignity, the title of Emperor, and his hopes of turning the tables on us down the line."

Now the debate had begun, and Mon allowed it to bloom. She moved to a seat on the edge of the couch, engaging with the others at eye level. Marjolos objected to the entire plan. Even if they were successful, he argued, they'd be vulnerable to Palpatine's *next* scheme. The only viable option, he claimed, was to roll back the proclamation of Empire and restore the Republic as it was. Doroon wanted assurances that the admiralty and the judiciary would stay neutral through the process. Norve-Gloss insisted that Mon was underestimating the public backlash. "Palpatine will use the state-owned feeds to rally people against the bill, and we'll be throwing away our careers."

Mon parried and countered every argument, trying not to show her pleasure. Marjolos was proposing to repeat the strategy the Delegation of 2,000 had attempted, and it would be no more successful a second time. Doroon was right about the military and judiciary, and Mon would be happy to see the senator take charge of securing those relationships. Norve-Gloss's concerns were reasonable but only reinforced the need to act swiftly, before Palpatine could broaden his influence over media outside the Core Worlds.

Sometimes her answers led to more questions or gruff resistance. But for Mon, this was the joy of politics—the backroom conversations with brilliant minds and mediocre bureaucrats, building a coalition that could stand despite its differences. The game of negotiation and compromise and promise-making was what she was good at and what she loved.

Senator Zar posed the most complex challenge, framed as a question of ethics instead of power. "I'm not a fool," he said. "I'll accept votes from anyone who supports a worthwhile bill. But to build a majority coalition, we would need the help of members deep in the corporations' pockets, as you said. They will exact a price for their aid, and this enablement of corruption—this willingness to turn a blind eye to the whims of the powerful—is what brought us to the brink before. We must draw a line somewhere, or what is the point?"

Mon did her best to allay his worst fears, promising that their group would control the scope of the bill, that the act would focus on the relationship between Emperor and Empire, without giveaways or sweeteners. "I've heard those promises before," Zar said, but he ceded the floor and the conversation moved on. Mon wasn't sure she had his backing, yet the others had grown excited, passing around the datapad containing her one-page proposal.

Then came Bail. She'd seen him skulking, rubbing his beard in a show of consternation and awaiting his opportunity. When he spoke, it was with an orator's articulation.

"What about the Jedi?" he asked.

"I'm afraid I don't understand," she said. *So go ahead and make your speech.*

"The Supreme Chancellor—the *Emperor*—ordered the Jedi's destruction. He sent death squads against Republic citizens who volunteered to serve their galaxy. He needs to be held accountable, for that if nothing else, and the Senate must put him on trial for—"

"Absolutely not," Mon said.

But Bail wouldn't be deterred. "For his crimes, during which we can show the people—"

"The Jedi are *not* popular right now, and tying ourselves to them would play into the Emperor's hands. His supporters would say we were following in the Jedi's footsteps, attempting to overthrow his legitimate authority, and *that* would be the topic of debate instead of . . ."

They talked over each other while the rest of the senators shifted uncomfortably. Mon forced herself to be silent at last. She couldn't afford to look like she was bullying Bail or refusing to consider his concerns. It could cost her the sympathy of the entire group.

Bail had the grace not to look smug. "The Jedi deserve justice," he said. "I realize the idea is controversial. I realize many people blame the Jedi for starting the war. But I believe a full investigation of what Palpatine has done will only gain support as the truth emerges. If we want to take back power, we can lay the groundwork by revealing the extent of his evils."

Strictly speaking, it was nothing new. Bail had demanded answers about the Jedi before. But in public he'd avoided pointing a finger at the Emperor or painting the Jedi as martyrs, and to hear him speak bluntly was jarring.

Before Mon could decide on a response, Zar interjected, "The Jedi Council attempted to assassinate Supreme Chancellor Palpatine, and he was within his rights to declare their Order an enemy of the state. The result was tragic and the tactics aggressive, but the Jedi cannot be taken lightly. What 'crimes' are you referring to?"

Bail shook his head, as if the question were contemptible. "Palpatine saw the Jedi as a threat, and he found an excuse to wipe them out. He planned for it, he waited, and then he murdered them while playing the victim. You know it in your heart, and there's a path to showing the truth to everyone if we commit."

There was silence in the room.

"Will you excuse us a moment?" Mon asked.

The others nodded or squinted warily or simply rose. The older senators paused to gather their balance while the younger ones strode toward the doors. Bail kept his eyes on Mon, but she barely glanced at him, observing the progress of her colleagues until she and Bail were alone.

Bail was clever, and he was crafty. She trusted he knew—or believed he knew—more than he was saying. And while Mon wasn't predisposed to conspiratorial thinking, she suspected he was right about Palpatine perceiving the Jedi as a threat. It was conceivable, albeit unlikely, that Palpatine's people had baited the Jedi Council into attempting to oust him, then taken advantage of the situation to eliminate the Order as a whole—though the attempt on his life made it difficult to treat the Jedi purely as victims.

And although Bail was paranoid, although he'd expressed his dismay about the Jedi's destruction publicly, and although she knew him for his obsessions and his intractability and his utter demonization of the administration, this was the first time he'd suggested anything so grand and sinister. She could afford to hear Bail out if it would bring the discussion back on course.

"Tell me," she said.

Bail looked to the doorways, assuring himself that the others were gone. "I believe Palpatine was planning the destruction of the Jedi for years. He feared them more than he ever feared the Senate. And if we can prove *that,* then we can incriminate his whole sordid administration."

"How would we prove it?"

He had the audacity to smile. "I've been badgering the intelligence services for weeks to show me evidence of a Jedi conspiracy, evidence that Palpatine was right to destroy the entire Order. But he overplayed his hand. The Jedi Council used force to try to stop him—it's true. And he can try to spin that into something larger, act like that incriminates every Padawan, every *six-year-old child* in the Order—"

"I understand your theory," she said. She'd heard the reports of dead children at the Jedi Temple, yet the deaths of children had never ended any war in history. "What's your proof?"

"The administration finally caved and sent me documents implicating the Jedi Order as a whole, claiming even the children were in on the Jedi plot," Bail said. "I happen to know they're fake. That's all we need. We've found the loose thread, and we can tug until the entire tapestry of lies unravels. We reveal Palpatine's true face. We clear the name of the Jedi—"

"*No one cares about the Jedi!*" she snapped, and it was heartless but it was true, and Bail needed to understand. "*If* the documents are fake, *if* we can prove it—you're talking about a series of revelations we'd need to showcase for the public in the most convincing possible manner, and for what?"

"For justice, for truth, for the Republic, for democracy—"

"There are better ways! People don't change their minds in the face of evidence. People look for evidence that fits what they believe. And they've already made up their minds about the Jedi. If we start—"

"Are the people who *do* still care about the Jedi irrelevant? Are the Jedi not *people* themselves? There are still Jedi Knights being hunted, and if we prove what Palpatine's been up to, we may actually save lives—"

"No! Absolutely not!" She held up a hand, and to her surprise Bail stopped. He scowled as she caught her breath, closed her eyes, tried to refocus. "We need *allies*, Bail. We need *votes*. And the shortest path there is by appealing to the self-interest of our fellow senators. The Emperor has taken away our power, and we want it back—simple and universal. When you talk about Jedi and conspiracies . . ." She sighed, aiming for patience without condescension. "If we bring *ideology* into it, we're adding needless difficulty. This will be hard enough as it is."

"You won't even bring it to the group," Bail said.

"You already did that. Chasing after Jedi won't get us the coalition we need."

He was hearing her. He was angry, but he was hearing her. And she thought he understood.

"Are you in or out?" she asked.

"I'm out," Bail said. "Padmé would've been out, too."

He walked to the doorway with their dead friend's name on his lips, and Mon knew he hadn't heard anything after all.

CHAPTER 9
DECISIONS UNDER DURESS

They'd taken a battered civilian patrol craft the guerrillas called the *Dalgo* to a neighboring system, where they'd swapped the vessel's identification codes and flown another six hours through hyperspace to a muddy green world on the edge of what had been Separatist space. They skirted the atmosphere to confuse any scanners, made landfall at an abandoned dig-rig, then piled into a skimmer and started another six-hour trip across the swamps.

Soujen didn't mind the downtime. As the skimmer bounced and scraped over boulders and roots, he was belted into his seat, breathing the miasma and thinking about his purpose.

Had the Separatists still been fighting—if there had been full-scale insurrections on Raxus Secundus and Cato Neimoidia instead of faltering resistance on insignificant worlds—Soujen would have gone to join them. That had been the best-case scenario in the event of a military defeat: the reconfiguration of the struggle from a galactic conflict into a series of costly ground wars, unwinnable for a Republic lacking the stomach for decades of occupation. These were the circumstances Soujen had prepared for—he had endured hours of briefings from tactical droids, viewing five- and ten-year projections of a grueling struggle.

Yet the Separatists' loss had been more complete than that. Count Dooku and General Grievous had both been slain, and the Separatist Council members had vanished. The movement's surviving corporate sponsors—those interstellar conglomerates like the Techno Union and the Corporate Alliance whose worlds and wealth had been the Confederacy's paramount asset—had subsequently withdrawn all backing, suing for peace and groveling before the new Empire. Without leadership, financing, or a droid army, the Separatist forces planetside had largely abandoned their battles. Even the death of the Jedi hadn't much bolstered troop morale.

This was the status quo Soujen had pieced together from his time in the pod and his journey aboard the *Dalgo*. It was an assessment with flaws, he was sure, based on propaganda and what he could glean from Saw's guerrillas. Yet the lack of counterpropaganda suggested there was no substantial Separatist resistance. And while the guerrillas had reasons to lie, that did not make them liars.

Thus, Soujen's job now was to avenge the Separatists' losses, not to undo them. His directives accounted for this possibility in broad strokes: He'd been provided with recommended targets and punitive strategies to deploy against the Republic. Under no circumstances was the fight to be abandoned—continuing the war was a moral and strategic imperative. The Separatist cause was just, and if it was ever to be reborn, an ongoing guerrilla effort would provide the sparks to light the fire. (Revenge, too, was a righteous cause, but Soujen's handlers had preferred to leave that point implicit.)

The others watched him nervously as he read over suggested operations in his files, body bent as the skimmer passed among low-hanging tree branches. He could set out to assassinate the Imperial politicians who'd denied the Separatists their freedom, or target the admirals and generals who'd puppeteered the clone army. He could target the clones themselves and their creators on Kamino, in hopes that a blow to the Imperial military might ignite a Separatist resurgence.

Or he could abandon the outdated target lists and prioritize the traitors and cowards who'd failed the Separatist cause: the members of Parliament who'd been too quick to sue for peace, or military leaders who'd surrendered on the day the Separatist Council ceased contact. He'd need to study the news archives more deeply, but he was sure he could identify these collaborators, given time. He could even go after the Separatists' turncoat sponsors, hunting the new heads of the Trade Federation and the InterGalactic Banking Clan. After all, had the corporations stood steadfast against the newly constituted Empire, the Separatist military would still be fighting. Their punishment was entirely justified.

He wasn't short of targets, and the more he learned about the state of the galaxy, the longer his list grew. But the task seemed overwhelming. He fantasized about shortcuts—using massive weapons, biological and chemical, to wage a one-man war against the most secure of his enemies. He had no moral objection to collateral damage. *His* people had suffered massacres enough.

If the cache offered only weapons—if he survived Saw's band, reached the objective, and found that the Separatists had left him no detailed plan of action—*enough* weapons would be an answer in themselves.

The skimmer jolted to a halt. "We walk from here," Vorgorath called, and the sound of booted feet hitting mud filled the air.

Soujen reminded himself, *You're a long way from the cache.* There were other tasks to be done first.

There had been five in the skimmer: Soujen; the simian Vorgorath; Karama, the Republic deserter with the metal teeth; Nankry, the newcomer who'd attacked Soujen; and Rechrimos, a slender Rodian who cradled a scattergun like a child's doll. Soujen found Saw's absence telling. The man was willing to risk his crew while he remained secure in his hideout.

"How far?" Nankry asked.

Vorgorath shook his head, spraying droplets off his fur. It had been drizzling on and off since their arrival. "Less than a half hour, should be. We time it right, it'll be dark when we make it."

Half an hour turned into an hour. Grass, muck, and gravel seemed to snatch at their feet, forcing them to make each step with care or be forced off-balance. Rechrimos—speaking in a pidgin Huttese that Soujen could barely decipher—asked about using the skimmer, but Vorgorath insisted they leave it. They'd remote-pilot it to the target zone for extraction, but until then it would be too easily seen.

Eventually they crested a low hill and saw their destination: a collection of squat prefab buildings surrounded by a security fence. A flag bearing a six-spoked wheel rose above the compound, barely visible in the night. It was a moment before Soujen recognized it as the crest of the new Empire. Smaller flags bearing the outdated Republic design loomed over the main entrance, along with a sign identifying the site as a medical facility. Every pane of metal was smeared with rust, mud, or both.

"Surprised they haven't abandoned it," Karama muttered.

"Generator in the back is new," Soujen said. "Expensive, even for the Republic. They won't decommission the place."

Karama shrugged.

They spent twenty minutes observing patrol patterns and counting personnel. They saw no wounded—from the layout, Soujen suspected the facility wasn't intended for long-term care—but they spotted several medics moving from operating center to living quarters.

"They don't look armed," Nankry said. "Shouldn't be trouble."

"You think?" Karama asked. "What happens if someone sounds the alarm?"

"We shoot them," Soujen said.

Karama scowled and looked to Vorgorath. "We're really doing this?"

"We have orders," Vorgorath said.

"It's a medical facility."

"Have to hit back sometime," Nankry muttered.

Soujen waited in silence and watched the compound.

"Stay out of sight if you can," Vorgorath told them all. "But if you're caught, do what has to be done."

/ / /

Soujen killed the first guard two minutes after Karama reluctantly passed him a blaster. Nankry killed the second, slipping a knife between the clone trooper's helmet and his chest plate. Neither guard sounded an alarm. The group breached the fence and entered the compound.

The guerrillas worked together adequately, Soujen thought. They weren't tightly coordinated, but they were adaptable and trusted one another, relying on the eyes and ears and judgment calls of their comrades. Except for Nankry, they seemed aware of one another's weaknesses and desires. When Rechrimos became nervous, Karama took the lead. And the group never looked to Vorgorath to tear open a gate, despite his prodigious strength.

Soujen suspected they'd been quite good at combating Separatist droids, but it was clear they weren't used to fighting living beings. Only Soujen thought to collect the guards' comlinks and listen in to the patrols. And Rechrimos lingered at the first corpse, chanting softly and mournfully until Vorgorath urged him onward through the mist.

They reached a terminal on the outskirts of the main landing pad. A stand-alone system connected only to the fueling stations would be useless to them—they needed one linked to the rest of the facility. The rest of the group hunkered in the shadows, weapons ready, while Soujen hurried to the pale pool of light around the terminal. Using his right hand, he pulled a short length of cable from behind his left elbow. The sensation of the cable unrolling beneath his skin was disconcerting, but he ignored it and plugged himself into the scomp socket.

There was no direct mind-machine interface. He wasn't designed for it, and he had no desire to intertwine his brain with a foreign computer. Instead, his implants bridged the gap, displaying specifications and menus. The terminal was indeed connected to the rest of the facility, and Soujen awkwardly navigated its layers and ran security bypasses. He understood only half of what he was doing, but he'd been assured the implants' slicing programs were the best the Techno Union could provide.

He found it difficult to process his physical surroundings as he scanned the data from the terminal. If a patrol spotted him, they'd shoot before he could react. He hoped Saw's people understood that they needed him. The time for betrayal would come, from one side or the other, but not for a while yet.

Then he had it: a supply inventory embedded in a facility map. He memorized the content, closed the connection, and secured the cable in his arm before racing back to the group. "Secondary storeroom," he told them. "Let's go."

It was Vorgorath who killed the first medic. He'd opened the side door to the admin center and found himself face-to-face with a man wearing a surgeon's uniform and carrying a disposal bag. Vorgorath had lunged at him and covered the man's mouth. The surgeon had thrashed as he'd suffocated. Vorgorath had hauled the body and bag away, depositing both with the rest of the medical waste, and when he'd returned, he'd refused to look anyone in the eye.

Soujen caught Rechrimos staring his way, as if Soujen were at fault.

They proceeded into the mazelike building, listening to footsteps down corridors and monitoring the comms for any concern over the missing. They heard the rain start again, pattering against the roof. They arrived at the storeroom together, and Soujen used the microlaser in his right hand to melt through the lock.

Karama took the lead again inside, rifling through the shelves and presenting her findings to Soujen for approval. He looked over medical kits, respirators, and finally a bundle of tight-packed tubes of ugly green cloth, each the length of his arm.

"These should do," he said, passing them to Rechrimos.

"Sure of it?" Vorgorath asked. "I expected something . . . sturdier."

"That's not how it works," Soujen said. "Biohazard suits aren't built for combat. They're fragile. But so long as we don't tear them, they'll get us into the cache safely."

"And out?" Karama asked. "The pirates who found you . . . I wouldn't wish what happened to them on anyone."

He was surprised by the sincerity in her voice.

"And out, too," he said. "If we're cautious."

Rechrimos handled the tubes as if they were antiques as he distributed them to the team. Karama finished her raid of the stockroom, and they were all departing when a low wail came through the building's address system. Nankry and Karama swore in unison, but nobody looked surprised. They'd been lucky to go unnoticed as long as they had.

∅∅∅

The clones found them as they were leaving the admin center. There were only five troopers, but they knew the lay of the land and they weren't carrying delicate cargo. The fact that they were firing stun bolts wasn't especially comforting. Soujen suspected it was for the safety of the facility personnel, because he'd never known clones to take *captives.*

In the chaos and crossfire, Soujen and Rechrimos were separated from the group, forced back into the building while the others crawled toward the compound fence. Rechrimos lingered in the doorway, falling behind Soujen after a stray shot nearly blinded him. Soujen hurried into the halls, trying to recall the building's layout from the terminal map.

The Rodian was yammering, scattergun held one-handed and a compressed biohazard suit under one arm. They scrambled over the scrubbed-clean floors. Soujen couldn't understand the man, but he recognized his increasingly angry and strident tone. "Be quiet!" Soujen snapped. And Rechrimos complied—which felt like its own sort of warning.

They paused in an office, long enough for Soujen to start a small fire with his microlaser, igniting food wrappers and fruit rinds and a dead power cell in the wastebasket. The fire-suppression system would stop the flames from spreading, but even that would divert attention. As they hurried onward, Soujen pulled up his bioreadings for review. His heart rate was elevated but within normal range, and his combat hormones were kicking in. His calm was biologically grounded.

Rechrimos fidgeted with the scattergun, adjusting its power level. Soujen led them to another office, this one with a high window looking into the rain. He rolled a desk below the window, climbed up, tapped at the pane, then hopped back down.

"Transparent metal," he said. "Half a centimeter thick. Can you blast through?"

Rechrimos said something Soujen interpreted as a yes and clambered onto the desk. Soujen put his own weapon down as Rechrimos leveled the scattergun and pulled the trigger. The pane exploded outward, and Rechrimos jerked his head back.

Soujen was ready. He heaved himself onto the desk, clapping one hand to the Rodian's face. His other hand went to Rechrimos's neck, and Soujen jolted the man with electricity as he cut his throat with the microlaser.

He took no satisfaction in the kill, but Rechrimos had been nervous in all the wrong ways. Perhaps he'd intended to leave Soujen behind, or perhaps not. Soujen was taking no chances.

He cleared the edges of the window (ordinary glass—he'd lied about the metal) and wriggled through, covering the distance to the fence without incident. He rejoined the others just as the skimmer arrived, and he climbed into a seat beside Vorgorath.

"Rechrimos?" Vorgorath asked.

"They stunned him," Soujen said. "I couldn't let him be captured."

Vorgorath nodded. No one else said anything. The skimmer bounced away from the facility, careening through the rain as sirens wailed behind them.

///

They didn't return to the rig or the *Dalgo* that night. There was *other business*, Vorgorath said, which Soujen took to mean a payoff—they'd obtained their information about the facility from somewhere, and local sources were always the best. They took the skimmer to a nameless settlement an hour's ride from the nearest city, and Vorgorath wandered off while Soujen and the others made camp in a mud field.

The rain kept spitting, but they'd grown used to it. Nankry pried a heating coil out of the skimmer so they could gather in its glow, and they ate in silence until Vorgorath returned. When he did, he said it was time to celebrate their success and mourn their losses. Karama produced a flask of brandy and passed it around (Soujen declined) while the group told stories about Rechrimos.

He'd been a brickmason, they said, dedicated to re-creating lost construction techniques from the Duluur sector. "You wouldn't believe what people used to make houses out of," Karama said. She told how Rechrimos had learned to form bricks from animal waste and ichor and the frozen metal slush from some uninhabited world. Vorgorath commemorated Rechrimos's disastrous marksmanship.

The joviality of the conversation was a feint, a way to sidestep grief. Soujen had seen it in soldiers before, and he thought, *This isn't their first loss.*

The conversation turned to Saw and why he'd taken Rechrimos in, and Karama talked about being found by Saw in a Separatist prison camp. He'd seen something in *her,* a captured deserter, so why not Rechrimos? Soujen found himself admiring Karama's frankness, her willingness to admit to her failures, and when she caught him looking too closely, she only smirked.

"You've been with him the longest?" Nankry asked.

Karama shook her head and pointed at Vorgorath, who shrugged as if the question were a matter of opinion.

Nankry spoke to him: "What do you think he's planning? If we get into the cache, we load up with money and equipment like he says?"

It was her way of asking, *Was this mission worth it?*

"Could be there's no plan," Vorgorath said. "Could be Saw knows resources will matter but can't say when."

"Or it could be he knows *exactly* what he wants, down to the last drop of biotoxin," Karama said. "Thing about Saw is, he'll never tell you."

"He doesn't share his plans?" Soujen asked.

It was the first time he'd spoken. The others looked at him in surprise. "He wants you to believe whatever motivates you," Karama said. "He won't lie—not often. But why should he tell you something if he thinks you won't like it? Saw will step in front of a blaster bolt for you, but he needs you at your best. You start to slip, you drag the rest of the team down."

There was no hostility in the words. Only Nankry looked discomfited.

"He's not *here,*" Soujen said.

"We didn't need him for this mission," Vorgorath said. "Do not mistake trust for cowardice."

Soujen was unconvinced, but he said nothing. He left to relieve himself, then lingered in the cold as he sank into mud up to his heels. The stars were smeared and distorted by some atmospheric effect, leaving the whole world looking like a cosmic afterthought—the last, hasty brushstroke in some barely finished mural.

This was a world that would be forgotten—the world, the clones, the medic, and Rechrimos.

Soujen heard someone wading toward him. He glanced back to see Karama. She drew up beside him, peering into the dark as if trying to see what he saw.

"Real winner of a planet," she said.

Soujen shrugged.

"I hear it's gorgeous in summer, though," she said. "Colorful blooms everywhere, high as your head."

"What's it called?" he asked.

"Star charts say Polroth Five. Locals say Li'eta, I think."

Soujen nodded, and they fell silent.

It was some minutes before Karama said, "You're Xivalian, right?"

He frowned, considering his response.

"Alvadorjian," he said at last. "The Republic called us Xivalian, but Xivalia was never our home."

"I apologize. I don't know much about your people."

This, he supposed, was a question. He'd faced ones like it before, from those who were curious or pitying or intrigued to meet one of his kind.

He might have given Karama the benefit of the doubt. He might have extended some patience. Yet Karama still thought of him as *Hress*, the name he had offhandedly given Saw. If the name *Soujen* felt too true to share with strangers, then how much more of a violation was it to speak of the Nahasta clan? To speak of his brothers and fathers, of the Greater Wheel and the Lesser Wheel, of the Night of Cups and the high songs and the fasting season? There was little that was sacred to Soujen—less than a man *should* hold sacred—but his people mattered.

So instead of revealing secrets, he asked, "You know why we joined the Separatists?"

"I do," she said, then laughed. "I thought I did, but I also thought you were Xivalian, so . . ."

He smirked and rubbed his thumb against the eyespots on his neck. "Tell me what they told you."

"Your people are going extinct," she said, careful but not tentative. "Fewer born every generation. Some people call it a curse, but it's not. It's just a genetic quirk."

She paused.

Soujen nodded. "Close enough. Go on."

"The Republic never did enough to help. So when the Separatists promised you a solution, you signed on."

Soujen grunted. "The Republic failed us for centuries. Five of the seven clans agreed to support the Separatist cause, while the others maintained neutrality."

"I gather that's important."

"Important enough."

She knelt in the muck. After peering at the ground awhile, she reached down and stirred the mire. She seemed to pull up something in her hand, study it, then toss it back. Soujen couldn't see what.

"Doesn't make a lot of sense, does it?" she asked. "Not a lot the Separatists can do for your people now."

His lips twitched. "Why are you baiting me?"

"I'm not—" She seemed to reconsider. "I want to understand. Because I don't know much about you, and we're counting on you to keep us alive, and because—screw it—because I'm *curious*. Most troops, dropped into a situation like this, they'd think about jumping ship. You weren't even a true believer, and you've got no doubts about fighting on."

"I never said I didn't believe," he said. When she didn't respond, he went on. "The Confederacy was a better option than the Republic, for my people and for others."

"Faint praise."

He shrugged. He had no interest in debating the Confederacy's worth. "I began as a mercenary. I fought for the Confederacy for money. Then I accepted a bargain and was remade. Had the war gone differently, we might have met on the killing fields. Instead . . ."

Karama kept picking at the mud. "I get that. But what do you *want*?" she asked. "The Separatists are never coming back. You've got to see that. So is this an honor thing? Is it about vengeance? Justice? Peace?"

"Vengeance," he echoed. It had a ring of truth to it, though a part of him wondered whether the answer was incomplete, or whether he'd chosen the wrong word because it was the closest word at hand. His lips twitched again, and he brushed past misgivings and irritation. "I know my purpose."

She squinted up at him and stood. "Did you ever not?"

He considered the question. He considered the answer. He said nothing.

Karama sighed. "The Separatists killed three of my cousins and more of my friends. Before I deserted, I wasn't a combatant—I reported for the military news feeds. But I was taken prisoner just the same. Nowadays, I just want to set things right." She shifted her weight in the muck. "Thank you for explaining about your people."

She turned and walked three meters before adding, "Saw thinks you'll betray us. You probably figured that. For what it's worth, though . . . I don't think you have to. You may not like it—even Saw doesn't like it—but we are on the same side."

With that, Karama left. Soujen thought about following her. He thought about killing her, but only out of habit. He couldn't see the upside.

/ / /

After the others had gone to sleep, Soujen climbed into the skimmer and thumbed the comm controls, scanning frequencies and listening to the planetary broadcasts. There was no word of their attack on the medical facility, but he lingered on the news anyway. A heavily accented local was extolling the virtues of the Emperor on one channel. On another, two speakers debated the merits of AgriStar-modified crops.

A voice on a third channel froze Soujen in place. A man's baritone rumbled through the skimmer's tinny speakers: "You speak as if we all supported violence, but that is slander, sir. Many in the Separatist Parliament desired secession without war and opposed the military's excesses. Many risked much in search of peace. My sincere hope is that where our worlds' partnership with the Republic failed, our membership in the Empire will reward all parties."

"And what about reparations?" a second voice asked. Soujen barely heard the words.

"Speaking for myself," the first voice said, "I believe that civilians who suffered on both sides must be made whole. A punitive approach will not restore our union but divide us further. Any monetary compensation should be decided by the people's representatives in the Senate."

"And do you expect to join the Imperial Senate yourself, Mister Nulvolio? The grand vizier announced this afternoon that we are one month from Reintegration Day, when the Separatist worlds will officially reunite with the Empire."

"When the day comes, yes. I expect to enjoy the privilege of joining the Senate."

The interview ended there. Soujen turned off the comm.

He thought about the deal he'd made. He'd given his body to the Separatists, offered himself up for experimentation and transformation. He'd spent months adapting, recovering, and retraining, and then—as the direction of the war had altered—he'd willingly stepped out of the conflict to become a contingency plan and instrument of vengeance. He did not regret these things. He had accepted that he was alone in the galaxy.

Yet now there was a second survivor of the Confederacy that Soujen had known. Now Tychon Nulvolio was a collaborator.

Soujen looked toward the sleeping forms of the guerrillas—Republic partisans all, fighting not for independence but for the restoration of Soujen's enemy. What would the clans think of him if they knew what he had become? It had seemed such a small compromise, to go on a mission for Saw, to chat amiably with Karama. But now he saw his hypocrisy for what it was in the light of Nulvolio's perfidy. His fury grew hot, directed not at Nulvolio but at himself. He, too, was a collaborator.

Soujen had all he needed from this world: information, freedom, equipment. He could've killed the guerrillas, maybe should have, but their knowledge of his existence could do little harm. *Waste no more time here. They are not the mission.*

He powered up the skimmer and took off across the mud. Whatever had become of the galaxy, however little loyalty and dignity were left, Soujen would stay true to his purpose. No compromise was *small* when the battle was lost and all that remained was a soul, unblemished and made of fire.

CHAPTER 10
AN INAUSPICIOUS MEETING

"Please, Bail. Just give her to the droid."

Leia was wailing, red-faced and inconsolable, as Bail cradled her against his chest and made meaningless sounds to soothe her. It wasn't working. He had to turn his back on Breha to escape his wife's stare.

"You promised we would talk," Breha said. "Leia is fine. Eness can take care of her. She's not sick. She's just *cranky*."

"She's my daughter," he snapped, "and she has to know I'll come when she needs me."

His tone was too sharp, but was he really in the wrong? The girl needed to know her father, needed to bond with him and feel connected. To put her in the arms of a nurse droid felt irresponsible, no matter what the parenting studies said.

Breha didn't argue, but he felt her watching as he rocked Leia and gave the child his warmth and his love. He forced down his irritation (at Breha, at the world) and focused on Leia's tiny breaths, on her nearly imperceptible heartbeat, on the fragile elements of life that connected her to the uncaring galaxy.

Sometimes he glimpsed her mother, his friend, in the crinkle of her brow, and he wondered whether he was failing the woman.

After nearly an hour, Leia fell asleep and Bail took her to her crib, then left the nursery. Breha followed. He gave instructions to the droid, who proceeded inside and closed the door. Breha waited.

At last, he turned to face his wife. Her eyes were dark and worn.

"Your daughter is not a shield," she said.

She seemed to regret the words as soon as they were spoken. Breha knew, *both* of them knew, that they weren't the embattled roles they'd taken on. They were kind and passionate, true to each other and to themselves, and if the exhaustion of parenting and the death of friends were the static they needed to shout through to be heard, they would shout until they were hoarse.

Bail knew this on an intellectual level. Feeling it and acting it were more difficult. He stumbled across news clips of himself some days, candid holorecordings made for the Alderaanian archives, and he felt estranged from himself—as if everything that had given him vibrancy and joy had been wiped out along with Master Windu and Shaak Ti and Plo Koon and the others.

Breha held up a hand to forestall any reply and walked to the love seat, dropping onto the cushions. She gestured to the place beside her, but Bail took a chair instead.

"I'm worried, is all," she said. "You've been running nonstop since the Emperor, since the Jedi, since Padmé . . . You're hurting yourself."

"You know what's going on," he said. "The Senate is the galaxy's first line of defense, and it's barely putting up a fight."

"Then take a moment to regroup. Even for a few days." She sighed and lifted her chin, meeting his gaze. "Come home to Alderaan. We'll be safe. We can plan our next move—"

"Your next move isn't mine! Your responsibility—" Again his tone was too sharp. He rubbed his face and ran his hand through his hair, as if to remake himself. "You need to focus on protecting Alderaan, and there's no one who can do that better. I need to focus on the Senate and the Republic." Not the *Empire*. The name itself was an effort to make him forget.

"Palpatine isn't going to win or lose because you took a week to get your head together. You're not in a condition to work."

Breha loved him. She *knew* him. He reminded himself of this because her talk of patience reminded him of Mon Mothma, and that roused his pique.

"I'll think about it," he said. "I promise I will think about it."

She looked unconvinced. He rose, walked to her, and placed his hands on her shoulders. He felt his own muscles relax. "Believe me?" he asked. It was, in truth, a plea. *Times are hard, but our trust is not broken.*

"Think about it," she agreed.

And he would. He would fulfill any promise he made to his queen, though he knew this one would make no difference.

After a while, they climbed into bed, and he thought about the ghosts of the Jedi and the ghost of Leia's mother, Padmé Amidala, who had loved the Jedi so. He thought about the Emperor, and all the evil one man was capable of.

∕∕∕

Once Breha was asleep, he rose from bed, went to the safe, and tucked several thousand credits' worth of Nothoiin ur-diamonds into a hidden pocket sewn into his belt. He donned a plain black coat and proceeded out of Cantham House without notifying his security detail. He considered taking his speeder but decided on public transport, thinking the walk would do him good.

He'd spent the past week attempting to trace the origins of the data the intelligence services had provided him. He had no doubt that the transcripts of the Jedi Council meetings were forgeries. He knew the Jedi Masters well and had seen their fear and grief the day the Emperor turned against them. Obi-Wan Kenobi had been calloused by war but had never *become* callous. Master Yoda had loved children, loved play and instruction more than anything, and his pain after the massacre had bent him with every step. The hologram showing the Jedi meeting

STAR WARS: THE MASK OF FEAR

with the Separatist Count Dooku was cleverly presented but likewise unconvincing. No such meeting could ever have occurred.

Imperial Intelligence claimed the documents had been obtained from an operative who'd died shortly after delivery, which neatly circumvented the most obvious questions. The seals on the files met all standards for authentication, yet that was both a problem and an opportunity. If Bail could prove the seals *had* been falsified, that would be enough to show that Palpatine's purge of the Jedi Order was based on a lie. And if he could prove *that*—and better yet, if he could prove Palpatine's involvement in the forgeries—the people of the galaxy would remember all the Jedi had done for them. They would remember, and they would turn against their new Emperor. They would *care*, no matter what Mon Mothma claimed.

What else could Bail believe but this?

The weather was unseasonably cold—the weather control systems still hadn't been fully restored—and snowflakes spiraled to melt upon the walkways. Bail strode to the tram stop and boarded a nearly empty car. He slipped a hand beneath his coat, first checking his belt, then the curved grip of the Kueget blaster pistol he'd received as a gift some years before. He'd rarely had occasion to fire the weapon, but he was an adequate shot, and he'd been told the blaster was extremely forgiving. Its transponder sat in a drawer in his office; the weapon would not be tracked.

He switched trams twice and took a turbolift half a kilometer down. On Level 1313, there was no more snow, and his coat felt stifling. He moved through a night market, calmer than he'd expected for the hour, and smelled street food, spice, and urine. Someone shouted from a window above him. The merchants and buyers kept to themselves, proceeding as though history itself weren't collapsing and the rise of the Empire were only a rumor.

He knew roughly where he was going, but most of the street signs had been stripped to wire by scavengers or covered by graffiti, so it was an hour before he found the complex of vice dens, gambling clubs, and drinking establishments known as Hivetown. He pushed through curtains and ducked under holograms advertising services of dubious legality. He was sweating and exhausted by the day, but adrenaline kept him alert.

It occurred to him that being identified could cause him problems worse than scandal. He didn't fear for his reputation, but what if the administration claimed he'd come to buy spice or slaves? *Too late for that,* he told himself. Besides, a regime that forged documents to justify genocide wouldn't need *evidence* to come after the senator from Alderaan. Only his existence as a non-threat protected him.

He pressed on through intoxicated crowds, feeling his lungs burn from hallucinogens designed for nonhuman physiologies, and caught the attention of a massive three-horned brute standing at a bronze door. "I'm looking for Den Dhallow," Bail said, and the brute only stared at him. "He'll find it worth his time."

Still no answer.

But Bail hadn't expected one. "I know what happened on level thirteen thirty-nine," he said. "I bear him no ill will, but I must speak to him."

The brute produced a comlink and tapped it rhythmically with one claw, never taking his eyes off Bail. A moment later, he stepped to the side and the door opened.

Bail murmured a silent thanks to the gods of bureaucracy—and all the staffers who'd compiled the Senate Intelligence Oversight Committee's *Sector Report on Organized Crime*—then proceeded through.

The room beyond was a club within a club, where patrons silently focused on screens around the bar or whispered at their booths. Bail found the contrast with the outer rooms unnerving, but he dragged himself to an empty booth and shed his coat, contemplating again what would happen if he was recognized. Would he be in danger? Might he be taken hostage? He felt shame at the notion that his argument with Breha might be the last they ever spoke.

It had been foolish to come alone, he thought.

He did not leave.

He was joined by a shriveled Arcona with glittering amber eyes sunken into the fog-blue wedge of a head. "Thank you, visitor, for waiting," the Arcona said in a lilting voice. "You wished a meeting with Den Dhallow?"

"You're not Den Dhallow," Bail replied.

The Arcona wiggled their fingers, the equivalent of a shrug. "I am of Den Dhallow's circle, and his favored of six. You are unknown. Be grateful."

Bail paused. He'd played diplomat a thousand times, with rivals and judges and foreign adversaries, but rarely with so little information—and rarely while staking his own life.

Graciousness won out over belligerence. He could always change tack later. "I am most grateful," he said. "But I am in need of Den Dhallow's services. I understand he employs the finest forgers in the Core." *Or at least outside the intelligence agencies.*

"Den Dhallow's artistic re-creations are entirely legal," the Arcona said. "I cannot endorse any project designed to deceive, nor will any of the six."

"Deception is the last thing on my mind." He shifted in his seat, wondering whether the Arcona could smell his body odor. "I'm looking to hire someone to *expose* a forgery, to examine a faked authentication seal and help me understand who could make such a thing."

"Forensic work is outside Den Dhallow's usual business. You may wish to go elsewhere? If you are the victim of a confidence trick, the underworld police will gladly investigate. We would take no offense."

"This is an especially elaborate forgery, and not one the underworld police—or the upper-level security forces—are equipped to review. Your people may find the work challenging, but there would be appropriate compensation. Unless Den Dhallow's reputation is exaggerated?"

"*That,*" the Arcona said, voice buzzing beneath the lilt, "is an ill-mannered insinuation. We have shown you courtesy, and you offer insults. Perhaps we should not have granted an audience."

The Arcona stood. Bail knew he was being played, but what could he do? If he refused to show his hand, the Arcona would depart and Den Dhallow lost nothing. There was no bluff to call.

"My name is Bail Organa," he said. "I am a member of the *Imperial*

Senate from the planet Alderaan." He kept his voice steady but low, erasing any lingering informality and inserting a note of command. "I am funded by the treasury of House Prestor, and I am willing to negotiate a price. Refuse to help, and I'll hold no grudge. But I am in possession of forged documents, and I need to know where they came from."

The Arcona cocked their head and observed him a long while. "Please stay seated," they said, leaving for the bar.

Bail closed his eyes. Where *would* he go if Den Dhallow refused? He couldn't force the man to cooperate, but the galaxy had a limited number of top-tier forgers. Could he reach out to his contacts in the self-governed worlds of the Outer Rim? Friends whose loyalties might have changed since the war's end? All his public blather about investigating the Jedi's destruction was nothing. The administration didn't care. But this was much riskier. This was the threat that would draw Palpatine's wrath if Bail was careless.

Was there any chance that the documents were real, that the accusations against the Jedi were true?

He laughed bitterly to himself. *You're the only one who knows the truth, and even you're starting to doubt it.*

/ / /

Bail thought back to the day the Jedi died. He'd borne witness as the troops descended on the Temple, seen clone soldiers gun down a child without pause or humanity. Palpatine had painted the execution of the Jedi as a bloodless necessity, the surgical excision of a security threat, as if a child were no different from a battle droid.

Maybe that was simply *war,* Bail thought. Maybe sending clones against droids had helped them all pretend that war *could* be bloodless, that with skilled hands and advanced weapons, they could spare anyone important and pretend soldiers were commodities. Maybe the people of the Republic had learned the wrong lessons and come to believe that because they cared about preserving life so deeply, any death that *did* occur must be justified. To believe otherwise would be to accept complicity in slaughter.

The worst of it was this: The child Bail had seen gunned down at the Jedi Temple *had* been a combatant. The Jedi trained their youngest apprentices for battle, and Bail had seen the child fighting, cutting clones through with a burning blade of plasma before the survivors had ended his life. There was no moral equivalence between the child and the clone battalion, yet it meant Bail could not picture the victim as fully innocent. The clones who'd died were no older than the child, conscripts in lab-grown bodies.

Much later, he had spoken to the last of the Jedi. They had consulted in secret, and the wizened Master Yoda had told him about Palpatine's obsession with dark arts, his cruel joy as he'd carried out his plan. Palpatine was steeped in the mysteries of the Sith, Yoda had said—the ancient anti-Jedi cult—and surely had been his entire life.

"All he has done, his manipulation of events, I will not guess," Yoda had told Bail. "Too arrogant was I to see. Too ignorant I am to know."

Bail believed the master's story. Yet who could he tell? He'd shared a stilted, sanitized version with Breha, but the Emperor's lurid wickedness had seemed unbelievable in the kitchen at Cantham House, with Leia asleep in the nursery and normalcy spackled over the broken galaxy. He'd failed to articulate the depths of Palpatine's evil.

He might have told his story in public, but what then? He'd have been arrested for aiding the Jedi, and he had no evidence of Palpatine's membership in the Sith cult. Moreover, who would care if he did? If Mon was half-right, if few cared about the Jedi, internecine heresies would mean nothing to the galaxy at large.

So he was alone with the truth. And left malnourished and unshared, that truth would seem less likely each day—until he would remember it only as a dream, having failed to act on its horrors.

CHAPTER 11
INTERVENTION

"What's he doing, anyway?"

"Getting himself killed, looks like. Killed if he's lucky, worse if he's not."

"I meant—"

Haki flapped a hand at Chemish and was rewarded with silence. A spice dealer and his entourage passed them, and Haki cried after the group, pleading for a few credits or a single death stick, then settling back against the alley wall when she was duly ignored. "I know what you meant," she said. "None of your business, is it? You're just along for the ride."

Chemish screwed up their face, wanting to protest but knowing better than to try. Haki smiled happily, then resumed her study of the portal into the netherworld that was Hivetown.

She'd planned to take the evening off, maybe take in a show in the Arts District. But she'd checked in on Bail Organa because she was, despite herself, a dutiful woman. And when Organa had abandoned his security detail to go flying like a fool into the depths of Coruscant, she'd decided to follow, and when she'd decided to follow she'd realized she could use backup, because her judgment was clearer than Organa's.

It would be good experience for Chemish, assuming they both survived.

"You know my uncle Edvi is Alderaanian?" Chemish said. "Really likes Organa. Lot of the neighbors do, too. Thought he was like Palpatine, pushing back against the corporations and the lifers in the Senate."

"Who said he isn't? Our spying on him doesn't make him a terrorist. He might be an idealist, might be on the take, might be an addict . . . Whatever the case, he's *trouble*. What's our job, again?"

Chemish suppressed a smile and shook their head. "Stability."

"That's right. The Empire is unstable. New governments, postwar governments, they always are. Mothma, Organa, and the rest of them—doesn't matter if they're plotting to overthrow Palpatine or if they're handing out flyers. They could topple the whole Empire by accident, because that's what instability means."

Which was true, as far as it went, if farcically exaggerated. Mon Mothma and Bail Organa and the rest of their delegation were more dangerous to themselves than to the administration. Nonetheless, Haki had a job to do, and Chemish needed to learn the basics before the nuances.

"Never get attached to a politician." Haki lowered her voice as a wrinkled Chevin stared their way, then lumbered into Hivetown. "Coalitions come and go, and they're not so different in the long view. Our job's to protect the Republic."

"The Empire."

"Exactly." Haki winked. "Now, what's your assessment of our situation?"

Chemish frowned but didn't hesitate. "Organa could be up to something, but he didn't look like he knew where he was going, yeah? So whatever he wants, he's new to it—which puts *him* in danger, because everyone here is dangerous."

"That all?" *Don't disappoint me. Your eyes are younger than mine. There's no excuse.*

"He was carrying a blaster. Might mean something, but there's senators who carry them everywhere, so best not to read into it."

"Good enough." *Excellent!* "So all that means *what* for you? You're surveillance, remember."

"If I'm not told different? One of us stays outside, the other follows Organa and keeps watch for anything compromising. Anyone he meets, we follow them if we can, but stay on the primary target if not. If things get hairy, we place a call to local security. Otherwise, let things play out and report in after."

She slapped Chemish on the shoulder and squeezed. "You're learning. Now we're going to do something else, because I've been at this most of a century and I know better than you."

They went into Hivetown together and played the roles Haki assigned: Haki the disheveled old woman searching for her son-in-law, Chemish her impatient caretaker who could pass out credits while Haki pleaded for sympathy. Chemish was a passable liar and, if anything, looked too comfortable among the thieves and addicts. It was a reminder to Haki that however naïve Chemish was when it came to spycraft, politics, or the galaxy at large, they hadn't lived a sheltered life.

It didn't take long to find someone who pointed them to Organa's trail, and Haki decided a change of approach was needed when they located the bronze door to the inner den. "Stay out here," she told Chemish, offering a few final instructions before engaging the bouncer in conversation. She took a gamble and offered a considerable sum as a bribe straight off. Anything else would've taken more time than she'd allotted.

The bouncer took her money (she wondered whether Intelligence would bother reimbursing her), considered the matter for a good thirty seconds, then allowed Haki through. Beyond the bronze door was a club within a club, and Haki shifted into a slouch, teetering just enough to suggest infirmity as she looked for the senator.

She spotted him at one of the booths, looking up at a slender Arcona pushing a steaming amber shot glass toward him. Two burly figures stood at the Arcona's side, blocking Organa's exit. "You must drink," the Arcona said, as if they'd been arguing about this for some time.

Haki couldn't hear Organa's reply, but he was frowning, clearly uncomfortable. The bartender was watching the Arcona and Organa. The other patrons were taking pains to look elsewhere.

"You must drink, Senator," the Arcona repeated. "A guest sups of the meal his host provides."

Haki stumbled forward, weaving her way in a roundabout manner toward the booth.

"Does that mean you've reconsidered?" Organa asked. "Perhaps I could drink with Den Dhallow himself?"

Den Dhallow. The name was familiar. Was he a blackmailer? A forger? Organized crime had never been Haki's specialty.

She could piece the particulars together later. By the looks of things, Organa was trying to strike a deal and Dhallow, sensibly, wanted nothing to do with the Imperial senator. Maybe he knew Organa was on the outs with the administration, or maybe Dhallow had other reasons—Haki could think of plenty. Haki supposed the Arcona intended to pump Organa so full of spice he wouldn't remember his own mother, then dump the senator on the street and pretend they'd never met him. An acceptable outcome for Haki, but only if Organa didn't choke to death in the throes of an overdose or get himself shot resisting. Being unpopular with Intelligence wasn't a crime punishable by death, and she could imagine how fast Bariovon would pin the blame on her if anyone asked why Organa hadn't been protected.

Besides, Haki was *curious* about a senator who laughed at Jedi treason and slunk to dark places during the night. She was curious what was so important that a new father would risk himself. Easier to get the answers from Organa than from Dhallow and his crew.

"I will insist—" the Arcona began.

Organa's hand slid to his blaster.

"Where'd you go? Where'd you go?" Haki slurred as loud as she could. She was wobbling three meters from Organa's booth, then two. It got her a glance from one of the Arcona's guards and no more.

We're doing this, then. Mercy.

She took another swaying step forward. Then, with a lurch, Haki threw herself into the guards and tumbled at their feet. She tried to grab them as she went down, twisting and swinging so they couldn't seize her. Then she bobbed upright again, catching one under the chin with her scalp and elbowing another in the groin. Her head stung and her joints ached, but she hadn't been caught yet.

"Sorry, sorry," she muttered, but she couldn't count on being under-estimated anymore. She slipped her Telltrig blaster free as the guards squeezed her from either side, and she loosed two shots, the soft fizzle of the silenced discharge lost in the chaos.

"Time to go, dear," she said, without a glance at the senator. She was watching the rest of the club now. The bartender was speaking into a comlink.

She heard a clatter behind her as the Arcona went down and Organa stood at her side. He gripped his blaster in one hand as if it were a club, his expression fierce and unyielding. "Who are you?" he asked.

"Name's Haki. I'm going to bring you home to your family. Though if you think your friend here was on the level"—she pointed to the Ar-cona with the toe of her shoe—"you're welcome to taste whatever's left of that drink."

"I'll pass," Organa said, and they ran together.

CHAPTER 12
NOT A SEPARATIST

They sprinted through the dens of Hivetown. Behind them was a commotion and ahead was a clamor, and Bail could only think, *We are all fools and dead men.*

He'd barely caught more than a glimpse of his rescuer. She was dressed in rags and furs, an ash-skinned woman with a noseless face and a mouth that extended nearly to her drooping ears. She was just far enough from human that Bail would need to be wary of assuming too much from her expressions, of projecting his own people's habits onto her.

But that was a problem only if they survived. He had no doubt he'd been in danger. He trusted his gut, and everything about the Arcona's posture had felt wrong. Now, though, with Den Dhallow's people pursuing, he might be worse off. Haki shoved him through a curtain into a long hallway, and he glanced back to see whether she was following. He thought he saw her call to someone, gesturing at a human in the crowd. A moment later there was the sound of a blaster bolt and a cry—"The Separatists were right!"

"Messy sort of distraction," Haki said. "Good ones always are."

Then they were on the streets of Coruscant, racing into the night, and Bail heard a fire crackling and smelled smoke, and he prayed that no one else had paid the cost for his foolishness.

CHAPTER 13
TRUTH, LIES, A LITTLE MORE TRUTH

"Drink," Haki said, pushing a canteen across the picnic table. "You're dehydrated."

The senator stared at her soberly. She'd seen a zeal in him as they'd run through Hivetown, but now, sitting in a brambly little pocket park two levels up, he looked almost mournful. Part of that really would be the dehydration—humans were terrible at retaining fluids—but something deeper troubled him.

Eventually he took the canteen, peering into the water and sniffing it before taking a cautious swig. "Where do you want to begin?" he asked.

It was a gracious way of declaring, *I'm not saying a word until you explain yourself.*

In her younger days, she'd have come prepared with a false name, props, and a whole supporting cast. Now she had only Chemish, and Bail had already seen them shooting into the air. Anyway, Chemish would need time to safely extract themselves, and these days Haki preferred to improvise. "I'm with Senate Security," she said. "Been threats on your life lately, so we figured best to keep an eye on your apartment. I admit, I got worried when you left without your bodyguards. Got a little curious. Good thing I did."

It was pleasingly close to the truth. She couldn't tell whether he believed her, but he nodded and said, "Thank you."

"Sorry I didn't think to get pictures or evidence. That lot assaulting a senator, have to figure the underworld police would want to know."

"Dhallow is untouchable," Organa said, "and his people only turned violent after—"

"Well, yes." She sighed, then winked. "We made quite the team."

The senator seemed unamused. Haki undid the knot in her hair and checked the power supply on her sidearm, low but adequate as long as nobody pursued them. Organa kept staring across the park, at the scaffolding and platforms and descending groundscrapers that filled the sky. He was shivering slightly, now outside the warmth of Hivetown.

"The fire," he said. "Suppose anyone was hurt?"

"Oh, I doubt it. Maybe some smoke inhalation, but Hivetown sees sparks like that twice a month."

"And the Arcona's bodyguards?"

Ah, she thought. *Now we come to the problem. One of them, anyway.*

"Couldn't be helped. If I'd tried to stun them, they would've broken my neck, if not yours."

"Too many people have died," he muttered, though it didn't seem directed at her. "Too many have died, and nobody cares."

You'll get over it, she thought. Men like Bail Organa always did—he'd fret for an hour and then forget. But she made sure to nod sadly and wait a spell, then said, "Can I ask you something personal?"

The senator waved dismissively. "Ask."

"You've got a newborn at home? That right?"

His smile softened the chilly air, and Haki was confident she'd made the right move.

"Leia," he said. "She's our first. War orphan."

"First is a trip. Second is easier but never easy as you expect—you figure you've been through the worst, then the babe turns out to have their own personality. The third, though . . . the third is sheer joy."

"How many do you have?"

Not a one, she thought. *Not anymore, not since the first days of the war.* But that wasn't a fact for manipulation or cajoling. That was for her and her alone.

"Five," she said. "Twelve grandchildren, if you can believe it."

"Are they all on Coruscant?" He'd roused himself to engage—against his better judgment, perhaps, but she had him on the hook.

"Oh, I'm only here lately myself. Raised my kids on Tsaokallus, down the Perlemian hyperroute a few parsecs off Metalorn. Not like this at all"—she waved an arm to encompass the entire planet—"but it's where my pop raised me, and we did all right."

"Tsaokallus." He frowned in concentration. "Mid Rim world. One of the old independent colonies that rejoined the Republic, what, sixty years ago?"

"Sixty-eight. I remember the day."

"You must've been young," the senator said. "Inspired to service?"

"You could say. Stayed out there a while, but I was proud to join Senate Security when the chance came. I know what life is like without the Republic."

"Something the rest of us will have to learn."

Haki shrugged. "If you say. The Imperial reforms don't seem right to me, either, but it's all over my head." *Plant the seed, then move on.* "Suppose we should get you home. Wouldn't mind stopping for a bite to eat, if you're willing to take it slow."

He protested, she said it wouldn't take long, and they found a kiosk catering to overnight factory workers and bought a pair of meat pies fried in pastry shells. They ate while they walked, and Haki shared plausible tales about her children. The senator occasionally broke into laughter and offered his own anecdotes in return.

Once Haki was wiping her fingers and Organa had lapsed into silence again, she said, "If I can be nosy, it seems you've got a good wife, good child, fame and fortune . . . Don't seem right you're dealing with Den Dhallow's crew."

"It was a poor decision," Organa admitted.

She'd need to drag it out of him. "Figure you weren't there for spice. Dhallow's no dealer. You won't tell me if he's blackmailing you, I suppose—"

"Blackmail's not his game."

"Right." She tried not to smile. "He's a forger? If you've got tax troubles, there's easier ways."

Organa peered at her and brushed the crumbs from his beard. "What do you know about Dhallow's forgery operation?"

"Not much. Mostly signets, visas, ledgers for up-and-coming corporations. Very good if he doesn't cheat you."

"In your experience"—he was cautious, as much (she suspected) about her as about what to say—"could Dhallow forge a seal that would pass inspection by the security services?"

This was a delicate moment. Men with obsessions were easy to manipulate, and the death of the Jedi had dominated the senator's life, in public and in private. Now Haki knew why he'd been so excited by the documents from the Jedi Archives—he believed they were forged.

She couldn't share the senator's interest in the Jedi, but if she played her hand wisely she might find the opportunity she'd been seeking. Or she might find something entirely unexpected. This was the intoxicating thing about spycraft, the moments where instinct and foresight came together, the moments when—Haki recalled the words of a mentor—you stood in a dark hallway seeking a door to somewhere new. You might not know how many doors there were or where exactly to find them or even where they would lead you, but your mastery of the craft would guide you. An hour before, she couldn't have said what door she'd expected the senator to open. But now she was close and knew what she hoped to accomplish.

"In my experience," she said, "Dhallow's work is excellent. But excellent forgeries come apart pretty fast in the lab."

"What if he's using a new technique?"

"Suppose he might be, but he's about money, not art. He'd be advertising it every which way, and I've heard nothing. There something that worries you?"

The senator shook his head. "Nothing I can speak of."

"You have clearances I don't, and I respect that," Haki said. "But I'll need more if you want my advice."

Had she played the part of security agent too well? He needed to believe she was loyal but mysterious, capable of offering him resources he lacked. She'd thought she'd overdone it, but now—

"Suppose I had evidence," Organa said, "indicating that members of the administration had justified key decisions based on falsified intelligence. I'm accusing no one—"

"Of course."

"—but I have a responsibility to learn the truth."

Haki counted to ten to show she was taking the situation seriously. "If you want to know where the forgery came from—and if your experts can't disassemble the seal, and Den's aren't interested—I'd ask who's motivated to put such a forgery together."

"Yes," the senator said, sounding disappointed.

"You checked the Separatist propaganda mills?" she asked. Sloppy, but it got the conversation where she wanted. "They churned out thousands of holos and documents during the war . . . most not very good, but they'd have a motive."

"I considered it. I even checked against the inventories of propaganda sites our people raided, but I didn't find a match."

"Doesn't mean there's no connection."

"Maybe not. But the trail's gone cold."

"Think so?" She stopped walking, and the senator turned to face her. "If the forgery's good as you say, there aren't many folk who could put it together and fewer who'd want to. You'd need a first-rate organization with technology on par with the Imperial intelligence services. And the Separatists always did have an edge on us there, Techno Union sponsorship and all."

Organa appeared ready to argue, but she didn't give him the chance. "If I were in your position, I'd take advantage of the war's end. See who's in custody. See who might know about a dangerous forgery crafted by a team of dozens inside Separatist Intelligence. You won't find anyone worth interviewing on Coruscant, but if you made the trip to the Separatist worlds, talked to folk in person . . ."

"Quite the plan," the senator said. His tone was guarded, but she could see the spark in his eyes.

"Just a thought," Haki said. And since his suspicions were growing anyway, she took the next step. "Of course, you'd need security. There's still fighting. And even if you keep the trip quiet, you'll want someone to watch your back, keep you from making a mess of it."

High above, a tower switched its evening lights to a softer daytime setting. You never saw dawn this deep in Coruscant, Haki thought, but the message got passed down all the same.

The senator studied Haki, looking at her face and then her garments and equipment. He was, she was sure, trying to figure out who she really worked for; whose side she was on; and most of all, whether he could trust her.

"You have suggestions of who I should talk to?" he asked. "Among the Separatists?"

"I could make a list. Take a little time and research."

"You have two days," he said. "I can make it home on my own."

The senator left her behind, and Haki was satisfied with the outcome. He saw her as valuable, which was as good as trustworthy. He'd taken the bait and believed the documents implicating the Jedi had been forged (*might* have been forged, at least) inside the Separatist Confederacy. That theory seemed unlikely to Haki, who saw no reason to doubt the documents' authenticity. But it gave Organa hope, and it gave her a path offworld.

Her job was to monitor a watch list of senators for indications of disloyalty. Organa's desire to authenticate classified documents was only marginally interesting, but a secret trip into Separatist space certainly warranted investigation . . . and who better than Haki to tag along?

She could be away from busywork and junior agents and a superior officer who saw no value in loyalty. She could take care of people who mattered, agents who'd disappeared. And if the fates were generous beyond compare, she could bring Chemish's brother home from Separatist space. That was what professionalism demanded. It was what decency demanded. She hadn't been able to save her own children, but they had been adults, they hadn't been her responsibility, and they hadn't risked themselves at Haki's request believing Haki had their backs.

She couldn't set things right, but she could make the effort. And knowingly or not, Organa was going to help her. The door was wide open, and she was leaving the dark hallway.

Haki shuffled through the streets, ready for bed and satisfied by a good night's work.

CHAPTER 14
"WHAT WILL WE MAKE OF THE FUTURE?"

Every trouble of the Senate was magnified and catalyzed by the sheer size of the institution. This was an unflinching law of politics, and Mon knew it as she knew gravity—as someone bound by its constraints in all ways, at all times.

Thousands of senators and thousands more nonvoting representatives served the congress, with each member officially equal to any other. Political historian Barouth Regorab had likened the difference between a planetary government and the Galactic Senate to that between a rural community and a metropolis: "When a person depends upon their neighbor for assistance during the harvest—when strangers are few and familial ties bind the farmer to the freighter captain—the greatest danger is shunning or exile. Mollifying your peers becomes a matter of survival. You have an incentive to iron out differences, or if necessary to bury any radical beliefs that would put you at odds with your community.

"In a city of millions, however, a person may build a tailor-made community inside the larger organism. Anger your neighbor and you may move in with a friend. Become an outcast among your co-workers and you may take a job with a competitor. Diverse arts and philosophies may flourish without the flattening effect of more tight-knit communities, and differences may be celebrated. Yet a lack of common ties can also cause neighbors to see one another as rivals. Ideological opponents can be dismissed without need for engagement. And good people may slip through the cracks, lost in the chaos and written off as *someone else's problem*."

So it was with the Senate. Coalitions, committees, task forces, caucuses, and other cliques, both permanent and transitory, abandoned well-meaning debate and kept one another at arm's length. Corruption flourished in the shadows. Unofficial hierarchies and centuries of accumulated rules and traditions made it impossible for newcomers to understand the esoteric rituals and power plays, let alone tackle galactic problems with any speed.

In the days following her conference with the Delegation of 2,000 leadership, Mon navigated the highways and throughways and back alleys of the metropolis that was the Imperial congress. She met with its representatives in state offices, home offices, sports clubs, and gymnasiums, working her way through a list of targets longer than any she'd previously assembled. She won meetings through persistence and guile, concocting bills and causes and gossip to earn her audiences before revealing her true purpose. And she enlisted the other delegation leaders in her efforts. Streamdrinker tackled the Expansion Region senators, reporting progress to Mon six times a day. Doroon operated more discreetly, tapping corporate consultants and retired officials to feel out which senators might be won over. Breemu and Norve-Gloss focused on Delegation of 2,000 members prone to peeling away.

All of them understood the invisible power structure that overlaid the Senate. Newly elected representatives hoping to change the universe soon discovered they were only names in a roll call. If they were loyal to their coalitions and remained in office long enough, they could aspire to a decent committee assignment. If they were lucky, their committee might be relevant to their constituency back home. Most never made it that far, using their offices to position themselves for corporate employment or planetary government jobs after their terms ended. These senators' votes were best purchased through their coalition leadership, with rare exceptions. Mon had Zar chase down any who might turn on their usual coalitions, any who held grudges or might be courted and flattered.

The next-largest category was the roughly 10 percent of representatives who handled the bulk of the work. These were diligent, dedicated people content spending years of their lives proposing mild reforms to things like fuel subsidies—things that few outside their committees understood. They recognized that good government is, by and large, unexciting, and they said what their coalitions expected them to say about the controversies of the day before returning to the trenches to fight about cross-species starship safety overrides. Mon had spent her early career earning her stripes among such lawmakers, and her nostalgia for that period grew daily. She met with these senators gladly, happily debating the finer points of her plan with her oldest colleagues.

Finally, there were the true power brokers. Fewer than fifty representatives led the major coalitions, charged with whipping up votes, steering the public debate, and wrangling junior members. Nowadays, Mon was among these privileged few, and she'd rarely had the time or inclination in recent years to speak to anyone outside the Senate's inner circle. If Bail had joined her, she would've sought his help pursuing Senate leadership. His charisma would've been an asset, and his absence would create doubts.

Yet the coalitions were vulnerable in ways they hadn't been in living memory, and if she was to drum up support for the Imperial Rebirth Act and snatch power back from Palpatine, she would need to pursue every avenue. She needed her usual allies, and she needed to identify senators who were susceptible to persuasion. No potential vote could be discounted or taken for granted.

Mon's sparring partner for the afternoon was Lady Nadrian, Senator DuQuosenne. The doyenne of the Yabrenito Cluster, DuQuosenne had held significant sway in the decades when Yabrenito had been at the height of its cultural influence—when it had been a prime exporter of innovative music, daring performance troupes, and interactive entertainment. Now, however, Yabrenito's influence had waned, and DuQuosenne was approaching her second century in the Senate. She still had colleagues who would follow her lead, but she rarely deigned to involve herself in real policymaking. Even the war had barely stirred her.

"Let Emperor Valorum run things as he likes," DuQuosenne was saying, afloat in her sphere and balling her tendrils. The J'feh's bulbous, milky eyes were nearly lost in the mists of the contained atmosphere. "He promised me the stellar cruises would be restored. The universities, the cultural ambassadorships—"

"Emperor *Palpatine,* of course," DuQuosenne's protocol droid said, wiping an errant speck of dust from the meter-wide sphere. Someone had painted a flowering vine curling around the droid's left arm, giving it the appearance of an art piece as much as a machine. "The cultural ambassadorships for Core World scholars really did have an outsized effect on tourism, tax migration, exports of wine and theater—"

"And Yabrenito's interests *have* been neglected for too long," Mon interjected, "but what good are promises when the regime can't be held accountable to follow through? That's all we're proposing—a bill that ensures the needs of our constituents *cannot* be forgotten, even when the Emperor's attention is elsewhere."

"The Emperor," DuQuosenne muttered, then gurgled something in her native tongue that Mon couldn't understand.

The droid seemed to recoil with alarm. "You'll have to excuse us," the droid said to Mon. "The senator tires easily. May I see you out?"

DuQuosenne said nothing more, so Mon allowed the droid to escort her through the suite of offices, past a chamber patterned with glowing circles on the floor, and to the door back to the Rotunda. There, the droid paused and asked, "When will the final text of the bill be ready for review?"

"Not before we vote, I imagine," Mon said. "A week or two for the draft language. What did she say, exactly?"

"She's taken to challenging visitors to the game of firepath. A stimulating pastime, but the risk of incineration is high."

Mon decided there was nothing to say to this and merely nodded.

"There is a matter that the senator did not mention," the droid said. "I hesitate to raise it in her absence, but given how busy she's been—"

"How can I assist?"

"Palpatine's support for the Yabrenito Cluster has been consistent, and we are grateful. However, he's been less favorably inclined toward the Breksky-Oward bill, which the senator has long been a proponent of."

Mon didn't attempt to hide her surprise. "The droid rights bill?"

"With the Separatist atrocities only recently behind us, prevailing sentiment is very much against the recognition of synthetic life," the droid said. "While the senator certainly wouldn't expect full integration of Breksky-Oward, protections for advanced intelligences would fit neatly within the Imperial Rebirth Act. We are redefining so many things."

Mon tried to read guile in the unchanging metal of the droid's features. She'd heard rumors that DuQuosenne had made her protocol droid her de facto chief of staff, but this was an unexpected turn.

"The bill's language is very much in flux," she said. "But I hope that if the end result is satisfactory, the senator would offer her support?"

"No doubt," the droid said. "Assuming, of course, you have the allegiance of the former Separatists?"

"That's in progress," Mon said. "But I won't bring a bill to the floor if I don't have the votes."

★★★

She didn't have the votes—not even close, and not even if the ex-Separatist worlds *did* come on board. Too many of the Delegation of 2,000 had given up. Senator after senator had seen the direction the galaxy was going and thrown in with Palpatine. Senator Malé-Dee, one of the delegation's most ferocious voices, had simply said, "The people have spoken. What does it matter if I believe they are wrong, when I am their sworn servant? Is it not the truest act of democracy to trust the public will?"

Others were more or less self-serving. Several delegation members, Initios Idi foremost among them, had argued that the Emperor's age and the injuries the Jedi had dealt him suggested his reign wouldn't last, saying, "In a handful of years, the Emperor will be gone. That will be our time, and moving prematurely will only exhaust us."

Mon's arguments that the grand vizier or others in Palpatine's circle would succeed him were dismissed. Separately, Senator Ghoghos of Demesel had confronted Mon in the Senate corridors after she'd spent days trying to arrange a meeting with him.

"I joined your delegation because the war was dragging on and my people were dying," he'd said. "Turns out the man we tried to ruin put an end to the fighting. Palpatine can dissolve the Senate and put me to work in the coaxium mines, and I'll still call him a hero."

Ghoghos wasn't alone. Outside the delegation, there was a new crop of senators elected during the war. Even the ones who hadn't been handpicked by Palpatine thought of him as the chancellor who'd restored galactic peace.

Mon was certain she could make up for those lost votes elsewhere. She spent her evenings concocting paths to victory with her strategy droids while Perrin muttered at holovids in the next room. But it would take time, and that was where the trouble *really* started. If she was chasing votes among the Xenoform Interests Caucus and the Nonmonetary Trading Committee, that meant she wasn't pursuing votes from the reintegrating Separatist worlds. And if she didn't secure the ex-Separatist votes before those representatives were inducted into the Senate, who knew where the balance of power would settle?

Palpatine's people were doubtless working the ex-Separatists already with promises and threats. Mon didn't even have a full list of their names—the administration kept adjusting its plans for Reintegration Day, now less than a month away. Who would be permitted to rejoin the Senate and who was considered a security threat remained in flux. The candidates she *did* know about were mostly away from Coruscant, back on war-ravaged homeworlds, cut off from galactic communications.

She was tallying her latest numbers—the droids gave her bill a 6 percent chance of success—when she received a call from Lud Marroi. "I have something for you," he said. "Rumor has it you've been rallying Separatists."

"Ex-Separatists. If I were, I doubt I'd be having much luck."

She wasn't surprised he'd heard something. Lud always had his ear to the ground. As long as the particulars of the bill didn't leak, she wouldn't fret overmuch.

"The administration is urging any Separatist Parliament members they've approved for senatorial positions to keep a low profile," he said. "Can't have them making themselves targets before Reintegration Day. Given how dependent the Separatists are on Imperial mercy—"

"No one's going to defy the administration before even being inaugurated. I understand. Is that all you called to say?" She wasn't *really* annoyed at him, but she could've guessed the bad news and didn't need someone rubbing it in her face. *Six percent, indeed.*

"Actually," Lud said, "I called to offer a solution. I scored you an invitation to the COMPNOR-Alpha summit tomorrow."

"The what?"

"A chance for Palpatine's new regional governors to mingle with select members of the Senate and judiciary. Might be some military attendees. A few ex-Separatist senators will be at the opening-night gala. The administration wants to showcase how the Seppies' gripes about the Republic have been fixed in the new Empire."

"As if they could afford to argue."

"There is that. You'd be present for the same reason. There are spots reserved for existing senators still on the fence about the Imperial reforms. They think they can win you over."

She'd be unwelcome at best, and the ex-Separatists would be surrounded by people vying for their attention. But it was a lead, and it was about time *something* went right.

"Why are you helping me with this?" she asked. By which she really meant: *Why do you keep helping me?* It wasn't Lud's assistance itself that felt remarkable—they'd always done each other favors, even at a cost. It was his steadfastness during these difficult days.

Lud paused, then said, "You're a strong-minded person. I don't want you running into any walls when there's a door still open."

You're worried about me. You think I'll do something foolish, and you're worried.

It had been a long time since anyone had worried about her that way. She tried not to show it in her voice. "Well, I'll try not to make a mess of things. Thank you."

"You should invite Perrin. Give you a bit of moral support while you're surrounded by the enemy hordes."

She laughed. "If he's not busy already, I'm sure he'll find a reason not to go."

"More's the pity," Lud said, and she thought he sounded pleased.

⫻⫻⫻

She invited Perrin anyway, and he told her he had other plans but offered to change them if she needed him to work the gala. She didn't, she said, and that was that. He didn't push, he didn't offer to come anyway, and she didn't tell him she could use a friend.

She spent the evening leading up to the gathering with Zhuna, sorting through research her aide had compiled about the other attendees. "I couldn't find a proper guest list," Zhuna said as Mon buttoned her white gloves and adjusted the drape of her belt, "but it's looking like imperialists from all branches. You're going to stand out."

"Then I may as well wear the red scarf instead of the beige," Mon replied, trying to seem nonchalant.

Zhuna was smart, capable, and too young to share Mon's many fears. When it became clear that Mon could do nothing meaningful to prepare, Mon shifted to a secondary project—convincing her aide to share more of her homelife or her hobbies or anything at all unrelated to work.

When Zhuna had first taken the job, Mon had thought she was merely a private person. Mon respected privacy. But she'd heard her aide gossiping freely in the Senate canteen and telling tales of her days off to other staffers, and Mon had realized that Zhuna simply wasn't comfortable sharing with her *boss*. So they'd developed a custom: Mon never pressured the girl but took pains to mention a night at the opera or gripe about family affairs on Chandrila. Then Zhuna would reply, not with an anecdote of her own, but with an exquisitely bland smile and mischief in her eyes and words along the lines of "How fascinating!" Zhuna was full of the inchoate energy of youth, and every erg of it was bottled up in Mon's presence. Mon was desperately curious, but she would never, ever pry.

While Zhuna checked the traffic reports, Mon thought of how Perrin, too, had confidence Mon would never ask too much, and how when they were together things could be wonderful, and when they were apart neither thought of the other. Mon looked at Zhuna and thought, *Don't marry too young, because the companionship is glorious and the loneliness is awful.*

Zhuna offered to ride with Mon to the gala, and Mon allowed her aide to quiz her one last time on the confirmed guests. The event was at the recently renamed Imperial Military Forces Museum, and Zhuna accompanied her until the security cordon, leaving Mon to present her credentials alone. Inside, among the exhibits of preindustrial armor and antique military uniforms, a predominantly human crowd of senators and judges mingled with functionaries from the executive branch. Clone troopers stood guard along the walls, camouflaged by the displays of armor, weapons, and other paraphernalia of death. Mon wondered how the clones felt about serving as ornamentation, but she forced herself to focus.

She wasn't wandering long before a barrel of a man introduced himself as Governor Rhaygus Strentine, newly appointed overseer of six sectors along the Mid Rim. He looked like a cantina bouncer, and she didn't recognize his name. "Glad you're here with an open mind," he told Mon after they'd exchanged pleasantries, and he ushered her to what he referred to as the "tour group."

"The theme of the night," the governor said, looking at her but clearly speaking to the group, "is 'What will we make of the future?' My job's not to answer that but to get you all on board with the 'we.'"

Mon surveyed her companions in the tour group. They were perhaps thirty in total, including Senator Malé-Dee of the Delegation of 2,000; several members of the Millennial Planning Committee, plucked out of obscurity; a gaggle of masked emissaries from the Viyentine government; and, toward the back, the only three nonhumans present (a peculiarity that had to be deliberate, though *why* someone had weighted the guest list toward humans perplexed Mon). Among the three, she found her target: Ta'am Khlaides, a reptilian Delrakkin who'd shed most of her dun scales with age.

"Let me tell you a story," Governor Strentine said as he guided the group past a decommissioned hovertank. "This whole governor business is as new to me as it is to you, and"—he let out a half cough, half snort—"when the grand vizier offered me the job, I didn't have a clue what I was getting into. Frankly, I wasn't smart enough to ask about the responsibilities or the pay. What I asked was 'Why me?'"

She barely listened, edging her way toward Khlaides. They'd never been close, but they'd worked together on the Interstellar Communications Committee early in Mon's career and long before Khlaides had left the Senate to join the Separatist Parliament. She tried to catch the woman's lidless eye as the governor spoke.

"The grand vizier smiled, told me that when Palpatine decided he wanted folk to fill the gap between small-scale planetary governments and the Imperial administration, he had three requirements.

"First, no politicians. I respect the hell out of you all, but the Emperor figured if he pulled from the Senate, you'd bring Senate habits with you. You're good with rules. Huh! Good at designing them, good at working within them. But if those rules were working right, we never would've had a Separatist crisis."

The governor paused as a parade of servants passed by, offering the tour group savories and sweetwine. Mon used the distraction to slip alongside Khlaides and murmur the woman's name.

"I saw you," Khlaides muttered. She didn't turn her head, instead lifting a hard-shelled invertebrate from a food tray and crushing the creature in her jaws. "What is it you want?"

Mon tried to recall whether she'd made an enemy of Khlaides before the war. She didn't think she had. She started to respond, but Governor Strentine was urging them forward.

"Second rule of choosing governors," he said. "The Emperor wants fighters. Now, not all of us were in the Republic military. I was part of a volunteer militia on Ord Mantell. Governor Tabril over there"—he gestured toward a slender man studying a trophy case—"was a combat sur-geon. We've even got a university professor who took up arms to defend her students. But the point is that we all understand the special deprav-ity of civil war. Not one of us will let it happen again."

"Meaning the Emperor only wants governors willing to kill," Mon murmured.

Khlaides bared her teeth. "We were all willing to kill. Some of us didn't speak of pacifism while voting for slaughter. What do you *want*, Mon?"

The governor was introducing Malé-Dee to one of Palpatine's judi-cial appointments, laughing and rasping as he did. Mon kept her voice low. "I was hoping to speak in private, and soon. I'd like you involved in a bill I'm preparing."

"Me? Or any Separatist at all?"

She didn't recall Khlaides being so blunt before, either. "I'd like you, but I'll take anyone I can get who's rejoining the Senate. I need every-one I can win over."

Khlaides turned to face Mon fully, studying her with a hunter's gaze. Mon felt small and exposed, and she stiffened her back. "You're toxic," Khlaides said. "Anyone can smell it. I'm lucky to have escaped execu-tion. Associating with the mastermind of the Delegation of Two Thou-sand would spell the end of my career at the least."

"What about your responsibilities?" Mon asked. At this point she had nothing to lose. "What I'm offering could mean everything to your people—"

"My people need to be heard. If the Emperor lops off my head, you think he'll let another senator take my place? Or will he give my planet over to the *governors*?"

Khlaides shuffled forward as the tour group moved on. Mon fol-lowed, but Khlaides moved up close to Governor Strentine and the swarm of judges, officers, and imperialist senators accumulating around him.

Strentine kept talking, drowning out Mon's thoughts.

"Third—and this one's embarrassing—the Emperor wants people with big ideas. Huh! That's what the grand vizier called them—big ideas.

What he meant is that the Emperor wants people who loved the Republic but who wanted to make it better. The vizier said that democracies don't really try things that are bold and new, because people get scared or bogged down in lawmaking or just stuck in a rut. They may know things aren't working right, but they're scared of change."

She was coming to hate Governor Strentine. His folksy affect, the coughs and harrumphs, his matter-of-fact way of assaulting the principles of democracy—the combination was repulsive.

But Strentine wasn't her problem for the night. Her problem was Khlaides. *Think, Mon* . . .

"The Emperor doesn't just want to reform government. He wants to reform society, wants us imagining what kind of people are the foundation of a strong, prosperous, and peace-loving nation of the sort we haven't had in a century. Governor Mestichan has some exciting notions about family structures, and he plans to work directly with the senators from his worlds to bypass the bureaucracy and create a whole new way of living over five years. If everything works out, the Emperor could make his reforms galaxy-wide."

"What's your *big idea*?" Malé-Dee asked.

Strentine laughed and smoothed his graying hair. "I didn't put you up to that, did I? No, I did not. I grew up on Jedha, the pilgrim moon. Gave me a different perspective on the Jedi, the Cult of the Force—excuse me, *Church* of the Force—and all the rest. Saw what happens when people give their time and credits to showy mystics instead of putting real effort into cleaning up their homeworlds.

"Now we all know how loyal and selfless the Jedi turned out to be, huh?" He laughed again. "I get it. I do. Easier to devote yourself to a cult than to the Republic, because the Republic screwed us over time and again. But maybe if we run the Empire right, people can find fulfillment building something real instead of devoting themselves to some cosmic power . . ."

And on and on.

Throughout her career, Mon had chosen to act as if her adversaries were sincere, to treat their ideas with respect and seek common ground. Overall, the practice had served her well. However satisfying it was to call out hypocrites and liars, it rarely helped negotiations. But she wondered about Strentine. If he was sincere, he was espousing the rhetoric of a thousand tyrannies. If he wasn't, he was a monster, advocating for what he knew to be monstrous.

He introduced them to the other governors, and some of them shared their own "big ideas." Governor Vashin had thoughts on "species compatibility," a term Mon knew only as an archaic euphemism employed by human supremacists. Governor Ordiron had a theory that droid labor devalued organic life, and this, too, had a precedent Mon recognized: Talk of the moral value of toil was a long-standing tradition among Outer Rim slavers.

She kept up with the tour, aware she was doing nothing to win Separatist votes yet hypnotized by the veiled cruelty of the governors. It was too fantastic to grasp. The idea that someone might legalize slavery within Imperial borders felt as impossible as rearranging stars. One could imagine the outcome but not the tools or the process.

Yet the governors seemed entirely serious. Throughout the evening, they spoke passionately about the need to avert another civil war that would cost trillions of lives. They showed images of their children and grandchildren—few of the governors were younger than Mon—and expressed concern for their descendants' future. They claimed that the Republic had been bound to collapse sooner or later, that without Palpatine, victory over the Separatists would have been followed by famine, by infrastructure failures, by existential problems the hidebound Senate had been unprepared to meet.

The end of the war was a rare opportunity, they said, a once-in-a-millennium moment in which expectations could be reset and the old ways of doing things re-examined—and Mon found she agreed with this, felt a flash of angst and jealousy at the realization that the governors had the sort of chance she'd always craved. They said the Emperor had laid claim to the moment instead of allowing the Republic's slow degradation to continue, and they were determined to chart a safer course into the future. If the governors and the administration made mistakes, those would be discovered and corrected in time, but it was better than re-entrenching "failed traditions."

Eventually Mon stepped away from Strentine and his ilk, leaving the tour group to lean against a glass case containing what a plaque obliquely described as an "early tribal bowcaster." She needed to catch her breath. To regroup.

"Are you well?" a voice asked her.

"Of course," Mon said reflexively, turning to face the speaker. It was one of the other nonhuman attendees, a diminutive Gossam woman whose ornamented neck seemed to tug down her wrinkled face. Slate-blue skin clashed with a patchwork dress decorated with gold thread. "It's a lot to take in."

"You're crying," the Gossam said.

And she was. Mon touched her sleeve to her cheek to dab away a tear. She made herself smile brightly. "I'm so sorry. I didn't catch your name?"

The Gossam rose onto her toes and inspected Mon's face. Her lipless mouth almost pursed. Then she nodded, apparently satisfied. "Have you heard of the Courtsilius Wax Revolution?" she asked.

The phrase was familiar, but Mon hadn't heard it in decades. She cast her mind to her teenage bedroom and her library of foreign histories. She'd learned to read Low Core Basic to interpret the letters of Evord the Incinerator, purchased an original manuscript of *Porayne's Guide* with her name-day money . . .

The Courtsilius Wax Revolution. It came to her and she swallowed bile. She remembered the recordings of speeches and cheering crowds, and the atrocities that had followed—the extermination of 10 percent of the planet's population.

"The Chrysalis Party," Mon said. "I remember."

"Not many do." The Gossam's eyes rolled in her bulbous head as a security team approached the tour group. She lowered her voice. "Tychon Nulvolio. You want our support, you talk to him. Even Khlaides will listen."

Then the Gossam was gone and Mon was looking at a black-clad officer flanked by two clone troopers. The clones halted, transforming into exhibits in the gallery.

"Senator Mothma," the officer said. "You need to come with us."

"Is something wrong?" she asked.

"There's been an incident at your home."

///

They wouldn't tell her anything during the speeder ride, and it felt like a cruel game. When she demanded to speak to their superiors, they said they couldn't permit it. They'd be at the scene soon, they said, and they called her "senator" and "ma'am," and for all she knew they were ill-informed and well-meaning and doing their best to navigate a difficult situation. Nothing in her heart believed it.

The speeder tore through the night, oblivious to traffic and wind. When it drew up outside Mon's apartment, there was a small battalion of vehicles on the landing pad: speeders from Coruscant and Senate Security, unmarked speeders she didn't recognize, an armored troop carrier, an emergency medical transport. The transport hovered with its warning lights on as medics maneuvered two gurneys toward its doors.

The medics appeared unhurried, and this comforted Mon until she realized what that could mean. She leapt onto the platform, prompting a shout from the officer who'd brought her. She cried out Perrin's name.

The two bodies on the gurneys were covered in silvery blankets. The medics looked up with alarm as Mon approached, and now they were shouting, too—but she heard none of it. "This is my home. That's my *husband!*" she said as clones hurried toward her from the apartment. "Let me see him. Let me see!"

A gloved hand grasped her arm, and she turned to look into the barrel of a pistol. Her assailant had no face, only a white helmet. For a moment she was sure the clone would kill her.

Then Perrin yelled, "Let her go!" and he wasn't on the gurney but sprinting from the apartment doors. The clone didn't release her, and Perrin leapt, absurdly, onto the clone's back. The clone dislodged his attacker with one swift shrug, dropping Perrin onto the landing pad while keeping his own hand on Mon. Now, she thought, the clone might kill them both.

Yet at *this* moment Perrin was alive. She felt joy.

There was more shouting, and the clone let go of her arm. Perrin scrambled upright. His nose was bleeding, but he seemed otherwise unharmed. Mon embraced her husband, and he clasped her even tighter.

Someone—the clone, perhaps—was saying, "She didn't ID herself! How was I supposed to know?"

"What happened?" Mon asked, muffled by Perrin's shoulder. He smelled of drink and vanilla cologne. "On the gurneys, who—"

"Zhuna. They got Zhuna." He spoke as if somehow that made sense.

She gripped Perrin so tightly that he groaned. Then she let go and returned to the gurneys, and the medics let her see the body of her young aide. Zhuna's face was unrecognizable, beaten with some blunt instrument, and Mon had seen death before but it had never seemed so brutal, so meaningless. Nonetheless, it felt like a fitting end to the night, so much so that for long moments she believed the killers had been Governor Strentine and his cohorts, or perhaps the Empire itself, made manifest with barbarous intent.

Eventually they took Zhuna away. When Perrin told Mon what had really happened, she felt agony and vindication.

CHAPTER 15
NO ESCAPE BUT DEATH

The rain picked up during the night, leaving Soujen sodden and filthy when he abandoned the skimmer at dawn. The cool, humid air and the dim sun refused to dry him, and at times he waded hip-deep through muck. Perhaps, he thought, he'd sink into the mire and be lost to the galaxy, to be rediscovered by some farmer's children generations down the line. His body would rot, but his implants would last. They might fetch a few credits in a salvager's market.

He did not sink, and the clothing Saw's troops had provided warded off the chill. By midmorning he spotted a road, but he kept his distance, concerned that Saw's people or Imperial patrols might be watching. He daubed his face with mud to obscure his features and cinched his hood over his scalp plating. Yet traffic was light, and to his surprise there were no checkpoints. The locals appeared to move freely, despite their world's proximity to what had been the war's front lines.

Had the Empire dismissed its enemies so quickly? If so, it was to Soujen's advantage, but the notion chilled him worse than the wind.

He'd wondered briefly during Li'eta's creaking twilight whether he'd acted in haste—whether his disgust at Tychon Nulvolio's collaboration with the Empire had clouded his senses. Was allying himself with Saw's guerrillas truly a comparable sin when he could always dispose of Saw later? Was aiding one enemy to strike at another such a betrayal of self? Or had abandoning the guerrillas merely soothed his ego and given him an excuse to avoid discomfiting arrangements?

He'd found himself recalling the scents of oil and serranite dust. A memory swallowed him. He was six years old, thumb rolling against his practice palette, and the paint he'd attempted to mix turned darker and darker despite his efforts to produce a shining incarnadine. The result was a dull umber, no matter how many colors he poured into it. His eldest father had caught him before he could hurl the palette in frustration and told him, "It is what you made it, and the change is past undoing. Put it to its proper use."

The decisions had been made. The moment of introspection had passed. He was alone on Li'eta, and he would find his way to the Separatist cache without the guerrillas. Then he would determine how best to punish the galaxy.

///

Soujen reached Quovel'cha around midafternoon, the city rising from rocky hills like an island in the mire. It wasn't a true city by galactic standards—Soujen doubted it hosted more than a few hundred thousand inhabitants, including the occupying Imperial troops—but according to the skimmer's maps it was the closest the planet had. The squat buildings were of mud and ferrocrete, and great pits led to underground colonies. There were pumps and syphons everywhere, apparently built to suck away floodwaters. Soujen paused to wonder what culture, what species had first adapted to this dreary environment by building *down* instead of *up*. But the wonder was hollow. He had no room in his life for idle curiosity, and he'd seen a hundred cities on a hundred worlds that, no matter their plumage, were all unremarkable at their core. He trekked on through streets sparsely occupied by workers and speeders and battery vendors.

In the city center, he finally encountered checkpoints and patrols. He recognized a tension in the Imperial guards and saw the nervousness of the civilians, and this comforted him until he saw that there were no recent blast points in the ferrocrete, no signs of insurgent attack or even much damage from the war itself. One sector of the city had suffered bombardment long ago—he caught glimpses of sodden ruins—yet the entire area was cordoned off, haplessly awaiting restoration. He came to suspect the city hadn't seen violence since the war's first year. As he observed a checkpoint, he noticed a farmer's speeder truck and watched the driver converse with the Imperial officer on duty. Soujen couldn't hear the words, but he could discern the tenor of the exchange. It was the driver who asked most of the questions while the officer performed a cursory search. The officer kept shaking her head, not friendly but familiar, as if she'd heard the farmer's queries more than once that day. She was offering reassurance. The farmer's nerves remained unsettled.

The pieces fell into place, and Soujen felt like a fool when he realized why the people of Quovel'cha were afraid—news of the attack on the medical facility had surely reached them. They had become accustomed to the occupation, servants of the Empire who cleaned buildings and sold food to the troops. They feared a resurgence of violence, but not from their Imperial masters.

There were no Separatists other than Soujen on Li'eta—just cowardly citizens, the Imperial troops, and Saw's embittered Republic guerrillas.

There had been Separatists once, though. He wondered how many had been executed, how many had fled, and how many had simply given up the cause.

Soujen had no money. He considered robbing someone, but that risked attracting attention. He was a stranger of an uncommon species and therefore easily identified. So far, he hadn't seen signs that a large-scale search was underway for Saw's troops—maybe the Empire assumed they had fled the planet—but he didn't wish to push his luck.

So he camped in the abandoned sector, in the burned-out shell of a roofless house. Blankets rotted upon broken beds, and looters had stripped the home's consoles of all panels and wiring. Ash, mold, and grime covered the walls. If anyone had died in the bombing, the bodies had been removed, but otherwise the place had no upside. This assured Soujen of privacy. Fresh water wouldn't be a problem, and while food was trickier, theft would attract less attention than assault. Satisfied with his situation, Soujen nested beneath one of the broken beds to escape the rain and attempted to sleep through the rest of the afternoon and night.

The next day he set to work. He studied the Separatist Intelligence files on Li'eta within his databank. The files were incomplete and outdated, but they gave him context and leads. He found the redaction of key fragments more amusing than frustrating. If the Empire ever captured him and decrypted his databank, Li'eta would be far from its top priority.

Perhaps, if he reached the cache, he'd find files of more recent vintage—not just a plan of action but updated dossiers on half the galaxy. For now, he'd work with the resources at hand.

He left for the inhabited sections of the city and found a gap behind one of the flood pumps from which he could observe passing traffic without being seen. The information in his databank helped him better distinguish the natives from the migrants, and the migrants from the refugees. Those born on Li'eta were mostly humans and humanoids. They spoke with their own accents, wore ornamentation on their boots, and had ritual scars on their thumbs. (None of Soujen's files explained the scarring.) The natives seemed least bothered by the Imperial presence. Non-natives were more apt to keep their distance from the patrolling troops, and none appeared to be among the day crews that took Imperial transports to nearby bases.

Once evening fell, he switched to his next task. The Separatist Intelligence files had suggested the presence of sympathizers—even assets—in Quovel'cha, though there were no names or dossiers included. There were, however, the coordinates of a street corner that had once served as a dead drop. Soujen investigated the neighborhood from there, looking for someone who fit the profile of a Separatist operative keeping watch on the drop point. If such a person was still here, he thought, they would be a non-native, but not a recent arrival. They would be someone with resources useful to the Separatist cause and a stake in Li'eta's future, perhaps with a family but more likely a loner—someone who didn't need to fear for loved ones.

He chose his candidate at last: a middle-aged woman, human but without a thumb scar. She was the proprietor of a machine shop specializing in vehicle repairs, with a window overlooking the dead drop. He didn't know her name.

He could have tried the drop, but he doubted it had been used in years—and after two days he was growing impatient. He broke into the second-floor bedroom of the woman's shop and awaited her return, wondering whether he'd reasoned correctly.

/ / /

When the screaming and threats were finished and they'd come to an understanding, he sat across from the woman at her dining room table and watched her fidget. He hadn't shown his blaster—she'd been frightened enough when he'd grabbed her in the dark—but just in case she tried to run, he'd chosen the chair nearest the stairway. The apartment smelled heavily of scented oils, barely masking the odors of metal and grease from the shop.

"You worked with the Confederacy of Independent Systems?" he asked. "There's no reason to lie."

"Yes," she told him. She looked toward the stairs. He smiled to reassure her, but she only flinched.

"I'm not here to turn you in," he said. "I'm here for assistance."

"The war is over."

He shrugged. "No war is ever really over."

She didn't seem to find that comforting, either.

"What do you want?" she asked.

"Nothing difficult. Safe transit offworld and enough credits to pay my way."

"Where are you going?"

"I'm not choosy. Anywhere more central than Li'eta."

She was silent awhile.

"You killed those medics on the news?" she asked.

Soujen shrugged again. "Does it matter?"

She spat on the floor. "You really screwed us. You know that?"

Soujen waited. He was in no hurry, and the woman was no threat. Anything she said to him was potentially useful, and if blowing off steam made her more cooperative, then that was useful, too.

"My grandson," she said. "I don't get to see him these days, but he goes to that new school, the one the Empire slapped down with all the propaganda holos. It offends the eyes and ears, but at least they feed the kids. Now they've shut it down—temporary, they say. Afraid it's a target, they say."

"Collective punishment," Soujen said.

"Oh, hell, probably. But righteous resentment doesn't fill stomachs. People around here *like* not being in a war zone. They like not sorting through rubble for the dead. They like the money the troops spend. You want to get the fires roaring, you needed to fuel them five years ago. Prove to these people the Confederacy has something to offer, because the Empire's at least making fresh promises."

He watched her. Her anger seemed genuine, though that didn't bother him. It *disgusted* him, but only intellectually. He'd never expected ideological loyalty on a planet that had accepted its occupiers so readily. The real question was whether her anger ran deep enough to become a problem, whether she'd run to the Imperial garrison the moment he set her free.

"I tell you this," he said. "Help me and I will leave. I will never come back, and I will never trouble you or Li'eta again."

She sighed and licked her cracked lips. "The Empire," she said. "Everyone stationed here, they still call it Polroth Five. They've been here long enough to know better, but they call it that anyway."

"Never let them take your name," Soujen said, and he felt she understood.

"Getting offworld isn't as easy as it used to be. You know about the chain codes?"

Soujen shook his head.

"They're rolling them out to the little planets first—smaller populations to manage. One code per person, lets the Empire track everyone coming and going."

"There must be ships off the official record."

"On Li'eta? Not many, and none I know." She twitched in her chair, as if she wanted to stand and pace but knew better. "No one knows how to fake chain codes proper yet. But half the real chain codes are still buggy, so a decent fake'll likely get waved through. Could take a few days, but I can figure out something. Assuming there's no more attacks, nothing to put the Empire on higher alert—"

"No more attacks," he said.

They discussed details of how long she'd need and when to make contact, and when Soujen was content, he asked her to rise and turn around. He stood behind her and pulled the back of her shirt over her shoulder, pressing his right hand against her bare skin. He triggered his microlaser at its lowest setting—the woman gasped, but then the process was over. "I've implanted a tracking device inside you," he said. "If you attempt to turn me in, I'll know. Do you understand?"

"I do."

Satisfied that she believed his lie, Soujen left and disappeared into the night.

▰▰▰

After that, all he could do was wait. Any preparations he might make for his journey, any attempt at acquiring weapons or intelligence, was too likely to alert the Imperial forces. He waited with neither patience nor anxiety.

He discovered that the mud he'd been using to conceal his features became gummy and pliable after drying, and he learned to combine his clothing, mud mask, and hood to disguise his species without drawing undue attention. The costume wouldn't hold up on close inspection, but it let him walk through Quovel'cha without special caution. His contact at the machine shop had provided him with enough credits for his meals, as long as he was thrifty. He ate Li'etan vegetables and salted tubers.

On the third day, he began visiting a cramped cantina in the pits. He bought exactly enough drinks to keep him in good stead with the owner. (He'd never had a taste for intoxicants, which had saved him from the path of his eldest brother.) Mostly he sat in the corner and listened to the updates blaring from the vid display: Imperial propaganda, local reports of no interest outside Li'eta, and sports recaps. Something called "rocket racket" was popular with the locals.

Tychon Nulvolio's interview with an unctuous Imperial reporter was played frequently—the same broadcast he'd heard the night he'd abandoned Saw's guerrillas—and by the fifth time it no longer made him recoil. Instead, Soujen watched Nulvolio, studying the man's eyes, lips, and breathing to determine what had turned the former Separatist leader into a collaborator.

The people of Li'eta had been bought off. That was easy to understand. Tired of war, they'd eagerly accepted a tightening yoke in return for a school, an infusion of cash, a promise that the galaxy would be different now that the Republic was called an Empire. They surely knew that the galaxy would *not* be different, but with the fall of the Separatists, they had no incentive to act upon the truth.

Yet Nulvolio had *believed*, hadn't he? Soujen had known the man so very briefly, but he felt confident in that much. Nulvolio had believed that those wronged by the Republic could come together and achieve something better for themselves. He had believed that action was necessary and death preferable to complicity.

Or was Soujen just desperate to think that Nulvolio had been an honest man? Because if he *hadn't* been, if Nulvolio had never believed what he claimed, what did that say about Soujen's own road?

On the fifth day came his scheduled meeting with the woman from the machine shop. She let him into her home shortly after midnight, and they went to the dining room. "Did what I could," she said, sifting through a small satchel on the table. She didn't meet his gaze. "Identichip and chain codes, credits, accessories. You're now a pilgrim headed to the Kathol Rift. Had to signal the old network, from when the war was on. It's what we could pull together."

She pushed the satchel toward Soujen. He took it without looking. The woman was nervous, which meant little. But she'd had time to stew in her fear and humiliation, and that too often led to bravery. So he watched her.

"No difficulties?" he asked.

"None to speak of. Questions about *why*, but I didn't say." She rapped knuckles on the tabletop. "I'd like to hear myself who sent you. Is there someone in a bunker out there, calling the shots? Someone take over for Grievous or the chief of intelligence or another muck-a-muck?"

"The source of my authority doesn't matter."

"Matters if the war's coming back to Li'eta."

He scowled and began sorting through the satchel himself. He rummaged through an identichip, datapads, strings of beads, and chewing sticks. "I told you I wouldn't return," he said.

She screwed up her face, then shuddered as if a ghost had left her body. "You'll want to get to the port tonight. Docking bay eight. There's a cargo flight waiting for you."

He couldn't have said whether it was the words, the tone, or the plan that troubled him. "If you did your job, a passenger flight is safer."

"You'll want a captain you can trust, one of our people. Anyone else might recognize you—"

"You're lying," he said. A guess, but why would she protest otherwise? He drew the identichip from the satchel, turning the card over in his hand. "I'm surprised at you."

She started to step backward, then halted and attempted to steady her breathing. "I tried. I didn't lie. I reached out to the old network, like I said, but I warned you things were messy! I told you no one wants to bring the war back! The others would've turned you in if I hadn't spoken up."

Soujen scowled. It was difficult to sort truth from fiction when everyone involved was plausibly a coward or a bastard.

The woman kept talking: "I made the arrangements, though! The chain codes *might* pass, that flight I called—"

He saw her reach under the table. He almost permitted it. Learning whether she'd sold him out to the Imperials or whether ex-Separatist agents were waiting to ambush him would have helped. So would learning whether the ID she'd provided was valid. Instead, he cut her throat with a burst from his microlaser. His identichip, her body, and the blaster she'd concealed under the table all hit the floor at once.

He stood still awhile, and his own breathing accelerated. He trembled as the scent of blood reached his nostrils. He wanted to tear the shop apart and scream at the woman and the cowardly ex-Separatists who'd failed him, who'd failed Li'eta. But he did not. He slammed a palm onto the tabletop, and that was release enough.

After that he sat down and thought, trying not to get distracted by loathing. He still needed to leave Li'eta. He needed a ship. Those facts hadn't changed. He was in a city full of Imperials, who wanted him dead or arrested; a few ex-Separatists, whom he could now assume wanted him dead or vanished; and civilians, who wanted to stay blind to their own complicity. His position was precarious.

Less than an hour later, he reached a dispiriting conclusion. He hauled the body into the main shop, strung it from a repulsor platform with a length of cord, and used his microlaser to burn a message into the wall: The Confederacy lives. Free Li'eta. Free Onderon. He left the door open and departed well before sunrise, bitterly curious to see who would take the bait.

/ / /

He returned to his cantina the next day and the day after. The murder in the machine shop made local news, as Soujen had expected. The reporters speculated about a Separatist underground and a connection to the medical facility "massacre." For the most part, though, the vid display showed the same mix of propaganda, sports, and agricultural forecasts. The bartender kept his eyes off Soujen, and Soujen increased his tips appropriately.

He wondered whether he'd overestimated his quarry and hidden too well. He began to envision backup plans—brutal, public, and high-risk. He'd need enough hostages to outlast a siege.

Then, three days after the murder, a newcomer arrived in the cantina. The man strode toward Soujen's corner, backlit by the gray afternoon light seeping through the door. Soujen recognized his stature and gait even before he saw the man's hooded face.

"All lies," the man said, gesturing with a mist-damp hand to the vid display. It was showing an interview with a scholar of the early Republic who was explaining how the Emperor's reforms were bringing the nation, "in many important ways," back to its original intent.

The man reached Soujen's table. "Join you, stranger?"

Soujen nodded. Saw Gerrera flicked his coat and slid into the seat across from him.

Soujen looked to the doorway again without moving his head. He scanned the cantina and saw none of the other guerrillas. They were likely stationed outside, but it was possible Saw had come alone.

"You saw my message," Soujen said.

"It's a good place, Li'eta," Saw declared, as if Soujen hadn't spoken. "Seen its troubles, but it's preserved its identity, and credit to it for that. The Clone Wars should never have come here, yet the Separatists wormed their way into every world that suffered from Republic corruption and overreach. Too many cracks in the wall, it turns out."

Soujen did not understand, and he was irritated by the irrelevancy. But he nodded. The bartender was polishing his bracelets. If anyone was listening in, Soujen couldn't find them.

"You made that mess on the news to, what—lure us out?" Saw asked. His voice fell. His tone was cool. Soujen had no trouble hearing over the rain. "You figured that we need you to get to the Separatist cache, so we'd come looking. And you need us for reasons you hadn't anticipated before deserting. Looking for transport, something of the sort?"

"Something of the sort," Soujen agreed.

"Do you intend to take me captive, or just kill me and hijack my ship?"

"Either will do." Soujen thought for a moment. "I didn't expect to be located so swiftly. I thought *you'd* try to lure *me* out."

"You weren't easy to find, but credits work wonders." Saw grunted thoughtfully. "Before you take up arms, then . . . can I tell you a story?"

Soujen considered refusing. Then he nodded. Saw grinned nastily, as if Soujen had fallen into a trap.

"I come from Onderon," Saw said. "Old world, stuck in its ways. But we were proud of our royals, proud to stand on our own, to not get embroiled in disputes between Republic loyalists and Separatists. It wasn't our fight—until the Separatists arranged a coup to put a new king on the throne.

"Now, this new king, first thing he did was lie about how he took power. We all knew it was a lie, but some folks decided to believe anyway, because it was easier than arguing. The new king got rid of the old king's advisers, appointed a new council, made sure the military answered directly to him. Enacted new laws in the name of stabilizing things during a time of transition. Is this starting to sound familiar?"

You've told me this story, Soujen thought. Though he realized as he listened that it *wasn't* the same story. The beats were the same, but the words were altered, the phrases and emphasis rearranged.

Saw had been practicing. Not for Soujen's sake, but for another audience. Soujen understood that if he'd been awake during the rise of the Empire—if he'd been a believer in the Republic instead of the Separatist Confederacy—the tale might have resonated.

"Go on," Soujen said.

"I fought for the Republic," Saw said, "because I wanted to free my king and my world. I succeeded at the first, but when Palpatine declared himself Emperor it was clear I'd failed at the second. Orders came telling us to surrender our weapons, the names of our allies, to the governor assigned to our system.

"The *governor assigned to our system.* Not our king, but a stranger sent to take the reins from us, from our rightful leader. We pledged ourselves to a Republic, and they expected us to fall in line for an Empire." The words were heated, but Saw's tone remained matter-of-fact. "For a couple days, my people and I—we watched. Then we said no.

"The Empire asked again, less politely. We said no again. Then the Empire tried to kill us, and there it was—the new regime exposed, the lies about peace and stability exposed. Makes you wonder what else they're lying about.

"The rest you can more or less guess. I knew if I gave up fighting, everything we did—everyone we lost—would have been for nothing." There was a hitch in Saw's voice, but it, too, seemed practiced. "One battle leads to the next. Strategies change. The Clone Wars may have ended, but another civil war is about to begin—which means we all have a decision to make: You can either adapt and survive, or die with the past."

Now Saw was done. He watched Soujen, and Soujen imagined Saw speaking the words in cantinas and town squares and cemeteries throughout the sector, preying on the lost and the damned. Saw had tested his speech on the pirate ship and seen that it wasn't the time, refined it in the caves, and each iteration was more compelling. His *intensity,* combined with an engineer's attention to word choice, pitch, and rhythm, granted him an unholy magnetism.

Soujen knew what Saw wanted. Soujen wasn't a fool, nor a man easily manipulated. And yet . . .

"How many recruits have you won this way?" Soujen asked.

"All of them," Saw said.

Soujen thought of the dead woman in the machine shop, who, despite her loyalty to the Separatists, had still betrayed him. He thought of her invisible contacts, the other Li'eta Separatists who'd preferred to see him dead over continuing the war.

He thought of Vorgorath and Karama, and their loyalty to Saw.

"You don't talk much about the future," Soujen said.

"What's the point?"

"Do you truly believe you can fight the Empire?"

Saw laughed. "Even the Separatists never planned to conquer the Republic. I'm not mad. My aspirations are simple: freedom for the occupied worlds, starting with Onderon and extending . . . well, as far as we can take the fight."

"By what means?"

"By whatever means necessary, military included. Though that shouldn't surprise *you.*"

This was the weakness of Saw's pitch, and Soujen wondered if the man was honing it as they spoke—if he'd have a more satisfying answer next time.

But Soujen had his doubts. If Saw really wasn't mad, then he understood he could never overpower the Empire, no matter how many guerrillas he recruited or how he struck back. The vast and ruthless machinery of a million worlds could hold Saw's forces at bay with a fraction of its real strength. All Saw could hope for was to be *trouble,* to endure through counterterrorism operations and crackdowns and blockades, bleeding the Empire here and there, until his opponents decided Onderon and its ilk weren't worth the bother. Even then, the Empire would have no reason to fully withdraw, only to reach an unspoken accord with Saw's forces: Onderon could hold on to a dream of self-governance as long as the guerrillas and the Empire kept killing one another forever.

That was the balance of power that Saw could hope for. That was the promise he was making his new recruits.

And if that was the case, so what? What did Soujen care about the guerrillas or the fate of Onderon?

"What about *your* future?" Saw asked. "What is it you want to accomplish?"

"You know," Soujen said.

"Vengeance, I suppose. Is that all, though? In your midnight fantasies, do you dream of ruling a Separatist Confederacy of your own? Is there nothing else you seek?"

No mention of the Alvadorjian people. Saw hadn't spoken to Karama, then. Or Karama had chosen not to speak of Soujen. This pleased him obscurely.

"There is nothing," Soujen said. Saw did not understand the nature of the clans and their curse, or what had set Soujen on his path. Karama didn't, either, though she had tried.

Saw squinted at him and laughed again. Then his expression turned pensive in a way Soujen hadn't seen before. "Your purpose is pure." Saw said. "Hard to believe, but I've seen nothing to make a liar of you. You are an agent of a higher cause who has been transformed, body and soul, by your service. I see beauty in that, and whatever comes I am grateful to have known you, to know such a thing is possible."

Saw seemed to recognize Soujen's bemusement-turned-disinterest and shrugged. "I can help you fulfill your purpose," Saw said. "I told you that before, and you lied to me and abandoned my people. I should execute you for your crimes, as I wanted to do when I found you. But now you've seen what the galaxy looks like. You know the limits of possibility. So I'm asking you to come back. Rejoin me in our fight against the Empire."

Saw had many reasons to want Soujen dead. Soujen knew too much about his operation. Soujen had murdered Rechrimos. But Saw could've delivered a bomb to the cantina or tipped off the Imperials if he'd wanted to cut his losses. He could abandon his search for the Separatist cache and simply be rid of Soujen. Soujen didn't doubt the man's sincerity.

And although Soujen didn't believe in Saw, the man's words had crawled into his brain anyway. *You can either adapt and survive, or die with the past.* Soujen's methods had left him in this wretched cantina, wearing a mask of muck, with his grand plan stuck on Li'eta. Soujen had failed to locate ideological allies, while Saw had tracked him here and walked into the cantina, risking himself against Soujen and the Empire. Saw's methods were flawed and his motives foreign, but they served him well.

"You would've killed me if we'd ever made it to the cache," Soujen said.

"Possibly. I never did decide. If you'd stuck around, you'd have tried to kill me."

"I may still kill you," Soujen said. It was a perfunctory threat.

Karama had told him, "Saw thinks you'll betray us. You probably figured that. For what it's worth, though . . . I don't think you have to."

He did not trust Saw, but he had misjudged the man and miscalculated his own assets. Soujen had seen his path as a straight line—as a mountain to scale, forbidding but direct. Instead, there was a labyrinth of shadows to pass through. There were obstacles even the former Separatists would throw before him.

"If I were to return," Soujen said, "we would need to work as equals, at least until we're done with the cache. You would share authority over your people. You would give me free access to your files, your ship, and your weapons." He was not a leader by nature, but to command the guerrillas, even in part, would make his acquiescence less the act of a collaborator and more the act of a warrior seeking an alliance. It sufficed to make the taste less bitter.

Saw shrugged again and leaned back. "Authority, weapons, and the *Dalgo*. But not my files. Unless you intend to share every secret of Separatist Intelligence you possess?"

Soujen considered, and again he was reminded of how introspection rankled his sensibilities. Introspection was the first step toward hypocrisy. Yet he could overcome this.

"All right," Soujen said. "Let us lie to our enemies and not to one another."

"So be it." Saw glanced to the display, where one of the Imperial governors was dedicating a war memorial. Then Saw looked back at Soujen. "What's your name, soldier?"

"Soujen," he said, and it tasted like a promise.

CHAPTER 16
GOODBYES

"Say it again," Chemish spat, leaning over the tabletop. "Tell me again that my cousin is dead and I should treat it as a damn *vacation*."

They tried to speak again, found no words, and swore loudly. As if on cue, the neighbors in the apartment below began groaning in passion and a speeder raced past the balcony blaring undersector pop. The midday sun warmed the soft yellow walls. It all felt like another insult, like the universe didn't care what had happened any more than Haki did.

Haki kept puttering with the listening device under the safe house's sink. She switched out a power cell, tested the device to make sure it functioned, then clambered to her feet with a sigh.

Not now, Chemish thought. *You don't get to play the tired old woman now.* It wasn't an act Haki let slip often, but it was still an act, and Chemish knew it.

"You're right," Haki said, her voice an octave lower than usual. "It was a lousy thing to say. The point I was trying to make"—she met Chemish's gaze and did not smile—"doesn't matter, I suppose. How's the family taking it?"

"I don't know. I should be over there."

"Yes, you should. Shouldn't be worrying about me or the work."

Chemish shook their head and felt dizzy. Rage and nausea had been banding together to fight off grief all morning, but the war was going poorly and soon they'd accept defeat. "She *was* the work, Haki. You made her the work. You had me spying on family, and now she's dead—"

"Which means the work is over. Doesn't always end in glory. Usually doesn't. Lost a target of mine in a tram accident once after tailing them six months. Never did learn if he was dirty."

"That's not—"

"Not the point. I know. But Zhuna's gone, and there'll be other agents to watch Mothma."

Chemish stared at Haki. The moaning and the street noises continued, and the sunlight twinkled against the cheap tin cups on the table. Chemish tried to figure out something to say that wouldn't be humiliating, that wouldn't make Haki lose all respect for her apprentice, but that would still, somehow, give them what they needed.

"Tell me what to *do*," Chemish said.

Haki looked Chemish up and down. She closed her eyes, reopened them, waddled over, then wrapped her arms around Chemish's shoulders—as she had the first time they'd met, when she'd told Chemish about their brother's disappearance and how she was going to take care of Chemish as if they were her own. Chemish's life had changed, and Chemish usually believed that had been for the better. They'd stopped fearing for their future, stopped taking low-paying courier jobs that took them racing across the city through gang territories and across broken platforms. They'd stopped asking what the point of it all was and found a *goal*.

If they hadn't taken Haki's offer, Chemish told themself, Zhuna would still be dead. It wasn't the fault of the work. But it felt like it, somehow, and something had to be done.

"Right now, all you can do is mourn," Haki said. "Spend time with the family. Do that meditation you like. Call it bereavement leave, long as you need, and we'll talk when I'm back."

"Where are you *going*?" Chemish whispered. This was the worst form of weakness they could show, asking questions Haki would never answer.

"We'll talk when I'm back," Haki said. Her tone said, *This is spycraft. You wanted to serve the Empire, and service requires sacrifice.*

I can't do this, Chemish thought, but they nodded instead.

When Haki left, they called their mother to talk about Zhuna.

PART II
DAY

CHAPTER 17
A VISIT TO THE DARK PLACE

"*Senator Mothma? You need to come with us.*"

Each time Mon retrieved the memory of her arrest from the Dark Place in her mind, the details were different. She'd heard that was typical in cases of trauma. Humans weren't like droids or species like the Jenet, able to dredge up past events with perfect accuracy. The human brain had a perversity to it, and when it recalled a thing it also *changed* it, shifting details and filling in gaps. Humans were built to retain emotions—the impact of an event—and not *facts*.

Yet despite her imperfect recollection, Mon could not forget what had happened to her. Her body remembered clearly what her mind did not.

She'd been late to a meeting when they'd come for her, in the first days after the war's end. (How many had *they* been? Sometimes she remembered one officer, other times as many as three.) A freelance reporter had promised her information on administration infighting. She'd been leaving the Senate, heading to meet her source halfway to the Executive Center, and she'd been intercepted.

"*You need to come with us.*" Those words she remembered. She'd protested on the ride to the Judicial Forces center, but she hadn't resisted.

They'd come to a side entrance, and she'd been handed to a pair of out-of-uniform officers who'd marched her inside. She'd known something was terribly wrong. But what could she have done? Fought and run and become a fugitive? Was there a name she could have spoken, some appeal to authority that would've preserved her? She'd read that this sort of second-guessing, the sense that she was to blame for what followed, was also typical in cases of trauma.

"You're a senator, right? Interrogation rooms are all full. Can't put you with the general population, so you'll wait here until they're ready."

They'd said something like that.

They hadn't laughed, but one had smiled when they'd opened up what might have been a closet or a decommissioned toilet stall. Mon had stared in confusion before they'd shoved her in. She'd tripped, slamming her head against the wall, and she would've fallen if there'd been room to fall. The door had shut behind her, and there'd barely been room to turn around.

Her body remembered the room perfectly. It remembered the crack of pain when her skull had struck the wall and how she'd pressed her cheek against the cool metal to keep herself from vomiting. It remembered exactly how far she'd been able to stretch her arms and legs. There'd been no light, and the frigid breath of the air vent had become excruciating as the hours went on.

There had been fear as physical as blood or sweat—fear she'd been forgotten, fear of what would come if she were ever released. But often the pain exterminated her fear. Her litany of agonies was long. There was the sharp revolt of her muscles if she tried to move, the dull misery if she didn't, the pounding of her skull, the change in her body temperature from feverishly hot to deliriously chilled, the thirst, the hunger, the ache in her bladder. All these things had slowly annihilated any rational thought, any intellectual worry or desire for revenge or questions about why someone would *do* this to her. The thought that had come through most clearly, most coherently, was *Please let me lie down,* but the best she'd been able to manage was a sort of half crouch that spiked fire through her knees. She'd hallucinated for periods, colors and sounds more than anything coherent, but the visions had been night-mares as often as they'd soothed her.

Much later, she'd learned that she'd been kept standing in her metal coffin for thirty hours.

When she'd been released at last, her limbs had been too weak and too rigid to keep her body upright. She'd soiled her robes; the stains were obvious on the white cloth. She'd been stripped of all dignity with casual, deliberate cruelty. Eventually, she'd been taken to an interroga-tor. She could no longer recall his face.

He'd apologized for keeping her waiting. The Emperor had concerns, he'd said, about revolutionaries and anarchists in the Senate who might seek to take advantage of instability following the war's end. It was the Judicial Forces' job to thoroughly investigate anyone belonging to anti-government groups such as the Delegation of 2,000, anyone who'd been unduly close to the Jedi, anyone who'd had close ties to Separatists. De-spite Mon's worrisome associations, the Judicial Forces had found nothing to indicate she was a threat. The man had given her a choice: sign a loyalty pledge in return for her immediate release, or remain in custody until a hearing could be granted and a more thorough investi-gation could be conducted.

She had signed. She hated that she'd signed.

"One more thing," her interrogator had said. "The administration has authorized us to bring you back for questioning any time we want. You understand? *Any time we want.*"

She wasn't the only senator who'd been arrested, but none of them talked about what happened. You could tell who'd had the luxury of righteous defiance, kept in a low-security waiting room, and who'd been through hell, to their own Dark Place. Mon couldn't explain it, but . . . you could just tell.

///

Sometimes she blamed herself for provoking Palpatine. If she hadn't, maybe she'd have been treated differently.

She didn't think this often. It certainly wasn't true. She doubted the notion of the arrests had originated with the Emperor, despite his seal of approval, and she suspected arrestees had been chosen for gentler or harsher treatment virtually at random—perhaps to sow resentment and suspicion among allies.

When Bail Organa had held a media conference following *his* arrest, simultaneously affirming his loyalty to the new Emperor and criticizing the "overzealousness" of the security forces, Mon had certainly resented him. Bail had seemed almost proud of what he'd been through, as if it had made him a hero instead of chipping away at his soul.

///

This was what Mon thought about in the days after Zhuna's death. *Her* trauma. *Her* imprisonment. Not *Zhuna's* suffering.

Zhuna hadn't been murdered by the Empire—not directly, anyway. A deranged woodworker from Coruscant's gentrifying 1649th level had become obsessed with Mon during the war. Mon represented everything corrupt and unprincipled within the Republic, he'd decided. After the war's end, Mon had failed to show deference to the new Emperor. So he'd come to the apartment to murder Mon and her husband, entering through the patio doors using a black-market slicing kit and bearing a durasteel pipe key—a half-meter-long rod designed for opening Coruscant's sewer grates. He'd found Zhuna sorting Mon's outfits for the next day.

The investigators said Zhuna had somehow crawled from Mon's office into the living room and on to the kitchen during the assault. Perhaps she'd been searching for a weapon. After killing Zhuna, the attacker had spent a good forty minutes wandering the house until Perrin had arrived and called security. When asked why the security team hadn't attempted to stun the attacker, the officer in charge had said, "We don't use stun when lives are at stake." When asked why security hadn't detected the intrusion themselves, they claimed the patio door sensor was faulty.

Mon hadn't agreed to the release of information about Zhuna's prolonged, painful death, but word made it into the public reporting anyway. She failed to visit the family on the first day and then the second. She was busy relocating her life to a temporary apartment—one chosen by Senate Security—and reassuring her allies that, yes, she was fine and that the Imperial Rebirth Act would not be delayed. Perrin drank heavily, snapped at her for endangering herself when she left for public appearances, and eventually went quiet. He had his own trauma to confront and his own perfectly valid fears, but she was in no place to help him. She doubted they'd talk for a while.

And when she should have been mourning Zhuna, she was thinking about the Dark Place. Every thought led inevitably to that wretched cell. She felt guilty over that, but not as guilty as she felt over Zhuna's murder.

///

Mon had read stories about Republic prisoners of war and the tortures the Separatists had inflicted, the lies the prisoners had been told, the mental and physical degradations the troops had endured. What Mon had suffered felt laughable in comparison. She'd emerged with no scars, no lasting physical damage at all. Her imprisonment had been an attempt to intimidate, but the administration hadn't dared to go any further.

In the days after her release, she'd forced her mind to forget. Yet her body did not forget.

She was needed. She couldn't afford to wallow. So she spoke to her doctors. The medical droids adjusted her anxiety medications. That would help her bury the memory again, slam it into the little coffin closet and lock the door, though the droids assured her the door would open again sooner or later.

As long as it was later. As long as she had time to work.

CHAPTER 18
NAVIGATING THE
MINEFIELD

The war was over, but the fighting on Olkrastrus IV had never ended. It was true that the battle lines had shifted when the Separatists had withdrawn from the settlements: The civilian leadership, loyal to the Confederacy from the war's start but knowing they were beaten, had ceded power while the Separatist military had retreated deep into the wilderness. The clone army had begun door-to-door searches to uproot urban insurgents and converted the planet's aerial greenhouses into massive floating fortresses capable of leveling any Separatist bunker and casting kilometers-long shadows onto the Spiral Forest. Yet despite the clones' iron grip on the planet, the scattered Separatist troops kept fighting, and the shelling continued from above, an ever-present drumbeat proclaiming the glory of the Empire and the bravery of every clone sacrificed.

"*Holdouts*," Bail said. He walked with Haki down a wide boulevard. Ribbons of red and orange pollen colored the wind, leading from the spaceport toward the city. "We were told there were Separatist *holdouts*, as if it were only a battalion or two. The administration stopped sharing the clone casualty numbers, which should have been a tipoff, but— I didn't realize."

"Nor did I," Haki said. There was a flash of light, a clap of thunder, and the smell of burnt carbon as one of the floating fortresses annihilated some target beyond the horizon. "It does explain a few things, though."

They'd been stuck in orbit for almost two hours while Bail had demanded landing clearances from a series of increasingly decorated garrison commanders. Bail had been expecting resistance. He *was* a civilian, and his visit *was* unannounced. But he'd figured that someone, somewhere, would be eager to impress a senator. Instead, he'd had to threaten review by the Military Justice Committee just to get assigned a dock.

"Maybe that's why they haven't transferred Bana Rhuus to another planet," Bail said. "The man was sector chief for Separatist Intelligence. If he's working with the Empire now, his knowledge of the local resistance would be a reason to keep him close."

"And a reason for us to move quickly, before Rhuus is lost in the chaos. Assuming he's not dead already."

The woman who'd finally cleared them to land had insisted she could spare no troops and no lodgings for Bail's visit. Bail, who suspected the warning was one final ploy to be rid of him, had agreed to take his chances. Haki had offered to arrange a place to stay. As usual, she was vague about her resources and her past, though she'd let slip that this wasn't her first time on Olkrastrus IV.

Before leaving Coruscant, Bail had made several inquiries and turned up nothing remarkable on Haki. He'd obtained files showing that she was indeed a longtime member of Senate Security, though none of Bail's colleagues had ever heard of her. She followed none of the familiar protocols and carried no identification. But she'd also saved his life, and she'd provided him with a list of Separatist captives and collaborators who might plausibly know more about the forged evidence against the Jedi. Her list had been detailed and thoroughly annotated, and it built upon data he'd seen in classified intelligence briefings.

So Haki could keep her secrets for now. She'd proved her usefulness, and she was pleasant company. If she was intentionally steering him away from the truth, he'd find out sooner or later. His gut said, *Stick with her,* and he intended to do so.

Haki took Bail to a bombed-out slum where cables crossed the cratered roadways like tripwires. Rusting droids switched the cables' hookups as distant generators overloaded or fizzled out. Inside a quaint dwelling abutting the city walls, Haki was greeted warmly by an elderly man speaking a language Bail didn't recognize. Haki returned the greetings with a fierce embrace, and after a lot of pointing at Bail, they seemed to come to an agreement.

Their host introduced Haki and Bail to a dozen children and grandchildren, along with siblings, cousins, nephews, and nieces. A few of the younger family members spoke a dialect of Huttese, and Bail managed to convey what he hoped was appropriate gratitude. They ate a meal of mashed grains accompanied by dried berries from the Spiral Forest—tiny jewels of flavor, each unique in color and aroma, with hints of jasmine, rose, hot peppers, and saffron. Haki and their host spoke quietly while Bail entertained the youngest children, showing them sleight-of-hand tricks he'd learned from his great-grandfather. He kept an eye on Haki, but he could imagine no more comfortable lodgings.

After dinner, the adults chewed on shreds of bark while the children headed to bed. Bail strained to understand questions posed by the family about politics and galactic affairs: Did Bail's presence on Olkrastrus IV mean the Separatists were ready to surrender? Did he believe the Emperor would bring a permanent peace? Something about the tenor suggested to Bail that outside the house, these questions would be regarded as controversial. But he didn't have the language to ask why, and he answered as honestly as he could.

"They're frightened," he told Haki later, as they settled onto cots in the guest room. "These people have lived through horrors, and all they want is an end to the conflict."

"This part of the city is sympathetic to the Separatists," Haki said. "The family is . . . exceptional, in a number of ways."

"You've done business with them before."

Haki shrugged. "With our host's eldest daughter. She went missing during the last days of the war along with her fiancé, a gentleman from

Coruscant I liked a great deal. They still haven't heard from either. The family hopes they're both alive—captives, maybe—though they fear they're food for the forest."

Bail nodded. He worked off his boots, wondering briefly about the propriety of undressing with Haki present, and then decided she wouldn't care.

"Are we making things worse for them? A Republic senator staying the night . . . Their neighbors will see them as traitors." He sighed. "What happens when we leave?"

"There will be consequences," Haki said. "There always are. But they chose to help us."

That did little to ease Bail's conscience. He slept anyway. He dreamed of his daughter at the table, eating berries and laughing as the drumbeat of death echoed outside.

////

According to Imperial Intelligence, Bana Rhuus had changed sides almost immediately after the death of General Grievous, pledging himself wholeheartedly to his new masters and thereby escaping—or at least postponing—his trial for war crimes and treason. He'd previously run something called "the Factory," a massive propaganda outlet that produced everything from news and entertainment for Separatist shadow-feeds to detailed and credible dossiers smearing high-ranking Republic officials. The evidence against the Jedi didn't *precisely* match the Factory's past output, but if the documents had been a Separatist creation, then Rhuus seemed as good a place as any to start.

Bail acknowledged—to himself, if not to Haki—that there was no guarantee the Separatists had been involved in the forgery. The mission might turn out to be a waste, and he might regret turning his back on Mon's scheme to bring the Emperor of Evil down through bureaucratic trickery. (He admired that woman's intellect, but how deeply wrong she could be!) Yet Haki was right to suggest the forgeries had been created by a technologically sophisticated group and not a lone operator. And Bail thought it unlikely that Palpatine would've had his own intelligence services concoct fake evidence, when one Republic loyalist might have easily leaked the truth. Anything was possible—the Emperor's black heresies still boggled the mind—but if Bail let himself focus on anything but the next problem, the next step, he'd likely go mad.

According to files Bail obtained on Coruscant, Rhuus was being debriefed at a secure facility a dozen klicks outside the city. The next day, accompanied by Haki, Bail managed to talk his way onto a military transport and persuade the clones that he was, in fact, an Imperial senator. Getting through the gates was more difficult—the facility hadn't yet been equipped with chain code readers. But after multiple scans to confirm his identity and ensure they carried no weapons, they were finally admitted. "Trouble with infiltrators," one of the clones said. "Bomber took out one of the barracks last week."

Bail wondered what that meant to the clone, knowing that, in all likelihood, the Empire would commission no more of his kind—that every death brought his people closer to extinction. But it wasn't the time for those questions.

By late afternoon, he was face-to-face with Rhuus. They met in an office decorated with tactical grids and topographical displays, and the willowy Koorivar's slender horn made him seem even taller and thinner than he was. "This is, ah, unorthodox, Senator," Rhuus said, pacing like a caged animal. "Whatever you wish, *whatsoever* I can help with, I will. But know that we are indisputably engaged and can spare *very little* time."

"Cooperate and we won't need long," Bail said. "You used to run the Factory, correct?"

"I *supervised* the Factory, but I was not responsible for its output. I did not create it. It was my assignment, and I accepted my position without complaint."

Bail allowed himself a glance at Haki. She had her hands behind her back, studying the displays as if to emphasize her distance from the exchange. Bail suspected she was paying attention anyway.

"Be that as it may," Bail said, "your *supervision* would have given you knowledge of all major Factory projects. I'd like to know if your people were involved in anti-Jedi propaganda."

"Oh, of course. We regularly—"

"Not the standard vids. Not the pieces for public distribution." Not the propaganda that had slowly soured the Republic on Jedi involvement in the war over the course of years. "I'm interested in whether you ever forged the seal of the Jedi Archives and used it to falsify a Jedi Council meeting."

Rhuus stopped pacing, and his head swayed from side to side. "Oh? Oh, well, that *would* be an endeavor. I don't recall anything *specific* to that effect, but there were so many projects, so many *calumnies* and *vilifications* regarding the Jedi Order. Will you let me review my files? My memory isn't what it was, but the files don't change."

Haki laughed loudly. When Bail looked over, she cast him an apologetic glance but did not explain.

"How long would it take you?" Bail asked

"My priority is Olkrastrus Four until I receive new orders," Rhuus said. "Once the fighting's over and the holdouts are defeated . . . maybe a week or two after that?"

///

Bail cajoled Rhuus. He pledged to help Rhuus if Rhuus would help the Empire, and he offered him protection from anyone he feared. Rhuus played the fool, claiming there was nothing he could do.

So Bail shifted to intimidation. He pledged to have Rhuus's privileges revoked, to speak at Rhuus's trial and demand that he spend the rest of his life in prison. Bail wasn't proud of these threats, and he wasn't sure whether he was bluffing. But he needed a triumph.

Rhuus apologized without ceding ground and eventually was called away by the base commandant. It was only after Bail and Haki returned to the city that Haki touched his shoulder and told him: "That was *not* Bana Rhuus."

They were walking along a road overgrown with serpentine trees and colored by fallen needles. No one else was in sight. "How do you know?" Bail asked.

"While you were negotiating our landing yesterday, I was reviewing any documentation I could find on Bana Rhuus. I happened upon his childhood medical records, which mentioned an injury to his left hand that reduced the flexibility of his fingers. The gentleman *we* saw was holding his hand as if it were paralyzed. Pitiful overacting."

"You couldn't have mentioned it earlier?"

"Rhuus was known to use body doubles—several of the Separatist Intelligence sector chiefs did—and his defection was out of character. I'm guessing that the man we met *is* hoping for an Imperial pardon and has some genuine classified data he's been doling out to his captors. I wanted to see if he'd share something useful with us, or prove my theory wrong. Alas, he did neither."

Bail nodded. He wasn't sure he believed it, but he was willing to hear Haki out. "So where's the real Bana Rhuus? Leading the Separatist hold-outs?"

"He's not a military man, so probably not *leading* them," Haki said, frowning. "Hopefully not, anyway. I'd wager a credit he's still alive and onplanet, since otherwise his double would have no reason to keep up appearances. Our impersonator would rather be tried as a war criminal's body double than as the war criminal himself, but he won't admit he's not Rhuus until he's sure Rhuus won't come looking for revenge."

"So how do we find him?" Bail asked.

"Find him?" Haki seemed genuinely surprised. "I don't believe we do. I'd say we leave Olkrastrus Four and move on to the next Separatist on our list."

"Bana Rhuus was first on the list for a reason. I don't intend to leave just because we've hit a snag."

"I don't suppose you do. But I *am* supposed to protect you." Haki peered up through the trees at the airborne fortress above. "How much are you willing to risk?"

"Everything," Bail said.

The question seemed like an insult. He would risk everything, again and again, until the Jedi's legacy was safe.

Bail went to the official sources: the clone army, the garrison commander. He spent days arguing, pleading, and bargaining with what little leverage and credibility he had, and over the course of a week, he obtained redacted deployment maps and outdated sensor imagery, bringing them back to the house piecemeal. Haki conducted her own investigation, returning late at night and typing her notes with an expression of agonized concentration. Together, they assembled a picture of the war on Olkrastrus IV.

Bail was no general, but he'd learned to speak the language of soldiers over the past years. The main Separatist fighting force was half a continent away, hiding in a network of canyons and attempting to bring their factories back online. Secondary Separatist groups were scattered around the planet, ranging from bands of a dozen or fewer guerrillas to armies hundreds strong. Bail's conclusions were grim: If Bana Rhuus was in the canyons, they would never reach him. If he was with one of the guerrilla bands, they'd never find him.

But Haki's intelligence complemented Bail's. She pointed to places in the deep forest where Separatists had been seen, away from anything of strategic value. That's where they would find Bana Rhuus, she suggested—somewhere he could wait, hide, and plan, sending messages to his allies without being caught in the fighting himself.

They agreed that Rhuus's hideout might plausibly be in a valley not far from the city, and they decided to go without alerting the Imperial forces. If Rhuus got word of an attack, he would surely flee, and Bail had no delusions that he could organize an ambush. "We go to parley, not to fight," Bail told Haki. "Once the shooting starts, our mission is doomed anyway." She grudgingly concurred.

They set off into the Spiral Forest early on a foggy morning, laden with food, water, tarps, tents, and emergency beacons. Their host had given them silk veils to filter the forest's pollen and ease their breathing. Haki carried the maps. Bail carried the fate of the Empire.

They spoke little during the journey. Bail found the quiet dismaying. With only the distant drumbeat of the shelling for company, his mind went places the past days' hectic pace had concealed. He thought of

Leia. He thought of Breha, who'd exuded unspoken doubt when he told her of his plan. He thought of the Jedi survivors fleeing from the clone army and wondered how many of them, especially those he'd aided, were still alive.

He thought of Padmé Amidala, and how horrible her death had been, and how young she'd seemed, even at the end—even with betrayal and disaster tainting her existence. "Are you doing this for the Jedi? Or to honor Padmé?" Breha had asked him before he'd left, and he'd told her that it was all the same. Breha had shaken her head. "No," she'd said, "it's not."

But it was. Because Padmé's burden and that of the Jedi would pass down to Leia if Bail didn't act—Padmé's burden, Obi-Wan's burden, and the burden Anakin Skywalker had cast aside. It wasn't right. It wasn't right for a child to grow up atoning for the failures of a generation.

"Why are you here?" Bail asked Haki as they rested on a crag rising into the forest canopy.

He expected her to lie. But he wasn't after truth, only conversation.

"That's a big question," she said. "Maybe we have the Force to thank. Maybe you want to know about Heptooinian biology?"

"Take it as you like," he answered, taking a drink from his canteen. The weather was mild, but the trek had been difficult, with few paths and many branches and bushes to scrabble through. The streamers of pollen left grit on his tongue despite the veil, and his clothes were covered in bright stains.

"I believe in two things," Haki said, her voice suddenly somber. "Opportunity and responsibility. The first means there's no point in overplanning. The universe bounces you where it will, and the only thing you can do is watch for your chance and leap on it when it comes. Maybe it gets you where you're hoping to go, maybe not, but it'll get you *somewhere*. And if your chance doesn't come, you stir the pot and make trouble until opportunity appears."

"I've known senators who saw the world that way. Most saw Palpatine as their chance to hitch a ride."

"Well, that's where the second part comes in: *responsibility*. We have to be responsible for someone, whether it's family or species or planet." Haki waved a veined hand. "I grew up outside the Republic. We knew what war and famine looked like long before you did. The things decades of conflict do to a place . . ." She looked toward the city, then gestured to the sky. "You haven't seen the half of it, Senator. The Clone Wars were three years, and they were awful, but you won't know real awful until you've seen folk fight for a lifetime."

She waited—for what, Bail wasn't sure. He nodded to show he was listening.

"Well," she said, "the Republic saved my world. So I'm here to repay it. Before family, before species, before love. My responsibility is to the Republic."

"Only now there's an Empire."

"Republic, Empire . . . different name, all the same people."

Bail didn't have a response to that. He should have, but he didn't.

They set off again, beginning their descent into the valley where they hoped Rhuus was hiding. Haki guided them in a zigzag through overgrown stretches of forest, explaining, "Want to get close before they notice us. Might be autoguns, other defenses, so better not to march straight in."

Eventually they spotted mounds of rocks and a cluster of intertwined trees that seemed like a plausible hiding place, a sort of grand archway of stone and wood. They reached the valley floor an hour before sunset and rested again before moving toward the mounds. Haki swore she spotted movement among the trunks.

They made no effort to conceal their presence, standing tall and speaking loudly. "Whatever you do, don't look threatening," Haki said, seeming amused by the thought. Bail felt briefly insulted, but Haki was right. No one would mistake a senator and an old woman for an assault team.

Soon they were close enough to catch winks of light among the branches and boulders. Bail quickened his pace, and Haki abruptly caught his arm. "Don't!" she snapped, nodding toward the ground.

Bail looked down. His left heel was settled on a smooth surface he'd taken for a rock.

"Mine," Haki said. "Pressure activated. Don't move."

Bail swore. His skin felt suddenly too hot. "Can you disable it?"

"Possibly. But if I try and fail . . ."

He studied her expression, then looked to the trees ahead. He tried to resist the urge to grind his heel into the metal and feel out its edges.

"Hello!" he cried. "We come to talk!"

Haki frowned, then nodded and took several steps backward.

No one answered. Bail tried not to think of the mine, his daughter, or his wife. His heart was beating rapidly, yet he felt clearheaded. He was not *afraid*, though he should have been. This was bravery. This was purpose.

After several minutes, he tried again. "My name is Senator Bail Organa of Alderaan! I've come to talk to Bana Rhuus!"

It was getting dark. The wind was still. He felt sure there was motion around them. The urge to turn and look was strong, but he didn't dare adjust his footing.

"You're a long way from home," a voice said. It was modulated and seemed to come from the trees to Bail's right—from a hidden electronic speaker, perhaps.

"So I am," Bail said. "Which is why I'd appreciate your hospitality. It's been a tiring journey."

The voice laughed. It was not a friendly laugh. "I know about you, Senator Organa. I know that while you were calling for peace in public, you were secretly working alongside the Jedi and the clone army to sever our supply lines, bombard our planets, capture and assassinate our leaders. You are a hypocrite and an enemy of the Separatist Confederacy—a tool of the Empire. I see no reason to offer hospitality."

"We were at war," Bail said. The accusation of hypocrisy rankled— *I restrained the clone army! I worked with the Jedi to save lives!*—but he was used to hearing worse. "I don't imagine either of us has clean hands. But we do have a common enemy."

"Do tell."

"The Empire," Bail said. "If you know about me, you know I'm no friend of the administration. Palpatine and his grand vizier are mad with power, and you may have the tools to help weaken their position."

"Tools of what sort?"

"Information."

The voice paused. "I possess a great deal of information. Yet I am an exile, a hunted figure. If you brought down your Emperor tomorrow, I am sure it would benefit *you*. Can you offer a reason it would benefit *me*?"

Bail had expected this question. He'd considered it back in the city and concluded his best option was to lie, to promise Rhuus an amnesty he had no power to grant, or suggest he could remove Imperial troops from Olkrastrus IV. Or he might trade Rhuus some valuable strategic data, perhaps a way to strike at the local garrison.

"No," Bail said. "I can offer you nothing."

He was not a liar—not most days, anyway. And he certainly wasn't a traitor, ready to sacrifice brave clones for his own convenience. (A part of him asked, *What about for the sake of the galaxy? What about for the Jedi? For Leia?* But it hadn't come to that yet.)

The electronic voice laughed and abruptly cut out. Bail felt the mine shift under his heel and flinched, nearly falling. But a moment later he was still alive, and a figure emerged from the archway.

It took him a moment to recognize the man. Rhuus's body double had lacked the layers of grime and pollen, the military fatigues, and the missing right foot replaced by a primitive metal peg. The real Rhuus had suffered in the Spiral Forest, and though Rhuus was surely his enemy, had committed atrocities during the war, Bail nonetheless found himself full of pity.

Pity would get him nowhere. He wiped the expression from his face.

"The mines have been disabled," Rhuus said. "Tell me what you're looking for."

Bail did. He told Rhuus of his suspicions about the Empire's use of Separatist propaganda. He argued that indisputable proof could open a path to Palpatine's downfall. Haki did not interject, and she drew no attention from her position behind Bail, playing the role of silent body-guard.

Rhuus listened, once or twice asking clarifying questions. When Bail was done, Rhuus rubbed the pollen from his forehead and said, "Two years ago, an emissary from the Techno Union came to the Factory and asked to borrow several of my agents—not mere forgers but *artists*, brilliant minds and skilled hands, psychological profilers and encryption experts. The emissary made it clear I was to ask no questions about her project. I would create a story for internal consumption to explain my operatives' leave of absence that was in *no way* connected to her.

"I was a man of some influence in Separatist Intelligence, Bail Organa. My propaganda swayed *worlds*. I turned brother against brother and showed the true ugliness of the Republic to its most loyal troops. It was rare for my superiors to deny me information, or to poach my agents for their own operations."

"What makes you think this operation was related to the forgery of Jedi materials?" Bail asked.

"Perhaps it wasn't," Rhuus said. "But aside from their artistry, the only trait these agents shared was their familiarity with the Jedi Order."

Bail felt a chill, the thrill of the revelation entwined with the fear of its implications. Part of him was tempted to turn to Haki, to see whether her read was the same as his. But he kept his focus on Rhuus. "Where can I find your agents?" he asked.

"In their graves," Rhuus said. "But fear not: I have a lead for you. The Techno Union woman may yet be alive. She made it to the end of the war, I know, though my sources since then have been . . . reduced in number."

"Tell me," Bail said.

Rhuus did, and they spoke a short while longer. Rhuus did not bid Bail well or wish him safe travels back to the city, but he expressed hope that they would not meet again. Bail took that as both a warning and the most sincere benediction he could hope for.

The old war criminal was who he was, and whatever the Separatists' gripes—however valid their complaints that the Republic had failed them—their leadership was not made up of kind or virtuous or heroic people. It was good, Bail thought, to be reminded of that.

Good he had no need to carry one more regret.

"Best we get moving," Haki said when Rhuus had disappeared into the archway. "It'll be full dark soon, and we're far from the safety of the city."

CHAPTER 19
A SECOND VISIT

They camped in the Spiral Forest that night, not far from the valley. And though Haki was tired and cold and felt—reasonably, she thought—*old*, she waited for Bail to fall asleep and went back the way they'd come, back toward the archway, picking her way through the minefield, knowing it was foolhardy.

She slipped past the sentries and into the caves formed by overhanging trees and rocks, and she felt lucky when it turned out there was no labyrinth, just a few small camps. She quickly located Rhuus, asleep on his back. She knelt behind him and gently cradled his head. Her left hand caressed his scalp while her right placed a needle against his neck.

He knew better than to shout when he woke. She injected him with a half dose—enough to relax him—before beginning her interrogation, asking questions in a soothing tone not so different from the one she'd used while rocking her sons to sleep. Rhuus answered with little resistance.

They were all dead, was the short of it. Haki's operatives in the sector; Chemish's brother, Homish, and his fiancée, who'd lived on Olkrastrus IV for a year; other agents she'd visited in the worst days of the war and pledged her support to, listened to, comforted, even held after especially bad missions. Rhuus had purged them all after the rise of the Emperor, in those vulnerable moments when the intelligence services had turned their eyes inward and neglected their agents in the field. Rhuus had seen the opportunity and acted like any good spymaster would.

Haki wasn't surprised. And maybe, she told herself, some of her agents elsewhere had survived. Maybe there was still hope.

Opportunity and responsibility. Was that what she'd told Bail?

She injected Rhuus with the rest of the dose before departing— enough to cause his heart to fail, as long as no medic found him first. She felt she'd been more than merciful. She didn't have time for justice.

CHAPTER 20
NO ONE FEELS POWERFUL

The memorial service took up most of the morning. Mon was the third speaker, after Zhuna's mother and boyfriend, and she'd come prepared with anecdotes about Zhuna's devotion to service and her growth over eighteen months as Mon's aide. After significant deliberation the night before, Mon had decided to acknowledge the horror of Zhuna's death in a passage about the woman's commitment to politics. "To truly uphold democracy is an act of humility," she'd said as forty faces watched in displays of grief, dignity, and frustration. "Democracy is the choice to accept that one's most cherished beliefs and foundational principles may not win the day. It is a willing abnegation where we bequeath power to those we may view as wrongheaded, unfit, or abominable. It is the paradox of holding true to ourselves, even as we accept when the vote goes against us and the desires of others prevail. Zhuna understood this and never gave in to hubris or despair. She understood that democracy is the foundation of virtuous government. Her killer, though he claimed to love our nation, possessed neither understanding nor love."

It was, she thought, a good speech. Zhuna's father embraced her tightly afterward, thanking her for coming when so many of Zhuna's family members had been too scared to attend, and Mon sleepwalked through the pleasantries and commiserations and all the rituals of death. She busied herself studying the service program while two of Zhuna's stepsiblings cursed Mon's name and called her an appeaser, a coward unwilling to stand against the imperialist movement that had killed their sister. One of the cousins, a youth someone called Chemish, escorted the pair away.

Perhaps they're right, Mon thought after she'd left the service, surrounded by an escort of twenty security officers. Someone had publicized the location. Imperialist protesters called for Mon's head on her way out, accusing her of exploiting a tragedy for political gain.

But that was over now. She left the protests behind along with Coruscant, reclining in the white leather seat of her shuttle and preparing for the meeting ahead.

Her attempts to contact Tychon Nulvolio—the man she'd been told led the ex-Separatist voting bloc—had yet to bear fruit. The man was a ghost, emerging for an interview or two and then vanishing. If she didn't speak to him soon, it would be too late. She had to be ready by the time the ex-Separatist representatives were reintegrated into the Senate. She'd lost nearly a week in the aftermath of Zhuna's murder, which gave her less than three weeks to go.

For the moment, she would focus on securing votes elsewhere. Zhuna's murder had slowed her progress, but she could forget the horror now and focus on tomorrow.

The shuttle took her out of Coruscant's stratosphere and into the void of space. She'd always enjoyed space travel—not *hyperspace* travel, with its cerulean fury like the heart of a cosmic storm, but passage between planets and moons, where everything seemed permanently fixed in a still and silent emptiness. She watched the glittering jewel of Coruscant fall beneath her, its facets winking with artificial lights, then turned toward Hesperidium. The moon's lights were fewer and clearer, penetrating its thin atmosphere in multicolored splendor, and great shadows described settlements and spaceports. The shuttle accelerated toward Hesperidium, slowed as her pilot proceeded through security checks and financial evaluations, then began a rapid descent toward one of the outlying ports.

Hesperidium was an unnatural paradise—a once-lifeless rock, the least of Coruscant's four moons, transformed into a resort and patchwork nature preserve by Coruscant's wealthiest citizens. There were parks that simulated a dozen biomes, mountains cultivated for climbing, and violet oceans traversed by massive yachts. At this moment, Hesperidium was in a simulated pastoral phase, favoring imported wood and eschewing the use of droids. Even the shuttle guidance signals were designed to look like great torches, their holographic flames crackling in the wind.

From the spaceport, Mon passed through more security checks and then took a carriage (in fact a speeder dressed up like a racing fathier) to the Axiom Club. After one final checkpoint, she entered the central lodge, a vast structure of wood, stone, and glass, smelling of a Chandrilan springtime and decorated with the holographic heads of mythical beasts. The space could have held hundreds, but it was occupied only by the three beings she'd come to meet.

"Senator Mothma!" the first called, stepping ahead of the others. Arvik Cornade was a burly man twice her age, with an elaborate mustache and a small cranial implant. His footsteps echoed on the polished granite. "Right on time."

"Master Cornade. Please, call me Mon," she said and took his proffered hand in both of hers. Cornade smiled but, she noticed, did not return the offer of familiarity.

He introduced her to the others, though she knew them by reputation. Baron Shkan-Shkan Yew was officially ruler of an obscure Nothoiin colony world, but his ancestors had invested their fortune in a variety of industries—plastoid manufacturing first among them. Now Baron Yew was one of the wealthiest men in the galaxy, with minority interests in half the public megacorporations. Hasalia Prederiko lacked Yew's pedigree but had her own sources of influence. She was chief financial officer at General Trade Galactic, an obscure holding company that owned several hundred shipping and retail firms. Many of those firms did legitimate business, but it was an open secret that the rest were fronts for the Crymorah crime syndicate.

Cornade was the founder and chief executive of Cornade Mining and Assembly, perhaps the most profitable corporation founded in the past century. Cornade, Yew, and Prederiko together possessed enough money to buy sectors or feed trillions. It made Mon's own inheritance seem a pittance. She considered herself fortunate and privileged, and she felt no envy, but it was a reminder that wealth—like power—was relative.

"We'll grab a bite first," Cornade said, leading the way deeper into the lodge. "The baron's snippy when he's not fed, eh?"

Mon tried to smile enough to acknowledge the comment and not enough to irritate Baron Yew. Prederiko laughed openly, and Mon suspected her own discomfort was the reason for Prederiko's joy.

They consumed a meal more intricate than any Mon had eaten in years—small plates of bite-sized cakes and truffles and gilded birds. Her whole body seemed to warm or cool with each dish, and the flavors summoned memories of her childhood, of forgotten dreams she'd had during her school years. She did her best to take it in stride, engaging Cornade in boisterous conversation about his resumption of control over business interests on Separatist worlds and speaking to Baron Yew quietly and politely about his stepdaughter's struggles with depression. Mon's research had turned up the least about Prederiko, so she asked few questions of the woman, and Prederiko said little in return.

Finally, when the meal was over, the baron said, "We can speak freely now. The administration is watching the Senate closely, but the lodge is secure. My people have completed their scans."

"Yes, Senator," Prederiko said. "Tell us all about the Imperial Rebirth Act."

She hadn't mentioned it to them in arranging the meeting, but it was no surprise that they knew. She expected they had connections to half the senators she'd brought aboard.

"I'd be delighted," she said, and started with her usual summary of the bill, its goals, and how she intended to sell it to the public. She explained how it would diminish the Emperor's authority while allowing him to save face. The three power brokers listened politely, but it was clear Mon was saying little new to them.

She modulated her approach. "Over the course of his career, Palpatine has shown great deference to organizations like yours. Your lobbying efforts are always entertained. In his early years in the Senate, Palpatine was keen to offer you key contracts and deregulate the bureaucracy on your behalf. If I may speculate, I would say he *respects* you as fellow players in the game of influence.

"Yet times are changing. The administration has spent enormous effort demonizing corporate interests and decrying the influence of the ultra-wealthy. Often, Palpatine has likened successful businesspeople to criminals," she said, avoiding even a glance at Prederiko. She thought she heard the woman snicker. "Palpatine has the instincts of a populist, and he's very good at the rhetoric. He's already nationalized the Banking Clan and has shown his willingness to absorb other organizations when he deems it prudent. Yes, the Banking Clan had already sided with the Separatists, and from Palpatine's point of view perhaps they'd grown too greedy—gone too far and become an enemy. What I'm telling you is that I don't believe it *matters*."

Cornade looked irritated—he'd been closest to Palpatine personally, spending time with the man when Palpatine had been a mere senator from Naboo. Baron Yew had his eyes half shut and his hands clasped together, as if he were focusing on Mon's words and tuning out the rest of the lodge. Prederiko was leaning back in her seat and nodding along.

"Palpatine's power is now unconstrained," Mon went on. "He may be your ally at this time, but your very *existence* depends on his favor. Can you guarantee he will not come to see you as an inconvenience? Do you think the Senate will be able to protect you if he wishes to seize one of your businesses? Or freeze your accounts? Or, if he prefers to be subtle about it, launch an investigation into your affairs, with the outcome predetermined? Under our new Galactic Emperor, you are vulnerable in ways you've never been before, and your reliance on him will only grow.

"He has been your friend, but you cannot afford the risk that he will turn against you. Better to check his power now. Can you honestly say the old system treated you so poorly?"

She smiled sardonically at this. That was a risk, but she'd found that powerful people, despite their inevitable complaints about all government bureaucracy, often had a sense of irony.

Her hosts were silent a moment. Then Baron Yew said, "Palpatine won a civil war and wiped out the Jedi Order for good measure. Perhaps we are past the point of restraining him. Perhaps all we can do now is ensure we do not become his enemies."

"Man's got a point," Prederiko said.

"Let's talk and shoot," Cornade said. "Mon, you ever handle a rifle?"

✇ ✇ ✇

Mon had, in fact, handled a rifle, though she loathed every aspect of target shooting—the icy touch of a metal barrel, the tactile feedback of a trigger, the whiff of a discharged blaster bolt. Her aim was also poor, a fact the others found greatly entertaining.

Maybe it was a subconscious act of self-sabotage. She had, after all, been able to lob a smashball with formidable accuracy in her youth. Call it her body revolting against the notion of handling a machine designed to kill. *Your mind may compromise, but you have the heart of a pacifist.*

Then again, it had also been a while since she'd had her vision checked.

They hunted aerial droids on the lunar plains. The machines had been built for this, hand-painted to resemble birds from a dozen worlds and programmed to emulate their species' songs. They flew and dodged shots in spectacular patterns, whole squadrons spiraling like troupes of dancers. They were nearly real. Prederiko fired a few perfunctory rounds, but the afternoon belonged to Cornade and Baron Yew, who took to dialing up the droids' agility when they realized Mon was hopeless.

They mostly talked about the war, which was similar, Mon thought, to talking about the weather. For years it had been the uncontrollable force around them, defining their daily lives and conversations. Even these power brokers, so removed from the existence of ordinary people, had been affected by the blockades and supply shortages. They knew people who had joined the Separatists and knew people who had died.

"You don't appreciate what it's like," Cornade told her, "to have twelve million employees pleading for evacuation before the enemy arrives. Waiting for support, waiting for the bombardment, all relying on you. That was the worst day for me, but there were plenty of others like it."

"I know responsibility, Master Cornade," she said.

"I'm sure you do, but your job is to represent your people's wants and needs. Senators speak up—they can't act alone. I've got the better part of a trillion people looking to me to keep their families fed, keep them safe, keep them employed. I've got half a dozen senators in my pocket, but I'm the only one who can flip a switch and ruin planets."

She didn't argue. Cornade took another shot at one of the droids as it swept overhead, looping gracefully out of sight.

"Why didn't you ever petition for corporate Senate representation?" Mon asked. "You might have gotten it."

"You looking to become Senator Mothma of Cornade Mining and Assembly?" he asked with a wink. Then he shrugged. "Always seemed like too much trouble. You look at the Trade Federation, and what did having representation get them? Easier to remind senators that their constituents rely on me and that my interests are their interests.

"Funny thing, though," he went on. "Maybe I was wrong to dismiss politics. Always figured there was nothing the Senate could do that we couldn't undo or ignore or work around, but I never guessed we'd see a war in my lifetime. Turns out we were as vulnerable to circumstances as anyone."

Mon thought about what she could say to that—whether it would be useful to point out that the outsize influence of businesses like Cornade's had helped spur on the Separatist crisis in the first place, or that the Separatist cause had been backed by many of Cornade's peers.

But her purpose wasn't to humble Cornade, merely to gain his allegiance. She said nothing and fired her rifle into the black and empty sky.

///

Later, over dinner, Baron Yew asked Mon about her own experiences in the war. She let instinct guide her answer. He would recognize an attempt at manipulation, any effort to play upon his sympathies, but she'd been building connections with people unlike her for decades. She trusted herself.

She told the baron about a day early in the conflict, when the Separatists had come for Chandrila. The Republic hadn't yet realized the extent of the Separatist aggression, and the planet had been unprepared. Mon had been trapped in Hanna City, sending urgent calls to Coruscant until the Separatists had jammed all transmissions and they'd watched the ships take position above the capital.

Chandrila's defense forces had been negligible—practically nonexistent—and incapable of damaging Separatist dreadnoughts. So all they could do was raise the deflector above Hanna and watch the bombs fall.

It should have been terrifying. Perrin had been offworld, so Mon had gone to her assigned bunker alone, watching streaks of light and the colorful splashes of coruscating energy as the bombs hit the shield. She'd stood with members of the planetary government, wondering whether any of them would survive—or if they *did* survive, whether they would have a planet left to govern. She'd imagined being a senator representing a ravaged world of broken cities, spending the rest of her life not in pursuit of galactic betterment but simply seeking respite for the Chandrilans who remained.

It had occurred to her, too—though she did not mention this to Baron Yew—that the Separatist attack might have been proof of her own foolishness. Perhaps her insistence on peaceful solutions had left Chandrila weak and exposed. Perhaps Chandrila had been wrong to elect her, wrong to believe that military strength was more apt to create conflict than prevent it.

"Yet you did survive," the baron said.

"We survived," Mon replied.

Hours had passed. The shields had held. The people of Hanna City had stopped cowering in their homes and emerged into the streets and plazas, shouting defiantly at the sky as the bombs kept falling. Soon the tenor of these gatherings changed, and instead of shouting, the people began to cheer, treating the explosions and the electric iridescence of the shields as a pyrotechnic display, oohing and aahing with each blast. The officials in the bunker had emerged then and joined the celebrations, half-fearful and half-exhilarated, knowing the Separatists might change tactics at any time. But until they did . . .

Well, until they did, there was life.

After seven hours and seventeen minutes, the Separatists had moved on. Mon's world, her career, and her beliefs had remained intact.

"What was the purpose of the attack?" the baron asked.

"I never found out," Mon said. "I suppose they wanted to make us afraid."

/ / /

After dinner, Cornade and Yew made their excuses and thanked Mon for her company and thoughtful conversation. They left her alone in the lodge with a glass of shining blue wine and a promise from the baron to host next time. Prederiko escorted the others out and made it clear that Mon was not to follow.

Almost an hour later, Mon had taken a single sip of the wine and Prederiko had returned at last. "I'd almost given up," Mon said, which was undiplomatic but almost true.

"You're the optimistic type," Prederiko said, leaning on the back of a chair carved from the skull of some enormous raptor. "I figured you'd wait."

"So?" Mon asked.

Prederiko laughed. "You don't like me, do you? You don't like them, either, but with me you're not afraid to show it."

Was she so obvious after all? Mon shook her head. "If we're being frank—I *do* like them. I don't agree with them about many things, but

I find Master Cornade and Baron Yew to be thoughtful and well-intentioned, even if they have their blind spots."

"Whereas I . . . ?"

"You profit off misery. You uphold the interests of people who bring nothing but pain to the galaxy."

Prederiko shrugged. "My business is entirely aboveboard. I can't imagine you're implying otherwise. But as far as I'm concerned, I contribute just as much as those two. The galaxy doesn't need more metals and droids and plastoid, but it *wants* them, and someone might as well employ a few trillion people to fulfill those desires." She lifted a finger, frowned, then lowered her hand as if changing her mind about something. "The reason you don't like me is because you don't want to be the *sort of person* who would like me."

"You're probably right," Mon said. "I am sorry—genuinely sorry—if I offended."

"You're forgiven. I'm used to it. You want to know if we're supporting your bill?"

"I do."

"Well, I won't keep you in suspense." Prederiko paused a beat longer than necessary. "We're in. Provisionally, anyway. We'll call in what favors we can and encourage our friends in the Senate to make the right decisions for their constituencies. Counting votes is your job, not mine, but figure we can swing maybe eighty, ninety senators your way."

"I'm glad to hear it. What's your support *provisional* upon?"

"Nothing outlandish. But if Palpatine's going to stop looking out for us, we need assurances that our operations can move forward whether he stays in office or not."

"Specifically?"

"I'll get you a list. For decades, the baron's been fighting off a movement that would force the old royal families to either divest from corporate holdings or abdicate their titles and inheritance. He's worried that turning the Galactic Emperor into a figurehead will only encourage the anti-royalists. A provision protecting the rights of nobility is the main thing he needs, along with the lifting of some embargoes from the run-up to the war."

Mon nodded. Some of the reform-minded senators would balk, but she doubted she'd lose more than one or two votes. "I can look into it. What else?"

"Cornade's going to ask for the stars and sweets on his pillow, but that's just who he is. Again, I'll get you details—hell, I can get you draft language—but the only thing he'll really insist on is something protect-ing droid labor and manufacturing. He's terrified the backlash against the Separatist droid armies is going to ruin his business. Don't really blame him."

Mon recalled her conversation with Senator DuQuosenne, and her promise to the woman's protocol droid that she'd attach a rider protect-ing droid intelligence. But she needed Cornade's influence more than DuQuosenne's. Maybe she could find something else to offer the sena-tor.

"And you?" Mon asked. "Does the Crymorah want any amendments to the bill?"

"To the bill? No. I'll talk to my sponsors, but so far as I'm concerned, you should get our full backing. No conditions, no provisions."

"Why?"

"You said it yourself. Whatever the Emperor gives us he can take away, and that's too great a threat to ignore. There are people . . ." Pre-deriko wrinkled her nose, seemed to play out a conversation in her head, then nodded. "There are people—not *my* people, but people in related lines of work—who see the administration as being extremely friendly to them. They're taking great interest in the regional governors Palpatine is appointing. Feel like they've got new partners, folks open to mutually beneficial relationships.

"I think that's probably true. But I'm cautious by nature. I like to hedge my bets. The way I see it, if *anything* goes wrong at all . . . Once the knives come out, my people and I would be first to go."

Mon couldn't help but laugh.

"That's the argument I've been making to the Senate."

"It's all the same, right? Politics. Business. *My* business." Prederiko smiled. "I'll get you your votes. Only thing I ask is that you keep my name out of it."

"Gladly," Mon said.

They left the lodge together, and Prederiko escorted Mon as far as the carriage back to the shuttle port. "One other thing I can offer," the woman said as they came within sight of Mon's gaudy vehicle. "The intelligence services are watching you. You ever need them off your back awhile, let me know."

"You have someone inside?" Mon asked.

Prederiko shrugged. "They're short-staffed. They can't watch *everyone*. All you have to do is provide a few leads—real, not real, doesn't matter—and we can pass the names along, watch the spies all run in another direction for a few days. Works like a charm."

"Unless you're one of the people they start watching."

"Well, that's why you don't send them after your friends. The more plausible the leads, though—the more people you point at who are undermining the administration, or, well, look like they *ought* to be—the longer the watchers stay busy."

"I appreciate the offer," Mon said.

They said their farewells. It wasn't until she was on the shuttle home that Mon realized she hadn't actually declined Prederiko's offer.

🌢🌢🌢

When she returned to her apartment—which was not her *home,* because her home was still a crime scene and deemed *insecure* by Senate Security, but rather temporary living quarters assigned to her and Perrin—she discovered her belongings were out of place. Someone had pawed through her drawers and left her casual shirts rumpled. Someone had left her datapads on the wrong side of her desk. She was confident the *someone* was not Perrin.

She felt a vague sense of disgust and violation, tempered by the fact that she'd seen so much worse of late. So what if Imperial Intelligence or the security bureau had searched her lodgings, not even bothering to conceal their work? It was better than murderers coming for her, better than being arrested. It was life now. It was the Galactic Empire.

She was getting used to it.

CHAPTER 21
SNAPSHOTS

When Chemish needed to think, Chemish climbed. Their mother called it "Troubled Spiderling Syndrome." Haki called it a self-destructive tendency. But climbing had saved Chemish's life in the days after Homish had died. If it had also nearly killed Chemish three times as a teenager, so what? Sometimes that was the cost of sanity.

So Chemish scaled the Agrunan Spire, scrabbling from trellis to piping to transmitter nodes, contorting their body to reach the next handhold and the next. They were sweating profusely in the midday heat, and the wake of passing speeders teased their hair. Now and then one of the spire's residents shouted obscenities or encouragement, or threatened to call Coruscant Security. Chemish had started at Level 4168 and ascended thirty meters freehand, using only magnetic gloves and grip stockings. They looked up, left, and right, but never behind and never down. They'd keep going until they had answers.

Chemish wasn't *political*. Zhuna hadn't been, either, despite what everyone said at the funeral. The two of them had grown up together in the Duros Blocks, less than an hour's ride below the Federal District, and the most *political* they'd gotten was when Zhuna's uncle's stepdaughter Macy had run for a seat on the block council. Zhuna had been fifteen, Chemish had been twelve, and they'd plastered the block with posters—until Macy had missed the first debate thanks to a double shift at the atmosphere scrubbers. After that, they'd believed what everyone else on the block seemed to believe: Palpatine was all right, Noodra Machik and Bail Organa and a couple others who weren't afraid of the corporations were all right, but the rest of the Republic was a bunch of crooks. The Clone Wars only reinforced those views, but Zhuna had done well in her second year at university and had somehow ended up with Senator Mothma—

Chemish struggled to bend their knee and get their foot onto a rattling air circulator. They weren't sure it would hold their weight, but to their left and right were flat windowpanes and durasteel. If Chemish wanted to avoid backtracking, the air circulator was the only way up.

So had politics gotten Zhuna killed? And if not, what *had*?

Politics had damn well mucked with Zhuna's death. Chemish thought about the memorial service three days prior, where Senator Mothma had talked about her own greatness in the guise of talking about Zhuna. When Genlee and Nych had started in on the senator about doing nothing to protect their stepsister, Chemish hadn't really disagreed. They'd pulled the others away to avoid a scene, but screw Mothma and all her anti-government plans.

Then there had been the crowd outside, the imperialist protesters who'd aimed their anger not just at Mothma but at the family, at Zhuna's mother. Chemish hadn't understood in the moment, but they'd watched the news feeds after. Some of the protesters said Mothma was twisting the facts of the tragedy to smear the imperialist movement— that Mon was blaming the killer's politics instead of his obvious derangement. There had been uglier claims, too—paranoid arguments that Mothma had arranged Zhuna's death for political gain. Haki had opened Chemish's eyes to the messiness of government, but Chemish knew a grotesque conspiracy theory when they heard one.

Politics, Chemish thought, seemed to twist up everything. It twisted up people, Mothma and the protesters alike, instead of pushing them to make things better.

The air circulator held but made a cracking noise under Chemish's foot. They moved quickly to the next grip.

They'd wanted to ask the protesters, *Why do you think these things? Why are you here? Even if you're right, how will yelling at our grieving family convince anyone?* But the family had needed Chemish, and they'd all gone home and welcomed in the neighbors and everyone who'd been too scared to come to the memorial. Chemish had thanked folks for the potluck dishes and the offers to do laundry, walk the pets, or do anything else Zhuna's mother needed. And there had been tears, and swearing, and Zhuna had still been dead, and Chemish, eventually, had gone to bed.

Chemish had taken snapshots of the memorial protesters with a concealed cam in their top collar button. Later Chemish had retrieved the images and stared at the angry faces. Chemish had tried to find any news reports about the murderer himself, but there hadn't been much, just a name.

Chemish felt for the next handhold, and their glove touched gravel. They pulled themself into a rooftop garden and lay flat on the ground, panting under the warm sun.

"Your brother told me you have the mind of a detective," Haki had told Chemish. But what Homish had told Chemish, over and over, was "You have the mind of a philosopher."

Why had Zhuna died?

It was a foolish question. A childish question. It was all Chemish could think about.

///

Haki had said that their job wasn't politics or law enforcement but *stability,* and that maintaining stability usually involved giving people what they wanted.

She'd first said the words early in Chemish's apprenticeship, when they'd met in parks or tram cars or Homish's storage unit instead of the safe house. Haki had delicately broached the idea of Chemish reporting back on what Zhuna had to say about her time in Mothma's office, and Chemish had asked why the administration wanted to spy on its own senators.

"Senate ever make much of a difference in your life?" Haki had asked. Chemish had said, no, of course not. Haki had smiled bitterly and replied, "You forget about the war? Think about it this way. Senators may never improve the status quo, but they can break it. Stability stops sounding so bad after a while, you look at it like that. You won't ever catch me saying the administration is perfect, but it won't break itself out of spite."

Chemish thought this made sense, mostly, though sometimes they wondered whether Haki believed it herself. They'd tried to ignore their questions and do what Homish would've done—do what would honor him, prevent another war and, incidentally, earn Chemish enough credits to escape the Duros Blocks someday. A life of spy work would mean a life of lies and a willingness to take orders. But what career didn't? The fact Homish had found a way to do good *and* make something of himself was a miracle. Chemish was just following his thread through the maze—his last, unwitting gift to his sibling. And if Haki had always been a little cagey about how *official* Chemish's apprenticeship was, what did it matter as long as their partnership continued?

It was for all those reasons and more that Chemish, the morning after their climb, had come to an outlying office building half a kilometer from the Senate Rotunda. Haki had said not to worry about work, but Haki had also emphasized the value of unexpected opportunities. And anyway, Haki was gone, off on her secret mission for who knew how long.

"You said you're a courier?" the bureaucrat asked.

"That's right," Chemish said. "Small goods, mostly. Documents now and then."

"Corporate clients? Government?"

They sat in an unornamented cubicle, and Chemish tried to recall the advice they'd received at the memorial. "*Everyone adored Zhuna. We'd love to hire someone from the family. Come down when you can, be your-*

self, and we'll work with you to find a position." Nothing enormously useful, especially when *be yourself* wasn't an option.

Chemish knew they were out of their depth. They didn't dress or talk like a Senate staffer, but if they could get inside, they'd have a whole new set of sources. Even if they failed, they might be able to make a personal connection, build a link to Mothma's other staffers. Chemish could still prove their utility and be Intelligence's eyes in Mothma's office, even with Zhuna gone.

"Independent businesses," Chemish said. "Thrizka owns the grocer's, sometimes makes loans to good customers. He trusted me to handle it. I'd run a bag stuffed with five hundred credits across the sector."

It was an anecdote that would've opened doors in the Duros Blocks. The bureaucrat didn't seem impressed.

"Any clients I'd have heard of?"

"Doesn't seem like it," Chemish said.

The interview never recovered from there, and though Chemish emphasized their relationship with Zhuna, the bureaucrat seemed disinterested. There was no tour of Mothma's offices, no chance to reconnect with anyone who'd appeared at the memorial. Chemish managed to contain their disappointment until they made it home, at which point the questions and anxieties unspooled again. They lay in bed staring at the stained ceiling and wondered what would happen if Haki never returned. Or if Haki did return and learned about the interview, what if she decided Chemish had acted too foolishly? What if Chemish lost their connection to the work of the Empire, and to their brother, and had to return to courier work until the day they slipped in the rain and fell so far that their body was lost forever?

What if they could've saved Zhuna?

What if? What if?

///

Chemish threw up. Chemish climbed. Chemish pretended to meditate. Chemish checked for signals from Haki and spent a day in the safe house cleaning every surface and looking for hidden messages that would tell them what to do.

They knew they were being irrational. They knew all their questions were one question. It just didn't matter.

/ / /

The second memorial service Chemish attended was outdoors, under a false sky projection in the Abbo-Suer District. There were no protesters, and half as many attendees as there'd been at Zhuna's.

Chemish stood in the back, listening to the ritual recitation of some Mid Rim creed and anecdotes from the troubled life of Thalvus Agyomenidus. Thalvus had been raised without a father. Thalvus had run cargo for six years before returning to Coruscant. Thalvus had bought the singing wood he'd used in his furniture shop from some world nobody had ever heard of, and that had changed his fortunes. There was a lot of talk of wood. There was not a lot of talk about how Thalvus had fallen in with a group so radical, so utterly supportive of Palpatine, and so derisive of his foes (real or perceived) that Thalvus had considered it reasonable to attempt a political assassination.

Chemish wasn't surprised, really. They watched the assembly the way Haki had taught them, without obvious interest. Chemish matched the faces in the small crowd to the faces they'd seen protesting at Zhuna's memorial. They kept watching those individuals when they filed out afterward and walked three blocks to a dive bar, where they drank and talked about their spouses and very little about politics, at least as far as Chemish could overhear.

These people hadn't killed Zhuna, not unless there really was a conspiracy, and Chemish didn't think there was. But they were the closest Chemish could get to asking Thalvus Agyomenidus, *Why did you kill my cousin?*

So eventually Chemish bought a round and introduced themself as "Homish Grayline" and said they'd seen the group at the memorial and asked if they would mind company. Chemish wasn't a reporter or with Coruscant Security. They'd just gotten angry about Senator Mothma using the tragedy to her political advantage, and Chemish figured they'd come and see for themself what Thalvus was all about.

It came out in more of a rush than Chemish intended—Haki had warned them they were no good at lying yet—but the group waved Chemish to a seat. A balding man with pale skin who kept an umbrella between his knees introduced himself as Laevido and said, "Thalvus was an idiot. Probably not as daft as the girl he killed, but he was old enough to know better. That girl . . . you don't blame the young for their mixed-up politics."

"Thalvus really did it, then?" Chemish asked.

Laevido snorted. "If he didn't, the fix-up was damn thorough. No, Thalvus did it. His spirit was admirable, but his methods . . ."

"How'd you know him?"

"He was one of our regulars."

Chemish asked the obvious question, and by the time the night was over they had an invitation to join the imperialists at their next meeting. Maybe Haki would've been proud, or maybe Haki would've scolded Chemish for wasting time infiltrating a band of the administration's supporters.

But Haki wasn't there, and Chemish wanted to *know*.

CHAPTER 22
THE CACHE

The *Dalgo* alternated propulsion methods, switching abruptly from sustained thruster bursts to antigravity repulsors. It would coast some, barely heavier than a needle, then thrust again, all the while descending through pale-rose clouds and past the peaks of dead skyscrapers. Whenever the pilot transferred power, the crew lurched in their seats, and not even Saw looked comfortable. But there was no escaping the sensor net over Eyo-Dajuritz. All they could hope to do was confuse it.

The smart thing was to keep your head low and stare at the deck plating between your knees. But the farther the ship descended, the more all of them, Soujen included, eyed the narrow viewports lining the crew cabin. Soujen glimpsed sparkling alloys beneath stone-flecked arches, saw black veins that might have been vines or cables or water marks running down the skeleton of a tower. To his right, Vorgorath whispered something like a mantra.

Saw seemed not to have heard. "Now we enter the realm of the dead," he said.

Eyo-Dajuritz was a fossilized ecumenopolis. Eons ago, it had been a city-planet like Coruscant—a feat of architecture, of geo-engineering and materials science, with metal towers rising from every meter of sea and surface to house a population of trillions. Yet Eyo-Dajuritz had been dead when the Republic was young, and even the name and nature of its constructors were now lost. Over millennia, the oceans had shifted and the atmosphere had changed. The world's lower levels had been submerged. The framework and foundation of the towers had eroded, the marrow of their bones leached and replaced by sediment and stone. The structures had been alchemically transmuted from one material to another, and many of the great skyscrapers had collapsed—causing more destruction, splitting mountains and raising clouds of dust to blot out the sun. Yet a few towers had remained upright for reasons that puzzled researchers, and Eyo-Dajuritz, monument to one of the oldest cultures known, had endured.

Today, Eyo-Dajuritz was one of the wonders of the galaxy—far from the major trade lanes, but host to a dozen floating settlements from which archaeologists and scientists labored alongside tourists and locals. The planet had been studied endlessly, depicted in fiction and documentaries ten thousand times over. But its mysteries were many, and its surface remained forbidden to the public. So much of its architecture had been lost already; to risk more would be profane.

So people said. So people believed. Soujen and the guerrillas were going down anyway.

Soujen didn't remember Eyo-Dajuritz, but he had been here before.

"We're past the sensor net," the pilot called.

"Can I throw up now?" Nankry asked.

Karama laughed. Soujen unbuckled his safety harness and made his way into the cockpit, looking down at a jade ocean and a shore of glinting wastes. "We're close," he said, pointing. "Farther inland, south of the three-pointed tower."

"Got it. Landing's going to be tricky."

"We can walk," Soujen said.

He heard Saw approach from the cabin. It satisfied him that Saw didn't interrupt or correct him as he guided the pilot. Saw had agreed they would be equals, *partners,* and so far he'd kept his word. He'd instructed his people to accept Soujen's orders, and the guerrillas had adapted.

"You're confident?" Saw asked when Soujen had straightened and turned around. "You were asleep when those pirates found you."

"This is the location," Soujen said. "I'm certain."

Because for all the things the Separatists might have kept from him, the location of his own hibernation pod wasn't one of them. This was what he was made for, to acquire the weapons of his defeated sponsors and use them.

"We'll get the gear ready," Saw said. "You lead the way."

⫻⫻⫻

"We don't know how the pirates found it," Soujen told the others as they trekked through the ruins. "They might have stumbled on a Separatist vessel making a delivery. Maybe they found coordinates while they were scavenging wreckage from a fleet battle. What matters is that they came unprepared."

"They messed up," Nankry muttered, laughing to herself. None of the others joined her.

The *Dalgo* had landed on a strip of eroded shoreline free of any debris, several hours' hike from the cache site. No one had suggested using the ship's cannons to make a clearing closer to their destination. Walking through the hushed city felt like rummaging through a grave. Even the sound of distant wind and the acridity of the jade sea seemed like violations. Soujen didn't understand why it should be so, what spell the ruins of Eyo-Dajuritz had cast. But he felt it mattered that this was a place older than empires, republics, and confederacies, untainted by the galaxy's conflicts.

"There will be no defenses around the perimeter," Soujen said as he climbed the slope of an ancient wall. "Not unless the pirates left their own. But the entrance will have a variety of traps. Past the entrance, the upper level will be clear of Separatist security, but there's a good chance that's where the pirates found our bioweapons stash. If they opened it there or broke a container, the whole cache could be contaminated. Touch nothing, *breathe* nothing, unless you're wearing protective gear."

"You said 'the upper level,'" Karama said. "How big is this place?"

"Heavy equipment and anything too large for the main shaft should be on top. Middle sections will have the handheld stuff—credits, blasters. Should be a databank there, too—intelligence, slicing programs, anything they couldn't load on me directly. That's assuming the layout hasn't changed—which it might have, because they brought in excavation droids to expand the cache over time and open new levels down below. Make room for a new headquarters or places where troops could hide under siege."

Someone swore. Soujen shrugged. "The Separatists built the cache to help us fight a war even after we were defeated," he said. "You want to do the same thing, so be grateful."

They were thinking about Separatist brutality, he knew. They were thinking about loved ones killed, everything they'd done to stop Soujen and his kind, and now they were ready to take up the weapons of their enemy.

Saw also seemed to recognize his people's thoughts. He waved them to a halt. "You think I like this?" Saw asked. "I didn't want help from the *Jedi*. I certainly don't want help from the *Separatists*. But it's where we are, and we've cut no deals. Think of what we find as spoils of war."

You cut a deal with me, Soujen thought, but he wasn't foolish enough to say anything.

Saw kept talking. "I'm not offering you a chance to back out. You're here, you knew the risks, and any one of us could die badly, same as the pirates. But this is the way to arm ourselves for survival. For revolution, should it come to that."

Vorgorath growled out, "For Onderon," and the others joined him. Soujen did, too, because Onderon was as good a planet to fight for as any and the lie didn't offend him.

/ / /

They spent the night a short distance from the coordinates of the cache. "Better to go in daylight," Soujen said, more for the others than himself. His optical implants could handle the dark.

He watched Saw. The man was blunt and hard and sometimes impatient, but the guerrillas looked to him as if inspired. Even Karama, whom Soujen had begun to respect, seemed to think of Saw as a force more than a man—not right or wrong, not good or evil, but a storm she was following to its natural end.

It had been different with Soujen. His recruiter had been a man of ice, not fire.

They'd found Soujen among his people. To this day he wasn't sure whether they'd come for him or his brothers, and it didn't really matter. He'd returned from a job in Hutt space, and there they'd been—slender, ocher-skinned strangers in great metal suits, speaking to his fathers in the Nahasta clan. They were Separatist representatives from the Techno Union, and with them had come Tychon Nulvolio. Nulvolio had seemed diminutive beside the others, though he'd stood taller than Soujen's eldest father. The Separatist's ashen skin and red-washed eyes had given him the appearance of infirmity.

"The outsider desires our services," Soujen's eldest father had told Soujen. "The choice is yours."

They'd gone to speak outside the Lesser Wheel, while Soujen's nephews spun colors and filled the air with the scent of oils. "Your people's curse could be a gift to the galaxy," Nulvolio had told him, his voice a resonant baritone. "I know your story. I know of the defect that ravages every one of you, resulting in fewer children with each generation. I know of the disdain you face from worlds who once believed your curse might spread beyond your species, and that those same worlds now call you thieves and killers, hoping it will justify their past misdeeds.

"I know, Soujen of the Nahasta clan, that the Republic has done nothing to secure your future, failed to provide your people with treatments that could cure you in five generations. But the Separatist Confederacy is prepared to do what others will not."

"Many have said that before," Soujen had said. "Yet the forty and nine clans are now seven."

Nulvolio had smiled and shown pointed teeth. He'd tipped his head back, taking in the oils' musk. "Would you let the seven become one? Would you let one become none, for fear of betrayal?"

He'd spoken with bureaucratic dispassion, and Soujen had despised him for that—for putting so little value on Soujen's species, and being inured to centuries of suffering—yet he'd respected Nulvolio as well. Nulvolio made no pretense of care or shared ideals. All that was left was the bargain.

They'd continued their conversation into the night. Soujen's people, Nulvolio said, were "biologically mutable" to the Techno Union's specifications. That mutability had made cross-clan breeding difficult, but it also made his people promising candidates for cybernetic implantation.

"The Republic has its Jedi," Nulvolio told him, "and it is the Jedi who hold their broken alliance together. Discontented worlds fear the Jedi warriors. Bickering worlds put their faith in Jedi diplomats, accepting deals and signing treaties that cannot survive outside a Jedi parable."

"You need people who can fight Jedi," Soujen said.

Nulvolio shook his head. "I respect the Jedi, as should you. Their loyalty to the Republic is admirable, but when a dying animal is suffering, when its natural end has come, the kind thing is not to prolong its survival. The Jedi refuse to *let the Republic die* and allow its worlds to forge their own futures. The Jedi refuse even to step aside.

"I do not expect you to fight the Jedi. That would be beyond even the Techno Union's capabilities. I *do* expect you to be an agent of equivalent utility, to strike where a droid army is insufficient. When blood must be shed, you will shed blood, as you have proved willing to do. When stealth and guile serve the Confederacy, you will employ those skills. You will not be a symbol or a hero as the Jedi are, but you must be every bit as loyal. In return, I will be loyal to you and your people until my death.

"This is the way of our Confederacy." The lines around his eyes had darkened. "Each member true to its goals, and each member true to every other."

By the morning, Soujen had agreed, and the rest of the clan had sworn to fight as well. There were other volunteers for the Techno Union's experiments, from other clans and other species, but Soujen never learned who they were.

///

The entrance to the cache was nothing more than a broad hatch set in a basin surrounded by the broken tiers of an amphitheater. The hatch might have been easily missed if it hadn't been surrounded by scorched rubble. The pirates had not made their entrance subtle.

Soujen led the way, with Nankry and Karama waiting a short distance behind. All three were clad in the biohazard suits they'd stolen from Li'eta. Farther back, in comms range but beyond the reach of any explosives or other deterrents potentially wired into the hatch, were Saw and the rest of the guerrillas.

"Descending," Soujen muttered. The plastoid lining of the biohazard suit rubbed against his lips and his scalp plating. It also stank of chemicals. "Shielding may disrupt the signal, so stay close."

There had been a ladder leading inside, but the topmost rungs were shattered. Soujen could see the floor below and almost leapt down the five meters before remembering how thin the suit was. He'd tear the soles if he didn't move carefully. So he lowered himself into the hatch headfirst, stretching to grab the first intact rung and hauling himself deeper upside down. "Bug man," Karama said over the comm, and it sounded almost affectionate.

He arched and flipped carefully backward onto his feet at the bottom, in a narrow corridor leading to a blast door. The door was barely ajar, as if it had been forced open with limited success. A computer port appeared to have been disassembled and sloppily reattached. Soujen connected anyway and found his vision flooded by warnings and security checks. His implants resolved most automatically, though the final authentication was manual. He entered the keyword Nulvolio had given him.

SARCOPHAGUS.

Then he had the keys to the facility. Multiple systems—the autoguns, the gas vents—had already been damaged or shut down by the pirates.

Others remained untriggered—a general destruct sequence, energy stores designed to detonate when doors were forced open—and these he disabled. Dark spots in the program suggested deeper layers to the system, closed even to him.

He disconnected from the panel and spoke into his comlink: "Come on. Going inside."

Karama and Nankry brought rope for their own descent, and when they'd all assembled at the blast door, they crept in together. Lights flared on automatically. The corridors were wide enough to move a speeder through, and it occurred to Soujen that the cache's builders must have filled in the entrance after digging out the first level. They spotted evidence of the pirates' raid: a wrecked maintenance droid, carbon scoring on the walls, a door that had been cut through with a torch. Somewhere, Soujen thought, they were bound to find a corpse, but the biohazard suits would filter out the smell.

They split up to assess damage and inventory the level. Soujen stepped into cramped hangars and storage bays carved directly from the bedrock. The pirates had taken their share of loot, but much remained: portable weapons platforms, mortars, cannons, artillery shells, and turbolaser power supplies. Enough weaponry and equipment to level a city. Karama recited her findings over the comm, uttering each word with a combination of wonder and disgust. "Geo-lances. Energy shields. Ore extractors. Like they wanted someone to build a factory from spare parts."

"Nankry?" Soujen said. "What are you seeing?"

There was a pause. "Medical equipment, mostly. There's a whole sort of infirmary? Looks like something was hauled out, lots of wires and tubes and scratches on the floor."

His womb. Where he'd been stored.

"Anything still working?" he asked.

"Maybe some, yeah. Not seeing any bacta, but maybe that's somewhere else."

Soujen heard her breathing catch.

"What did you find?" he asked.

She didn't answer. He repeated the question.

"Can you come here?" she said, her voice small.

Soujen and Karama arrived in the medcenter at the same time. Nankry faced away, apparently wedged into a doorway leading into the next compartment. The pirates, Soujen guessed, had forced the door open by hand, failing to move it more than fifteen centimeters. Nankry had attempted to sidle through, twisting her body to fit.

"Are you stuck?" Karama asked. She was holding back laughter.

"No," Nankry said. Her voice was still quiet.

Soujen approached her. Nankry was between the metal door and the frame, but she did not, as she said, appear to be stuck. Soujen was taller than Nankry, and he managed to look over her head into the room beyond. There he saw the source of her terror—a meter-high stack of canisters, beside which lay two more canisters, dented and punctured.

"Tell me it's food. Tell me," Nankry said.

"It's not food," Soujen said.

He understood now. If she went into the room, she'd be immersing herself in the toxins. If she tried to back out, unable to turn around, she'd very likely tear her suit on the door.

"I'll guide you," he said. "Don't tense up."

He placed his hands on her shoulder and waist. Gently, he coaxed her back out of the doorway, sometimes verbally and sometimes tugging her, smoothing down her suit, using himself to pad the space between her and the metal frame. As he did, it occurred to him that he could easily end her life, tear the suit minutely and let the bioweapon begin its work. Nankry had tried to murder him once already, and he'd killed Rechrimos for less.

As Nankry leaned into him, Soujen imagined eliminating all of Saw's guerrillas one by one. With his access to the security systems, he could lock doors and reactivate defenses with ease. He could take everything, take their ship, and then . . .

He glanced toward Karama, who stared his way. He couldn't make out her expression through the shield of her suit.

"You're free," he told Nankry, and she was. She looked as if she was ready to crumple to the floor, but she held still, allowing Soujen and Karama to inspect her suit and ensure there was no breach.

"Thank you," Nankry said when they were done.

"Plenty of ways to die, still," Soujen said.

But not at my hands. Not today.

Was he staying true to his bargain with Saw? Was he growing soft? Or was one the same as the other?

He pushed down the thoughts. But he would be watchful.

CHAPTER 23
THE ILLUSION OF PROGRESS

The gas giant Balagash had seventeen moons, and the Republic had fought the Separatists on every one. The eighth moon, Balumbra, lacked the sapient gardens of Rhoremone and the fierce warriors of Ma'a. But of all the moons, Balumbra was the most defensible, formed from rare and precious metals resistant to blasting and bombardment, and perpetually sheltered by the orbits of three of its larger siblings.

"Best stay behind for this one," Bail told Haki as they left their vessel for the pocked streets of the Balumbra spaceport. Above them, through the magnetic shield, Balagash burned with its pustulant green light. "I had to call in a favor to get access to the prison. Your presence might invite questions."

"Shouldn't be any trouble, a place like this," Haki said. "Have a chat with today's Separatist. Give me a buzz if you need anything, eh?"

Bail set off, and though Haki should have been bothered, all she could feel was relief. They'd made four stops since the business with Bana Rhuus and the Spiral Forest, and each time Bail had found some new lead, some obscure bit of information that convinced him that the next stop, the *next* revelation of their dreary journey, would make everything fall into place. The Jedi would be exonerated, he'd expose the administration's lies to the galaxy, and so forth. He hadn't said as much out loud, but she knew what he was hoping.

It was implausible. It was exhausting. It might, she supposed, be true. Yet she'd set Bail down this path not to find out what became of the Jedi but to give her an excuse to touch base with her agents across the galaxy. She'd met failure at every turn and had her worst fears confirmed: The purge of those operatives abandoned by Imperial Intelligence was near total. The Separatists had taken their vengeance, and there had been death upon death.

And what was the harm, really? The war was won. Who cared whether a few moles inside the Separatist military disappeared? What use were the neighbors, the lovers, the housekeepers, or the children of Separatist officers who'd passed on information to the Republic during the fighting? Could Haki place Gereth Novam, a handyman for one of the Separatists' chief tacticians, in the household of Mon Mothma? Could she use General Hryoth's mistress in data analytics? Of course not. Her spies in the Confederacy had served their purpose and could be cut loose, to hell with their lives.

Still, if Haki was anything, she was thorough. It was conceivable some agent had left a message on Balumbra with an unlikely tale of survival, so she set out into the alleys of the port, weaving past market stalls and housing hatches. Balumbra was a mining colony turned garrison, all trenches and tunnels carved into the lunar surface, and Haki's feet hurt after fifteen minutes of walking. But that, too, was the way of things. She'd had a colleague years before who'd liked to say, "Spycraft is more satisfying when you spill your own sweat."

The local dead drop was the wiring box of a long-deactivated traffic signal in the residential district. She was in sight of it when she took note of a pair of humanoids she'd first spotted at the docks. They'd kept their distance, frequently splitting up and taking detours before reappearing in her peripheral vision, but they were clearly tailing her.

She passed close enough to the wiring box to confirm that there was no scrawled marking—no message, no secret survivor, and no hope to distract her. She was free to be angry and focused.

She didn't know the colony well, but she could work with what she'd seen. She never broke stride, continuing past the traffic signal and working her way down increasingly narrow and ill-lit trenches away from the crowds. As before, her pursuers kept their distance, often lingering a turn or two behind her. If she'd overestimated them, she would soon lose them altogether.

Finally, she reached the rock face at the end of a half-completed trench, glancing back to confirm her pursuers hadn't yet followed. Trying not to conspicuously grunt or wheeze, she scaled the rock to the lunar surface above. Once there, she dropped to her belly and slithered through the dust, keeping an eye on the trench below and waiting for her pursuers to come investigate.

Her patience was rewarded, though not in the way she'd expected. She heard scrabbling and realized that one of her pursuers had decided to be *clever*. He was climbing to the lunar surface himself, planning to peer into the dead-end trench to see what had happened to his quarry.

She was waiting when a jade face rose over the trench edge. "Hello," she said, pressing the barrel of her blaster to the man's forehead. She scooted into a kneeling position. "Suppose you're looking for me?"

The man blinked. He looked less frightened than he did confused. "I don't—no one's going to hurt you."

"Certainly doesn't seem like it," she said. "Call your friend up and let's talk like adults."

/ / /

Ten minutes later, she had them half-stripped, face down in the dust as she pawed through their belongings. They tried to convince her to listen, that they just wanted to talk. She ignored them as she checked over their blasters (identical DC-17 pistols, barely used or extremely well maintained) and their comlinks (scrubbed of identifying marks, running high-end encryption). She was trembling as she pieced together possibilities.

"Who are you working for?" she asked, gesturing at the jade man with her weapon.

"Imperial Intelligence," he said.

"Your assignment?"

"Monitoring and protection of Senator Bail Organa of Alderaan."

"And who do you suppose I am?"

"Haki Zeophrine, Senate Security."

She guffawed. She waggled her silenced Telltrig at the man, getting too close—close enough for him to lunge at her, if he wanted. "Haki Zeophrine of *Imperial Intelligence!*" she snapped. "Who put you on this project?"

"Orders from Nauk, Signals Section—"

"*Signals Section?* How does any of this relate to signals intelligence?!" She was shouting now, and the most awful part was that she could imagine how it had happened. Signals had intercepted Bail's message to the moon's prison asking for access, which had made their section chief curious. Maybe Nauk had acted without consulting anyone, or maybe he'd reached out to Haki's superior, Bariovon, who'd never read Haki's report to begin with and figured she was still on Coruscant. Whether the error had been caused by ego or carelessness didn't affect the outcome. "There are Separatists still killing our troops, *our people,* and you lot decided to double up on watching one fool senator? Go home—"

The fire suddenly went out of her voice, and she tucked away her weapon. "Go home," she repeated. "Tell your superiors I've got the situation in hand and they can talk to Bariovon if they doubt it. Bail Organa is being watched carefully enough. You should do something useful with your lives."

///

Bail swept aboard the tiny Alderaanian shuttle with his usual fervor, calling Haki's name and marching to her bunk with an expression that mixed pomposity with grim satisfaction. "We've got it," he said. "This one wasn't aware of the forgeries, but he knew the Separatists were preparing an arsenal of sorts, weapons and information to deploy in case of a loss . . ."

She barely heard him, though the words fermented in the back of her brain anyhow. He was talking about Separatist vessels, special cargoes, and how he and Haki might track what they'd been up to, whether by analyzing flight recorders or interviewing captured crew members, when at last she cut him off.

"Senator," she said. "Maybe it's time to turn this over to professionals."

"What are you talking about?" he asked.

"We've been at this awhile." She sat up in her bunk and looked at him with a smile as sympathetic as she could muster. "It was a good try, but every lead you've found has been vague at best, and you're chasing a trail that might well be an illusion. Let Imperial Intelligence figure out if you've got something. You're a senator, and I'm an old woman. We're probably fooling ourselves."

"I don't trust Imperial Intelligence."

Points for that.

"You're worried they don't want the truth," she said. "I think you should give them more credit. There are hardworking people there, the same hardworking people you trusted during the war. They can't all be in on some conspiracy, can they?"

"All it takes is one person to manipulate the flow of information. To edit reports, to give critical assignments to the wrong officer." Bail shook his head in frustration. "There's more going on than you realize, Haki. This is a matter I must pursue."

He headed into the cockpit, and she followed. He was a fool and her agents were dead and she wanted to go home. It was all she could do not to shout, *There's no point! Don't you see?*

"Senator," she said, "even if you're right about everything, the Jedi aren't going to come back. Not even if they're exonerated."

He stopped walking and turned. She was almost chin-to-chin with him. They'd never talked about the Jedi, not to each other. She'd done what a good security officer was supposed to do, pretending she hadn't heard his conversations with Bana Rhuus and others, pretending she hadn't figured out what he wanted.

"The truth has to be known," Bail said.

"And what if it is? What then?"

She knew the answer. If he credibly accused the administration of incompetence, complicity, or malice resulting in the unjust execution of the Jedi, there would be riots and disorder and a functional inability to govern until the dust settled. While politicians wrestled for power, there would be misery in the streets—misery for the victims of the Clone Wars, who didn't care about their leaders as long as relief shipments arrived on time, and for troops and spies, too, who needed leaders who prioritized their safety and not the good name of dead Jedi.

She knew better than to say it aloud.

Bail spoke, not unkindly. "Haki, you are here because you were right. I needed protection. And you are *very* clever. I am grateful for your assistance. But you are not my partner or my adviser. You can leave if you like, and I'm happy to arrange transport, but there will be no more talk of giving up the mission. Am I understood?"

She knew how to look professional and accept an order. "Of course, Senator. I apologize if I was out of line."

"Good. Let's take a look at the data we've got."

She watched him pull up logs and star maps. She kept her expression blank. What choice did she have? She couldn't return to Coruscant without Bail Organa. She'd promised Bariovon regular reports, even if he wasn't bothering to read them. She could resign today, and maybe those bunglers from Signals Section could pick up where she left off, but more likely Bail would continue his work with no one guarding, no one watching . . .

And she realized, with a sinking feeling, that he really might be onto something.

Nauk's Signals Section operatives had been interested in Bail for a reason, and while Haki could assume that reason was general disorder in Imperial Intelligence, she'd been making a lot of assumptions lately. Maybe Nauk, or someone higher up, was genuinely concerned about Bail's investigation. She'd assumed the trail Bail was following would end abruptly, yet it hadn't ended. She'd assumed Bail would be lost without her, but she'd barely assisted him since the Spiral Forest. She'd been so focused on her hunt for her missing agents that she hadn't reassessed the possibility Bail might stumble upon something genuinely disruptive—some hidden truth that could wreak havoc on the galaxy, unleashed for the sake of Bail's ego and the memory of the dead Jedi Knights.

She couldn't afford to be dismissive anymore. She couldn't afford to be careless and lose herself in self-pity.

"The Separatists left a cache," Bail was saying. "In case of their defeat . . ."

For the first time, she realized she might need to stop him from finishing his mission.

CHAPTER 24
EXCHANGING PARTS

They'd spent the day cataloging and organizing the site, sealing off sections that were awash in nerve agents and other biotoxins. Saw was in no hurry. Neither was Soujen. The work was slow and tedious, and moving equipment back to the ship would be slower and more tedious yet. But revolutions were rarely glorious things. They were grueling, painful, and best handled with extreme deliberation.

The work helped Soujen avoid thinking about the future, but he couldn't escape contemplation altogether. He'd need to make decisions soon, and soon he'd discover whether the cache's contents would resolve that problem. Maybe he'd find a weapon deadly enough to bring down the Empire. Maybe he'd find the coordinates of a dozen other caches and a dozen operatives like him, all waiting to band together. Maybe the cache's databanks would reveal that the Separatists had planned to betray the Nahasta clan, that every planet in the Confederacy had loathed Soujen's people, and that their covenant had been a lie. That way he would owe them nothing.

Or maybe he'd find a message from Tychon Nulvolio explaining everything. Maybe he'd find a plan drawn up in the dying days of the

Confederacy, instructing Soujen precisely how to proceed. All he asked for were enough resources and guidance to continue along his path.

In the night, as he took his turn at watch and walked among the trillion ghosts of Eyo-Dajuritz, Soujen let his mind drift to his life before the Separatists. There were particulars he couldn't remember, not *concealed* like the dark spots in his databank but lost like dreams during his modification. Yet the broad outlines were there.

He remembered his eldest father teaching him the Art as a child. Soujen had been skilled for his age, weaving colors together on the Lesser Wheel, combining oil, minerals, and bioluminescent microbes, whirling, pressing, and purifying them, until he had a paint never before seen in the galaxy, unique to him—a shade of sunset orange that turned violet at one angle and fiery at another, or one of the family of true blacks that leached color from its neighbors. The merchants of his clan sold their colors to artists and weavers and luxury speeder manufacturers. (Aratech considered its paint source a trade secret, but among the clan there were no secrets.) The elders of his clan distributed the profits among the families, but the colormakers themselves held a special honor. Their tradition had endured for millennia when so little else did.

Soujen had not become a colormaker. He'd been angry as a child, understanding that his people's natural state was not one of poverty and inanition. They'd been cursed, they'd been shunned and despised for their curse, and the Republic had promised them aid and provided none. The clans had lashed out and demanded things be set right. Nothing had been set right. So it had been for centuries.

Thus, Soujen had turned to violence. He'd become a mercenary like his fifth uncle, and that had earned credits more easily than colormaking. And, he could now admit, it was more *satisfying* than colormaking. A life devoted to family was a life of hurt—of migrancy, of discrimination, of watching his clan slowly die. The life of a mercenary was likewise full of hurt, but he could reflect that hurt onto the uncaring universe. It was close to justice, using blasters and fists on those who ignored his people's plight.

The worst hurt of all had been the agony of modification. He'd left his

clan and journeyed to the shrouded world of Skako, where he'd under-
gone tests and scans and surgeries. He'd lived for months in a laboratory, seeing the same faces, eating the same food, smelling the same
methane atmosphere every day.

There had been so much pain. Yet even in the laboratory, there had
also been kindness. Dr. Ro-Yai, who led the surgeons, had been gentle
to a fault, compassionate with every touch and every incision. "The galaxy is unkind," Ro-Yai had told him once. "You must be brave when you
face it again, brave for the cause of our Confederacy and your people.
For me you do not need to be brave. For me, you may let yourself hurt,
and I will try to heal you."

Soujen's eldest father had been *good*. Ro-Yai, too, had been *good*.
There were few truly good men in the universe.

He was thinking about Ro-Yai when Karama found him that night,
telling him Vorgorath would take his place on watch. They walked back
toward the camp together, then kept on walking. Their arms brushed as
they drifted into the ruins and navigated roadways with red moss and
crisp yellow grass. They slowed as they approached a denser zone, where
fossilized structures rose out of the ground like the skeleton of some
world-spanning beast. Without speaking, they both seemed to understand that going farther would put the architecture of antiquity at risk—
that they could be banishing the ghosts of Eyo-Dajuritz to oblivion.

"Do you want to go back?" Karama asked.

"No," Soujen said.

She entwined her fingers with his. His implants fed him sensory data
about the oils on her skin, the microbial life under her nails.

"Why do you bother?" he asked. "The war ended for you. Whatever
Saw says about tyranny, you could go home."

Karama snorted. "Not much home left. Part of why I joined him in
the first place. Maybe he's wrong about the Empire, maybe he's right,
but the government wants me dead, and I've been doing this too long
to change course."

"Haven't we all?" he asked.

They were both silent again. If she had been of his people, been of the
clans, he would have called up one of the low songs from his throat and

harmonized with her. He would have revealed his ancestry through the notes, exposed the intertwining lineages of Nahasta, Bayubay, and Rejardain, paying tribute to his forefathers in clans dead for a century. The moment was apt for such a thing. It was apt for joy and sensuality.

But Karama was not of his people, and he had not sung since his modification. He was still of the Nahasta clan, still Alvadorjian, but he had replaced pieces of himself with another ancestry entirely.

It was of this second nature that he spoke when he told Karama, "My death is mine to choose."

She shook her head, perplexed or worried or both. Soujen took her hand and brought it to his lower abdomen. His skin felt cold—the power source implanted there was well insulated and produced no stray heat. "I possess three weapons—the shock device in my palm, the microlaser, and my battery. The battery is attached to a self-destruct system. My death is mine to choose. That does not make me unique, but the knowledge . . . it is clarifying."

"In what way?"

"Every moment is a choice. For you, too, but mine is explicit. I choose to live, and I choose to act."

"Some people might use that against you."

"The self-destruct is under my control and mine alone," he said, but by her expression that hadn't been what she meant.

Afterward they talked about trivial things, about whittling, ghosts, and the strange creatures of Onderon—anything but their mission or Soujen's past. Karama understood loneliness and survival, he thought. It was why they'd been drawn to each other.

They were sitting in the dirt when they saw the light—a streak across the sky that flickered in and out. Soujen tensed, and he felt Karama's muscles tighten. A moment later, Saw's voice came through their comlinks: "Get back to camp. Unknown vessel just landed, and we need to be ready."

CHAPTER 25
A STRANGE INVITATION

"I promise, it's entirely adequate," Lud said, pushing the gravy toward Mon. "Wipe the taste of Hesperidium right out of your mouth." Mon laughed and shook her head, but Lud insisted, and she scooped up a helping with her flatbread and ate gracelessly. The rich, savory sauce dripped onto her chin. She barely glanced about to check whether anyone had seen.

Lud had been solicitous toward her since Zhuna's murder, leaving daily messages of support and offering invitations to meals, without insisting and without regard for how complicated his own schedule was. Mon had said no until she'd said yes, and now, sitting with him, she remembered what it was like to have a friend.

She didn't have many—not outside politics beyond a few classmates she saw once or twice a year and not many *in* politics, either.

Maybe that was why she'd stayed with Perrin all this time. She looked up from the plate, caught Lud's gaze, and rebuked herself. *Those are dangerous thoughts.*

"You really can't tell anyone about Hesperidium," she said. "Honestly, I shouldn't have mentioned—"

"I heard yesterday. There was speculation about you and the Commerce Guild . . . ?"

She sighed. She trusted Lud, but she had no intention of telling him about Cornade and the others, and she didn't intend to let him guess who she'd met through process of elimination. "Can we drop it?"

"Of course," Lud said. "But can I say one thing? You don't have to tell me anything. I'm not *asking* anything. I just want—"

"There's a reason we don't talk about our projects."

He waved off her objection. "Two minutes. That's all."

She looked around the restaurant. It was packed with the lunch crowd, maybe a hundred dockworkers jostling over trays. "Two minutes," she said.

Lud steepled his hands and gathered his thoughts. "You're whipping votes outside your usual coalition. Everyone knows that, and certainly I respect the effort. It's hard enough keeping my allies in line—I can't imagine winning over my opponents.

"However . . . the people you're dealing with? If you're—and again, I'm not asking you to give anything away. I won't even watch your expression." He turned to the stained wall as his voice fell to a murmur. "If you're building a coalition to oppose the administration, I wish you'd consider the optics."

"What *optics*?" she asked.

"The *optics* of you assembling a group of the most privileged people in the galaxy. Corporate tycoons, senators from royal families and the wealthiest worlds in the Core—"

"As opposed to humble men like yourself, from working-class worlds like Troithe?"

He scowled. "You promised me two minutes."

Mon held up her hands in surrender.

"Palpatine is a populist. The reason he appeals to worlds like Troithe is because people there see him making real changes in their lives. He cracked down on the corporations. He ended the war. He's promising that the era of out-of-touch politicians and twelfth-generation nobility shaping the galaxy for their own benefit is over."

"He's—" she began. *He's not giving power back to ordinary people.*

He's only shifting who holds it. He and his cronies don't care about your world any more than they care about mine.

She stayed silent.

"What you're doing," Lud said, "is only proving him right. The Delegation of Two Thousand was . . . well, it was mad and foolish and an utter failure, but at least it was idealistic. It was built on principle, and people saw that even if they didn't understand what the principle *was*. Now *I* know you're acting in what you believe is the best interest of democracy. I know you, Mon. But—"

"But my coalition of the rich and ultra-powerful symbolizes what everyone hated about the Republic, is that right?" She pushed her chair back, and Lud turned toward her. "I think your two minutes are up."

He called her name and apologized as she stood. She told him it was fine, that she just had business back at the Senate and she'd stayed too long already. She looked away when she saw the hurt in his eyes and hurried out of the restaurant, telling herself, *He's not the one who gets to be injured, and he's not the one who gets to be angry.*

She shouldn't have cared what he thought.

The commercial spacedocks were packed at this hour, and she had to push through throngs of people and past hoversleds laden with crates and cages and boxes of produce. She should've had security with her. The threats on her life were coming in rapidly since Zhuna's death and Mon's "politicization" of the tragedy. But she hadn't wanted anyone looking over her shoulder while she met Lud—at least, anyone other than the usual spies, who she assumed were tracking her every move and who, if she was lucky, might bother to intervene if she was attacked.

As she maneuvered toward the tram, she nearly bowled over a squat man in a farmer's cloak and cowl. She apologized instinctively as he caught her wrist to keep from falling. But he hurried on, and she managed to board her car moments before it sped off for the Federal District.

She didn't think of the encounter again until she was back in her office, trying to comprehend the way Zhuna's replacement had configured her calendar. Her wrist itched, and she rolled up the white of her sleeve to see if she'd somehow scratched herself.

There was a rash forming, blotchy and red, with each splotch centered on a darker brown dot. She began to scratch, then abruptly stopped as she saw the red blotches spreading like a stain. The brown centers grew larger and darker. She thrust her arm away, as if she could distance herself from whatever was multiplying within her flesh; at the same time she cried sharply and stumbled away from her desk.

She needed a medic. She'd been infected, she thought, poisoned when she'd boarded the tram. But there was no pain, only the faint itch, and even that hadn't increased in intensity. The spread of the blotches slowed, creeping to a stop. The dark spots were bleeding together, seeming to form patterns.

There were *words* appearing on her flesh, no larger than the labels on a control panel: TYCHON NULVOLIO WILL SPEAK TO YOU.

Someone was calling to her through the office door, asking whether she was all right. She suppressed her trembling and called back. "I'm fine! I just dropped something."

The ink shifted and wriggled again, forming new words from the old: NO OBSERVERS. NO SPIES.

Was it a statement or a demand? The itch became a burn. She wanted to clasp her wrist and squeeze, but she didn't dare touch the rash. The dark spots drew together and welled like a droplet of sweat, then ran down her wrist and fell to the carpet. A few moments later the tattoo had fully expelled itself and drained onto the floor. All that remained was the rash, already paler and less angry than it had been.

She dropped into a chair and caught her breath. Her panic—her fear that she'd been witnessing her own assassination—caught up with her. She began shaking and tried to recall whether she'd taken her anxiety medication.

She was fine. People were trying to kill her, but this hadn't been *that*. She was fine. She permitted herself five minutes to pull herself together. She drank a glass of water, though she wasn't thirsty. She stuck her head outside the office to question her new aide's calendar skills.

Then she began to plan. Whatever the intent of the message, she couldn't risk meeting Nulvolio with the intelligence services tracking her every move. The ex-Separatists were the key to passing the Imperial

Rebirth Act, and if the administration knew what she was doing, it would apply pressure or halt the reintegration of Separatist worlds altogether.

She told her aide she was going for a walk and left the Senate building. This time she allowed her security detail to follow as she strolled through the crowd of federal workers. The throngs seemed less familiar every day, full of new staffers and bureaucrats, young and old but nearly all human. With their dreary outfits and tight shoulders, they looked as if they were carrying the fate of the galaxy instead of fixing the plumbing of democracy.

Mon entered a public comm station and opened a channel to Hasalia Prederiko, chief financial officer of General Trade Galactic and go-between for the Crymorah underworld syndicate. "You made me an offer," Mon said. "If I could provide names . . . ?"

You said you could get the spies off my back if I turned in the right people.

"I can make arrangements, yes," Prederiko said. "Really, it's a pleasure to help."

She'd thought it through in her office. The decision hadn't taken long. "Senator Erashe. The aide to the chief courier, Raave Galdon. Ungol Ungrave, Senator Palok's chief of staff." All three were plausibly of interest, each well positioned to view sensitive material and either antagonistic toward the administration or embedded deep inside it. She doubted any of them would suffer serious repercussions from an investigation. "Bail Organa, too," she added. Because what would it hurt? Someone had to be watching him already, as they were watching her. He'd suffer no additional harm, especially having already run offworld, refusing to involve himself in the Rebirth Act.

She heard Prederiko calling to someone in the background, then return to full volume. "Erashe, Galdon, Ungrave, Palok, Organa. That all? Not exactly enough to keep the administration up at night."

Mon hesitated, then added, "Senator Lud Marroi."

It's not personal, she thought. But he was close to the administration and known to associate with *Mon Mothma,* one of the administration's leading opponents. Who could say what he might really be up to? The intelligence services would look into him and find nothing. He was too well connected to get in trouble for something he'd never done.

"Give me a day," Prederiko said, ending the call.

Mon left the comm station and headed back toward her office. She could regret her choices after the Rebirth Act passed.

CHAPTER 26
THE CACHE (AGAIN)

"They were terrified of Republic victory," Bail said as he paced in the cockpit. "Strange, given how close they came to winning, but Separatist Intelligence and a select group inside the Parliament didn't believe their luck would last. As it turned out, they were right."

Haki thought he was speaking to himself more than to her. He was putting together all the fragments they'd collected since leaving Coruscant. She'd put them together, too, but she was listening now.

The ship glided into atmosphere, repulsors humming into action to ensure they felt no more than a shiver underfoot.

"They ordered the creation of caches full of weapons, credits, droids, even Separatist personnel who could continue the fight if the Confederacy was defeated," he went on. "They stocked supplies for electronic warfare, for propaganda. The caches had everything anyone needed to cause chaos inside the Republic. Why not evidence to frame the Jedi for crimes?"

"Perhaps," Haki said, "we should focus on finding the Separatist Parliament members responsible. They might have answers, whereas we barely know what we're looking for."

"We know enough," Bail slid into the copilot's seat beside Haki. "Only one cache was ever completed, at least according to our friend on Balumbra. This is the place."

Eyo-Dajuritz *might* have been the place, Haki conceded. They'd spent almost two days cross-referencing Separatist secrets with military sensor logs Bail had pulled from who knew where. Eyo-Dajuritz had been in the right sector and had seen unexplained visits from Separatist vessels during the time of the cache's supposed creation. None of the Separatists they'd spoken to had offered *coordinates* for the mysterious cache, but Bail had found a solution for that, too, requisitioning detailed topographical maps from Eyo-Dajuritz's historical preservation agency. If anything had shifted even minutely during the Separatist visits, it would be recorded.

Bail was smarter than Haki had given him credit for. He'd have never made it past the Spiral Forest without her, but after that he'd been like a hound on her leash, following a scent and heedless of the danger. She *had* to help solve the puzzle. If he'd caught on, if he'd sent her away, he'd have sought help elsewhere and there'd be no one watching him now. And someone had to alert the adults in the administration if Bail discovered something that could throw the Empire into tumult. She hadn't believed it possible when they'd left Coruscant. Now she did.

At least she'd blocked his last few messages home—just a tweak to the ship's comms had done it. If he was onto something real, if Haki needed to conceal anything, she wouldn't need to worry about silencing the Queen of Alderaan, too. She'd sent a report about Eyo-Dajuritz to her superiors as well, though who knew whether anyone would read it.

Bail was talking his way past the port authorities as they approached, something about a Senate commission to examine possible damage to historic sites. Haki leaned back in her seat and resisted coaching him in his lies.

She missed teaching. She missed Chemish.

The fossilized megastructures peered out from the clouds as they made their descent. Haki studied them through the viewport with a coroner's eye, wondering what had killed the world—whether war or plague or civil unrest. The unimaginably ancient structures bore no tell-tale scars. Maybe this was why Eyo-Dajuritz maintained its place in the galactic imagination, Haki thought. It represented the hope of a natural death, when so many civilizations came to more gruesome ends.

They crossed from day into night and chose a shallow lake for a landing pad, not far from the jade ocean and away from the delicate, fossilized buildings. "Maps suggest a sinkhole about three kilometers out," Bail said. "We'll take a look, see if it's anything. If not, we'll check the other candidates."

Soon they were picking their way over treacherous ground with hand-lights. She didn't bother suggesting they wait until daylight. Bail was too anxious and excited for her to shorten his leash now.

After a while, she asked, "Why did you lie to them? The Eyo-Dajuritz authorities?"

Bail grunted a few meters ahead of her. "We're close. There are people who don't want this secret uncovered. No reason to give them a head start."

"You're clearly not worried about any Separatists at the cache," Haki said. "Do you *really* think Imperial authorities are going to come and stop us?"

"I think this administration is capable of anything," he said. He stopped to look at her, shining his light at her midsection. His expression was shrouded in darkness. "I think if people knew what I was attempting, many would dismiss me as a crackpot spinning conspiracy theories. But some would try to stop me. Whether they believed I was right or not, they'd try to stop me out of loyalty to the regime." He shrugged in the dark. "And some would agree the truth is worth uncovering, no matter who it bedevils. I can't predict where any one person will fall when they're tested."

He seemed to be waiting for an answer. She didn't offer one, and he resumed his trek.

She'd pushed too hard on Balumbra. He knew who she worked for, or he suspected, or he suspected that he knew. But that went only so far. He hadn't tried to look further into her background or find another body-guard. It was possible Bail felt that she'd learned too much already and that he had no choice but to see his bet through, to hope Haki would ultimately stay loyal to him. If that were the case, Haki thought, she could at least take some pride in what she'd achieved.

There was the hint of a rosy dawn as they approached the target co-ordinates. They'd begun their descent into a sort of amphitheater when Haki caught a whiff of body odor on the breeze. She suppressed a twitch, keeping her shoulders square and her head down as her eyes searched for motion in the dark. There was nothing, which told her their observers were professionals.

She increased her pace to reach Bail's side, but it was too late. The night flashed crimson as a particle bolt seared the air between them, shattering the silence of the ruins. A second bolt flew closer to Haki, and this one she traced to the rim of the amphitheater, roughly thirty degrees to their right.

"Go!" she yelled. "Other side! Go!" And her blaster was in her hand, suppressor off, snapping off sizzling energy in the direction of one of the shooters. When she saw a plume of dust and fire rise where one of her shots had landed, she felt momentarily saddened—every missed target meant a piece of antiquity obliterated. But she ignored the thought. *Survival first.*

Bail ran, firing wildly with his own sidearm. But he was struggling not to tumble down the slope, and their adversaries had him pinned. Haki yelled again, "Get back to the ship!" and tried to draw the assailants' attention, firing at four, five points along the amphitheater rim. Whoever they were, they seemed more intent on immobilizing Bail and Haki than killing them. But they weren't *averse* to killing.

She'd be damned if she was going to let them have an Imperial sena-tor. Troublesome as Bail was, she'd almost started to respect the man.

Figures were sprinting over the lip of the amphitheater as their com-rades' barrage forced Haki and Bail to the ground. Haki shot one of the runners, heard her mark's last wail—then felt two hundred kilograms of muscle and bone slam into her. First one, then three attackers grap-pled her, yanking her pistol away, and she was only a frail old woman being slammed to the ground by younger beings from stronger species. She called to Bail one last time, but she couldn't imagine the senator had escaped.

She tasted blood, felt her battered face start to swell, and closed her eyes.

CHAPTER 27
THE PRICE OF FAILURE

"**W**here are we going?" Mon asked, but nobody replied. "Where are you taking me?" she tried next, and one of the crew members gave her a six-eyed glare, saying a word in a language she couldn't understand.

The instructions had come over two days, via methods nearly as odd as the tattoo: a message carried by a trained hawk-bat; a code word spray-painted on a garbage bin at the back of an alleyway; a clothier droid in a tourist district that, when given the code word, told her where to meet her transport before wiping its own memory.

If it really was Tychon Nulvolio reaching out, he put no trust in her ability to elude her watchers. And perhaps he was right to doubt. She had no way of knowing whether Prederiko had succeeded in diverting the intelligence services' attention. Mon had done all she could, selling out her friends and telling no one about her journey, and she was keenly aware she had left herself exposed.

If she died inside the rusty freighter she'd been brought aboard, no one would ever find her. If someone at the other end of her flight locked her in a tiny cell and interrogated her every day of her life, she could expect no rescue. She'd understood these risks, and she had acted anyway. Still, she was afraid, and she cursed herself for that.

The crew did not allow her inside the cockpit, but otherwise she had the run of the ship. Nobody present spoke any language she was familiar with, which she suspected was by design, to avoid accidental revelations about the ship's identity or point of origin. The vessel did carry cargo, but every crate was unlabeled and covered in peeling red paint. Mon wasn't sure whether the crates contained anything at all.

After two days' travel, the vessel landed roughly, and Mon was blindfolded and loaded into a rickety speeder truck. The crew was neither forceful nor deferential while handling her, and Mon wondered what would happen if she resisted. The ride was brief, only twenty or thirty minutes, after which Mon was hoisted out and led from a damp, breezy walkway to an echoing space that smelled of mildew and must.

Her blindfold was removed. The crew members were gone. She was now accompanied by a figure in loose black armor with a rifle slung over one shoulder. There were no markings on the armor, and the figure's face was concealed by a mask and respirator. "This way," the figure said, leading Mon onward.

They walked together through a maze of crumbling brickwork, illuminated only by the helmet light of Mon's escort. The low ceiling was supported by stone archways replete with decorative flourishes. From the puddles and the stains on the brick, Mon surmised that the maze flooded periodically. She supposed she was underground, and the historian in her busily speculated about the catacombs' origin and purpose. An early sewer system from some culture especially proud of its architecture? Or perhaps the maze served some ritual purpose, trapping some fell beast (real or mythical) at its center.

These thoughts occupied and soothed her until she reached a chamber larger than the others. Power generators and portable consoles had been installed over scraped bricks, and insulated cables wound their way up three tiers protruding from the room's five walls. A pentagonal dais of the usual brick stood in the room's center.

Mon had the impression of a temple devoted to some faded religion—

an impression reinforced by the figures lined up on each tier, facing the
dais but looking toward Mon. For every individual physically present,
two others existed in hologram, yet there were more gaps in the tiers
than figures. Mon recognized Ta'am Khlaides among the assembly,
staring with her predator's eyes. Others she knew by reputation alone,
former senators who'd sided with the Separatists years earlier or Separatist parliamentarians elected after the secession. Some were dressed in
travelers' robes and work boots. Some, mostly the holograms, wore formal or ceremonial attire.

Mon did not react with alarm or fear. She hadn't expected an intimate meeting, hidden from all eyes. But neither had she expected this
congregation in darkness.

Were the Separatists better organized than anyone had known? She
couldn't help but think of images of the Confederacy's representatives
sent out across the galaxy during the height of the war, these same faces
calling for victory over the Republic. What had she stumbled upon
now?

One figure descended from the tiers and approached the dais. He was
ash-faced and red-eyed, a willow of a Pau'an male who stood a head
taller than Mon. She knew him immediately.

"Senator Mothma," he said.

"Representative Nulvolio," she replied, lowering her eyes in deference.

This was as she expected, at least, but she knew so little about the
man. He had never served in the Republic Senate, but he had been chief
of staff to Aguth Omak, the secessionist senator from Sluis Van. Once
the war had begun, Nulvolio had faded from public view. Only after
Omak's death had he drawn attention, when he'd run for and won
Omak's vacant seat in the Separatist Parliament. Mon couldn't guess
whether that election had been fair or utterly corrupt, but Nulvolio's
prize had been a position of middling importance within the Confederacy's civilian government—a government whose real power was jeal-
ously hoarded by the corporate council and the Separatist military.

Recently, Nulvolio had spoken in interviews about the privilege of
joining the Imperial Senate—how he was looking forward to represent-

ing his world after the reintegration, how it was time for old wounds to heal, and so on. Palpatine's administration had clearly approved of his Senate induction, but seeing him now, with an assembly of ex-Separatists behind him, Mon wondered whether Palpatine had underestimated him.

"We welcome you to this, our shadow Parliament," Nulvolio said, drawing his lips back and showing his fangs.

"Was I mistaken to think your Parliament dissolved?" she asked.

"Oh, not mistaken," Nulvolio replied. "And if the administration had its druthers, those of us who were once comrades would never again gather outside the public eye, never *plot* and *scheme,* nor speak a word without preapproval. Yet our worlds share common interests, and so at times we meet to discuss our common cause. You understand our need for security."

"Until the reintegration of your worlds is complete, all of you are vulnerable to reprisals," Mon answered. "I *do* understand, and I will do anything necessary to protect your secrecy."

The room seemed to whisper. The domed roof echoed back every murmur and holographic hiss.

"We met here in the war's final days," Nulvolio said, "when Raxus Secundus was no longer secure and none of us knew whether we were destined for execution. But in earlier times, before the secession, this was a place where we planned and dreamed of unfettering ourselves from the Republic's antiquated systems. We imagined alliances that would allow our planets to flourish, and we pretended that our corporate sponsors would fall in line once they saw the zeal of our people." There came a grinding sound from the back of his throat. Perhaps it was laughter. "It was a good dream, Senator. You would have appreciated it."

"I might well have," Mon said. "I always believed that Separatists and loyalists had more in common than we pretended."

"Thus, you come to us now."

"And you brought me here, to the place where your ideals met reality. Symbolism is everything in politics."

Nulvolio grunted and appeared unimpressed. "I am told you are forming a coalition to take back power from the Emperor. But we know the price of failure. We know the price of demanding a voice when the powerful refuse to heed us."

He gestured at one of the farthest tiers, and there was a flash as several holograms winked out of existence and others formed beside them. Separatists dismissed, and others welcomed to the assembly? Mon didn't understand. She wasn't even sure whom she was making her argument to—if she won over Nulvolio, would the others follow? Or had Nulvolio decided to back her already, leaving her to win over the rest?

And what if she failed?

"You've all suffered—" she began. Yet as soon as she spoke there was yelling from the tiers:

"You know nothing!"

"She'll start another war."

"He'll take everything!"

Nulvolio brought silence with another gesture. Mon couldn't help feeling the scene had been rehearsed.

"Our responsibility is to our own people," Nulvolio said. "It is by the grace of the Emperor that our worlds are still inhabitable. While he demands we pay for the harm we inflicted, assigns us debts that will take generations to satisfy, we must be grateful our voices are to be heard at all. This is not sycophancy or craven acquiescence. This is the reality of our situation. To turn against the administration would be to risk all we have left."

Suddenly, Mon *did* understand. Nulvolio hadn't invited her to debate policy or lobby his coalition through speeches and promises and deal-making.

She was being put on trial, to be judged by Nulvolio with his allies bearing witness. And as with any good show trial, the outcome wasn't what mattered. What mattered was that Nulvolio was seen as fair and wise, as a leader whose keen mind should not be questioned going forward. Mon was a prop in Nulvolio's power games, present to help him secure his position within his fragile coalition.

As long as I know the rules, then.

"You want to speak of responsibility?" she asked. "Let's speak."

CHAPTER 28
AN INTERRUPTION, A SECOND INTERRUPTION

They'd bound the two prisoners' hands and feet with sealant foam, light as cloth and hard as duracrete, before dragging them into the upper levels of the cache and thrusting them into a storeroom the pirates had already cleared. Karama hadn't been happy about exposing the prisoners to possible contamination, but Saw and Soujen had both agreed: As long as anyone lingered on the surface, they all risked discovery.

Besides, the guerrillas had scrubbed most of the level. Soujen put the odds of the prisoners' death by biotoxins at less than 20 percent. The guerrillas kept their hazard suits on anyway.

Once the prisoners had regained consciousness, Saw took the lead in the interrogation. Soujen mostly watched, observing faces bruised and crusted with blood. He'd never enjoyed extracting intelligence, and Saw was more personable anyway.

The exchange started badly. The man claimed to be Senator Bail Organa of Alderaan—a statement backed up by his diplomatic documents and Karama's memory of public hearings after the Separatist secession. The woman claimed to be Haki Nevzal, the senator's secretary and personal aide, though when Saw asked her about the modified pistol she carried, she only whimpered and pled ignorance. Vorgorath, already enraged by her killing of Qaterman—one of Saw's more capable troops, albeit slow to duck—had throttled her. Saw had dismissed Vorgorath and Karama from the room, and now it was just the four of them.

"I know why you're here," Organa said. "But the war is over. Reintegration is barely a week away. There's no point fighting for a Confederacy that's gone."

Saw looked to Soujen and arched his brow. Soujen turned and watched Haki. The woman had her knees pulled up to her chest and her back to the wall. Her eyes were downcast, but he felt, nonetheless, that she was watching him.

"We're not fighting for the Confederacy," Saw said. "Not most of us."

Organa frowned up at him. "Scavengers, then? Arms dealers?"

"Discarded believers. My name is Saw Gerrera, of Onderon."

Organa's posture shifted subtly as something registered in his brain. "You ran the militia. We supplied you, trained you—"

"You pushed us into fighting and contrived to wipe your hands of us if we lost. You wanted Onderon at no risk, and you got it. Don't take too much pride in that."

Organa didn't flinch. "What are you doing *here*?"

Saw laughed. "You go first."

Haki made another whimpering sound as tears ran down her cheeks. "Please," she said. "Whoever you are, just let us go. You brought us here to kill us? Ransom us? No one will care. The administration won't pay for him. I'm an old woman. We can't help you, we're not worth anything, just let us go . . ." She said more, but it was lost first in the snuffling, then the bawling. Organa shifted closer to her, leaning against her as if to offer what comfort he could with bound hands.

"Are you alone?" Saw asked.

Organa did not answer.

"Where's your ship? Are you being tracked?"

Again, Organa did not answer.

"Why did you come here?"

Finally, Organa replied. "For centuries, Alderaan has opposed all un-regulated arms trading. So far as I'm concerned, there's no good reason for *anyone* to have these weapons."

"You learned about the cache," Saw said, "and you came to investigate it? To destroy it?"

"The war is over," Organa said.

It was almost convincing.

The questioning went on longer, but Organa revealed nothing. Haki continued blubbering, pausing only to plead in increasingly incoherent ways for her life and Organa's. Soujen finally left the storage room, and Saw followed.

"You believe any of it?" Saw asked.

"I believe he's a senator," Soujen said. "Otherwise, no. We should kill them and finish here as fast as we can."

"Why kill them?" Saw sounded curious but not disapproving.

"Anything else gets complicated. Complications ruin missions. Better to keep it simple."

Saw looked to the storeroom door. He reached out toward it, as if to touch it, then seemed to think better of it. Suited or not, it was wise to be cautious.

"They killed one of my people," Saw said, and there was a sharpness to his words before his voice fell. "They *are* a threat, but the senator could turn out to be useful."

"The Imperial senator is your enemy," Soujen said. "His government wants you dead."

Saw peered at him. "The Separatists called us terrorists. I didn't mind that, even embraced it sometimes, but I need you to understand. We weren't squeamish, and we didn't always follow the Republic's 'rules of military conduct'—the laws about perfidy or how to treat a captive. Yet we *did not* target civilians. We were not *murderers*."

Then Saw turned away.

Saw controlled his emotions well, Soujen thought, but his old loyalties were showing. "*We* were not murderers," he'd said, leaving unspoken the accusation: *Unlike you.*

Soujen shrugged. He would need to be cautious around his *partner.*

/ / /

They loaded hoversleds with weapons, power cells, explosives, cases of
Republic credits and Hutt peggats and unstamped nova crystals. Most
of the false identity documents would be outdated under Imperial rule,
but they took any originating in Hutt space, the Corporate Sector, or
other independent polities. They left the bioweapons alone. That frustrated Soujen, but he understood Saw's rationale. They had to hurry
before someone came looking for the senator, and *hurrying* was a sure-
fire way to end up like the pirates.

Soujen left the others to rapidly explore the lower levels. The main
databank was there, the arsenal of secrets Nulvolio and the others had
believed would serve him in his one-man war—and he lingered over
the machinery, skimming files and downloading documents virtually at
random. Little of it seemed relevant with the war so thoroughly lost.
What did he care about the generals' plan to pacify Coruscant, or who
in Separatist Intelligence had questionable loyalties? He memorized
and erased the antidotes for various toxins. He transferred great stores
of data into his implants, enough that red warnings began to flash in his
vision.

This was *why he'd come,* and he had no time to study. All he could do
was offload files and hope the answers he desired could be found later.
Perhaps the weapons and other equipment they carried out would suffice. Perhaps a doomsday plan meant for times such as these was buried
beneath layers of encryption, waiting for him to expose it. This wasn't
the ideal way for the mission to proceed, hurried and scattershot, but
what mission went smoothly? He might find success despite the distraction created by the senator.

These were desperate thoughts, though, and desperate hopes. He admonished himself for craving easy answers. The fantasy of a doomsday
plan might need to give way to cruder alternatives. But the files would
provide *something.*

Below the databank, on the lowest level shown on his maps, there
was another hatch built into the floor. It was crudely fitted and resistant
to opening. Soujen supposed the excavation droids had installed it as

they extended the bunker deeper. He was considering cutting it open when he heard footsteps and turned to see Karama in her hazard suit.

"Saw's been trying to reach you," she said. "Trouble topside."

He abandoned the hatch and rushed after Karama through the tunnels. They found Saw calling out orders at the sleds, but Saw shifted his attention to Soujen as he approached. "*Dalgo* just called in," Saw said. "Imperial military transport is approaching."

"Did they spot the *Dalgo*?" Soujen asked.

"We don't think so. They may not even know where the cache is. They're flying low and slow, like they're scouting the area."

"Looking for the senator?" Karama asked.

Saw nodded but looked to Soujen.

All of this had been predictable, Soujen thought. *Inevitable.* His subconscious had been assessing variations of this scenario since the senator's arrival, yet he'd deluded himself into hoping for more time.

"If we left now," Soujen asked, "how much of the equipment could we bring?"

"Maybe a quarter of what we were hoping for," Saw said. "Still enough to supply our people for a year. But we'll never get it to the *Dalgo* without being spotted."

"We could bring the ship to the cache, load and run under fire."

It was a bad idea, and all of them knew it. They'd be easy targets in the bowl of the amphitheater, even with the senator and his assistant as hostages. Worse, they'd be moving volatile equipment. It would be a miracle if they made it to the *Dalgo* without the explosives or the power cells being struck and going up in flames.

"What if we ditched everything but the money?" Karama asked. "We'd still be better off than when we started. We could leave the sleds behind, split up, and rendezvous with the ship on foot instead of throwing ourselves against Imperial troops."

"Maybe." Saw didn't sound convinced.

Soujen wanted to believe there was a way to take everything they'd gathered and still escape the planet. If they were already down to a quarter of what they'd hoped, losing anything more was an insult. But he'd told Saw: *Better to keep it simple,* and he'd been right. The priority was survival. He squeezed his rage, compressed it into a stone inside his mind.

"Two options," Soujen said. He had Saw's and Karama's attention. "First, we show the enemy we have hostages—give them a reason to refrain from bombing and force them to move in on foot. They'll surround the cache and try to wait us out, so we give them a deadline—say we'll kill the senator in an hour if they don't withdraw. That way they can't afford to wait for reinforcements—they have to come in after us.

"We can turn the cache into a kill zone and bring in the *Dalgo* to flank. We eliminate their troops and break out."

Saw closed his eyes, appearing to imagine the battle. Then he nodded slowly. "The problem is timing," he said. "For all we know, more transports could be minutes away. If we bet wrong about their reinforcements, we die."

Soujen didn't disagree.

"What's option two?" Karama asked.

"We could seal the upper levels, lay traps, and descend. The excavation droids who constructed the place might have built another exit, or they might be waiting on standby on the lowest level. We survive long enough, we order them to dig us a way out."

"Assuming they're operational. This doesn't sound *less* risky," Karama said.

Soujen scowled. "It may not be. But so long as we're alive, there's the chance the situation changes."

Saw swore. Karama flinched. Soujen guessed she wasn't used to seeing her commander indecisive. Both of them were struggling to maintain their composure, and every slip irritated Soujen. *We need to act now.* Even if he prioritized his own survival, he needed the others to preserve anything valuable from the cache.

"What about the prisoners?" Saw asked. "If we go into the lower levels, do we take them?"

"If we do, we guarantee the enemy will pursue instead of holding position," Soujen said. "But we'll have hostages if we need them, and I don't think they're a danger. If we leave them behind or send them to the surface . . ."

He'd taken hostages more than once, but that had been long ago, during his days as a mercenary. The memories had shattered when the implants had been forced into his body, and all he had left were impressions and images, children crying and snipers in their perches.

What mattered with hostages wasn't their value but what they were valued *for,* whether someone wanted them back or simply wanted them not to talk.

"If we send up the senator, the Imperials will still come after us," Soujen said. "But their options will multiply while ours decrease. I say we bring the hostages with us."

Saw grunted and nodded. "Agreed. But we'd better get them into hazard suits."

CHAPTER 29
THE CITY BELOW

The guerrillas told them nothing. One freed Bail from his bonds, hammering at the hardened foam until the insulation shattered. As Bail worked chunks of the stuff off with his elbows and knees, another guerrilla helped Haki. A third kept a weapon pointed at them from across the room.

"Gear up," a woman said, flashing metal teeth and tossing two bunches of green cloth onto the floor. "We're putting you to work."

Bail scowled. Haki sniffled. Neither of them asked any questions as they dressed. Each had been allocated half of a torn and burnt biohazard suit—damaged, Bail supposed, in the fighting when they'd been captured. *Better than nothing.*

Then they were separated, Haki marched down one corridor and Bail down another. Walking was difficult. He'd been in his restraints long enough that his legs had stiffened, and he'd been badly bruised when he was captured. Every muscle ached, and his entire face stung. But the pain was tolerable, and he felt strangely lucky not to hurt worse. More troublesome was his body's new unreliability. One wrong shift of his hips, one wrong transfer of weight to his heel, and his legs collapsed beneath him. His escort had to catch him twice. A third time, Bail hit the ground and felt pain spike his knees.

But you're alive, he told himself. *You're alive and where you need to be. The cache is real.*

He was led to an underground hangar where a dozen speeder bikes were lined up, their mechanical innards splayed across the floor. One of the guerrillas was on his back, hurriedly removing fuel cells and repulsors, while another was stacking choice pieces onto a hoversled and muttering into a comlink.

"You're here to help," Bail's escort told him. "You do what you're told. Twitch wrong and we take the hazard suit back. You don't want that."

"What's the rush?" Bail asked.

The woman swore and gestured vaguely at the bikes. "Just get to work. No one wants to shoot you, but we can't afford dead weight."

He went to the bikes and knelt, achingly slow, beside the guerrilla performing the disassembly. "How long do we have?" Bail asked. "It would help to know."

He couldn't see the guerrilla's face, but something growled inside the suit.

Bail did what he was told. He popped out stability bolts and stacked parts onto the sled. He looked for ways to sabotage the operation, but all he could think to do was balance the cargo so that it would tumble off when the sled got moving—and this, he decided, was pointless. His body urged him to act, flooding him with adrenaline despite its pains, but while his instinct was to run, he had no plan and not enough information to formulate one. He knew Saw Gerrera only as a name in reports passed over his desk—a fighter from Onderon, a man neck-deep in anti-Separatist operations, a man who'd operated independently and, it was rumored, with very little *restraint.*

But why had Saw turned against the Empire?

Had he turned against the Empire? He'd said his people were "discarded believers."

Hell, maybe Saw—with his brutal tactics and disdain for Republic authority—had been recruited by the administration for deniable operations. Maybe Saw and his guerrillas were present on behalf of the Emperor, wiping out the evidence Bail had come to secure.

Or maybe you're seeing conspiracies everywhere. Worry about survival. Worry about Haki, who's frailer than you.

When they'd finished gathering high-end speeder parts, they moved to another storeroom one level down. This time they loaded unmarked boxes onto the sled, each box heavy enough that Bail staggered as he tried to lift it. By the end he was wheezing, and his partner had told him to sit and stay out of the way.

"What's in there?" Bail asked.

"Unprocessed hypermatter," his partner told him. "Unstable, too. Drop a box and we're all dead."

It might have been a lie. Still, Bail was glad he hadn't rigged the stacks on the sled to topple.

Soon the guerrillas were gathering, and a dozen or so troops moved sleds down the corridors. Bail and Haki were both given sleds of their own to push along. Haki kept her head down, keeping up her display of meekness, but Bail was relieved to see she hadn't suffered further harm. Neither Saw nor their other interrogators were present. None of the guerrillas seemed to question their absence.

They descended to the bottom of a central shaft. Power and network cables were strung across the floor of the sublevel, and Bail nearly tripped as he followed the group. Through an open doorway, he spotted banks of computer terminals and data storage units.

He nodded toward Haki. "We need access," he murmured.

"Hush," Haki whispered. She didn't look at him.

"We've come this far. If there are answers, that's where we'll find them."

"No. Look."

Bail followed Haki's gaze. Their second interrogator—the taciturn Alvadorjian who'd watched them with cruel eyes—had emerged from one of the terminal rooms and was speaking quietly to three of the guerrillas. The guerrillas began sorting through the sleds' cargo, and it was several moments before Bail realized they were gathering small cylindrical devices.

"Detonators?" Bail asked.

"Combination ion-kinetic detonators," Haki said. "Our captors mean to wipe the databanks, trash the hardware, and likely kill anyone close."

Bail's first chief of staff had told him that his skill as a politician was his rare mix of intensity and integrity. True, he often acted rashly, and he'd never possessed the gamesmanship of a Palpatine or a Mothma. But he could stare his opponents down and, at least some of the time, make them believe what he believed. Breha called it his Jedi mind trick.

Bail understood its limits, understood that blundering forward, powered only by righteousness, could doom him. But right now it was the only tool he had.

"Stop!" he called, striding toward the Alvadorjian. One of the guerrillas grabbed him before he'd made it three steps, and Bail didn't struggle. He kept his voice level, almost casual. The muscles in his bruised face burned with every word he spoke. "None of us benefit if you destroy the data in there."

The Alvadorjian turned to observe him. He approached Bail and waved the others back. "And what do you think is *in there*?" the Alvadorjian asked.

How much did he dare to say? If Saw and his band *were* working for the Empire, they might eagerly destroy anything that could incriminate the administration. At best they were unpredictable.

Too late to reconsider. He'd committed to his path.

"There may be information about the Jedi," Bail said, too low for anyone other than the Alvadorjian to hear. "About what happened when they were murdered. There may be more to their story than any of us know."

The Alvadorjian seemed to consider this. Then he turned to the guerrillas and gestured. Two of the three glanced back at Bail, but all of them headed into the terminal rooms with their detonators.

"I am here only in service of the truth." Bail's voice rose in volume but stayed steady. "You fought for the Republic once, and whatever you see yourselves as now, you feel bonds of loyalty still. You are children of Onderon, if nothing else. The information in the databanks is irreplaceable. If the fate of the Empire matters to you, for good or ill, I urge you to preserve it."

The Alvadorjian gestured the rest of the group forward. One of the guerrillas pointed a rifle at Bail. Bail's voice rose to nearly a shout. "If the truth frightens you, then lock me inside. Or shoot me now, so long as the data survives—"

The guerrillas carrying the explosives had emerged. The Alvadorjian pointed toward the nearest terminal room and thunder shook the passage. The air felt charged with static and flame and smoke billowed from the doorway. Bail's vision blurred as his hope died.

"That was the first databank," the Alvadorjian said. "I'd prefer to detonate the others via motion sensor, to catch our enemies in the blast. But if it'll quiet you—"

Bail was yelling again. "Show some blasted curiosity! Show some *interest* in the galaxy!" His thoughts were on fire, and the pain and exhaustion and fear were gone. "This is madness!"

The Alvadorjian stomped past him. As Bail turned, the man stepped behind Haki and clapped both hands over her biohazard hood. "You might be useful," the Alvadorjian said. "She is not. I won't kill her, not yet, but I can take her eyes one by one and no one here will stop me. Only you can stop me, Senator."

Bail stared in shock. Inside her hood, Haki mouthed at him, *Not now. Not now.* She stood very still.

He felt a thickness in his throat made of rage, shame, and sorrow. He breathed the acrid smoke. He bowed his head in acquiescence and swallowed his humiliation, endeavoring to please his captors, to be the good hostage. Enough blood had been spilled already.

///

They descended into the lower levels, and Bail watched the Alvadorjian carve open a hatch with an industrial laser torch. Saw Gerrera joined them and consulted with the Alvadorjian before telling the others, "It's time to go."

The guerrillas—twelve in total, fewer than Bail had expected—seemed to understand. They lowered the hoversleds through the hatch, then followed with their prisoners. In the darkness below, the sweep of handlights revealed cave walls and soil and uneven ground, with barely enough room to walk without crouching. Whatever machines or droids had dug the tunnel had done so with little regard for comfort. Some of the guerrillas seemed dismayed, and Bail found this gave him bitter pleasure. Inside the hole where his hope had been, he could still find strength for resentment.

They resealed the hatch, shutting out the last light from the cache. Saw retrieved a fresh set of detonators from the sleds. "We'll follow the excavators' trail and mine the tunnel at irregular intervals," he declared. "Don't make it predictable. They'll spot most of the traps, and that's fine. Point is to slow them, not kill each and every one."

"Clones?" one of the others asked.

"Confirmed," Saw said. "Word from the *Dalgo* before departing was fifteen troops on the ground. Expect reinforcements sooner rather than later."

Bail said nothing as they marched into darkness. He thought about the databank the Alvadorjian had destroyed and what might have been stored there. He thought about the assault on his body in the amphitheater and what he'd nearly allowed to become of Haki. He thought of how foolish he'd been to come as he had, and when he noticed himself spiraling, he forced himself to focus. The situation was dire, yet there was more to be lost.

If he'd been home, he would have spoken to Breha. He would have walked through his gardens. He'd have sought a way to approach his circumstances not with passion but with detachment, because passion had already buried him.

He could not do these things beneath Eyo-Dajuritz. Instead, after a time, he listened for the voices of the dead Jedi Masters. He asked for their guidance and prayed for a reply, and he tried to clear his mind instead of cursing his own inadequacies. He sought the pragmatism of Master Windu, the tranquility of Shaak Ti, and the irrepressible warmth of Plo Koon. He had known none of them intimately, but scant encounters had made him a better man.

He went through the motions of meditation—as much as he could while walking. He steadied his breathing and emptied his thoughts. He felt no tranquility, but the sounds of footsteps faded and the lights ahead of him floated in the darkness like stars. Eventually, he began to ask himself questions.

What do Saw and his band want?

He brushed aside the frustrated answers, the sarcastic answers, and looked to facts. If Saw's crew was planning to murder a squad of clones, they weren't with the Empire. Most likely, the guerrillas were outlaws. Perhaps terrorists in the making—as they'd fought the Separatists, now they planned to fight the Empire with the Separatist weapons they'd stolen.

Bail imagined the clone troopers triggering the explosives. The image of white armor splashed with crimson was vivid. No matter their part in the destruction of the Jedi, the clones were still victims, forced into lives of violence. Now Saw's guerrillas were ensuring these clones would never live to escape their roles. The guerrillas were too cruel, too cynical, or simply too loyal to question despicable orders, and none of that boded well for Bail, Haki, or the troops on the surface.

The rough tunnel descended sharply, and Bail struggled to climb down a rocky incline that opened into a wider cavern. He considered his next dilemma.

What do the clone troopers want? Why are they here?

If they were chasing Saw—tracking down outlaws pillaging military-grade weaponry—then they were unaware of Bail and Haki, who had simply stumbled into the conflict.

The alternative was that the clones were actively looking for Bail. But no one knew about his voyage to Eyo-Dajuritz except Breha and Haki. Breha had no reason to send clones to his rescue, and Haki . . .

Haki had wanted him to stop searching. She'd said so multiple times. And she had secrets of her own.

Could Haki have called the military to—what? Arrest Bail for seeking to expose the administration? Could the troopers have come to erase the cache's databanks themselves, just as he'd feared Saw and his guerrillas had intended?

He had no answers.

They stopped to rest, eat, and drink. The guerrillas removed their hazard suits, and Bail and Haki stripped as well, exposing their faces to the cool, still air and the scents of rust and moss.

Even in his state of bitterness, with only pinpricks of light to see by, Bail recognized the majesty of Eyo-Dajuritz. They sat among the fossilized foundations of what had once been skyscrapers—the bones of mountains, glittering with mica and metal, expressing secrets with every atom.

Bail spoke softly as Haki passed him a canteen. The nearest guerrilla wasn't closer than three meters. "I'm sorry," Bail said. "For what that monster nearly did to you. For inciting it."

"The perils of being a bodyguard," Haki said flatly. "Think nothing of it."

"I've endangered you enough already. If I can protect you, I will."

Haki didn't reply. Bail looked to the guerrillas, then back to her.

"The clones," Bail said. "Any idea where they came from?"

"Lots of possibilities. Could be after Gerrera and his crew. Could be Eyo-Dajuritz calling for help after two ships landed on forbidden soil."

"You don't think they're after us?"

Her expression was lost in the shadows. "I don't *think* so, though I suppose anything is possible. I don't think they know we're here at all— not unless someone's tipped them off."

"Huh." Bail put the canteen to his lips, more to buy time than out of thirst. Though he *was* thirsty—the sip turned into a lengthy draught. "We made ripples out there, interviewing Separatists across the galaxy," he said. "Someone could've figured out what we were up to, someone who wanted to stop us from embarrassing the administration."

"And you think the clones came to look over our shoulder? Politely confiscate any data we find?"

"I think it's possible someone wants us dead," Bail said. Because it *was* possible—Bail had been shedding his camouflage as an impotent senator for weeks. If Palpatine finally saw the danger he posed, he would extinguish Bail easily as he had the Jedi.

It was possible. Was it likely, though? He couldn't be sure anymore.

"Or if not dead," he went on, "at least shuffled off the road we're walking."

"Plenty of people want us stopped," Haki agreed. "But I'd worry about the ones in front of us, not the ones who might stage a rescue."

The guerrillas flashed a light in their direction and indicated for them to rise. Bail did so, feeling soreness suddenly return to his legs and weariness afflict his mind.

Haki was brilliant. That had become clear. She was also watchful, and whatever her blind spots it was telling to see her dismiss the notion that the Empire might be as dangerous to them as the guerrillas.

He would do whatever he could to save Haki from torture and death. But he wasn't sure she was his ally anymore.

CHAPTER 30
THE TRIAL OF
MON MOTHMA

"**C**owus Roont, the so-called 'Fifth Sage' of Dwartii and one of the founders of the modern Republic, enumerated three responsibilities of a democratic representative. First and least of those, to Roont's mind, was the responsibility to speak for one's constituents and act on their behalf—to be their voice in the chambers of power, a proxy for their collective will."

Mon spoke to the silhouettes and holograms that limned the catacombs with ebony and azure. She did not look at Tychon Nulvolio, though she was aware of his presence. She circled the dais, moving not to block him from the assembly's view but to position herself as his equal. In turn, Nulvolio shifted so that he might appear to loom above her, to encompass his role as judge. They danced together.

"The second was the responsibility to one's own conscience. Roont believed that to be nothing *but* a proxy for the will of the people was to discard a profound ethical burden. She wrote, 'At times of crisis, the representative must always defer to her own moral compass.'" Mon offered the driest of smiles. "No matter how dire the polling."

No one laughed. That was fine. Her job right now was to impress them. Persuasion and bonding could come later.

"Why," she went on, "did Roont elevate the individual conscience above the collective agency of the citizenry? It is because she saw the third responsibility as the most important: the responsibility to democracy itself. As long as an elected leader prioritizes the continuation of democratic government, as long as that leader respects the rule of law, the people may always choose new representation to better serve their needs. Future generations may atone for the mistakes of the past. Yet should the engine of democracy break down, she wrote, 'a citizenry will forever be left at the mercy of unaccountable leaders.'"

Nulvolio was circling her now. Mon stopped. She allowed him to step in front. He turned slowly as he spoke, looking at her while he addressed the room. "A compelling argument to put the lives of our people at risk," he said. "The Empire could bring famine, plague, death to our planets by doing nothing more than refusing to grant us aid. We depend on shipments of medicine and food because our factories and fields were burned. Raxus Secundus *still* lacks running water! We cannot save ourselves, because the only abundance in the galaxy is in the cradle of the Empire."

That she could have argued with, but it wouldn't have won any sympathy from the assembly. Besides, getting drawn into the details was nearly always a losing move. She acknowledged the point with a curt nod and let him continue.

"Cowus Roont hardly reckoned with a situation such as ours. History is no guide for what we face today," Nulvolio said, and Mon refrained from rolling her eyes. "You speak of maintaining the *engine of democracy,* yet as far as I see, that time is long past. Did our worlds not demand to be heard before we turned to secession? Did we not serve that engine by crying out and demanding the Republic listen, while you, Mon Mothma— you and your peers in the Senate—made only gestures toward change?

"And when it became clear that no change was coming, when our worlds chose to leave, how did the Republic respond? By granting emergency powers to the Supreme Chancellor, by forming a Grand Army the likes of which had *never* been used before—"

"You know I opposed the Military Creation Act," she snapped. *Showing a bit of spine won't hurt you.*

"Oh?" Nulvolio asked. He gestured broadly toward the assembly. "Did you oppose the *use* of the clone army? Did you urge Republic citizens to lay down their weapons and permit the free passage of Confederacy vessels? The full recognition of Confederacy sovereignty?"

"Perhaps I would have, if your corporate sponsors hadn't immediately begun strangling the Republic—and if you hadn't attempted to assassinate Padmé Amidala, one of the most fervently anti-war senators in congress." She raised a hand, low enough to avoid offense. "But you're right. I'm not without blood on my hands. Both of us, *all* of us"—she swept her gaze over the gathering—"failed to maintain the democratic machinery. We had years, maybe decades, during which we could have prioritized the continuation of the Republic over the problems of our individual homeworlds. The war was a tragedy, and it could have been prevented if both sides had taken a longer view.

"Now the Republic has fallen, but there's still life in the old ideals. If we continue to keep our heads turned, tend to our own planets instead of uniting to repair the damage, then who can say we weren't warned? Who can say we didn't know how terrible the results could be? We cannot fail our galaxy a *second* time."

" 'We cannot fail our galaxy a second time,' " Nulvolio repeated. There was no mockery in his voice. "That is the warning you bear for us, and it is a powerful one, I grant you.

"Yet accepting that premise, we remain what we are—injured, broken, and with a strength the Empire fears. Which brings us to a question you have not addressed: Why should we follow *you*, Senator Mon Mothma of Chandrila? You who failed, by your own admission, the most important test of your career? You who could not prevent the war, nor secure the peace, nor *win* the war once it began.

"You who organized the Delegation of Two Thousand, whose grand ambitions made it an easy target for the Supreme Chancellor. You who stood beside every politician, Palpatine included, when it served your purposes—and you who broke every alliance when it strained convenience.

"You seek votes to strip the Emperor of his power. Well, of course you do! What options do you have to maintain your position and escape a decline into insignificance? While *we* stand among the ruins of our worlds, tasked with securing the present as well as the future. *We* have already tasted the price of rebellion, and trillions suffer for it every day.

"Can you, with your history of errors, assure us of victory? Can you even assure us that our worlds will fare better under your vision than under Palpatine's? Why should we trust *you* to guide us, Senator? Why follow a woman who aspired to the chancellorship and became despised by the galaxy, marginalized for her embrace of unpopular causes, who never took the steps to produce results?"

This is the moment, she thought. The assembly was watching, and Nulvolio was ready for a verdict.

But he was giving her an opportunity, as well. Nulvolio had made no commitments, had said nothing to limit his options. He had accepted the premise of her proposal—that they shared a responsibility to the future—and he could still graciously deem her a worthy ally and attach his reputation to hers if she defeated every trap along the way. He was overseeing her trial, but the outcome was not preordained—because whatever happened, Nulvolio would benefit.

There *were* words that would win the assembly over. She only had to find them.

She could ask them, *Who else do you have to lead you?* It was a fair argument, but it would fail her.

She could tell them, *The Emperor and his advisers have revealed their strategy. They have no more secrets, no more tricks. And I know how to move against them.* This was also true, but asserting it wouldn't convince anyone who didn't already agree.

She could plead, *I'm not here to lead you. I'm here as part of my coalition, and I seek partners.* But that would be a lie, and it would only prompt the question, *Why should we put our faith in your coalition?*

She drew breath and thought through a thousand scenarios until the first words came to her lips.

"You say I have a track record of errors. Perhaps that is true. Time and again I've been tested, along with all of us, and my victories have been few.

"But I have *survived*. I have come back from every failure. The people of Chandrila have reelected me. My influence in the Senate has waxed and waned, but I've never been powerless.

"I've seen thousands of senators come and go. I've been attacked, arrested, spat on, mocked, and I've never hidden. I am *still here*. My friend and my aide"—*I'm sorry, Zhuna*—"was murdered by a man drunk on Imperial propaganda, a man who sought my life, and I have not flinched. Imperial spies watch me, and I do not cower. Did anyone else have the resources or the influence to find you?

"For that matter . . . would you think of putting anyone else on trial here for the crimes and failures of the Senate during the war? You wanted a reckoning, and you chose *me*. That alone is recognition of my role. If Palpatine is responsible for the actions of the clone army, then I am responsible for the failures of the peace process. I wielded the power then, and I still do.

"I am not asking for your loyalty. I am not asking you to believe that I am a savior or a visionary, or to forgive my crimes against your people. But what we face is a fight for survival—our own survival, yes, but also the survival of democracy in this new Empire.

"So I ask you, when survival is what matters, when the tools at hand are the tools of the Senate, will you slink into the shadows to be forgotten by history, hoping for Palpatine's crumbs? Or will you recognize that the reasons you hate me are the reasons I can devise a way to restore the engine of democracy?"

She could barely see the faces in the shadows, but she sensed disdain and disappointment. The holograms vanished and reappeared in strange patterns, like lights strung around a cheap cantina. Nulvolio was behind her now, ready to lower the axe.

It isn't enough, she thought. *It's close, but it isn't enough.*

"Mon Mothma," Nulvolio said. "You ask us to risk more than you have ever risked. The consequences for Chandrila, for your home, are nothing compared to what awaits our planets."

"I know," she answered, staring ahead.

"For us to follow you . . . we would need to believe your dedication to *our* preservation was equal to your dedication to yourself, to your world."

She forced herself not to close her eyes. "I understand."

She heard the scrape of metal against metal. In the darkness of the chamber, a monitor screen flashed. She looked ahead into her own face and saw the image of Nulvolio behind her, towering over her, a pistol leveled at the back of her skull.

"Would you die to restore democracy to the Empire?" Nulvolio asked.

"I would," she said.

"Would you die rather than see the worlds of the Confederacy punished for your actions? Would you offer yourself and Chandrila as a shield against retribution?"

She hesitated for only a moment, long enough to consider the consequences. Long enough to consider whether she wished to escape them. "I would." She closed her eyes. Perhaps it was all a demonstration. Perhaps it was an execution. Either way, it wouldn't last long.

"Would you turn the implementation of your plan over to us? Tell us the names of your allies, the promises you've made, everything you've done, and allow us to see this project through?"

"No," she said.

Nulvolio paused. "Why not?"

"Because the others trust me, not you. Because the public will never accept a bill pushed by former Separatists. And because if you try and fail, then I *cannot be* your shield."

She opened her eyes. On the screen, she saw Nulvolio return his pistol to his robes. He stepped around her, swept his gaze over the assembly once more, then turned to face her and extended a hand like a claw.

She took it.

"Let us proceed," he said.

CHAPTER 31
THE ART OF SHAMING

Chemish didn't have a proper job anymore, not since Haki had accelerated their training and offered Chemish a stipend. Chemish still made the occasional package run for appearances sake, delivering credits, machine parts, and spice for whoever asked—but, really, they had lots of free time. That gave Chemish a chance to get to know Laevido and the others who'd been at the memorial for Zhuna's murderer.

What Chemish had learned was this:

Laevido carried his umbrella everywhere and was the de facto leader of the imperialist activists living in the Level 4040 residential blocks. Similar groups flourished all over Coruscant, Laevido claimed, but the self-declared "4040s" were among the oldest. Laevido had worked in weather control for twenty years before deciding he wanted an education, and university had shown him that democracy rarely ended well (no matter what Republic propaganda said). He coughed when he laughed and could make any anecdote riveting by pacing it just so. He liked detective stories and bawdy comedy, and Chemish kind of loved him.

Dakhmi was a feather-haired Omwati, the only nonhuman among

the 4040s and the youngest besides Chemish. Dakhmi was studious and angry and, according to Laevido, had lost everything that mattered in the war. Fowlitz was a shuttle pilot by trade and a Kloo horn player by avocation, and the 4040s had taken to attending his band's performances and chatting in the clubs and bars afterward. Erinya and Jayu were a married couple who seemed more interested in socializing than politics—at least until Jayu had her third drink and started complaining about the Jedi, or Erinya began talking about her work with the underworld police. There were others, too, dozens in the inner circle of the 4040s and hundreds associated with the group, and Chemish met them at school fundraisers and speeder races as often as at rallies or private gatherings. They were a sprawling, dysfunctional family of activists and hobby soldiers and losers and parents striving for a better future, and Chemish felt at home with them. Often, Chemish wondered whether Zhuna's murderer really had been the exception. Whether the 4040s were a potential source of informants and agents for Haki and Imperial Intelligence instead of a threat to be watched.

"It's a strange thing to have come as far as we have," Laevido told Chemish one morning as the group bagged litter, painted walls, and repaired lifts throughout a decaying housing complex. "Some people think we've done our part, that the Emperor can do the rest."

"But things are unstable," Chemish said, peeling a cracked, severed cable from a hallway wall and tossing it into their garbage bag. "There are senators like Mothma who want to go back to the old ways."

"Oh, there's that," Laevido said. "Mothma and her ilk, the radicals pressing for reintegration of the Separatists, people inside the administration trying to sabotage the Emperor and the grand vizier . . . I had high hopes for Bail Organa, but word's come down he's just as bad as the rest. Going to need to watch him closely." Laevido appeared distracted a moment, then returned to his train of thought. "We'll stand against them all, but our cause is bigger. You know why?"

"Why's that?" Chemish asked.

Laevido ran a hand along the wall. Abruptly he plunged a thumb into the instaplast surface and ripped out a handful of rotting insulation. He looked at the material in disgust and dropped it into the bag. "Twenty years ago, barely anyone supported reforming the Republic, tearing out its guts and starting over. Maybe Palpatine heard about us. Maybe he came up with his Imperial project on his own. But we laid the ground-work. That's what politics and advocacy are good for."

Chemish considered this. Laevido wanted engagement, wanted a conversation, and if Chemish only asked questions, he'd become suspicious. "I never trusted politics," they said. "Always seemed like a distraction from actually getting things done, or a way to chase power."

"Usually it is." Laevido looked satisfied. "That's why executive authority is so important. But even in an Empire, when a visionary leader stands supreme, it's the people who lead society by example."

"Like what we're doing now?" Chemish asked.

"What we're doing now is modeling acceptable behavior, showing how a community ought to operate. Today we're building a place of safety for poor folk who've been ignored too long. Tomorrow . . . tomorrow we may need to show someone what's *not* acceptable in the new Empire."

"How do we do that?"

Laevido chuckled softly, wrapping an arm around Chemish's shoulders. "By making an example of *them*."

Often, Chemish wondered whether Zhuna's murderer had been the exception. Now and then, though, Laevido said something that made Chemish certain they bore watching.

/ / /

Chemish never told the others their real name. They never went directly home—not even to the safe house—from a meeting with the 4040s. They took every precaution Haki had taught them and a few they'd learned as a courier, shaking muggers and addicts on dangerous routes.

Maybe it was paranoia. If nothing else, it kept Chemish's mind busy.

The 4040s held regular protests outside the offices of Mon Mothma and other members of the Delegation of 2,000. After several visits,

Chemish began to distinguish those in the crowd who were there to yell from those there to observe. The observers marked the arrivals and departures of senatorial aides, recorded speeder traffic, or performed other surveillance in plain sight. Their technique wasn't professional, but it didn't need to be.

One evening after Fowlitz had just finished a show, Chemish asked Laevido what the 4040s were doing with the surveillance data—and insinuated that they might be interested in surveillance work themself. "I used to watch the gangs outside Thrizka's, make sure security knew the schedule. Not so different, right?"

The group had just settled into the club's back room, swapping gossip, rumors, and praise for the governors. Masks in the images of pre-Republic generals stared down at their table from the wall, and the dim light glimmered on Laevido's balding scalp. "You're too smart to play tracker," Laevido said. "It's grunt work."

"I'm good at grunt work," Chemish said.

Laevido laughed. Erinya wandered over to the table, and they talked about the street and skyway closures planned for Separatist Reintegration Day, and whether the administration would permit protests. Then Dakhmi came with drinks, and someone bought Chemish something green, frothy, and strong. Dakhmi complained about the senators, professors, and rabble-rousers who said the administration favored humans—because who could believe *that* when the grand vizier was Chagrian?

And as the hours passed, Chemish realized they'd drunk too much, and their skin was becoming warm, and Laevido had been asking them questions awhile, and Chemish hadn't asked any of their own.

". . . offworld," Laevido was saying. "Have you ever been offworld? You can tell me."

Chemish hadn't, and they wanted to say so. Instead, they said, "I'm starting to feel sick. I should get home."

"We'll get you home," Laevido said. "Stay until we're all ready, eh?"

"I feel sick," Chemish said, because they weren't sure whether they'd said it already.

Laevido smiled and put a hand on Chemish's wrist. "You're doing fine. What you drank—it's brewed from the glands of a deep-sea creature native to Courtsilius, and it enhances emotions, especially shame. Most people with a conscience find it *very* difficult to lie after partaking, and I thought we could use an honest conversation."

Chemish fought down an instinctive panic. It was fine to look scared, they thought. Fine to look insulted and violated. By the time they thought these things, Laevido was in the middle of another question: "I want to understand why you're here with us," Laevido said, "because I would like to help you on your journey. But you need to be totally honest. What drives you here, my friend?"

What would the 4040s do if they found out the truth? Chemish worked for the regime, the regime the 4040s supported. But then there was Zhuna. *Don't tell them about Zhuna.*

Chemish's lips were already moving. "Family," they said.

"How's that?"

Don't tell them about Zhuna. Don't tell them about Zhuna. All Chemish could think about was the news reports, about their cousin dragging herself to the kitchen as her assailant beat her to death. They wanted to lie, but just the idea caused Chemish to flush. They couldn't live with the thought of deception, wanted to weep at the idea of being untrue to others and themself.

Somewhere Haki's voice seemed to say, *This is the job.* "Living your truth" *is a luxury.*

"My brother," Chemish said. "My brother was in the war, and we weren't really as close as I tell people, but he was so smart and so *good.* And he traveled. He saw more than the three rotten sectors of Coruscant where I've spent my whole life. He got out. He got *away.* I love my family so much, but I don't want to grow old watching the triplets and paying for my aunt's apartment and . . . My brother got away, and I want to be like him. I want to serve. I want to see things and know things, and I want to get out."

"You want purpose," Laevido said.

"I want answers, more than they've got here."

Laevido nodded and squeezed Chemish's wrist. "Find a worthy cause, and the answers will come on their own."

Chemish forced a wretched smile, then puked into their glass.

/// ///

That was the end of the interrogation, and Chemish managed to exaggerate their own intoxication until the 4040s didn't dare try to transport them home. Chemish was allowed to pass out on the couch of the club, and they found their way to the safe house the next morning, taking the usual precautions to make sure they weren't followed.

Chemish was exhausted, hungover, and ashamed of baring their pathetic soul to the 4040s. It had been careless of Chemish to drink— but they hadn't been *entirely* careless. Chemish hadn't forgotten to activate the device sewn into their jacket sleeve. Now, sitting at the console with a cup of rose tea, they downloaded the recordings and ran the playback at double speed. They listened to Laevido's questions, and they listened to what came after, while Chemish had slept.

There was talk about Chemish and about sports. And eventually, after most of the 4040s had left, there was an exchange that made Chemish sit bolt upright, ignoring their exhaustion and need for a shower. They listened to the end and replayed the exchange:

"We are doing *something* for the reintegration, right?" Dakhmi asked.

"We are," Laevido replied. "The Emperor wants to invite the Separatists home, and we can't stand in the way. But we can make sure they don't feel *welcome*, and we can make sure no one takes advantage of the chaos. I'm waiting for word, but there are plans in motion."

That was all. No specifics, nothing actionable, but enough to chill Chemish's skin.

Haki had left instructions for how to make contact in the event of an emergency but warned Chemish that messages might be unlikely to get through. Chemish sent a coded signal anyway, a request for contact without details. The signal would work its way along hyperspace relays until coming to rest in a satellite over Ord Tiddell, where Haki might discover it minutes or months down the line.

Chemish showered. They made breakfast. They forced themself to just *be*, to listen to the music and the yelling from the street and to taste savory synthetic meat with its bitter sauce. They would forgive themself for the mistakes they'd made, or at least try to forget them.

After that, they would need to decide how long to wait for Haki's reply, and what to do if it never came.

CHAPTER 32
WHISPERS IN THE VAULT

The "vault" at Cantham House was neither as grand nor as secure as the name implied. Queen Breha Organa of Alderaan saw it as little more than a glorified closet—a closet with a field-reinforced door and shelves of classified datapads, yes, but still a dim and musty space with pale-yellow lighting and stale air, conferring no dignity.

The vault's walls were ordinary durasteel, and the door itself was (she'd been told) vulnerable to various forms of electronic slicing. Nonetheless, no signals could penetrate the enveloping particle globe. No communications could be sent or received. For this reason, Breha met Trayus Castolle, chief of the Royal Guard, inside. She mustered what dignity she could, standing straight-backed against cabinets that contained several million credits' worth of ornamental jewelry for use at state-sponsored occasions.

"Tell me what you've learned," she said. Castolle—scarred hands, scarred eyes, but with cheeks and chin as smooth as a youth's—bowed his head. When he looked up again, he stared only at Breha's chin. "From the beginning," Breha added.

"The beginning would be the threats, my Queen," Castolle said. His body displayed the discipline of motionlessness, and his voice echoed weirdly in the vault. "They began after the Royal Consort's detention by Imperial Security and continued after his release. Nothing extraordinary, nothing worth acting on, mostly addressing him as a senator and ignoring his connection to the House of Organa. Citizens angry he wasn't showing more deference to the new Emperor. As a precaution, and in recognition of the recent lapse at Senator Mothma's apartments and the murder of her aide, we increased our vigilance and coordinated our efforts with Senate Security."

Breha hadn't shared the Royal Guard's "increased vigilance" with Bail, though she'd known about it at the time. The Royal Guard was her responsibility. Senate Security was his. "Go on," she said.

"We discovered evidence of a surveillance operation focused on Cantham House and the Royal Consort's Senate staff. I would describe the operation as . . . organized but inexpert. We were able to identify several suspects as members of a political action group calling itself the '4040s'—imperialist militia types. Again, out of an abundance of caution, we decided to perform an unscheduled search of Cantham House for any monitoring equipment."

"Which is how you found the listening device in my husband's office."

"Yes, my Queen. The technology is sophisticated—several levels above what we'd expect from the 4040s—but we can't say anything more for sure."

"Oh, there's a great deal we can say for sure." She tried not to inject blame into her tone. Castolle wasn't at fault. "My husband is being spied on—by one party at least, possibly by several. You mentioned coordinating with Senate Security?"

"That's right."

"I've heard several complaints that the additional officers they provided have been unusually inquisitive—that they've been *thorough* in their searches of the estate and that their questioning of the staff verges on intrusive."

The scars around Castolle's eyes twitched. She knew he wanted to study her face, but his training wouldn't allow it. Here, in total privacy, she could have urged him to feel at ease, could have afforded the lapse, yet to do so would have been a distraction for them both. Breha had opinions, so *many* opinions, on the class structures of Alderaan, and for the entirety of her tenure as queen, those opinions had been less pressing than the crisis of the day.

"You suspect the security forces planted the bug?" he asked.

"Do you? Speak freely, Guardsman. Tell me I'm being paranoid, because it would be a great comfort."

"At this juncture"—the formality fell out of his voice, the stilted tone became a mutter—"I don't have a clue. Senate Security had access, but motive is a political question. You pay me to stay away from politics."

She laughed darkly and nodded. She wished Bail were there. But that was the problem.

Officially, her business on Coruscant was personal: She'd come so that she and Bail could bond with their new daughter as a family. There was truth to that, but her visit had other motives as well. The transformation of the Republic into an Empire had implications far beyond the Senate, and dozens of planetary heads of state had come to the capital to quietly confer about the political fallout.

Those meetings were dwindling in frequency as the dust settled. They'd been enlightening, if not strictly productive, with a burning focus on the proposed system of regional governors.

"You're confident my husband was the primary target?" she asked.

"If you're being surveilled, it's with an additional level of discretion."

"What do you recommend?"

"Still speaking freely? I suggest you decamp for Alderaan immediately and advise the Royal Consort to return as well. Coruscant is an environment we cannot control. Once you're back at the palace, we can reassess protocols and decide on next steps."

It was a reasonable suggestion, and Breha rejected it with barely a thought. Castolle didn't need to understand, and he wouldn't ask, but she bore responsibility for two billion lives. She was Queen, ruler of House Organa, protector of her people, and—

No. That's not why you're doing this.

Bail's last message had said he was headed to Balumbra to continue his investigation into the framing of the Jedi. He'd made no contact since. Breha knew him. She knew the dangers of his mission, and she believed with all her heart that he had encountered something terrible.

Bail was brave and strong and might well return to her unaided. He might well not need her. He had stared down more than one threat to his life during the war. But *he* was the target of the spies on Coruscant. He had made an enemy of the administration, and if Breha *was* needed to unravel the net around her husband, she would not be able to do it from Alderaan. That was not an expression of duty toward her people but an expression of love toward her husband, and if she tried to justify one as the other, then she would only fail all her vows. If she was to be selfish—if she was to put her husband and daughter above her planet—then best to be clear about it.

"We will stay here," she said, "until the situation requires we do otherwise."

"What about the princess?" Castolle asked. "If there is a danger here, should she be moved?"

Breha was unprepared for her own outrage—and Castolle must have noticed, because he flinched. *You would take away my child?* she thought. Her frustration rose like the tide until it drowned her thoughts of Bail and she blamed him for running away, leaving her as Leia's sole protector while he put himself in who knew what dangers.

And just as quickly as it had risen, the tide subsided, and what was left was love and compassion. *The joys of motherhood,* she thought.

"You're right, of course," she said with a sigh. "Leia needs her parents, but not at the expense of her safety. Have one of your people ready to evacuate her to Alderaan at a moment's notice. She'll stay only as long as the threat remains hidden."

She dismissed Castolle. Alone in the privacy of the vault, Breha sagged under the weight of her world and her family.

CHAPTER 33
THE HAUNTING
OF BAIL ORGANA

The farther they went, the more Eyo-Dajuritz revealed its true self. The caverns became large, malformed pockets full of stale air stinking of red moss. Stalagmites rose and merged with the fossilized support beams of decayed megastructures. They walked through forests of pipes and conduits and aqueducts, passed through chambers like the faded remnants of theaters, houses, and shopping centers.

Here and there they found a signpost, a statue, or a wall that had been newly shattered, its broken edges still bright. This was the trail of the excavation droids that had come from the cache, and each time the group discovered something broken, they silently gathered. They had troubled Eyo-Dajuritz, the ancient graveyard of a lost species. They had troubled the planet, and the least they could do was mourn.

Sometimes voices spoke to them. Someone's comlink would activate, untouched, and those nearby would hear the soft static of background radiation. The hiss would pitch up and down, the pops would jump in volume, and—so subtly that the process was impossible to recognize until it was complete—the static would transform into an alien whisper speaking a forgotten tongue. For a minute or two the voice would speak incomprehensibly. Then it would dissolve back into static and the com-link would deactivate.

"Old broadcasts," Saw told the others. "Something still transmitting after all these eons."

Saw was probably right, Bail thought. None of them suggested aloud that the voices were ghosts. And unlike some of the guerrillas, who grew tense when the voices came, Bail found the voices comforting. They were a reminder that no matter how long ago a people had been lost, no matter how thoroughly they appeared to have been purged, *something* was always left behind.

The passage of time was difficult to judge. Bail dozed uneasily during rests and always woke tired. Meals were irregular and carefully rationed. Perhaps they'd left the cache ten hours ago, or perhaps thirty. They'd abandoned the biohazard suits long ago. He used the stops to engage the guerrillas in conversation, and though they were resistant at first, he wore them down. They were anxious, listening for sounds of pursuit and eyeing the dwindling supplies of water, and he sensed they were relieved by the chance at simple dialogue. He tried to hide his own dis-like and mistrust. Learning their names helped: Vorgorath. Chee'nobin. Raloph. Nankry.

"Is everyone here from Onderon?" he asked Karama, a young woman with metal teeth, as they made camp in the valley of what might once have been a tram station.

"Originally?" She frowned. "Onderon or close to, mostly."

"It's a beautiful world," he said. "I was there before the war, at an in-terplanetary summit of royal courts. I was only decoration for my wife, so I had plenty of time to tour Iziz."

"The city's not what it was," Karama said.

"Not much is, present company included."

Karama laughed. He could tell she didn't want to.

He spoke for a bit about the palace and the zoo, though he didn't get much more than grunts and occasional smirks in reply. If he'd had more time, he could've done more with his audience, but he knew he had to move things along.

"The Jedi. Did you ever meet any?" he asked.

She looked at him sharply.

He waved a hand, casual as he could. "I know Saw and his people were trained by Jedi—Jedi and a clone captain. I read the reports. I promise, you wouldn't be spilling state secrets."

She'd been checking and rechecking the contents of one of the supply boxes. The other guerrillas were scattered, some around the camp, some scouting, and some laying traps in the tunnels. They had privacy, and though Bail feared pushing too hard, he doubted he'd have another chance soon.

"Jedi and a clone," she repeated.

"Ever expect to use Jedi tactics *against* the clones?" he asked.

She snorted. "You think these are Jedi tactics?"

"No," he said. "Neither do you."

Karama looked ready to stalk away. But no one else was there to guard him. Haki was working with one of the other guerrillas to collect water off the cavern roof.

"Cheap shot, I know," Bail said. "But sometimes how you fight matters more than the cause itself, and it's never too late to change."

She drew a long breath, then released it.

"You didn't press for military support on Onderon," she said. "You wanted the Separatists out, but you weren't willing to sacrifice Republic lives to do it."

"That's not—"

"I followed the debate, Senator. I talked to your spokesperson. I know the line about Onderonian neutrality, how the Republic didn't want to interfere with its sovereign authority. But the fact you secretly sent help anyway doesn't make you noble. It just makes you a hypocrite."

Her posture had changed. He adjusted his own. "You were a journalist?" he asked.

"For the Grand Army's news feeds. I wouldn't exactly call it *journalism,* but it was what the troops heard on the front."

"Where did—"

She cut him off. Her face had grown flushed. "We're not backstage, and this isn't a friendly interview."

"And if I offered you one?"

She wanted to leave. He could see that, but he could also see she wanted to take the bait.

"Not an interview, then," he said. "We'll do it like a media conference. Ask me any one question and I will reply truthfully, to the best of my ability. And I'll ask you one in return."

She scowled but didn't move. He had her, not by manipulation or lies but by empathy and curiosity. Things that made it harder to kill a hostage.

She asked, "When the Empire came after us, after Saw, and told us to surrender and stand down, did you know?" She held up a hand and seemed to backtrack. "You won't admit to knowing. Would you have done anything about it if you had known?"

"I didn't know." He thought the rest of the question through and added, "But I wouldn't have stopped them."

Of all the outrages perpetrated by Palpatine, all the horrors inflicted by his regime, demanding the disarmament of a local militia seemed to Bail like the least of them. And knowing what the guerrillas had become, knowing they tortured prisoners and collected bioweapons and would wipe out the secrets of the Jedi . . .

"What's your question?" Karama asked.

"Have you ever killed a clone?" he said.

"No." It was cold, flat, and unmistakably a lie.

But that was something. It meant whatever extremes the guerrillas had turned to, however tight a grip Saw had on them, not all of them were proud of the blood on their hands.

Maybe, Bail thought, he'd be able to use that. But he damn well didn't see how.

///

After another few hours, Saw called a stop. "We can't march forever," he said, "but we can't linger. We'll get four hours' sleep, hope the clones are still disarming the cache." No one looked happy, and no one could say whether the excavation droids had dug a way to the surface somewhere in the caverns. But the group moved to secure the perimeter and bed among the rocks.

Haki nodded to Bail, and they waited until the others had grown quiet. They huddled against one another and the cavern wall.

"You're all right?" Bail asked.

"Tired," Haki said. "There's a pain in my chest I can't shake, but I'm alive. You?"

"They were easier on me when they first took us," Bail said. He wasn't sure whether it was true—he hurt badly and often. But Haki moved with a strange stagger, and her veins were growing dark. "You shot one. They wanted to punish you for that."

Her eyes fluttered shut. "I'm going to miss that pistol," she said, "assuming we survive."

"I don't think they intend to execute us."

"No, but give them long enough and they will. Gerrera thinks of himself as a persecuted savior, and anything that doesn't reflect that enrages him. The others believe in Gerrera. They can convince themselves of anything."

"You've heard of him before?" Bail asked.

"Seen the reports, like you. Man refused to disarm and has been escalating since then—piracy, supply hijackings, the like. Funny thing . . ." She laughed. It was a wet sound. "You know Saw Gerrera was being considered for a governorship before this all went down? The administration likes military boys who don't get squeamish, likes folks with charisma who are attached to their homeworlds."

How do you know that? Bail thought. At some point she'd stopped pretending. Or maybe her injuries were making her delirious.

"Of course," Haki went on, "all that went out the window when he made an ass of himself. The administration also likes folks who'll take orders, and it turns out he's not that. So they've been hunting him awhile. You know his type. Little dictator with a ball of hate to bounce off the wall when he's lonely."

Bail grunted. He did know the type. "What do you suggest we do?"

"Need to get away," Haki said. She didn't sound entirely focused on the conversation. "Running won't work. Fighting won't work. But Gerrera's afraid of the clones, and rightly so. We need a hiding place—somewhere we can disappear. When this lot has to choose between searching and moving on, they'll move on."

"And then?"

"We wait for the troops. With the booby traps Gerrera's set, with no lights and no supplies, only a fool would go back through the tunnels."

It was a sensible plan, Bail thought, and he trusted Haki's survival instincts. But it wouldn't do. "We have to get back to the cache. We can't know for sure all the data was destroyed, and we can't trust the clones to preserve it."

Haki's lips twitched. She glanced about, and when she looked at him again, she was no longer the cowardly senatorial aide, nor was she the woman who'd called herself his bodyguard. Her expression had lost all warmth, and her dark eyes were keen and unkind.

"You're paranoid," she said. "The clones are the only way we live to escape. If you can't accept that—"

"They followed us for a reason," Bail snapped, "and you see that as clearly as I do. If that reason is to wipe out evidence exonerating the Jedi, to destroy data that would embarrass the administration—"

"Then *so what*?" Haki asked. "Suppose it's true. Suppose your documents were spun out of stardust and Separatist imagination. What *good* does showing proof of the administration's malfeasance do anyone?"

"Truth matters. The Jedi matter," Bail said. He forced himself to keep his voice low. "And it matters if our government is run by a cartel of criminals and power mongers. It matters that people know—"

"So they can do what, exactly? March in the streets until Palpatine steps down, ashamed of the trouble he's caused?"

"The Senate and the judiciary won't stand for what he's done once they know the extent of it." He was saying too much, but he'd kept it inside too long, and Haki's words had elicited a moral revulsion. To be silent was to be complicit in the death of the Jedi. "The Jedi were heroes, and once the investigations begin, they won't stop. People will rally behind the facts."

He wanted to say more. He wanted to paint an image of Jedi survivors standing in the Senate chamber, reporting all the atrocities they'd seen—Obi-Wan and Yoda delivering accounts of the Emperor's evil, unveiling a truth that even Mon Mothma would accept.

Yet Haki was watching him with something like loathing, and she jutted a thumb toward the guerrillas. "The only people you'll rally are people like *them*. Ex-soldiers who mastered violence during the war and not much since. If you work long enough and hard enough and make convincing-enough speeches, I'm sure you can create an army of Gerreras who'll make threats on behalf of your lost cause.

"Palpatine's administration will justifiably see them as a threat and begin to crack down. These angry, embittered people will fight back, perceiving themselves—as Gerrera does—to be victims. They'll begin bombing barracks and military transports, saying they've been forced into violent action, saying they're only trying to protect themselves and demanding Palpatine's resignation. The ordinary citizenry of the Empire will rightly consider these people to be lunatics and radicals."

Bail began to retort, but Haki wouldn't be silenced, and he feared they'd draw attention from the others. She was sweating feverishly, and at times she tripped over her words. "Soon enough they'll be so convinced of their cause, so certain that justice has been denied them, that they'll start attacking nonmilitary targets—probably tax offices at the start. Everyone hates tax collectors, and you can always say you're stopping the government from funding whatever you hate most. The radicals will lose their last supporters in the Senate. They'll give a bad name to Jedi sympathizers. But they'll be so buoyed by their aggrieved righteousness that they won't quit. They'll start attacking spaceports, tram stations, cafés and bistros and cantinas frequented by government workers. They'll still call for 'justice for the Jedi' now and then, but they'll develop a whole new ideology unique to their circumstances. Parts of it, little paragraphs deep in their manifestos, may actually make sense.

"That, Senator"—Haki took a deep breath and smiled, white lips peeled back over gray teeth— "is the *most* change you can hope to create. You can inspire a terrorist movement destined for failure, capable of destroying thousands of lives over the course of decades."

Then her intensity vanished. "Or maybe you bring the most compelling proof imaginable to the Senate. Maybe Palpatine expresses his fury at the incompetence of his intelligence services! How could they have *believed* those Separatist lies about the Jedi? How could they have failed him? Maybe he tosses away a few mid-level bureaucrats, maybe Isard and Chivolney resign in disgrace. Maybe it all ends there, the Jedi are exonerated but remain quite dead, and everyone is happy . . . except you, I think? You have it out for the Emperor, and I do not think that would satisfy you."

He waited. He watched her breathe heavily.

When Bail spoke, his voice, too, was soft and without force. "You'd rather a madman rule the galaxy than risk standing against him?"

He wanted to know. He wanted to understand.

Haki shrugged. "Madmen come and go. I've lived a long time, Senator. I saw a lot of bad regimes on my homeworld, and the worst thing isn't tyranny but *fear*—not knowing whether a war's going to start, not knowing if someone's speeder is going to explode as you're walking to market. Scars a person for a lifetime, and every conflict plants the seeds for the next."

"And massacring a group like the Jedi? That leaves no scars?"

"Suppose it does. Doesn't mean the answer is to keep cutting. You're a father now. What are you *really* doing in this cavern? Your job's to give stability to Leia, not knock down everything for your personal sense of justice."

"They killed the Jedi children, too."

Haki looked away. "Then there are no orphans, and they aren't our responsibility."

There was a call from the tunnel, one of the guerrillas setting traps returning to camp. Bail scooted away from the wall and winced at the ache in his back as he lay on the rough ground.

"Get some rest," he said. "You need to heal, and neither of us is thinking clearly."

Somewhere, the ghosts were watching.

CHAPTER 34
THE HAUNTING OF
SOUJEN VAK-NHALIS

"They're planning to escape," Soujen said. He walked alongside Saw Gerrera at the front of the company, over rough terrain that might have been a cemetery.

Saw didn't spare him a glance. "Why wouldn't they be? Do they have a plan?"

"Not a solid one. Hide when the chance comes, wait for us to move on."

Soujen had looked across the cavern and spotted the senator and his aide conspiring. He'd adjusted his auditory implants, narrowed his visual focus to their lips, and done his best to interpret their conversation through the static of Eyo-Dajuritz.

He'd heard them talk about the Jedi and the seeds of insurrection. He thought he'd understood the gist, but what surprised him was that he'd *cared*. His body had tensed as if he'd been hearing something momentous, and he'd replayed the conversation in his mind while the rest of the camp had rested.

Why did he care? He still wasn't sure. What use was the information to him?

"We should kill the secretary," Soujen told Saw. "She's dangerous, and she has no value. Without her, the senator won't be difficult to control."

Saw grunted. "It's good to have a second hostage—one to use, one to make an example. Besides, they haven't made trouble yet. We kill the woman, the senator won't be cowed. He'll just accelerate his escape plan, and thwarting even a fool's plan would cost more time than we can spare."

Soujen didn't argue, but he thought to himself, *You're less than you pretend to be.*

Saw readily spoke of war, revolution, and death. He drew people to his cause with a natural charisma weaponized through methodical refinement, and he was readying himself for years of battles. He was familiar with asymmetrical warfare. But if he was less squeamish than his people, he still resisted habits he wrote off as *Separatist*, habits he would need to learn if he was to survive.

Soujen would not be the one to teach him. He had enough to worry about.

///

The voices were unpredictable. They could stay silent for hours and then, unprompted, begin jabbering in Soujen's mind. The others had removed their earpieces and hidden their comlinks, but Soujen couldn't tear out his implants. The ghosts of Eyo-Dajuritz had free rein to mock him and express the enmity of eons.

Soujen couldn't understand the words, but he didn't doubt the ghosts' intentions. The guerrillas, the Imperials, all of them were intruders on a world that should've been left in peace. They'd dredged up spirits, and those spirits now watched as foreigners trekked across sacred soil and trampled primeval monuments. Soujen recognized, where the others did not, what it meant to lose a civilization—for a species to wither and disappear. He understood the hatred such a species would have for all who came after. What loathing the dead must have for all who blithely disregarded a cosmic inequity.

Only Karama seemed to notice that Soujen was troubled.

"It's this place," he told her as they crossed a chasm bridged by a chain of crumbling stone disks.

He had no desire to discuss it further, but she looked across at him as they maneuvered a hoversled over the span. Her skepticism was obvious. "You were going to torture the secretary, back in the cache. You were furious."

He scowled but did not answer.

"Did you find what you wanted? In the databanks?" she asked.

"No."

"I'm sorry." She paused. "I don't know what you were hoping for, but I wish you'd found it."

"We found enough," he told her. So he'd told himself. But although the plunder on the hoversleds would be useful, it gave Soujen no means to exact vengeance on a galactic scale. And the files he'd managed to extract (the rest were gone now—*You kept the data out of enemy hands*) had little that was relevant: write-ups of past Separatist psy-op campaigns and weak points in Republic blockades long since dissolved. There were hundreds of documents still to examine, but only two had carried meaning so far:

The first file had contained a list of Separatist caches, their locations and timelines for completion, and the names of ranking Separatists compiling an overriding strategy for use in the event of the Confederacy's defeat. The master strategy document was to be finalized roughly one year after the construction of the first cache. According to Soujen's reading of the timeline, Separatist Intelligence had barely begun work on the project by the war's end. In all likelihood, there was no doomsday plan in place, no clear directive as he'd desired—just Soujen and whatever resources he could muster.

The second file had contained a stylized picture of his body and his implants, neatly annotated, with pages of documentation outlining his abilities and his restrictions. He read about programs concealed in his software, hidden in the dark places of his databank. The Separatists had built in safeguards, means of controlling their operative, ways to induce pain and ways to shut him down entirely. These did not surprise him.

An attached personality profile described him as "not unintelligent but lacking formal education . . . possessing self-destructive tendencies, a deep-set rage, and a profound incuriosity about the world around him. The project," the file said, "will provide him much-needed purpose and an excuse for violence—his drugs of choice to escape self-reflection." There was more—about his species, baseless speculations about the "traumas" of his childhood, patronizing notes suggesting that, in the eventuality of Separatist victory, Soujen could "overcome his personal challenges" and rise to a position of leadership. He was "still capable of love and courage." He skimmed portions and deleted the file before reaching the end.

The author was unlisted. Perhaps it had been Tychon Nulvolio. Perhaps it had been Dr. Ro-Yai, who had seemed to care for Soujen. Neither, he thought, had ever really understood him. He considered discussing the matter with Karama, but he couldn't bring himself to broach it—not in front of the ghosts.

///

They next rested twelve hours later. By then they'd nearly lost the trail of the excavation droids. The caverns were so vast that the guerrillas struggled to find breach points. The group wandered an underground city, passed through fossilized pyramids, and followed trenches in the cavern floor two meters deep—the tracks of some gargantuan train system. On occasion, they heard a faint rumble from the tunnels behind them. They debated whether the sound indicated pursuit—the clones setting off traps—or if it was merely the rock settling.

When Soujen attempted to sleep, the ghosts whispered. He distracted himself with the files he'd downloaded from the cache, searching through meaningless reports on troop deployments and secret projects that would never be completed. When he dreamed, he dreamed of Eyo-Dajuritz as a once-living thing, the rotting corpse of a world whose flesh had decayed and whose bones gleamed from under piles of soil and the tarry void of space. Eyo-Dajuritz turned to him as Soujen stood on an endless plain under a red sky, a land without land, and the world screamed at him in static, screamed without words: *I will consume you, and the seven clans will suffocate in my stomach. I am a planet, and in eons I will still be here, whereas you will only nourish me. You will disappear from memory with your people, who have no homeworld to remember them.*

He fought as a million hands grasped him. Fingers wormed into his ears, pushed soil up his nose. Thumbs punched through his scalp plating and touched his brain. He tried to use his shock conductor, his microlaser, all the weapons of his body, and all of them were gone.

Then he was no longer fighting the ghouls of Eyo-Dajuritz. The hands became wind, and the soil became sand. The air shimmered with blue and red lightning as the clones marched toward him and he shot back, barely able to see through the veil of dust. "Get down!" he heard. "Get down!" And he dropped back into a bunker as a detonator erupted and sent a flaying wave of sand overhead.

This was a memory, or an illusion of a memory, and he knew what was coming.

There had been six of them. This had been before the implants, in the first few months of the war, when the Confederacy had contracted him for a mission on Leyoye Prime. The mission had gone well. He'd planted the bomb and escaped the city, only to find himself without a means to exfiltrate.

Thus, he'd joined the Separatist forces trapped on the planet with him. They'd fought to survive without battle droids or starships, suffered as the Republic pushed their lines back kilometer after kilometer. There had been six of them in his unit: Poan of Riek, Delsh Oquan, Baby Yezz, Seebee One, Bargaz Barnok, and Soujen. Then there had been five, then four, until finally there had been Soujen and Poan. They had grown close, as beings grow close in the fields of war.

Poan had wept when he'd killed his first clone. The others had told him, "They're only clones," and Poan had agreed, but he said he wasn't sure he could fight against a real person—a person with a homeworld, family, and memories like his own. He'd been sure that diplomacy would end the war swiftly, and that even if the Republic Senate and the Supreme Chancellor remained unreasonable, the Jedi would set things right. Poan had told Soujen, "The Jedi believe in peace above all else. They won't take sides. They're not *political*. But they won't let this war keep going."

Poan had never met a Jedi until that day on Leyoye Prime—until a shadow in the sand had sped ahead of the clones and leapt, seeming to spring from sizzling particle bolt to sizzling particle bolt, bare feet touching fire. Poan had watched the Jedi bring her laser sword down and cut through the shell of a bunker, tossing bodies into the sand with a gesture, then moving to another bunker, and another.

Poan and Soujen had both survived that day, but they'd lost the battle and fled the field and seen dozens massacred. One Jedi had been a weapon capable of bringing ruin without a word or an army.

When Soujen woke on Eyo-Dajuritz, the ghosts were no longer speaking to him through the static. He stared into the darkness and saw the faded dream, saw the last glimmer of the Jedi's sword.

He understood, with the quiet force of a revelation, why he had reacted to the words of Senator Organa, why he cared that Organa had come to exonerate the Jedi.

The Jedi who had been a weapon of terror once could be a weapon of terror again, one that could be turned upon the Empire.

///

After he woke up, it took him twenty minutes to confirm what he'd expected and another twenty to interrogate everything his instincts told him. He then spent an hour browsing files from the cache, seeking alternatives one final time.

His superiors had understood neither his motives nor his methods. He was a man who used the tools given to him, and it was time to make the best of his circumstances.

///

Organa and his secretary were gone when Soujen went to check. Most of the guerrillas were asleep. The great underground city offered many hiding places, and for a moment Soujen feared he'd missed his opportunity. But as he scanned the electromagnetic spectrum and stared into a haze of radiation, the distant glow of Bail Organa and Haki Nevzal stood out like a beacon.

He stalked them in silence. He took care to tread on no artifact from the ancients of Eyo-Dajuritz. His eyes perceived a churning mist of energies, pulsing like the static in his ears. And just as voices had emerged from the static, he perceived figures coalescing at the periphery of his vision. He did not look toward them. He did nothing to summon their attention.

Saw had said the voices were stray transmissions from some ancient device. As the sounds persisted, Vorgorath had suggested that there were no voices at all, "only our minds straining to find meaning in disorder, like looking for shapes in clouds." Either might have been right. But Soujen believed in ghosts. He saw no reason to take chances.

The secretary spotted him first. She was helping Organa into a trench when some shift in the shadows gave Soujen away. Organa and the secretary began to run, and Soujen increased his pace, chasing them into the trench.

He reverted his sight back to organic baseline. If he couldn't see the ghosts, they couldn't see him, and now he had his quarry. He could hear Organa and the secretary fumbling along the trench, panting for breath. Soujen no longer concealed his footsteps.

He saw black against black but intuited their presence ahead. He adjusted the power of his microlaser and released a burst in the darkness—a spark, enough to illuminate his face for a fraction of a second.

"You'll never leave these tunnels." The senator's voice came out of the void. "Not if you kill us. The clones won't allow it."

They were words of defiance from a man who believed he was doomed. Soujen recognized the tone.

"I have what you want," Soujen said. It was a statement of fact, not an enticement. "I have the files to exonerate the Jedi."

CHAPTER 35
THE DEAL STRUCK

The negotiations went smoother than Mon could've hoped. Most of the assembly had long since departed from the catacombs, leaving only Nulvolio and half a dozen of his associates as Mon walked through the Imperial Rebirth Act. Their discussions regarding conditions and sweeteners were neither brief nor contentious, and when anyone took exception to the bill's language, it became clear that Nulvolio's word was all that mattered. Mon had been a pawn in his game to secure power over his coalition. But having won the match, Nulvolio was ready to put his capital to good use.

She drafted requested alterations, mostly related to the Emperor's authority over military deployments. When the conference finally came to an end, Nulvolio dismissed his associates and the Separatist representatives retreated into the shadows. Somewhere in the distance, Mon heard a repulsorlift, echoing and distorted by the brick catacombs.

"We're agreed, then?" she asked.

Nulvolio stepped back from the dais they'd used as a conference table. He studied her, then inclined his head. "We are agreed."

"You could have asked for more," she said. "You could have asked to have the burden of reparations lifted, requested additional funds to rebuild your worlds—"

"And you would have accepted, having no other choice. And the bill would fail to pass." Nulvolio's lips curled back. "I am not new to politics, only to your Senate. I have no intention of slitting my own throat."

"Then I think we'll work well together."

"Perhaps. Should your efforts succeed, that will be put to the test. What I've not asked for today I may ask for tomorrow, and if you refuse then I will commit to your destruction."

"In order to placate your allies?" she asked. "Or because you are a vengeful and dangerous man?"

Nulvolio laughed. He gestured for Mon to follow him, and they left the chamber through another archway, not the one she'd entered through. Nulvolio seemed at home in the catacombs, and Mon wondered how much time he'd spent over the years walled up in darkness. She wondered how war would have shaped her politics if she'd first taken office during a conflict that had stolen the lives of trillions.

"I meant what I said," she told him. "I'll do whatever I can to keep this from backfiring on you. Even if the bill fails, I won't let the administration blame the Separatist worlds."

She had enough blood on her hands and guilt on her soul.

Nulvolio said nothing as they walked on. In a small brick chamber much like all the others, he rhythmically tapped the mortar. Metal doors slammed down from the archways, and the room began to shudder.

"You'll receive safe transport back to Coruscant," he said. "You're certain you'll be ready by Reintegration Day?"

"We should have most everyone we need already," she said. "We're down to the last holdouts, and the final bill won't take me more than a day or two to polish. After that we'll want a vote as soon as you and your people are sworn in. Give the administration no time to counter."

Nulvolio nodded. "The eyes of the galaxy—and the Emperor—will be upon us."

The room came to an abrupt stop, and Mon had to catch herself to keep from falling.

"As good a plan as I can expect," he continued, "as long as you can hold your people together between now and the vote. I won't interfere with your work, except to ask one final thing."

The request didn't surprise her. Now, with all witnesses gone, was the time for personal favors. But after the show he'd put on, he wouldn't risk overreaching.

"Go ahead and ask," she said.

"Have you heard news from Eyo-Dajuritz?"

That *did* surprise her. "What sort of news?"

"Any unusual activity, any military action or disruption of the protected zones since the war's end. Your sources are not my sources, and I wish to know the moment anything out of the ordinary occurs there."

"Is something worrying you?"

"Nothing we need be troubled by for the moment. But best to keep me informed, for all our sakes."

She'd been to Eyo-Dajuritz only once, early in her career as part of a goodwill tour promoting Republic historical sites. She'd wanted nothing more than to visit the surface—to walk through a preserved city that had been old before the discovery of interstellar travel—and to this day, she regretted leaving the tour early to see to a succession crisis on Chandrila.

She'd read histories of Eyo-Dajuritz. She'd fantasized about *writing* histories of Eyo-Dajuritz. It felt disconnected from war and Separatists and Empire, and discussing it in the context of power politics felt like an insult to its historical significance.

"If I hear anything, I'll make contact," Mon said.

"It may be nothing," Nulvolio said as the metal doors slid open. "Pray it's nothing."

CHAPTER 36
EXONERATION

"The databanks have been wiped by now. I made sure the detonators would do their work," Soujen said. He watched the senator and his secretary while they stared toward him in the dark. The secretary was seeking a weapon, a shard of rock or metal, with one hand. Soujen permitted this. He could snap her neck before she could bring any bludgeon to bear.

"But I downloaded the databanks' contents," Soujen went on. "Not everything. Enough. I have what you're after."

"You brought a backup," the senator said.

Soujen extended the length of cable from behind his elbow, then let it spool back inside his body. "Of a sort. My body can decrypt files you could never access. I have tactical data, target lists, propaganda files— I was built to be the death of the Republic. I'll show you."

He turned his back on them and walked. He wondered whether the secretary would run or strike, but she sensibly did neither and blindly followed him with the senator. That was good. He would kill them if he had to, but now they were useful. It annoyed him barely at all that Saw had been right.

⫽ ⫽ ⫽

He borrowed a handheld projector from Karama, abandoned the secretary under Vorgorath's guard, and brought the senator into the mouth of a fossilized pipe. They sat across from one another as Soujen plugged himself into the disc and played his first recording.

Motes of light sprung up and formed the hologram of a young woman. Weeping and furious, she talked about the child she'd had stolen by the Jedi. She'd never agreed to give her boy up, she said, but the Jedi had taken him anyway, and she'd spent years searching for him, going from temple to temple. When she'd found him at last, she'd learned that instead of training him, the Jedi had thrashed him, tormented him, and treated him as a house servant.

Soujen's attention stayed on the senator. The man's expression shifted from confusion to outrage before hardening into a mask.

"Lies," the senator said.

"Yes," Soujen agreed. "There's supporting documentation, but it's weak at best."

The next recording showed a Twi'lek dressed in farmer's robes speaking to a shadowed and shrouded being implied to be a Hutt. The imager's focus frequently shifted to a metal cylinder clipped to the man's belt as the two figures discussed the exorbitant fees the Twi'lek, as a representative of the Jedi Order, would need to provide his services to the underworld. The Republic, the Twi'lek noted, was paying far more.

This time, the senator shook his head and laughed. "It's absurd," he said. "No one would believe it."

"*Someone* would," Soujen said. "Not most, but someone."

"That's not even a real lightsaber on the 'Jedi.'"

"Untrue," Soujen said. "The weapon was from the personal collection of General Grievous."

The third recording was a statement from a clone trooper lambasting the Jedi for incompetence and accusing them of prolonging the war intentionally. This recording was, as far as Soujen knew, unscripted and delivered by a real prisoner of war. It was not the most convincing of the three, to his mind—the actress anguishing over her lost child was sur-prisingly persuasive—but his files flagged the clone's statement as being of high value.

The senator didn't watch for more than a minute before slamming his palm over the projector. "Why are you showing me these?" he asked. "I know all about the Separatist propaganda operations. I know none of it's true. But that's not what I came for."

"Think of it as context," Soujen said. "You want to show your people that the Confederacy was escalating its efforts to smear the Jedi. You're building a case. Are you not?"

"Do you have the proof I'm looking for? Tell me or stop wasting my time."

Soujen studied the senator. Showmanship was not Soujen's specialty, but he needed Organa to believe.

"I have documents under seal of the Jedi Archives," Soujen said. "Re-cordings, too, all suggesting the Jedi would attempt to remove the Su-preme Chancellor by force." He looked to the projector until Organa removed his hand, then fed a new image to the unit.

Photons whirled and formed a two-dimensional image in three-dimensional space: the crest of the Jedi Order, a winged blade repre-senting fire and battle and triumph. The crest shifted to one side as ancillary text scrolled up beside it, meant to indicate the authenticity of the seal; the date of document creation and the date of sealing; the Jedi who had placed the seal; and a dozen other points of data that had re-ceived the Jedi's blessing, formalizing the inalterability of the docu-ment.

Aside from the marker of authenticity, the fields were blank—ready to be filled in by the file's possessor.

"I don't understand the techniques," Soujen said, "but I possess the raw data. Proof the seals can be forged, along with originals of the falsi-fied documents."

Senator Organa rose with a roar of triumph, nearly slamming his skull into the underside of the pipe. He grinned, seemed about to reach out to Soujen, then offered a sickly laugh. "I knew it. I knew."

"The files are useless without me," Soujen said. "I've keyed them to my biological signature, and if I die my implants will erase themselves. If you want to present your evidence to the Empire, you require my willing assistance."

The senator sat down again. "What do you want?" he asked.

"I'll think it over," Soujen said, climbing out of the pipe. "But I'm not your only problem. You'll need to win Saw over as well."

///

Soujen left Organa behind. The senator would not flee, not now. He'd make his own way back to the guerrillas, who were already preparing to move on.

Soujen considered his parting words and wondered: Was it cruelty that had made him lie about Saw? A way of punishing the senator for his crimes against the Separatists? A way to claim vengeance for the Nahasta clan and for Poan and all who'd died in the war, in one small and petty way? He hadn't *needed* to leave Organa in doubt, and now the senator would be fretting about how to make a pact with Saw Gerrera.

Maybe cruelty played a role. But so did pragmatism. Saw would need to be coerced into cooperation (or otherwise dealt with), and why not have the senator do the dirty work? Easier than expending Soujen's own credibility and easier than betrayal. He wasn't ready to sever his partnership with Saw—the plunder could still serve him, as could the guerrillas. Plus, Soujen couldn't have Organa worrying too much about Soujen's own motivations.

Because Organa's secretary was probably right. There was no better way to cast the Empire into endless war than by convincing its population they'd been betrayed. The Separatist movement was defeated, but there was still discontent and fury among thousands of worlds, fury that could be directed toward Soujen's enemies. Saw and the guerrillas were proof that there were people who'd take up weapons against their own government if properly inspired.

Soujen had no army. But over a decade or two, after enough spaceport bombings and kidnappings and pointless revolutions, perhaps he could inflict enough damage to begin balancing the scales.

CHAPTER 37
PRIORITY
INTELLIGENCE

"From the beginning. What's your name?"

"Chemish Runazha."

"And who sent you?"

"No one sent me."

"You told the front office—"

"I said I work for Haki Hakaryeung. I'm her apprentice."

Chemish was doing their best, but this was their third interview since coming to Imperial Intelligence, and Chemish's frustration was starting to show. Their latest interviewer was a bored-looking man, barely old enough to shave, who steadily tapped at a datapad he didn't actually look at.

Chemish had come to report on the 4040s, the imperialist activists who were planning *something* for the Separatist reintegration and who'd wittingly or unwittingly created the circumstances that led to Zhuna's murder. But no one seemed to know who Chemish was. Chemish was starting to wonder whether Haki had bothered naming them in the official records at all.

For that matter, maybe Haki Hakaryeung wasn't their mentor's real name. Or worse, maybe Haki wasn't part of Imperial Intelligence, and

Chemish had been recruited to spy on Zhuna and Senator Mothma by some rival faction—

"Sorry," the young man said. "Just to make sure I've got it right—can you spell your last name again?"

Chemish nodded slowly. Frustration could be good, they thought. Repetition could be good. They kept the mind from spiraling, like meditation. Chemish wasn't skilled at meditation, but they kept trying, and there was a reason for that.

When the conversation came back around to the 4040s, Chemish was ready. Chemish told the man about the group's leadership, how they'd harbored extremists before, and how they'd talked about *action* coming up. "I don't know what they're planning," Chemish said. "Maybe it's nothing. Maybe they just want to yell at the Separatists and show the galaxy that nothing's forgiven. But they're organized, and they're up to something, and I wanted to make sure somebody knew."

The young man asked questions, but they were mostly about spellings, dates, times—all the trivial bits that would fill out his report. Chemish stayed calm and wondered whether they'd be transferred to yet another questioner afterward.

There were no windows in the office, and the light seemed to cast a gray patina over everything. The man's sleeves smelled of garlic. He looked down at the datapad, reviewed everything he'd entered, then looked back to Chemish. "You said they'd been tracking Senate staffers during protests?"

"That's right."

"And they've been protesting at Senator Mothma's offices?"

"On and off, yes."

"I'd like to see the surveillance data."

You're missing the point, Chemish wanted to say. But it made sense. If Chemish had been their source inside Mothma's office—if *Zhuna* had been their source—then they were blind now. They wanted to fill in whatever they'd missed.

"I don't have a copy. I can tell you what I remember," Chemish said, and for the next two hours they reported everything they could recall. Other officers came in and out of the room, making their own queries about Mothma and her staff, and by the end Chemish began to wonder what was going on inside Imperial Intelligence.

When the interrogation was finished, and Chemish had provided their name and contact information once again, and the young man had consulted with one of his superiors awhile, an older man entered the room. His drab, gray-green uniform was immaculate and his grooming impeccable, and he dismissed his younger colleague before walking to each of the room's corners, tapping the panels that—thanks to Haki's training—Chemish assumed housed cams and pickups. Then the man bent over Chemish and said, barely audible even up close, "Homish was your brother? Is that right?"

Chemish felt a surge of relief—not just to be understood, but to be recognized for who they were. "Yes."

"Good man, Homish. I liked him. A lot of people liked him. So we're going to cut you loose. We're going to pretend you never said you were apprenticed to Haki"—he hesitated—"Hakaryeung, because that's trouble you don't need."

"What kind of trouble?"

"You don't need to know. Just . . . Haki is done. She's out, even if she doesn't know it. That's fine if you're one of her sources, less so if you're her apprentice. You understand?"

Chemish had questions—too many questions—and pared them down as fast as they could. They wanted to know more about Haki's trouble, more about the implications. But what were the odds they'd get an answer? Finally, they settled on, "If that's true, why would you tell me?"

The man snorted and shook his head. "I'm out myself, soon. Retiring, before Bariovon and his lot do to me what they did to her. Now . . ." He straightened up, snapped his fingers, and looked at all four wall panels again before saying louder, "Think carefully. Is there anything else you know about Mon Mothma? Anything at all you can tell us?"

Chemish stared and thought, *What have you done to Haki?*

But Haki could take care of herself. Chemish had their own problems. These people clearly didn't know about Zhuna, or they were pretending not to. They didn't know Chemish could talk about Mothma for hours, reciting her lunch orders, shuttle habits, and taste in popular music, everything their cousin had ever told them. And whatever was going on was too complex, too layered and fraught with internal politics, for Chemish to make sense of it.

Chemish wanted to be forthright and honest, and if they were, they'd never get back to the 4040s. At worst, they'd be arrested.

Chemish believed in the Empire and in the role of Imperial Intelligence to ensure stability. But they weren't an idiot.

"That's all," Chemish said. "Thank you for listening to me."

CHAPTER 38
A TRADE,
A COMPROMISE,
DEATH

They heard bombs going off one by one, faint at first then growing louder over the course of the day. With each clap, Bail imagined the deaths of clones—devoted men who'd never chosen this life. He imagined them crouching over the bombs and blown apart before they could disarm them, marching through tunnels and dead in a flash, or bleeding out while medics scrambled to strip their armor. He remembered Olkrastrus IV, where he'd stood atop a mine and talked his way to survival. The troops who hunted him now had no one to bargain with.

Once, after he heard a scream, he told himself in an effort to harden his heart, *They killed the Jedi. They cut down children.* But the clones were not the murderers. They were only the murder weapon, and every explosion felt like an assault on decency and righteousness. Killing clones wasn't much different from killing Jedi.

He no longer spoke to Haki, and Haki did not speak to him. Their divide ran too deep to mend for now. Bail guessed she was still looking for ways to escape and cursing him for his alliance with Soujen. Perhaps she would come around later. In the meantime, he helped Karama with the hoversleds, offered Vorgorath assistance with a makeshift map, and did his best to watch Soujen and Saw. Soujen had said Bail would need to deal with the guerrilla leader, but Saw had shown nothing but disdain for his hostages. For the moment, Bail's best chance was with the others.

He knew he wasn't thinking straight. It had been days since he'd had adequate food or water. His body still failed him at unexpected times, seizing up with pain, and he hadn't slept more than an hour or two in recent memory. His eyes ached from staring into the dark. Yet Soujen had offered him hope, and he'd be damned if he threw that away.

They came abruptly to their journey's end in a broad, flat cavern, with dozens of hollow pillars rising into the ceiling. Vorgorath was shining a light on a metallic hulk standing before an unmarked rock face. It was the wreckage of a Separatist excavation droid.

"Must have been low on power," one of the guerrillas said. "Tore itself apart trying to punch through."

"Then we look for another exit," Saw said.

They fanned out around the cavern. They discovered gargantuan stone doors like those of a hangar bay, sealed for epochs. They peered inside the pillars, but those were impossible to climb through. They returned to the excavation droid and argued over what lay beyond the wall. As the minutes passed, they all grew frustrated. Bail had suffered, but so had the guerrillas. They'd seen a companion die by Haki's blaster, risked their lives in the cache, marched with little sleep or sustenance. And now they were trapped.

"We should've fought back at the start," one of the group muttered. "Back when we were fresh. By now they'll have sent in a damn army."

"Regrets won't help," Vorgorath said with a snarl. "We need a way out."

"We don't even know where we are," another replied. "Tried boosting the signal, but we can't reach the *Dalgo*."

Saw and Soujen joined the group, maneuvering among the hoversleds floating serenely near the excavation droid. Another bomb went off, close enough to vibrate the rock.

"We've got to use the hostages," Karama said. She glanced toward Bail with a tortured expression, then looked swiftly back at Saw. "They're our only advantage, and we don't have time to come up with a better plan."

"Trade us, threaten us, you'll still be trapped," Haki said. She sounded disappointed. "They'll never let you get to the surface."

Saw shook his head. "You're probably right, but you may still be our best hope." He looked first to Haki, then to Bail, as if awaiting a counteroffer.

You're running out of options, Bail. You may as well try.

He straightened his back despite the weakness in his knees. "I believe the clones are here to destroy us," he said, looking from Saw to the others. "At the very least, I believe that the clones came to stop us from finding files inside the cache, and that they have no intention of rescuing Haki or me. Our safety means nothing to them. Turn us over and you'll only make yourselves more vulnerable."

A man behind Bail started laughing. Karama asked, "The databank files?" while the woman called Nankry shouted accusations. Saw watched in silence. Soujen, after a pause, stepped forward and spoke—voice low, yet able to penetrate the debate.

"I believe him," Soujen said. "But it doesn't matter without an escape plan."

Nankry swore twice, then asked, "Can't we blast our way out? Go where the droid was going?"

Saw scowled. "Vorgorath, what explosives do we have? What would happen if we tried?"

"There's enough detonite to blow a city. Quantity isn't the problem. Shaped charges, scans of the caves, reinforcement fields . . . we have none of them. We might collapse the cavern. Or we might blast a hole to nowhere."

"What about the doors?" Bail asked. "They must go somewhere."

This started another round of debate. Karama eventually proposed rigging both the doors and the wall to expand their options and confuse their pursuers. Vorgorath objected, but Saw agreed and ordered any of the guerrillas not trained in explosives to stand guard at the cavern entrance. "If the clones come, hold them off."

The guerrillas scrambled. Bail took his opportunity—what he suspected might be his last—and approached Saw. "We need to talk," Bail said. "About your mission and about Soujen."

Saw arched his brow. He shot a glance to Soujen, who seemed to have heard. The Alvadorjian shrugged.

There was a noise from the entrance. Bail heard the voice of a clone shouting commands.

"Talk fast," Saw said, and the shooting began.

/ / /

The cavern was alight with blue fire. Barrages of particle bolts struck the cave roof and sparked against the pillars, never connecting with the guerrillas but forcing them to stay low. It wasn't an attack but a siege, a means for the clones to exhaust and demoralize them before finally pushing forward.

"How do you suppose they'll come?" Saw asked. He had his rifle unslung, and crouched with Bail behind the excavation droid.

"You'd know better than I," Bail replied. "I've spoken to many clones, but rarely about tactics."

Saw grunted. "Tell me what you want."

Bail thought about everything he could say—everything he knew about the death of the Jedi and the true nature of the Emperor, about his mission to the cache, about Soujen and Haki and the politics of the moment. There was so little time. He had to play to his strengths and pray that Saw was cooperative—that the man's proclivity for violence was half an act, and that honesty and compassion would bridge the rest of the gap.

Give me strength, he thought, hoping the ghosts of the Jedi could hear him over the wraiths of Eyo-Dajuritz.

"Soujen has files that can expose the crimes of the Imperial regime," Bail said. "Files I came looking for, which he obtained from the cache."

"So?"

"So, with his help I can use that information. I can embarrass the Emperor. More than that, I can use it to launch a public investigation into all Palpatine's sins."

Saw gestured sharply and spoke into his comlink. Somewhere across the cavern the guerrillas returned fire. Then Saw nodded to Bail, and Bail continued, "If you want Onderon's freedom, if you want to hurt the Emperor, Soujen and I can accomplish more through politics and the media than you'll manage through blasters and bioweapons. You're stockpiling to fight a war, but your people . . . You chose not to surrender to the Empire, but you didn't *want* this fight. What if it's not necessary at all?"

"What if I'm wasting my time?" Saw asked with a sardonic smile.

"What if your work is finished?" Bail asked. *You want to be persecuted? Be persecuted. You want to save the galaxy? Save the galaxy. Just give me what I need.* "You kept your people alive. You won the war. You found the cache. Get us out, and this could be your last battle."

There was a break in the blasterfire. Saw looked worried and called into the comlink for a status report. Bail couldn't hear the reply, but Saw nodded grimly. "Prep for detonation." He turned back to Bail. "This can wait until we're free."

"It *can't*, though." Bail grasped Saw's shoulder, demanding his attention. "Because we're boxed in, and you and I both know this could go wrong. You need to prioritize. Do you want the supplies? Do you want the clones dead? Or do you want to get Soujen and me off this planet?"

The guerrillas were changing position. Bail saw lights moving out of the corner of his eye, but he kept his gaze on Saw.

"You know he's not one of us?" Saw asked. For the first time, Bail heard real anger slip into the man's voice, something concealed brought to the surface. "You know he's a Separatist? He came from *this place*. Separatist Intelligence chose him because of the crimes he committed, the ruthlessness he displayed—because they trusted him to embody the spirit of murder that drove the Confederacy."

Bail shook his head and released Saw's shoulder. The words were a blow, and he flinched but recovered. "I didn't know. What does it change? He has the files—"

"He will betray you."

"If he brings the files to the Senate, let him kill me. I'll consider my duty fulfilled."

To set matters right, he *would* die willingly. The Jedi would be avenged, the friends who'd fought and fallen for the Republic would have their sacrifices honored, and Leia would know her father as a hero instead of the man who left her to contend with the terrors of the galaxy. Bail's journey would be complete, and his death would be noble. Saw seemed to hear him, and the man's anger seemed to retreat into vague disdain—as if Saw had been right about Soujen and Bail but was disgusted nonetheless.

"Your codes," Saw said.

"What?"

Now Saw had purged even the disdain. His diction was clipped and urgent but otherwise gave away nothing. "Give me your codes—your diplomatic IDs, your Senate access privileges. You say you can strike a blow for Onderon if you steal one of my people. I want something in exchange, in case your plan doesn't work."

"They'll change codes the moment they confirm I was here. They may have changed them already—"

"Then I'm taking a risk, aren't I?"

Bail wondered how much of this Saw had gamed out. Had he been looking to extract Bail's authorization this whole time? Breha would've seen it coming. Even if it wasn't a ploy, Bail would be handing vital keys over to a man he didn't trust.

What would Saw do if he agreed? Bail felt the aches of his injuries and wondered.

The clones were shooting again. This time the blaster bolts were joined by sizzling flares launched deep into the cavern, sending light and shadow streaking across stone.

"Nobody dies," Bail said. "That's my condition. I give you the codes, you give me Soujen, and you give me your word that whatever you're plotting, you don't *kill* anyone."

"Conditions. You really are a senator." Saw made a sound of pure revulsion. "Good enough—assuming any of us live."

CHAPTER 39
FALL

The guerrillas were regrouping in the cavern's center, with the hoversleds arrayed toward their rear. That struck Haki as optimistic: Despite everything, Saw Gerrera was still hoping to keep the plunder out of the line of fire and haul it safely off Eyo-Dajuritz.

Haki was squatting behind a pillar, two meters from a flare that hissed and spat and smelled like a burning credit chip. She rotated her attention from the sleds to the guerrillas surrounding her to the distant forms of Bail and Saw as they waved Soujen over. She didn't know what those three were discussing, and she was too far to read lips, but she could guess the gist. Bail was cutting a deal with the terrorists, looking for a way to get himself and Soujen out alive so he could pursue his fantasy of exposing Palpatine's supposed crimes. He was cutting a deal, and he was cutting Haki out—not out of malice but out of pragmatism. She'd said too many careless things and lost his trust, and soon she'd pay the price.

You should never have left Coruscant, she thought. *You should've stayed behind and kept an eye on Chemish. You're too old for lies and cover stories and asset cultivation, Haki. You're too old for the work, plain and simple.*

But of course, she hadn't left Coruscant for Bail Organa.

The trio scurried to join the rest of the guerrillas now, half crawling to avoid drawing fire. Haki looked from Soujen to the sleds to the guerrillas closest to her. *You can do it,* she thought, *if you time it right.* Trouble was, she didn't want to. There was a very good chance she'd end up dead.

But what was the alternative? Letting Bail's myopia ignite another war? Yes, Haki's superiors were idiots, and Imperial Intelligence had abandoned its mission. Yes, the administration was doubtless corrupt, and the Senate no better. But war was a horror unique in the galaxy, and Bail, with all his privilege and righteousness, didn't seem to realize he was asking countless people to suffer for his idea of justice.

Maybe he wasn't callous. Maybe he genuinely, foolishly believed he could oust Palpatine cleanly on the back of public outrage.

You know what you have to do. Quit dallying and act.

No one was looking her way. Karama was behind the next pillar over, but the woman was taking potshots at the clones. Saw was calling out orders, and Bail had arrived among the sleds, crouching under cover and hiding his face as they all prepared for the detonation. Soujen had found a pillar of his own at the guerrillas' vanguard and was peering toward the clones emerging from the cavern entrance.

This was her chance.

Haki scuttled back through the cavern to a sled stacked with small, flat boxes. She hunkered behind it. No one seemed to notice her. She adjusted the sled's repulsors so that it moved with only a tap, and she nudged it along toward the guerrillas again. One of Saw's people glanced back but didn't seem to register what was happening.

Saw called out a countdown. Clones kept marching out of the mouth of the cavern, intensifying their covering fire as they spread to flank. Haki stood and ran with the sled. As she passed the flare on the cavern floor, she scooped up the stinking, smoking, brilliant rod and tossed it among the stacked boxes. Then another push and the sled was flying into the midst of the guerrillas, the blinding flare at eye level.

There was a moment of confusion as the sled flew by. Haki kept up her momentum, angled to one side, and snatched Karama's sidearm as she passed the girl. She dashed on ahead and aimed as well as she could in the chaos. Boxes on the sled began popping and bursting.

Haki spied Soujen's face and snapped off three shots.

Without Soujen, Bail would have nothing to bring home. Without Soujen, Bail was just another senator—and not the worst by a long shot.

Someone shouted Haki's name. She wouldn't live much longer. She saw her shots go wide, and now Soujen was looking toward her, rising from his crouch, predatory eyes finding their target.

She was adjusting her aim when the nerves in her arm caught fire and the universe flashed blue. She didn't feel herself drop the pistol, but when her vision returned, the weapon was no longer in her hand. Her sleeve was aflame, exposed skin blackened. She'd been hit by one of the clones, and all she could think was, *I'm on your side, you fools!*

Saw's voice called, "Detonate!" and thunder struck the cavern.

Everything was bright. The clones and the guerrillas stopped shooting. They stopped shouting, too, or the noise of the explosions reduced their shouts to insignificance. Maybe part of it was the pain—with every instant the agony in Haki's arm grew worse, and the parts of her brain processing sound, sight, smell, and taste began shutting down. Her entire sensory world was contracting around her body.

But she still noticed when the thunder was followed by an even louder noise, like a mountain splitting. The guerrillas were running at the hoversleds, and the clones had resumed fire. Soujen was raising his rifle, and Bail was exposed, an easy target, yelling at Soujen. The cavern filled with choking dust; clones and guerrillas looked toward the walls and the roof as rocks tumbled free and pillars liquefied and burst. Only Soujen seemed undistracted, and the barrel of his rifle pointed Haki's way.

Then came the flood. One moment they were standing in the rumbling cavern, and the next all of them were struck by a torrent of water—overturning the hoversleds, snapping the remaining pillars, and smashing into guerrillas and clones. For Haki, the deluge was almost a relief—not because Soujen, too, was washed away, but because the pain of her arm was nothing compared with the sensation of the water bludgeoning her, enveloping her, and ending her journey through the ruins of Eyo-Dajuritz.

CHAPTER 40
ANOTHER ARREST

The trip home was easier than the trip out, though Mon never learned where she'd met Nulvolio and the other Separatists. After departing the catacombs, she'd donned a blindfold, felt the cold hand of a protocol droid on her shoulder, and been steered up a series of ramps and across deck plating and plush carpet. By the time she was permitted to see again, she was aboard a midsize luxury yacht. She carried documents indicating that she was one Gon Raithra of Metalorn, traveling to Coruscant.

Mingling with passengers and crew members seemed unwise, so she spent the trip listening to the public news feeds and editing her copy of the Imperial Rebirth Act. She expanded the sections of the bill she'd drafted with the Separatists, wrote and then deleted an introduction putting the declaration of Empire in historical context, and went down a mental checklist of all the deals she'd made and broken. The clean, elegant bill she'd promised the Delegation of 2,000 now had dozens of pages addressing droid labor laws, carve-outs for Historically Recognized Royal Families, tariff-free status for imported white membrosia ("in recognition of the beverage's unique cultural importance"), and a section guaranteeing continuing employment for the

regional governors within a "robust and functioning" security apparatus.

It was a monstrous assemblage of stitched-together parts, but its
heart—the reassertion of the Senate's powers and the diminution of the
Emperor's role—remained. Mon was proud of it, and even the accumulated detritus felt somehow appropriate. It was democracy embodied, in
all its compromises and tradeoffs, all its messy imperfection.

She thought it might even pass. She'd need her droids to project the
final count—it was no use calculating votes by hand when there were
thousands of representatives in play—but it *might pass.*

The public feeds were promising a grand ceremony, days away, marking the reintegration of Separatist worlds. Profiles of the incoming senators and praise for Emperor Palpatine's generous but security-minded
policies alternated with discussion of opposition to the event and interviews with "ordinary" citizens planning to protest. It was delicately balanced, Mon thought, which suggested the administration was taking
public opinion seriously. She suspected the hand of Grand Vizier Mas
Amedda, aiming to keep people angry and wary of the defeated Separatists without thwarting the reintegration altogether. Without Separatist
representatives, the Empire couldn't control the Separatist worlds—
but Palpatine and Amedda wanted those worlds to know their place.

Things would get messy. All Mon could do was hope her coalition
stayed together.

When the yacht landed, she started receiving calls. Her senatorial
staff, who'd frantically tried to cover for her absence, came first. She told
them which meetings to reschedule and which to postpone indefinitely,
suggested stances on the usual scandals and crises, and instructed them
to prepare for the reintegration. There had been multiple journalistic
inquiries about her disappearance, and she offered up a few lines her
speechwriters and press secretary could spin into a statement. Her staffers were clearly nervous about being kept in the dark, but they did their
best to hide it.

She checked her messages as she departed the spaceport. There were
check-ins from acquaintances, which she ignored, and calls from worried Senate colleagues, which she responded to as rapidly as she could.

Zar, Doroon, and Streamdrinker had queries and status reports about their own recruiting efforts for the Rebirth Act—no disasters, though loyalties were fragile at best. There were updates on the investigation into Zhuna's death (she saved these for later) and warnings from Senate Security (deleted). Breha Organa, Bail's wife, asked vaguely and cryptically for a meeting. Mon wondered whether the Queen of Alderaan was concerned that Mon's spat with Bail would have consequences for her domestic political situation. It wouldn't, but Mon could understand the thought.

There was nothing from Lud Marroi, which shouldn't have concerned her but did. When they'd last spoken, they'd argued—and then she'd sicced Imperial Intelligence on him for her own benefit. Given the argument, she'd have expected a thoughtful apology or at least a strained attempt at humor.

She was thinking about Lud, exiting a tram onto the boulevards of the Federal District, when she realized she should call her husband. She'd warned Perrin she would be gone awhile, and though she doubted he'd been fretting, she didn't want him to learn of her return from her staff. She had her earpiece in place and the comlink in her hand when the midday crowd parted around her and three uniformed figures approached.

The figures spread out as they closed the distance—not encircling Mon, not *aggressive*, but making it clear she wasn't to run. She didn't recognize the pale gray of their outfits (the administration seemed to introduce new designs daily), but each figure had the bearing of a security officer. Each wore a sidearm on their belt.

"Senator Mothma?" the first asked. He couldn't have been older than twenty, but his eyes were hard and his voice confident—a boy who'd seen the war up close.

"Can I help you?" she asked. She didn't put down her comlink. "I'm in a hurry—we can talk on the way to the Senate."

"We need you to come with us," the boy said. The others stepped closer to her. "You're being taken into custody."

She ignored the memory of her body, the revulsion and terror etched onto her by her last arrest.

"Why?" she asked.

"We have questions," the boy said, "about your association with Bail Organa of Alderaan."

He turned and began to walk. The others stood within arm's reach of her. They were presenting her options: She could follow and cooperate, or she could be manhandled into compliance. She did not believe they were bluffing.

She followed.

Bail, she thought. *What have you done to us all?*

And if the intelligence services had begun watching him at her instigation, what had she done to him?

CHAPTER 41
NO MARK LEFT
ON THE GALAXY

After the flood came darkness and pain and struggle. Karama lost her rifle in the first deluge, but when a hoversled tumbled toward her, she caught it, ignoring where the metal cut her hands, and hauled herself aboard. She knew she should look for other survivors, watch for clones, try to salvage whatever plunder was left. All she could do was hold on and try to avoid being dashed against the cavern walls.

The flares burned underwater, casting rippling light against the fossilized architecture and warping the shadows of clones and guerrillas into midnight titans. When the initial tsunami subsided, Karama powered up her sled's repulsors and paddled on her makeshift raft, racing from air pocket to air pocket, following the titans and not caring whether she chased friends or foes.

How many hours did the journey to the surface take? Everything since they'd captured the senator seemed an endless series of steps and aches and hunger pangs. The past few days were like the last days of the war, or the days in the camp on Atoa. They were a smeared charcoal portrait of memory, the discrete moments lost and reduced to a dream of what *had been*.

Now she floated free. The hoversled drifted on emerald waters in a vast lake under a rosy sky. She could barely lift her head after the batter-ing tides, but she forced her throbbing muscles into action and shoved toward a distant flotilla of other sleds tethered to one another with rope and cables. Four other survivors stood there, waving. Saw was among them, because Saw Gerrera always survived.

Soujen was missing, as were the senator and his secretary. Karama wondered distantly whether they were all dead. Soujen was strong, and his augs might have preserved him underwater. She would hold hope for him later. She had none to spare now.

"The *Dalgo*'s en route," Saw told her in a muffled voice, helping her tie her sled to the others. "Should be twenty minutes out, and we can't wait for anyone else."

Karama nodded vaguely. She understood the rules of war. If you were left behind, no one would come for you. You always said the opposite, told your comrades you would die for them, but that only went so far. The group came first. The cause came second. The individual was worth nothing.

She wondered why she had such trouble hearing Saw. She thought at first it was water in her ears, and then, looking up, wondered if it was the noise of the patrolling starfighters sweeping over Eyo-Dajuritz and searching for—well, *them,* though also the lost clones and the senator and who knew what else. Yet the fighters were distant. As she focused, she realized the noise overpowering all the others was irregular and drumlike. She scanned the horizon, squatting and propped on one hand.

The *wrongness* hit her before the explanation, just a sense that some-thing was profoundly *off* about the landscape. Then her eyes caught a distant motion, and a line of shadows she'd taken for mountains shifted and dissolved. Something gargantuan was crumbling into the water, and the sky above the mountains turned dark with dust.

Frantically, she looked all about her. She could see to the horizon in all directions, and in all directions shadows were collapsing and return-ing to the soil.

She understood what was wrong now: There were no skyscrapers around the lake.

There were no fossilized megastructures stretching to the sky. There were no amphitheaters or roadways or skeletons of metal beasts. There was water and, here and there, islands that glittered in the sunlight.

Karama remembered what she'd been told about Eyo-Dajuritz as a child—the holograms they'd seen in school, the enigma that had captivated a class of ten-year-olds for a month before they'd moved on to mythosaurs and podracing. And she remembered Saw briefing the team about the sensor network, the pains that the Eyo-Dajuritz authorities had taken to prevent anyone from landing and damaging a single square meter of the ruins.

A body threw shade into her eyes. Saw stood above her, and he, too, looked to the horizon.

"It's a pity," he said. "But no regrets."

What have you done? Karama thought, trying to tell herself not to ask questions that had no purpose, trying to bury her reporter's instincts to record atrocity for posterity. She listened to the drumbeat of catastrophe, and she joined Saw and the others as they prepared to leave the world they had destroyed.

PART III
DUSK

CHAPTER 42
THE MEMORY
OF FAMILY

He'd stripped off his clothing, but he still felt wet and cold. The odors of saltwater and moss lingered in his nostrils. Soujen was tired in a way he hadn't been since before his modification. He wanted to sleep. He wanted to shut down all input to his brain and recapture the darkness of his hibernation pod. He did not wish he'd died underground, and he did not wish to abandon his mission. But he wanted to leave the universe awhile and rest.

Bail Organa should have been in no better condition, but he possessed a buoyancy Soujen did not—as if his survival were a wonder worth celebrating. From the caverns, Soujen had dragged the senator through the water and eventually to land. Organa had barely spoken— spitting and coughing and shivering as they escaped the scene of destruction and hid from the starfighters overhead. Eventually the senator had managed to point. "My starship," he said. Soujen remembered the trajectory of Organa's ship, and Organa remembered the direction he'd come from, and they made the trek while Eyo-Dajuritz collapsed around them, eons of history brushed away as if by a cosmic hand. The ghosts in Soujen's ear screamed, but then the static grew overwhelming and the screaming stopped and eventually the static went, too. Organa leaned on Soujen's arm, and Soujen half carried the senator.

At one point Organa had asked, "What about Haki?"

Soujen replied, "Haki tried to kill me."

"I forgot," the senator said. Then he vomited seawater.

Now they were aboard Organa's vessel—a fine ship, maybe the most expensive personal transport Soujen had ever been aboard. Soujen slumped in the copilot's safety harness while Organa took them out of atmosphere and into hyperspace. They had not been pursued. Soujen supposed Eyo-Dajuritz's desecration had fooled the enemy's scanners.

He found he didn't care. Nor did he care enough to assert dominance over the senator. Soujen should've been making threats, warning Organa not to act on his own, making clear his own physical superiority. But he didn't.

He wanted to rest.

///

A few hours later, Bail Organa brought him tea and aromatic biscuits. Soujen consumed them methodically without leaving the copilot's seat. When he was finished, he looked up and saw that the senator was watching him with a face that feigned compassion.

"You're not eating?" Soujen asked, wondering for an instant whether he'd been poisoned.

"I ate earlier," Organa said. "You don't remember?"

Soujen didn't. He said nothing.

"You carried me out of there," Organa said. "I owe you my life."

Soujen watched the senator shift position in the pilot's seat. He moved like an injured man, avoiding pressure on half a dozen points. Still, his voice was strong.

The senator had a plan and a purpose. He had come for the Separatists' files, and his mission was nearly complete. Whereas Soujen's mission . . .

Soujen's mission had barely begun. He had lost the bounty of the cache. He had compromised himself, befriended foes of the Confederacy, revealed secrets meant for comrades and kin to a woman he barely knew. He had sacrificed his allies, drawn the eye of the Empire, and nearly lost his life to the water and the ghosts, all for paltry gains—all to take the first step of a journey light-years long.

These thoughts—frail thoughts, half-formed—drifted across his mind like flotsam and disappeared, quickly forgotten. It was the ghosts of Eyo-Dajuritz who were to blame, he decided. The ghosts had cursed him.

"We struck a bargain, you and me," Soujen said. "Where are we going?"

"Coruscant, but we're taking the long way around, in case anyone observed our jump." Organa glanced at the console, then back at Soujen. "Once we arrive, I'd like to take you directly to the chief justice. She's one of Palpatine's appointees, but she's not the sort to deny facts when they're in front of her. She'll get copies of your files, record your testimony, make sure there's an unimpeachable record of everything."

Soujen tried to imagine standing before the Imperial chief justice. Out of habit, he started thinking of ways to kill her. He started thinking of ways to kill Bail Organa.

"What's her name?" he asked.

"The chief justice?" Organa sounded surprised, but he rolled with the punch. "Ayelowa Kefarra."

Soujen accessed his files and scanned his suggested target lists. There was no reference to the name. That helped. Ignorance was a sort of darkness, and darkness was a sort of rest. "And after?" he asked.

"We go straight from the judiciary to the Senate. Someone may want to detain you, but I think I can buy us time. Once we arrive, you'll need to testify again, but I'll walk you through it. It'll all be a show for the cams, and with every senator and half the galaxy watching, Palpatine won't dare shut us down. If he does, he'll only look worse."

Soujen considered.

"And after?" he asked again.

Organa bowed his head and looked back to the console. "You didn't exactly volunteer to be a prisoner of the Empire, I suppose."

"No."

"But the rest—you'd be willing to testify, give us the files?"

"Yes."

Possibly.

"What about your price?" Organa asked. "You said in the caverns that you would think about it. Saw Gerrera had demands of his own, but—"

"But Saw does not speak for me, no. My price," he said. "My price."

Did he have a price? If so, he would need payment sooner rather than later. If he went to Coruscant with the senator, if he submitted to even a fraction of Organa's requests, he was unlikely to ever escape that sinister world at the Empire's heart. To be taken prisoner was unthinkable, but the other options were little less grim. Perhaps he could arrange an alternative, record his testimony aboard Organa's ship. But surely the more dramatic the revelation, the more chaos he would cause in the Empire, the more blood in the streets. If Organa's efforts failed, then Soujen was left with nothing—nothing from the cache, not even his alliance with Saw . . .

He wasn't thinking straight. He needed time. He needed rest.

"Home," he said. "Before anything else. Take me home."

He sounded young and vulnerable, and he wished he *had* spent the past hours threatening Organa and putting the senator in his place.

Organa only nodded. "Give me coordinates, and I'll set course."

/ / /

The native metal-eaters were nearly gone from Ylagia. The iron jungles grew wild, their jagged spears rising across the eastern continent. Yet enough metal-eaters remained to keep the jungles away from the city fortresses, to preserve the towers rising from the mountain stone and the spiral roads like halos. Every Ylagian city was *art* first and foremost, and the inhabitants, indigenous and otherwise, seemed to accept the cost of conservation.

"Maybe that's why they let us stay," Soujen said, half to himself and half to Organa, as their ship skimmed the bladed ground. "Ten years my clan has spent here—a long time for my people."

"I understand," the senator said. "You're not the first of your kind

I've met. Your people have suffered a great deal, and the Republic shares the blame."

Shares the blame. Soujen smiled bleakly. The senator was *almost* taking responsibility.

"You see Ologage? The city?" Soujen asked. The ship was cresting the hills now, and the mountain rose ahead. The spires and platforms glittered with color, like waterfalls of hue, simple turquoise and umber on the lower tiers, and exotics on the upper levels—melancholigo and amberwise. "They buy their paints from us but only let us through the gates to trade. We're thieves and mercenaries and parasites, they say."

The worst of his exhaustion had left him during the flight. His physicality felt restored—he felt capable of moving, of fighting, of killing again. Part of him wondered whether a visit to Ylagia was even necessary now that he was no longer weak. Yet he heard himself, and he knew something inside him remained fragile. The Soujen Vak-Nhalis who had emerged from the pod as a weapon of Separatist vengeance would never have spoken cordially with Senator Bail Organa, no matter whether circumstances dictated an alliance.

They found a spot to land, a rocky ledge on the mountainside, and checked for signs of Imperial pursuit. They discovered none. Ylagia's few port monitors had more than enough traffic to keep busy, making it unlikely the ship would draw any attention. Still, the world had belonged to the Separatist Confederacy during Soujen's last visit, and he reminded himself to be prepared for changes.

He grabbed a comlink and a canteen before heading to the boarding ramp. "I'll be a few hours—no more."

The senator followed him. "I'd prefer to stay together."

Soujen shrugged and left the ship. He heard Organa's footsteps behind him, but he didn't turn around.

Ylagia smelled of rust, and Soujen heard the metallic murmur of the steel-boring beetles rise from the jungle below. By the time the clan had relocated to Ylagia, he'd begun spending most of his days offworld, but he'd visited often enough that the place had a soothing familiarity. He knew the mountain's paths, its caves, and its switchbacks. Not everything was the same—landslides had ruined sections of the trails, and he saw distant bombardment craters—but he navigated without difficulty. Organa struggled behind him, and Soujen could hear the man's rough breathing and occasional pained grunts. Yet the senator never complained, and Soujen never stopped.

After about an hour, they emerged from a last set of tunnels and into a narrow rift that ran below Ologage. A red-brown creek flowed among the rocks. Soujen followed it through the chasm, only to stop abruptly when he rounded the first bend.

"What is it?" Organa asked.

Soujen proceeded ten meters down the rift. "This was home," he said. "This was where we camped."

The shantytown was gone. Half a kilometer farther along, they found signs of what had happened: burnt scraps of cloth, fragments of sheet metal that had been the walls of huts, and greasy soot still clinging to the chasm walls where the stone had been sheltered from rain and wind. Someone had torched the rift the Nahasta clan had called home.

Soujen felt no grief and he felt no fear. There was only a tension, a sense of disorder that troubled him. He halted at the mouth of a cave that had housed the Greater Wheel. It was now filled with piles of broken clay and metal and the skeleton of a burnt speeder. He supposed his people had attempted to protect their belongings there.

He squatted outside the cave and flexed his throat, pursing his lips and expelling the air in his lungs. The sound he made, half a whistle and half a moan, trailed off after only a moment. He thought at first that he was out of practice, then realized his body was no longer suited to the high songs of the clan. The implants that gave him the ability to breathe where others could not also impeded his airflow.

He felt Organa's eyes upon him as he tried again and again, seeking the sounds, the notes, that were his birthright. Finally, he produced a child's tremulous tune, the keening and the birdsong woven together in one melody. He maintained it for only seconds before it came apart. He hacked and coughed until his implants kicked in and regulated his breathing.

But the song had done its work. From the depths of the cave emerged a spinning cylinder of a droid, floating three meters above the ground.

"Soujen Vak-Nhalis," the droid said. "You have returned."

Soujen stepped up to the droid, which descended to eye level. He leaned forward, kissed the droid's cylinder, then spat into the groove of its cycler before stepping back. "I give you my genetic code, my heart, for the archives," he said. "Keep it as you keep the stories of our people."

"That is my purpose," the droid replied.

Then it flipped open a compartment, and a thread of light shot past Soujen. He turned to see the light fixed on Organa's forehead.

The senator stood very still, his arms at his sides. His eyes looked at Soujen.

"Your guest?" the droid asked.

"My guest," Soujen agreed. "He may live, and he may listen."

"He appreciates the generosity," the senator muttered as the droid switched off its targeting laser.

///

The droid, the sacred archivist of the Nahasta clan, keeper of memory and keeper of life, told them what had happened.

The enemy had come only in the final days of the war. The city of Ologage had turned on the Separatists and pledged its loyalty to the invading Empire, but the Imperial Army had feared resistance. As a precaution, the Imperials had ordered all beings camped outside the city walls to depart.

They had been given a day's warning. A small number of clan members had evacuated—the Vak-Tiin family, Orchros Vak-Porouth—but after a decade on Ylagia, the clan had struggled to uproot swiftly. They'd had no ships that could hold the Greater Wheel, nowhere to run but the deadly iron jungle. When the incendiaries had begun to fall (an hour before the deadline), they'd huddled in the caves and hoped for a miracle—a rainstorm to douse the fires, or a Separatist rescue.

No intervention came. The clan had died that day. Only the archive droid had remained.

Soujen watched the senator on and off throughout the telling, noting Organa's shift from horror to anger. It was a subtle performance, expressed through a wrinkled brow, a clenched jaw, a soft, throaty scoff. Soujen wondered whether it was sincere or for his benefit—or, more likely, both. Organa was a politician and a performer by nature.

The triple suns were setting, and Soujen announced to Organa that he would spend the night among the ruins. Organa said that he would stay as well, and though Soujen considered requesting solitude, he decided it didn't matter. There were no secrets of the clan left to keep.

Nor was there anything to do, really. There were no bodies. Anything living had been reduced to ashes, bones and all, and the ashes scattered by the wind. Soujen and Organa had brought no food, so there was nothing to cook or eat. The droid had erased those sacred shards of the Greater Wheel forbidden to outsiders. So Soujen paced through the rift and steeped himself in memories of his fathers and brothers. Even those were hard to dredge up, because of the damage to his mind and because there was nothing in the rift to remind him of the family he'd once had.

"I am sorry," Organa told him when it was dark and they sat together in the cave mouth. "I know it means nothing, but I *am* sorry."

"Your people did this," Soujen said.

The senator paused for a time, then replied, "They did."

Soujen felt a spark of fury that failed to catch fire. "Have you ever wondered," he asked, "if you were on the wrong side during the war?"

"You want my honest assessment?"

Soujen nodded.

"I'm not sure there *was* a right side," the senator said. "I opposed the Separatist Confederacy because it chose violence when other paths remained. It seemed to me—it still seems to me—that its cruel tactics and disregard for life were inseparable from the greed that drove the Confederacy's corporate elite. I also acknowledge that many well-meaning people saw matters differently and opposed the Republic for good and moral reasons.

"I've come to wonder if the whole war was a sort of feint—half a misdirection on the part of those who desired an Empire. Palpatine and his cronies pushed and pushed until the fighting started. Count Dooku was a . . ." He paused. "The particulars don't matter. But by joining the war, all of us played into Palpatine's hands."

Soujen laughed wearily. "Which would make you as much a victim as my clan. Is that correct?"

"There's no comparison to draw."

"Convenient, how you're spared the burden of the Republic's sins."

Soujen stretched his limbs. To calm himself, he ran a self-diagnostic and confirmed his implants were fully functional. He stared into the blank spaces of his databank and found the darkness soothing. "I joined the Separatist cause and accepted modification because the Separatists pledged assistance to my people. But by the end, I believed. I believed in the side that didn't breed soldiers in vats or send *diplomats* to make peace with laser swords. I believed that even if the Republic was little worse than the Confederacy, it held too much power. The galaxy was better off divided."

Organa's face twisted up, but he didn't take the bait. He shrugged and said, "The modifications—how extensive are they? I was told there were experimental techniques . . ."

"They are *effective*."

They fell into silence. The darkness grew deeper, until Soujen could no longer see Organa's expression.

The senator said, "We could go to Alderaan."

"Instead of Coruscant?"

"We have medics who could remove the augmentations, if you wanted. We could get you a new identity, set you free to reunite with your people—one of the other clans, if you can't find the survivors of Ylagia." The senator's voice seemed to draw both strength and intimacy from the shadows. "There's still beauty in the galaxy, opportunities outside war and suffering. There's no shame in stepping away from the fight for a day or a lifetime."

Soujen wondered if he would have said as much in daylight. It seemed *off* for a man who'd caused such ruin seeking to exonerate the Jedi.

But what had driven Organa to make the offer, whatever need or ploy, was irrelevant. There was no departing from the path Soujen was on.

"No," Soujen said. "There's no reason to go to Alderaan."

/ / /

Soujen did not sleep, but his memories mingled like dreams. He saw his childhood practice palette, slathered in paint he'd ruined and turned to umber. He was six years old, and in his mind's eye he carried the palette as his eldest father took him on a trading mission. They came to the studio of a sculptor, promising colors to bring his statues to life, and Soujen craned his neck and peered at the slabs of basalt, laser-cut into the shapes of living beings. The studio smelled of burning stone. Soujen's eyes stung.

The sculptor was speaking—to his father or to Soujen?—and carving away at a pillar. Emerging from the rock was the jagged geometry of a man, with blunted limbs and facets instead of features. The sculptor said, "Each begins unformed. Each begins a potential philosopher, warrior, mother." With a flick of his wrist, he loosed a crimson arc from his wand that pared stone from the statue's arm. "But look! Child, I have made a mistake! Retrieve that for me!"

Soujen looked to his father, who nodded. Soujen scurried to the statue and lifted a shard of rock from the dented metal floor. It was nearly too heavy for his spindly frame, yet he presented it to the sculptor, who struck Soujen's arm and sent the rock crashing to the metal again.

The sculptor said, "No! Once done, a cut cannot be undone. The work is never complete. We may add wrinkles to a brow, and a storm may pock smooth skin, but we can never go backward. That which is lost is lost forever."

The sculptor began cutting again, flinging hot chips of stone into the air as larger shards rang upon the floor. With each cut, the statue became more real, more *true*, and its flaws defined it. "This is his fear I cut away!" the sculptor cried. "This is his compassion! These are his hopes! He has no more use for these—they are as dust!"

And as Soujen listened to the sculptor's voice, it became the voice of Dr. Ro-Yai, who had remade Soujen in the Separatists' laboratories. And the statue was Soujen, and it was hideous and perfect.

⫽⫽⫽

The vortex moon rose, and the sky churned. The senator breathed softly and turned on the rocks. The archivist hummed in the depths of the cave, then powered down.

Around midnight, Soujen left the cave and the rift and scaled the rocks to reach the city of Ologage, where the nighttime colors of the gates glowed fat and luminous after hunting and devouring the daylight paints. Soujen avoided the main checkpoint, following the wall half a kilometer before climbing a low and rusting barricade, arriving in the city slums. These were as he remembered, and the streets were quiet except for the occasional distant voice and the metallic hum that rose when the wind picked up.

He stayed to the shadows, moving toward the spaceport until he found what he'd been half-consciously seeking. Two uniformed young men walked at an easy pace toward the residential zones, pistols on their belts. Soujen couldn't identify their ranks or positions, but he recognized the surety in their posture. They believed they had taken the planet and were safe from Separatists, robbers, and drunks.

He stalked the men, awaiting his opportunity. He found it when they crossed a bridge over the Glittering District. He killed them both, not allowing either to scream, leaving one body on the bridge and the other below.

When he left the city, he realized he could remember very little—the look in the older one's eyes, yes, but even that might have been one of his victims from another time. War *reduced* people, he found. There were only a few ways people looked when they died, and Soujen had seen them all. War, like a sculptor's tool, pared away possibilities.

Back at camp, the darkness was starting to lift. The colors of the city shimmered like an aurora, igniting strange fires in Organa's flesh. The senator was already awake.

"Where've you been?" Organa asked.

"I needed time," Soujen said.

The senator watched him. Soujen wondered whether he knew somehow, or at least suspected. He tensed for an argument, readied barbs, threats, and accusations of his own. But no argument came.

"Are you ready to leave?" the senator asked.

"Yes," Soujen said, unsatisfied.

Whatever he had come to Ylagia to find, whatever delirious craving for simpler times had come to him in his weakness, it no longer mattered. His clan was dead. His body and spirit had been shaped by circumstances. If the ghosts had cursed him on Eyo-Dajuritz, so be it. What was done could not be undone, and there was no regaining what was lost.

CHAPTER 43
STANDING ORDERS

Her ancestors deserved the credit. Haki hadn't survived thanks to wit, or training, or even sheer stubbornness. She'd survived because some evolutionary precursor to the Heptooinian species had left her an organ that stored half an hour's worth of oxygen at the base of her neck—a vestigial organ frequently extracted from children but with occasional advantages when left intact.

So Haki hadn't drowned when the tunnels had flooded. She'd been lost in the dark with one arm burnt and useless from blasterfire. She'd carried the burden of her failures with Bail and Saw Gerrera, but she hadn't drowned, and that counted for something. She'd crawled and swum and wandered through the darkness, and she'd followed the faintest of lights back to the surface.

Then she'd slept on an island amid an emerald ocean. She'd bound her cauterized arm. And she'd swum on, ridden flotsam, following the starfighters above and hoping they would lead to an Imperial base camp.

She wasn't sure how long it had been since everything had fallen apart. She knew that she was exhausted beyond measure, that her body was covered in dirt and moss, and that she *stank*—oh how she stank. She knew she was ready to retire, but the job wasn't over quite yet.

She eventually spied a squad of clone troopers picking through the ruins of an islet—looking for traces of survivors, maybe—and she swam to them, calling to them. They pointed their rifles at her—which she'd expected. As she hauled herself out of the water, she recited her name and identification number. She said she was an officer of Imperial Intelligence sent to watch Senator Organa. Eventually they seemed to hear her.

"Where are the others?" their commander asked.

"Don't know," she said.

"Where's Senator Organa?"

"Don't know," she repeated. "Haven't seen another soul since the flood. I'd like to report in directly, if you've got comms."

The clone said he'd check with his superiors and wandered off while two others stood guard. Haki lay on the ground, too beat to do anything more. She listened to the clone's voice in the distance, but she couldn't make out words. The tone was curt and clipped, but they were clones. That was how they talked.

Still, something troubled her. Maybe it was the fact the clones didn't have standing orders regarding her at all. She now assumed her reports had brought them to Eyo-Dajuritz (if they knew about Bail, that seemed a safe assumption). So even accounting for bureaucratic miscommunications, they should've been briefed on her. Maybe it was something about the rhythm of the conversation she could only faintly hear, as if the clone were repeating to his superior everything she'd said, and all anyone was interested in was where the guerrillas and Bail had gotten to.

Haki had been a spy for a very long time. She'd lied and been lied to and learned to recognize when someone was ready to be rid of her.

The commander was coming back. The others minutely adjusted their stances, keeping their rifles aimed at Haki. If she'd been cleared, the efficient thing would've been to call them off then. But the commander didn't do that.

Haki realized, with no small dismay, that Bail had probably been right: The administration didn't want anyone leaving Eyo-Dajuritz with the knowledge of the cache.

The clones *had* been sent to kill them all. Her rescuers were nothing of the sort. Her reports hadn't been ignored, but had instead damned her. She'd been cut loose long ago, and she'd never even realized.

It felt like it should have been funny, but Haki didn't have it in her to laugh.

CHAPTER 44
THE ESSENCE
OF DEMOCRACY

"What will it be, then?" the senator asked. "After your testimony, it may be difficult to leave. You could be imprisoned, interrogated, even executed. I can speak up and argue for a pardon, but it wouldn't be unthinkable for Palpatine to bypass your right to a trial. The courts might support him if they consider you a Separatist combatant."

They were in the crew lounge of the senator's ship. Soujen ran his fingers across a bulkhead, feeling for tremors in the metal. His implants told him the ship was vibrating and he could hear the hum of the hyperdrive, but he couldn't *feel* it.

"I won't be taken," Soujen said.

"Then our plan has already failed."

It was difficult for Soujen to picture any Senate testimony at all—for him to imagine what he would say, or that the enemy would allow him to speak. The senator's initial plan, however—the interview with the judiciary, the transferring of files—seemed sound.

"No," Soujen said. "I'll do what's required. But I won't be taken. When that becomes inevitable, my cooperation will end."

Organa nodded slowly. He was saying something about connections, allies who might shelter Soujen in extraordinary circumstances, but Soujen wasn't listening. He had no intention of relying upon an Imperial senator for his freedom.

The Separatists had given him another option, to be used only in dire circumstances. It was one no one could take away.

///

Soujen had never seen Coruscant before, but the alien architecture and the suffocating web of metal seemed instantly familiar from orbit. It was as if the tunnel of hyperspace had cast him back to a primordial era when Eyo-Dajuritz still thrived.

That sense of displacement lingered as his eyes found satellites and space stations, as he saw the thruster burn of passing freighters and warships. From their angle of descent, he could see the sliver of surface where day was turning to night and the cityscape began igniting with artificial illumination. He saw clouds dissolve where the weather satellites worked furiously. The organism that was Coruscant still breathed, with a civilization of trillions dwelling upon its body. But both would die in time, and when they did Coruscant would look like Eyo-Dajuritz. Its skeleton would be stripped, and though it might take millennia, that skeleton would one day turn to dust.

Knowing the fate of the Imperial capital made it no less impressive now. Organa piped news feeds to the cockpit's vid displays as they slipped through atmosphere—Soujen saw boulevards thronged with shouting crowds and skyways blockaded by unmoving speeders. The images came quickly, stripped of sound and context, and Soujen struggled to comprehend the scale of what he saw. Did the people raising fists in anger and marching through drizzle number in the hundreds? Or were they millions?

"Protests," the senator muttered. He sounded grim.

"For us?" Soujen felt a fool for asking.

Organa shook his head and spoke without condescension. "No one knows we're coming. No one even knows this ship belongs to me—it's registered to the Alderaanian consulate. Believe me, I take our security seriously." The vids switched between shots of the protesters and studio reporters. "No, this is about reintegrating the Separatist worlds. In two days, it becomes official—the incoming Separatist senators are sworn in."

"Not Separatist anymore," Soujen said.

"No, of course. What a mess, though—reunited at last, and now some vocal minority is demanding, what . . . that we punish your planets forever? Lock you out of the Senate as retribution? The war is *over*, and there are bigger problems."

You think so little of us, Soujen thought. *You think we are defanged and glad of it—so grateful that the war is over, so grateful for our own defeat, that we would never wish you harm.*

He did not like Bail Organa.

He thought again of the senator's offer to take him to Alderaan and strip him of his implants, to make him less a weapon and more a man. To do so would have been to undermine the senator's own mission. What convictions did such a man truly have?

The screens showed clones lined up behind energy cordons. The protesters flashed holograms and yelled toward the clones, berating them and urging them to join the demonstrations.

Organa shut the screens off. "Trouble," he said, tapping the scanner.

As Soujen looked at the sensor readings, two airspeeders were already pulling into view, their flashing lights painting the clouds crimson. Out of sight but on-scanner were three more, englobing Bail's starship as it continued its descent.

A voice came through the comm: "Alderaanian vessel, proceed to your dock. Do not attempt to change course."

"What do they intend?" Soujen asked.

"Hell if I know," the senator said. "Not a lot of choice now, though."

"They know it's you."

"They *can't*. Maybe . . . they might suspect."

Organa's eyes were half-closed, brow furrowed in concentration. Soujen unbuckled his harness and leaned forward, looking between the airspeeders and, below, the boulevards and landing platforms. Rain was beginning to spatter on the viewport, but he caught flashes of light and movement through the haze. They were heading directly into the protests.

"Eyo-Dajuritz," the senator said. "They must have—"

"They tracked you," Soujen said at nearly the same moment. "They knew you were there."

"Haki." The senator spat her name. "She could've planted a tracking device, could've told someone. That's how they found us on Eyo-Dajuritz and that's how they found us now." He slammed a fist onto the console, growling in frustration. "I should've known. I should've thought of . . . There's been too much—too much going on."

"What do they want?" Soujen asked.

"I don't know. I don't . . ." For a moment the senator seemed lost, but then he regained focus, seeming to organize his thoughts aloud. "They won't want you to testify, but they may not know you're aboard. They can't possibly be sure of what I did or didn't find on Eyo-Dajuritz. They may not even—"

"They don't know for sure *you* survived. They don't know for sure that you're the pilot."

"No. But I don't know what that buys us. They'll learn soon enough, about me *and* about you."

Soujen stood as the senator kept talking.

"I can call for help," Organa said. "There are still people in the judiciary, in the security forces, who might run interference if the administration hasn't guessed what we're up to. That could buy us time to reach the chief justice."

Soujen pictured the brigade of troopers awaiting them. He pictured the senator surrendering and the troopers escorting them both away while Organa prayed for salvation from his allies inside the bureaucracy.

He pictured a summary execution. No one would ever need to know who had survived Eyo-Dajuritz.

Eliminate the complexity. Complexity results in failure. Simplify the mission.

He marched out of the cockpit and through the ship. The senator was calling to him, but he ignored the man, located the engine compart-

ment, and sorted through a tool chest until he found what he was looking for. By the time he returned to the cockpit, the ship was making its
final descent. He could see the clone troopers on the platform, their
white armor glistening in the rain while their black-clad superiors stood
behind them. A second row of troopers held back the protesters pack-
ing the connecting platforms, and brilliantly colored strips of speeders
stretched across the horizon, holding position and displaying holographic messages declaring, No Reunification, We Do Not Forgive, and No Votes for War Criminals.

He stepped behind the pilot's seat and pressed a laser welder to the
senator's temple. "I'm taking you hostage," Soujen said. "Do you understand?"

Organa tensed in his safety harness. "This isn't the way."

"I captured you on Eyo-Dajuritz and I brought you here. You'll be in
the clear. I'll have you as a shield. And if we're separated . . ."

Then what? Would Soujen find his way to the chief justice on his
own?

". . . there will be other opportunities," Soujen finished. "I'll make
contact if I can."

The ship bounced as its landing gear met the platform. The comm
was blinking, and a loudspeaker outside was insisting the occupants of
the ship exit one at a time. The clones hurried to surround the vessel, as
if they feared someone would escape from a hidden hatch.

"They'll have snipers. They won't allow you to take me," the senator
said as Soujen forced him to his feet and marched him to the boarding
ramp. "I can still get us out of this."

"I don't think you ever could," Soujen said. He keyed the door, and
they walked into the rain.

There were shouts—demands that Soujen put down his weapon, let
the senator go. There was the chatter of officers frantically calling their
superiors for instructions. And above it all was the roar of the protests.
The senator was yelling, too, urging the clones to do whatever Soujen
said, saying they mustn't fire. Soujen let all of it wash over him as he
moved forward, raindrops tapping his scalp plating and caressing his
face.

"I want a speeder," he snapped, though he didn't, really. Anything they brought him would be tracked. "Give me space or the senator dies."

He put pressure on the laser welder's trigger, exaggerating the motion for his audience. The welder was a prop—his microlaser would have killed Organa more neatly—but it did exactly what he needed, forcing the troops to back away. Soujen scanned for snipers, but the senator had been wrong to worry about that. The protesters' airspeeders kept any other vessels from taking position, and the crowd on the platforms gave him additional cover.

But the Imperials would come for him. As he approached the strip leading from the platform to the main boulevard, the roar of the protesters grew louder. The clones closed in behind him. If the senator was right, it was possible they weren't even concerned about bringing Organa in alive. But in public, before the crowd, they wouldn't gun Soujen and Organa down together. They needed to appear to be *trying*.

One of the clones was drawing near. The noises almost concealed his movements, but Soujen heard the squeak of his soles against the metal platform. He threw the laser welder backward in an arc that he vaguely hoped would hit the clone, and with his free hand he shoved Organa toward the platform's edge. It wasn't Soujen's intent to kill the senator, but the closer he came the more chaos would ensue.

Now entirely unencumbered, he dived onto the platform, letting his implants rebalance his body as he dashed on hands and feet. The shouting continued behind him, and he thought he heard Organa's voice saying, "I'm all right! I'm all right!" But Soujen didn't turn to look. The clones started shooting, yet Soujen was moving toward the protesters, toward the barricades and the second line of clones, and no one dared fire into the mass of bodies. In another moment, he was scuttling past the barricades, knocking clones aside. Then he was among the protesters, surrounded by hordes that hated the Separatists, hated *him*, but were too ignorant to understand what he meant for their Empire.

CHAPTER 45
NOT AN INTRUSIVE QUESTION

The interrogation room wasn't like the closet where Mon had been tortured. It was perhaps three meters on a side, with room to pace and good lighting. A table and two chairs, all of unadorned metal, gave her a place to sit. There was even a water dispenser built into the wall, perfectly functional. And though no one had provided her with a container, she could drink from her cupped hands if she got thirsty.

The room was not like the closet at all. But her body remembered the closet, and Mon found her spine hurt no matter how she sat or how much she paced, and her skin was hot and her heart rate rapid. She tried to hide it from the cams that were surely watching. She chose not to splash her face with water, because to do so would be to show weakness to the interrogators yet to come.

She wished, for a moment, that she'd called Perrin when she'd first landed. That instead of racing from Nulvolio's yacht back into the fray of politics, she'd taken a moment to speak to her husband, hear his voice, and remember what she'd once loved about him or still did.

Then she scolded herself for the wish. Her staff knew she was on Coruscant, at least, and they were better equipped for this contingency than Perrin. They would be sober enough to notice her disappearance and would act. They would ask questions, and given the administration had spirited her away in public view, they had a chance of getting answers.

Granted, whether they could pressure the administration into *releasing* her was another matter entirely.

Still, *possibilities* were what she chose to focus on, because as long as her mind was active, her body's memories could not roam free. When she finished imagining what her staff would do, she turned her mind to the question of what Bail Organa had done—what disaster he'd encountered or caused in his quest to exonerate the Jedi. When she'd finished with that question, she turned her mind to sports, tracing a smashball course on the metal table and re-creating memorable plays from the last Overring Tournament.

Mon had been locked in the room no more than three hours when her interrogator arrived, carrying a datapad. The woman was about Mon's age, dark-haired, with amber eyes and variegated, asymmetrical teeth. She wore the white uniform of the Imperial Security Bureau and hadn't as much as closed the door before she spoke: "Senator Mothma, I'm so sorry to keep you waiting. The anti-reintegration protests have started, and we're desperately understaffed. Half of my team is stuck in traffic, if you can believe it."

The woman slid into the chair across from Mon and waited a beat. The trick was obvious, but it almost worked. Part of Mon, the part that prized etiquette and diplomacy, wanted to say, *Of course it's not a problem.* Instead, she smiled tightly and asked, "Why am I here?"

"Just a few things to clear up," the woman said, making a show of studying the datapad. "Then we'll have you on your way to the Senate. Or I can arrange a ride to your home, which frankly might be easier with the skyways the way they are. Oh!" She looked up, as if suddenly remembering something, and produced a narrow, finger-length bottle from her pocket. "I wasn't sure about your schedule, so I brought these."

The woman slid the bottle across the table. Mon opened it and saw two sapphire teardrops at the bottom—a single dose of her anxiety medication.

Laying it on thick, aren't you?

The woman wanted to remind Mon of how much the bureau knew. How the bureau was in control. She wanted Mon to be afraid they'd swapped the pills for something else.

Mon took the bottle and downed both pills, feeling the tickle in her throat as they liquefied.

If the medication had been altered, so be it. She wasn't going to second-guess herself.

"Why am I here?" Mon asked again.

The woman met Mon's gaze, then returned to the datapad. "The fellow from your home security detail? The one who dropped your pills off? He mentioned he hasn't seen you in several days. Is everything all right with the apartment?"

"Yes, of course."

"I know the relocation was sudden, but it's for your own protection. You do understand that?"

"I do."

"May I ask where you've been, then?"

Again, the woman met Mon's gaze. Her pupils seemed to contract, as if they could squeeze the life from her subject.

"My business is Senate business," Mon said. "I'd need to know your clearances before saying anything more."

"What clearances do I need?"

"Even telling you that would be a breach. If you can provide me your code list, I can check myself."

If the woman really wanted to know, Mon thought, she'd be able to clear this bureaucratic hurdle. Then Mon would need to think up another lie. But she wasn't about to make anything *easy* for these people. If she forced them to work for every scrap, they'd focus on what they wanted most and wouldn't be inclined to go fishing.

Assuming they meant to ever release her.

"We can come back to that." Back to the datapad. "Let's discuss Senator Bail Organa of Alderaan. You know him well?"

"I know him."

"How would you define your relationship?"

"We are professional colleagues."

"Would you say you're *friends*? Rivals? Give me perspective. Give me context."

Mon shifted in her seat as the pain between her shoulders magnified. *Stay alert.* "We've had ups and downs over the years. In the past, we've shared many of the same causes, and that's led us to work and socialize together. But I wouldn't say we've been especially *close* outside the Senate."

The woman tapped at the datapad. "You've been to—oh, well, enough parties and galas and funerals together that my assistant wrote, 'See attached file.' He didn't actually bother attaching anything, but I'm presuming that means the list is extensive."

"I'm sure it is. We've both been in the Senate a long time. Pick anyone with a similar record, and I imagine you'll find we went to the same fundraisers and networking events because, frankly, that's *the job*."

"Have you met his wife?"

"Yes."

"Have you met his child?"

"Not that I recall."

"Leia?"

"Is that his daughter's name?"

"Do you *like* him?"

This caught Mon off guard. "Pardon?"

The woman tapped a finger on the tabletop. "It's not a hard question. *Do you like Bail Organa?*"

"I'm just not sure why it's relevant—"

"It's relevant because I'm *asking* you, Senator, and I don't think it's an intrusive question. Whether you believe it or not, I'm trying to do *my* job, and to do that I need to understand people. I need to understand relationships. And if I ask my questions in the wrong order, then it colors my investigation in ways that benefit no one. It sends me down the wrong paths. And then I have to bring in other people to ask *them* the wrong questions, and may my superiors be merciful if I start making the wrong arrests. Do you understand?" Abruptly, the woman flipped the datapad, turning it face down, and put her full attention on Mon. "Do you *like* the man?"

prisoned, such as Omchro of Abednedo, who had spent three months detained by the Mining Guild when the deaths of forty-two workers led him to call for a strike. Omchro had, in his waning years, produced a series of oil paintings depicting the cell he'd inhabited as a younger man, each showing cots, walls, and door from a different angle. She thought of Kehal Kehouris, who had led the Second Isobian Revolution to overthrow his world's noble families. He had spent the remainder of his life in an oubliette, scratching treatises into the wall, and was still regarded with disfavor in parts of the galaxy. But in her youth, Mon had been enraptured by his ardent (even violent) anti-royalism.

She thought of Lady Hasquil, cocooned for fifty years for acknowledging the sapient rights of the Mourushian Kelp, and she thought of Nermani Ulekt, who'd broken the Republic's quarantine to deliver aid during the Contagion of Tynna. Mon thought of these figures and knew she was nothing like them. The administration sought to humiliate her, but if she feared for her life, it was because she herself was *fearful*. What had she really sacrificed? What had she lost? Zhuna was dead, and the Separatist worlds had endured terror of all kinds, but Mon retained her title and assets and a station of comfort. To compare herself to martyrs was sheer hubris.

She was giggling at the notion when her second interrogator arrived.

/ / /

He was a stout man with a tilted nose and a miner's hands. "Senator Mon Mothma of Chandrila," he said as he entered, sliding into the chair across from her with an exhausted sigh. "You know why we're here, so we may as well be quick about it."

"I'm afraid I *don't* know why I'm here," she said.

The man ignored her. "Bail Organa of Alderaan. How long have you known him?"

"Since I first joined the Senate, I suppose."

"And how long ago was that?"

"You know the answer," Mon said.

"How long ago, please?"

"Thirteen years? Just about."

"And you've been friends with Bail Organa all this time?"

"Really, I had this same conversation with your predecessor—"

"*Friends,* Senator. You and Bail Organa are friends?"

"We're friendly colleagues. We're not social outside work, if that's what you're asking."

"What about the level fifty-ninety-one air race last year?"

"The what?"

"The airspeeder race. You had a private box. Was that *work-related?*"

She struggled to remember. Her head ached. Had she had some secret meeting with Bail at an airspeeder race?

She groaned when the memory came to her. "That was my husband, not me. He and Bail both have a love of vintage airspeeders—lots of chrome and snorting engines. There may be a charge to my credit account, but I promise you, if you check the ticket, you'll find it's in Perrin's name."

"We'll see about that," the man said. "But if your husband socialized with him—"

"Then you can talk to my husband," Mon said, sharp but not raising her voice. "We've covered this ground. We talked all about my relationship with Senator Organa. So unless you give me new questions, you'll get no new answers."

The man tugged at his uniform and leaned back in his chair.

"You and I haven't been talking five minutes, Senator. We've got a lot of ground to cover."

"What about the hour I spent with the other officer? The woman?"

"I don't know who you've talked to," the man said, "and it doesn't matter to me. Watch your temper and let's get this over with."

So she went through the same questions and tried to stay patient. He asked about Bail's politics, committees they'd served on, and bills they'd co-sponsored. All of it seemed straightforward. Only when the man began asking about more recent events did Mon force herself to think everything through. She could acknowledge the veterans dinner, but what about the meeting where she'd proposed the Rebirth Act? Was the administration trying to ferret out her list of allies?

"When was the last time you saw him?" the man asked.

She decided to tell the truth—or enough of it, anyway. "We were at an informal meeting off Senate grounds."

"When was this?"

She gave him an approximate date, and he didn't press her. He asked who else had attended, and she said she couldn't recall. "Senator Doroon, I believe. Senator Marjolos." Because if the intelligence services had been watching her then, they surely already knew who'd been present—even if Lud's countermeasures had prevented anyone from listening in on the discussions.

"Where was this?"

"Senator Lud Marroi's home. He wasn't present."

The man paused. It was a fractional pause, but he'd delivered every other question so quickly that it stood out.

"What did you talk about? You and Organa?"

Now it was Mon's turn to hesitate. *We argued about the Jedi.* Whatever trouble Bail was in, she couldn't imagine the truth would help him. And whatever their disagreements, she had no desire to see him endangered.

"I don't remember the particulars," she hedged. "Bail and I . . . we were both friends with Senator Padmé Amidala, before her passing. She was the one who brought us together, settled differences between the two of us. Honestly, Bail and I fought about *something*, but I don't recall what. I think we were both just angry Padmé wasn't around to set things right."

Where did that come from? Is that true?

The man nodded brusquely. "Did he mention anything about traveling?"

"Off Coruscant?"

"Off Coruscant. Not to Alderaan—a longer trip."

"Not that I recall."

"Do you recall him mentioning Eyo-Dajuritz?"

She frowned. "I don't."

"It's a historical site. On the protected planets list—"

"I'm familiar with it. I don't remember Bail ever mentioning it."

"I'm not asking about *ever*, I'm asking—"

"He did not mention it to me at that meeting, and I do not recall us ever discussing Eyo-Dajuritz."

"You sound confident."

Mon laughed, and the sound was louder than it should have been in the small room.

"Eyo-Dajuritz is one of the great wonders of the galaxy," she said, "and if Bail Organa were the sort of man to casually discuss lost civilizations and the xenoarchaeological record, I expect we wouldn't have needed Senator Amidala to bring us together."

Her interrogator appeared unamused. "You haven't heard, then?"

"Heard what?"

He scowled, and there was a tremor in his voice. "Eyo-Dajuritz is half ruined. Bail Organa was on the surface with a band of terrorists from the Japrael sector. Early reports say the terrorists blew a hole the size of a mountain in an ancient dam and flooded one of the empty lake beds." He shook his head rapidly. "I don't know what part Organa played in it all, and the terrorists have made no statement. It's an act of planetary vandalism, as I see it. But you'd better believe we'll find out what he was doing, with or without your cooperation."

The man lurched to his feet, swaying under his own bulk. With a mumbled "Thank you for your cooperation, Senator," he left the room and locked the door, leaving Mon to sit bewildered and appalled.

▱▱▱

Mon was alone again. Such destruction on Eyo-Dajuritz was difficult to fathom, and she wondered whether the story was a lie, another power play to throw her off guard. But it was too strange and specific. Something had happened there, as Nulvolio worried it would. He had warned her to keep watch and made her promise she would tell him anything she learned. She would have nothing for him until she was free.

Nor could she learn what had become of Bail. She felt oddly responsible for his fate, as if part of her believed it had been her duty to mend things with him, or she alone had driven him off. Bail was a grown man, and Mon knew that she had only done what was necessary . . . but she worried.

And she *had* given his name to Imperial Intelligence when she'd needed a distraction. She was not free of responsibility, though she suspected the act of *planetary vandalism* would have drawn Imperial attention regardless of her involvement.

Whatever the medication had been, it wasn't helping her anxiety. Vertigo consumed her even while she was seated. She felt nauseated, amusing herself with the thought that if she were to vomit, she could do it in front of the door. It would be the most childish vengeance possible, but she was tired and hurting and in the hands of a security force she no longer trusted. Childishness was one of few weapons left to her.

She tracked time by listening to the ventilation system and pretending to know how long each cooling cycle lasted. Ten minutes on, fifteen minutes off. That meant she'd been waiting two more hours.

She wondered how far her interrogators were authorized to go and what they really sought. They wouldn't disappear her forever—she told herself that, and it seemed likely. She'd get a trial. Too many people knew what had happened. And besides, Palpatine was ruthless, but the day-to-day administration of justice was carried out by the same people as always. Even her interrogators had probably served in Republic Intelligence or the other services during the war. She'd trusted in them then. She hadn't been naïve or averse to oversight, but she'd trusted them.

But somehow everything seemed more *fragile* now.

Where would the system hold, and where would it break?

////

Eventually the woman came back. She made no acknowledgment of the second interrogator, and Mon did not inquire. The woman did not apologize or attempt to feign affability. She sat with her datapad, looked directly at Mon, and asked, "How long have you known Senator Lud Marroi?"

"Nine years, I believe," Mon said.

The woman nodded as if this were a new and trenchant piece of data. "You've worked closely with him?"

"When we've been on the same committees, yes."

"Which committees were those?"

Mon listed off as many as she could remember, along with the years her tenures had overlapped with Lud's. For the first time, the woman made notes on her datapad.

The woman asked Mon about Lud's politics and his family. She asked how often Mon saw him. When Mon acknowledged the closeness of their relationship, the woman changed tack, focusing on the people in Mon and Lud's shared orbit. She asked whether Lud had requested introductions to any of Mon's associates or whether she'd sought introductions to his, and whether they'd ever traded Senate staffers or outside counselors.

"You said you had a meeting in his home," the woman asked. "Why wasn't Marroi present?"

"He wasn't part of the meeting. I needed a place to host, and I asked him if he knew anywhere neutral and secure."

Mon considered her prior interrogator's surprise when she'd mentioned Lud. Through her headache and nausea, she tried to put the pieces together: She'd set the security forces on Lud's trail, as she'd done with Bail. That had to be part of this mess. They'd found *something*, enough that she'd piqued their interest by referencing Lud unexpectedly, and now they were certain *she* held the key to unlocking Lud's secrets . . .

They'll destroy him, and it will be your fault. You'll say the wrong word, and they'll destroy him.

Bail was responsible for Bail, and Mon was responsible for herself. Lud had done nothing to deserve the scrutiny of the administration, and she alone might doom or save him.

"When you meet with Marroi, do you do so alone? With staff?"

"Alone, usually."

"Do you keep records of the meetings?"

"Only if there's staff around."

There was another problem, too. If Mon didn't end her interrogator's line of questioning, she might spend another day in the cell. She couldn't afford the time.

The woman began asking about the frequency of their meetings and whether that frequency had changed over the years. She asked whether Mon had talked to Lud about the new administration, and Mon said yes because no one would've believed otherwise. That opened up a second series of questions about Lud's politics and the opinions he'd ventured.

Mon concocted a solution and she hated it. She tumbled it in her mind as she struggled through the interrogation, and when she decided she'd find nothing better, she said, "*Stop.*"

The woman watched her.

I'm sorry, Mon thought, though she didn't know to whom she was apologizing.

"Stop," she said again. "I told you. We talk about politics . . . rarely."

"You mostly talk about sports," the woman said, not hiding her skepticism.

"We don't talk as much as you'd think."

The woman eyed Mon, waiting.

"Lud and I are having an affair," Mon said. "Or to be precise, *I'm* having an affair. Lud is just participating." She made her smile as bitter as she could, opened her mouth as if to say something more, and then closed it. The woman kept staring until Mon, to fill the silence, added, "We really *were* friends, before the war. It was politics and sports then, but things at home . . ." *You've spied on me and Perrin. You know what our home looks like.*

"Anyway, Lud was *available,* and that was that."

Mon took a deep breath. "It would be a scandal if anyone knew. Not even the staff realize. Lud would be pilloried by the media. Perrin would never tolerate it. You can't imagine how difficult things would become for everyone . . ."

There you have it. Now you have something on both of us.

There were follow-up questions, about the nature and length of the affair and about who had initiated it. Mon kept her story straight and resisted adding too many details. Meanwhile, the woman, despite her diligence, seemed to have lost interest in the whole conversation, as if it was all a bit tawdry for her.

Eventually the woman stood. "Wait here," she said, then departed.

Mon experienced no triumph. The lie felt filthy and too close to real, and she was still too sick to think straight.

/// /// ///

A few hours later, a junior officer entered the room and told her, "Senator? You're free to go."

Mon didn't believe it, though she stood and followed the officer into the corridor. Her head was still pounding, but the vertigo had ebbed, and she was able to walk without swaying or holding the walls. The officer did not speak, and neither did she—to do so would have broken the spell.

They left the detention area and approached a turbolift to the security bureau's central office. The door slid open, and a man emerged. Mon didn't recognize his face, but her body knew. Her shoulders tensed, and her heart rate accelerated until she thought she might faint.

He was the one who'd spoken to her after her first detention, who'd made her sign a pledge of loyalty, and said to her, "The administration has authorized us to bring you back for questioning any time we want."

He didn't glance in their direction until he was moving past them in the corridor. He flashed a smile at Mon, full of malice and unearned strength.

"Any time we want."

Then he was gone, and Mon was in the lift. Soon she was past the secure perimeter and on the main boulevard outside, leaning against one of the streetside railings and gasping for air above the bright abyss of skyscrapers and holograms. Her blood coursed with terror, but her mind, her intellect, knew only outrage and fury at the people who would treat her, treat *anyone,* as unworthy of dignity—as something less than *enemies,* because enemies could be respected. Enemies could be recognized for their virtues—for their valor, ideals, or skill—even when their causes were unjust. To treat people as obstacles whose removal was a source of pleasure was abominable. It was the antithesis of everything Mon had ever believed in.

No matter that she had succumbed to the same joys on occasion.

Part of her wanted to weep. Mostly she wanted to scream.

After a while, she noticed it was raining. She noticed the distant noises of traffic and something that sounded like a crowd chanting. She watched the lines of speeders along the skyways, like colorful ribbons tying Coruscant together.

She heard someone call her name. "Mon?"

She pushed off the railing and turned to see Bail Organa walking away from the security center, looking as if he, too, had seen hell itself.

CHAPTER 46
POSTMORTEM

Soujen's last act before disappearing into the mob had been to shove Bail toward the edge of the landing platform. Had Soujen known how slick the metal was? Had he seen Bail nearly fall into the depths of Coruscant? Bail had flailed, catching the arm of a clone trooper and swinging above nothingness for half a second. The clone had hauled him to safety, but it was as close to death as he'd felt since setting out with Haki. Even the flood on Eyo-Dajuritz had served as the culmination of threats—he'd had time to grow inured to the fear. The fall had been entirely unexpected. Only luck had saved him.

Nonetheless, it had served Bail well during interrogation. It left little doubt in anyone's mind that Bail had been Soujen's hostage. It meant Bail had been, for the most part, treated as a victim rather than a suspect. It meant he'd been able to request an examination from a medical droid, who confirmed that Bail had been beaten several days prior (allowing Bail to joke with his interrogators about applying for a combat service medal). It meant that while there were a great number of questions about why he'd gone to Eyo-Dajuritz and what he'd seen, his interrogators had accepted his declared ignorance of the terrorists' motives and operations. It meant he could play the roles of both fool and statesman.

The administration would search his ship. They'd searched him thoroughly enough—"in case the terrorists planted anything on you"—and they would find he'd brought back nothing to exonerate the Jedi, nor transmitted anything since leaving Eyo-Dajuritz. *Maybe* they'd worry he'd shared intelligence with someone on Ylagia, but only if they suspected he was in league with Soujen.

The only person who might contradict his story was Haki, and to the best of his knowledge, she was nowhere to be found. He half hoped she'd perished in the flood, yet admonished himself for his own callousness.

Now he was out. The interrogation was over, and he was hurrying toward Mon Mothma as she swayed at the edge of the boulevard outside the security bureau. He reached out to steady her, but she shook her head and gently pushed his hand away.

"I'm all right," she said. "I was in there a while, is all. What about you?"

"I was lucky," he said.

"No," Mon said. "You were *likable*, I assume, and we can all be grateful for that. Your charisma is a damned Jedi mind trick."

"Breha tell you about that?"

"Once, when I was complaining. Come on. We should talk, but not here."

She gave the bureau a backward glance, and Bail understood: *Not while we're being watched.*

He said in a murmur, "If you need cover, I can go ahead, meet you somewhere—"

She let out a sound so scornful he struggled to recognize it as a laugh. "Let them see us leave together. Let them wonder. I don't care anymore."

He nodded, not fully understanding and surprised by the bitterness and defiance in her voice. This was not the woman he knew. Something had chipped away at the polished surface, leaving her soul exposed. He wondered whether he'd changed half as much.

Mon trekked toward the nearest tram stop, and Bail kept at her side. "You heard about the protests?" she asked.

"Seen them. Impressive crowd. A lot of people holding grudges."

"Good. They'll give us anonymity."

"You're joking. They'll kill us if they realize who we are—"

She glanced behind them again, and again Bail understood.

Every tram stop near the protests had been shut down, so they had to disembark early and walk a considerable distance before the demonstrators were in sight. Bail drew Mon's attention to a street vendor selling rain gear, and they both purchased cheap unsized garments. The ponchos stank of plastic, but Bail hoped the hoods would conceal their faces.

They spotted no fewer than fifty clone troopers, two dozen Coruscant Security officers, and a handful of Imperial military representatives on the fringes of the crowd. Their weapons were uniformly holstered or pointed downward.

"The administration wants these protests," Bail said, nearly shouting into Mon's ear over the chants and cries. "They're a warning to the Separatists to stay on their best behavior."

"You don't know the half of it," Mon said. "The reintegration—it's going to get complicated."

"We really *do* need to talk," Bail said, flinching as something ignited the air—a floating holo-emitter showing cascading images of Republic war dead.

He felt Mon's hand on his shoulder, and he leaned in to hear her response. She squeezed the wet lining of the poncho. "I'm glad you're here," she said.

He realized he hadn't thought of their arguments and their differences since seeing her in the flesh. He slung his arm around her torso and pulled her against his side, and Mon didn't push away. Instead, she leaned into his body, and they walked on, each silent and seeking comfort in the warmth of the other. Bail couldn't remember such a moment happening before—even during the better days of their friendship, she'd always been untouchable—and he doubted it would ever happen again. But today was different. Today words were not enough.

◢◢◢

They kept their heads down and watched for cams and drones as they crept through the crowd. They found the unlocked entrance to a housing block, slipped away from the mob into a maze of apartments, and left via a back entrance two levels down. As they hurried through an alleyway, Bail proposed returning to Cantham House. If Breha and Leia were on Coruscant, they'd be there. But Mon was adamant. "Assume the house is bugged," she told him. "Assume everything is bugged." The message was implicit: *Don't contact Breha until we're done here.*

They walked twenty more minutes, until they were confident they wouldn't be easily found. They stopped at an outdoor auto-galley and bought plates of rubbery noodles covered in aromatic herbs. Mon consumed her meal with equal parts disdain and relish, like a woman who hadn't eaten in days. Bail forced down what he could and offered the rest to Mon.

While she ate, she talked. She seemed to be recovering her strength, focusing on her plate as much as on Bail while she described the coalition she'd built around the Imperial Rebirth Act. Separatists, corporate interests, the Delegation of 2,000—anyone outside of Palpatine's imperialist backers had been fair game. She'd assembled an alliance that Bail acknowledged was impressive.

When she finished her meal, he asked, "You're sure Arvik Cornade and his lot will stick with you? He's bound to profit under Palpatine, and he's taking an awful risk."

"I'm sure," Mon said dryly. She lacked her usual poise, but she sounded like herself again. "We had that conversation."

"You know what you're doing."

"But you don't believe the bill will pass."

Bail didn't. He thought about lying, but he shook his head. "It's just a lot of moving parts. Palpatine may not know the particulars, but he and the grand vizier are bound to have an idea of what you're planning."

"That doesn't mean they can stop it," she said.

"No, it doesn't. For what it's worth . . ." He hesitated, then shrugged. "If you get the bill to the floor, I'll vote for it."

"You won't like it."

He tried to imagine all the sweeteners and riders attached to the bill. "I'm sure I won't. I'll vote for it anyway. And damn anyone who doesn't."

Mon looked satisfied, as if she'd been waiting for the words. "Good enough," she said, straightening her back. "Now tell me what the hell you've done."

He did his best to be concise—and more honest with Mon than he'd been with his interrogators. But it was difficult to move from one version of the story to another so quickly. And he knew there were things he left out and things he colored in a manner bordering on deceptive. He told her he'd come to suspect that the evidence against the Jedi had been manufactured by the Separatists and knowingly used by Palpatine. He told her he'd gone searching for Separatist turncoats and prisoners who might have more information. He didn't mention Haki by name. He told her about his discovery of the cache and how he'd come to Eyo-Dajuritz. He saw Mon's body language shift in a way he couldn't read when he mentioned the planet.

But she didn't interrupt as he told her about Saw Gerrera and Soujen Vak-Nhalis and the deals he'd cut with both. He didn't dwell on the march through the caverns, but he told her (he didn't expect to be believed) about his theory that the clones had come to kill him along with the guerrillas—to wipe out the evidence that was, at present, locked in Soujen's head and missing somewhere in the bowels of Coruscant.

"Soujen's a nasty piece of work, Mon, but if anyone can outrun the security forces, it's him. And if we find him, he can still testify before the chief justice and the Senate. I think he sees it as the only way left for him to keep fighting—"

Mon was shaking her head, and all their disagreements came rushing back—all his disappointment in her, his frustration that she was too afraid and too cautious to make a stand.

"If he gets in front of the Senate," she said, "my coalition will burn to the ground. Everything will be filtered through the lenses of Jedi politics and Separatist terrorism, and I can't begin to guess at the fallout."

"People will begin to question the official story. Senators, citizens, members of the administration—they'll be angry about being used, being lied to—"

"And that's *if* Soujen gets in front of the Senate. It's just as likely he leads the security forces on a chase around Coruscant for the next week and we're treated to news coverage of a Separatist assassin running wild. It's already starting."

Bail began to argue, but he saw the direction of her gaze, and he turned in his seat. A billboard extending from a neighboring gallery displayed an image of Soujen and a caption warning of a terrorist threat to Coruscant. Bail swore, sighed, then nodded. "It's starting. But we're so close, Mon, and this is *important*. Something big is in our grasp."

And you have no idea what I've done to get this far. The risks I've taken for myself and my family. The risks I'm still taking.

He would act on his own if he had to. He'd gone without help this long.

Mon was holding up a hand, eyes closed and contemplative. When she reopened them, she looked more tired than before. "I won't say you went about this the right way. But you brought this to my doorstep, and you're correct—I can't ignore it, and it *is* important. It could realign everything in our favor if it's handled with extreme delicacy." Which Bail read as, *You don't have the skills to pull this off.*

She kept talking. "Here's what I propose: I may have sources who can locate your man before the administration does. That's not a guarantee. But it's a possibility, and I'm willing to look into it. However, it will take time. And I've already been away from the Senate for too long.

"Until Soujen is on his way to speak to the Senate, the Imperial Rebirth Act must remain in play—assuming the administration doesn't postpone the reintegration." She gestured at the billboard again. Bail didn't bother to look. "We do not give up on the Rebirth Act until there's either no other choice or we have a better plan in hand."

"I can accept that," Bail said. "What does it mean, practically?"

"It means if I'm going to call in favors to locate Soujen, I need to keep my coalition together in the meantime. My staff is barely briefed, so someone has to gather strays, count votes, and talk down potential defectors. Someone who can reassure everyone that the bill is on track, even when it's not."

"I'd volunteer," Bail said, "but I've been out of the loop myself. What about Streamdrinker? Or Doroon?"

"No one looks to Doroon for leadership. Streamdrinker's better, but he'll want to make changes of his own to the bill, and we can't afford ideological purity. Besides"—she pursed her lips—"you *left,* Bail. You ran away from the Rebirth Act, and you left us to fend for ourselves. Do you have any idea how much time we lost trying to secure the votes of your allies? How many senators were hesitant to sign on, knowing you hadn't committed?"

"I never tried to sabotage you." It wasn't an excuse. It was surprise that made him say it.

"You didn't have to. We managed, but even now there are holdouts who could make the difference—assuming, again, we don't lose the senators we've got. You're—policy isn't your strong suit. We both know that. But people *like* you, and they want you to like *them.* On my best day, my allies are invested in working with me. They're excited to follow you."

This had been an unspoken truth between them. They'd worked together often and divided tasks according to their strengths. But Bail had rarely heard Mon put it so bluntly. His instinct was to defend her and deflect the kind words. Instead, he said, "I can't guarantee anything. I've lost more fights in the Senate than I've won."

"Only because you choose the wrong fights! You can sit in your office, hate the bill, and call up whatever junior members idolize you. Give whatever magnificent speech you have to whenever someone in the coalition gets cold feet. You'll bring credibility for the true believers, and for the rest—just tell them nothing has changed. The bill is still mine. *Tell* them you feel it's watered down and compromised. Some of the fence-sitters will take that as a good sign, coming from you.

"Hell," she said, "even if it weren't for your terrorist friend, I might still need you to get this bill passed."

He thought it through. Part of him wondered whether Mon was trying to get him out of the way, but that was unlikely and ungenerous. She was risking a great deal putting her project in his hands. And she was right. He could handle it as well as anyone—and he would hate every moment campaigning for a flawed bill and pleading with hypocrites and plutocrats to fall in line.

That was manageable. That was politics. The question was, could he trust Mon with *his* project?

He could have, once. He could have trusted her, and if he were tempted to doubt or she were tempted to stray, Padmé's faith would have set things right. Both of them had trusted Padmé, and to betray her would have been to betray each other.

"Assume I say yes," he said. "Assume you find Soujen. Do you promise to bring his evidence before the Senate?"

She straightened her back, and he recognized the shift in her demeanor. She'd been treating him as a confidant, sharing her troubles and frustrations openly. When they'd walked in the rain, they'd been closer than they'd ever been, old friends and comrades in arms. Now, in a moment, she'd transformed into Mon Mothma the senator, the woman who'd aspired to become Supreme Chancellor and who'd learned every procedural quirk in the Senate bylaws, every bureaucratic angle and trick of political gamesmanship.

"I'll do everything I can," she said.

Bail almost believed her.

///

The luxury airspeeder that pulled alongside the platform was five meters long, painted an unprepossessing ocher. Its windows were tinted, and its repulsorlifts whined at a low pitch that suggested a lack of recent tuning or, alternatively, custom enhancements. Bail didn't recognize the vehicle, and he hesitated to step out from under the awning into the cold drizzle. He'd left Mon behind half an hour earlier, made a single call—all too aware that the security bureau might be listening—and now waited at the roadside with all the nervous energy of a teenage delinquent.

The middle side door of the speeder rose. The silhouette of a woman in the far seat called, "Get in!"

He nearly lost his balance as he dashed to the door, vertigo following the burst of energy. Then he was in the speeder, the door was humming shut, and Breha was holding him in an awkward half embrace encumbered by the speeder seats and Breha's safety belt. Bail clung to her shoulders, and she kissed his damp forehead and lips. They whispered meaningless things like "It's good to see you" and "I'm so glad you're all right," and it was a while before Bail even noticed that the speeder was moving again. The dizziness stayed with him, wrapped around his mind, and he felt cascades of gratitude, love, and inexplicable grief. He felt like a seafaring vessel battered by a tempest that had, at long last, set down its anchor. But the anchor did not lessen the storm.

Eventually he took in his surroundings properly. He still didn't recognize the vehicle. The driver's seat was occupied by Castolle, Breha's chief of the Royal Guard—a man who'd always seemed to maintain a simultaneous dislike of Bail and an absolute respect for him. Bail had never seen Castolle play the role of chauffeur, and he looked twice between the guardsman and his wife, then said, "Tell me what's been happening."

Breha's hands had slipped to his. They interwove their fingers as she shook her head. "You first," she said.

They began to argue, both of them gentle but insistent. Bail contended there was no time. Breha countered that he'd abruptly disappeared and returned as the hostage of a terrorist. He heard the tremor in her voice—an extraordinary thing for a woman as steadfast as Breha—and he acquiesced, hurrying through his story as well as he could, stumbling past whole weeks and moments of terror to race to the end.

It was the third time that day he'd recited the tale, and this was the least coherent telling yet. He'd let his intellect drive him with the security bureau, selecting every answer with care. With Mon, he'd endeavored to be purposeful and focused. With Breha, he had no filter and no agenda, and he could see the torrent of information and emotion frustrated her. He lingered on the land mine, his guilt over Haki, and his worry over Soujen. He barely spoke about Eyo-Dajuritz. The honest story, the story notched in his bones, was not the informative one. "There's no time for all of it," he said when she asked him to backtrack—to explain something more about Saw Gerrera. "There's too much, and there's no time." And something about his tone calmed her, and she listened to his broken tale with newfound patience and empathy until he finished.

"They're watching us," he said after, drawing his thumb along the veins on the back of her hand. "I would've contacted you sooner, but they'll be watching."

"I understand," Breha said. "They've been watching us, too. That's why"—she gestured at the interior of the speeder—"I've sent most of my staff offworld. There were threats accumulating, even before the protests."

He tried to make sense of this and failed. It was one piece of information too many, and it wouldn't fit right into his head. But he recognized Breha's sobriety and nodded. "Everyone's safe? Leia is safe?"

"Leia is safe." Breha squeezed her eyes shut, and her fingernails dug into Bail's wrists. "We should all be on Alderaan."

This, too, he failed to make sense of. He turned the words until he realized it was a rebuke.

"This is *for her*," he said, soft and urgent, as if it were something to conceal from their driver. "Everything I've been doing is for her. What we're doing will save her."

"Will it?" The tension and rebuke were still in her voice. But foremost there was empathy, even pity.

"Mon and I, we have a plan—"

Castolle spoke from the front of the speeder, words crisp and guarded. "We're out of the sector. No pursuers. I need to know where we're going, my Queen."

Breha looked to Bail and mouthed, "We are together." There would be more discussions, more arguing, and more tears to come. But they were together again, and she trusted him.

"I need to make some calls," he said. Then to Castolle: "And we need to get my chief of staff. There's a lot of work to be done, and promises to keep."

CHAPTER 47
THE ECSTASY
OF DANCE

Soujen kept moving, hours after he'd lost his pursuers. The security forces had split the mob of protesters like a knife, and he'd only escaped by running with the crowd as it retreated from clone rifles and police stun batons. He'd attempted to disappear, but he didn't know the city. Cam droids would spot him, or he'd stumble into sight of some unlucky security officer, and the chase would start again.

Yet the Imperial forces were a threat he knew how to confront. Urban warfare was urban warfare, even in a metropolis larger than any he'd encountered before. The mob itself had been more problematic, throwing off his senses and leaving him overstimulated and uncertain of the dangers all around. The protesters had come to send the message that there was no place for Separatists in the Empire, that Separatist sins were too great to be forgiven. They'd moved with a million limbs but spoken with one voice, wrapping around Soujen like a serpent, and he'd known that if they squeezed, there would be no escape.

He'd eventually slipped past the security cordon and away from the demonstrators, riding cargo lifts deeper into the city, where there were fewer Imperial troops and fewer cams. He'd wrapped himself in a red pilgrim's robe, stolen off a drunk in an alleyway. He'd passed through levels that smelled of saltwater and kelp—whole city sectors built for aquatic species, where transparent tubes connected spherical buildings and bulging eyes stared out windows.

He had no destination in mind. The farther he was from the protests, the better his chances at survival, at least for a while.

But to what end? He skirted a night market now, where he towered over ankle-high locals as they traded scrap metal and food, and where machine stalls trimmed tools and bolts of fabric to suit miniature hands. He was in enemy territory with his once-clear plan of action sullied by the facts on the ground. The senator and Haki had both claimed that evidence exonerating the Jedi could bring about a revolution, yet his experiences on Coruscant filled him with doubt. Would the mob protesting Separatist representation suddenly turn on the Empire? Would these beings living in Coruscant's abyss take up arms and march on the Senate kilometers above?

It was possible, but it was difficult to imagine. He thought back to the woman on Li'eta who had said, "Resentment doesn't fill stomachs. People around here *like* not being in a war zone. They like not sorting through rubble for the dead."

Survival came first. Reformulating his plan could come after. He wandered on. He glimpsed blurry images of himself on billboards, along with lists of his crimes, culminating in the "attack" on Eyo-Dajuritz. He saw public holo-terminals flash his face between liquor advertisements and announcements from the grand vizier. A loudspeaker announced lockdowns and searches of the Federal District. He wondered whether they would put a bounty on him, and what price they would set. He thought the last true Separatist soldier on Coruscant deserved a considerable sum. *Kill me and you end the war.*

He crossed a transparent metal bridge embedded with multicolored lights and arrived on a street alive with spice dealers, performers, and taxi droids, all catering to young humanoids dressed in what Soujen presumed were the latest fashions: synthleather jackets with angular collars and holographic overlays, skintight gauze-and-lace body wraps

with sparks flowing down their seams, patchwork coats with hems con-
stantly woven and unwoven by larvae. Against the glow of the wealthy
and fashionable, the mass of poorer figures—the hangers-on, the non-
functional addicts, the folk who clearly lived in this sector and hadn't
merely come slumming—nearly vanished into darkness.

High above, half-concealed by roadways and catwalks, a security airspeeder was descending and probing the area with its spotlights. With
his head low and his pilgrim's shawl tight over his face, Soujen followed
a group of humanoids too intoxicated to notice he wasn't part of their
clique, joining them when they proceeded through the triangular doorway of a nightclub. The airspeeder landed some distance behind, and he
heard the amplified voices of the underworld police before the thrum-
ming of club music drowned them out.

The club was busy, but there was space to move, with as many patrons slumped in booths or under tables as dancing; even the dancers
had the unsteady, graceless gait of celebrants who'd been on their feet
for hours, experiencing a cultish rapture, their sweat more spice than
salt. Humans and Duros predominated, and here and there Ithorians or
Thisspiasians writhed, lounged, or draped themselves over railings. The
wealthy and fashionable mingled with the manifestly impoverished. The
only things common to all the club goers were their youth and their
ecstasy. They laughed and moaned and smiled, or stared glass-eyed into
the walls as if they saw the secrets of the universe reflected in the metal
plating. The music was too loud for conversation. They took notice of
one another only to synchronize their movements, to dance together
and kiss.

The patrons seemed oblivious to their own extremes of privilege and
poverty—and surely oblivious to the sins of the Republic that had
brought so much opulence to Coruscant's aristocrats and left the lower
levels to starve, along with whole sectors of the wider galaxy. It mad-
dened Soujen. He walked deeper into the club.

Were the underworld police approaching the entrance? He couldn't
risk looking back. He crossed a transparent section of flooring and saw
Mon Calamari and Quarren—ancient species who'd shared a home-

world divided by the war—swimming together in a gargantuan tank below.

They were as oblivious to species and planetary lineage as they were to wealth and class. Soujen wanted to tear his scarf from his face and show them what he was, to ask whether they knew what the Republic had done to *his* people over centuries, and whether they understood the intractability of human domination.

Now he glimpsed an armored officer at the club's entrance, holding a stun prod in one hand.

Soujen moved past the bar and booths, down a corridor strewn with dancers defeated by the dance. He stepped over bodies and walked again through the fields of Leyoye Prime, where his comrades had lain in the dust, dying without blood or broken bones; dying by the fire of blaster bolts and laser swords, reaching toward him for help or simply to touch a living being. He'd walked on then, unable to spare time even for Poan, who had survived so long only to see his heart turned to ash. If he'd stopped, the enemy would have found him. He'd walked on then, and he walked on now.

How could the dancers fail to see that they mocked the dead? That their groans and laughter taunted the fallen?

He knew the police weren't confident of his presence. They'd have come in force, not by ones and twos. But they would recognize him if they found him. He increased his pace, leaving the bodies behind, and realized his heart rate had accelerated. He heard a snicker and tensed as if assaulted. He swung to the right, passing through another doorway and heading toward the sound.

He was in a narrow vanity lounge, with a mirror on one side and trashed sofas and restroom stalls on the other. There were three occupants—a man and a woman giggling on one of the sofas, and a second woman peeling holographic mesh off her skull at the mirror. Soujen glanced into the mirror and saw himself as in the news feeds, the ones proclaiming him an assassin, a terrorist, and the vandal who'd erased eons of galactic history. He saw the face of a killer, and he thought of all his crimes the Empire had failed to associate him with—the deaths, the bombings, the kidnappings, everything before the war and during it.

The club goers didn't notice him. Their laughter rose, and again he flinched.

"What are you laughing about?" he asked.

He'd meant to speak in his usual steady tone, but the words came out too loud and too ragged. The woman at the mirror and the one on the sofa looked his way, confused.

He needed to leave. He would be easy for the underworld police officer to find. Instead, he marched up to the sofa and looked down at the pair there. "Why aren't you at the protests?" he asked. The man shook his head. "Doesn't it matter to you?"

Soujen was close to shouting. He knew it was foolish, and he understood, in part, why he was doing it. The taste of rage obscured the taste of despair.

The man—clearly intoxicated—clapped his hands over his ears and said, "Go away!" The woman at the mirror moved as if to pass Soujen and return to the club. Soujen gestured with a fist and triggered his microlaser, casting a burning thread across half a meter of the mirror and cracking the surface. "Tell me!" he said, and the woman stopped where she was.

"We don't want trouble," the woman said. She was dark-haired, dressed in a coat that might have bought a year's worth of food for the Nahasta clan. Only the Nahasta clan was gone now.

"Tell me," Soujen said, "what you did during the war. When your Republic was blockading our worlds, caging us, did you volunteer to fight or did you let the clones do your killing for you? Did you even notice what was going on?"

He gestured at all three in turn.

The intoxicated man stared up at him with bloodshot eyes. "What war?" the man asked. "What war?"

Soujen smiled coldly, but the dark-haired woman suddenly spoke: "You're Separatist? You're Separatist. You think we didn't suffer? You took our *food*. We had whole levels starving because you cut off agricultural routes. Of *course* we fought back, and that was before—"

"What did you do?"

"—your fleet came to attack us—"

"What did *you* do?"

"I went to university! I worked in a habacha shop! You think I should've picked up a gun and—"

He aimed his microlaser at the woman on the sofa, the only one who hadn't spoken. He didn't recognize her species—the tendrils of her hair ended in thorny stickers. "What about you?" he asked. "Or are you like your friend? Did you know there was a war going on?"

"Yes," the woman said. Her voice was small, but she'd scooted over to shield her companion with her body. "Yes, I knew."

"And how did you spend the war years?"

She said something too quiet for Soujen to hear over the music. He adjusted the pickup on his implants and asked again.

"I was fourteen years old," she whispered. "What was I supposed to do?"

Now the woman at the mirror was speaking again, and Soujen couldn't hear her over the noise and the blood in his ears. *Age is no excuse,* he thought, but he didn't say it. In the chaos of his memory, he couldn't find the names of his brothers who'd gone to fight when they were twelve, thirteen, fourteen. Age had never been an obstacle to war, and even the Republic had known that, sending clones younger than his brothers onto the battlefield. His mind scrabbled for any thought beyond rage. The man's voice—*"What war? What war?"*—became the voice of Senator Organa offering to remove his implants: *"There's still beauty in the galaxy. There's no shame in stepping away from the fight for a day or a lifetime."*

He fired the microlaser in bursts, burning holes in the wall as the club goers cried out and dived. One lurched toward him to attack, and he kicked her hard in the jaw. He felt skin and bone break, though he doubted he'd killed her. There was screaming—from inside the lounge or out, he wasn't sure—and he hurried back to the hallway, clambering over the dancers' bodies as he moved to a back door and out into the street. The club music followed him, and he wanted to turn around. He'd been *soft*, and now he'd humiliated himself, thrown a petty tantrum and done nothing meaningful to right things—to steal the peace from people who did not *deserve* peace, who'd done nothing to fight the war and nothing to stop it. He could still fix it, he thought, but then he glimpsed the lights of the police speeder, rising like a predator, and he began to run. He couldn't stay. He didn't know what his mission was anymore, but he couldn't stay.

CHAPTER 48
GOING HUNTING

They'd had the shifts all planned out, starting seventy-two hours before the reintegration. "Large-scale, sustained protest is the name of the game," Laevido had told them. "Our job is to organize and inspire. And if we do it right, more and more people will show as we approach the Seppies' inauguration. It starts with us—the true believers, the real oddballs. Then the casual supporters join, and finally ordinary folk who don't pay politics a lot of attention but want to do the right thing.

"If we exhaust ourselves too early, though, the whole damn protest collapses. So you take care of each other. You need to go home awhile? Go home. When you're handing out water, keep some for yourself. Don't scream yourself hoarse today if you want folks to listen tomorrow."

Chemish and the other 4040s had taken in the instructions and cheered, and they'd marched on the Federal District under the eyes of the troops. They'd joined imperialist activists from across Coruscant, even some from offworld, and they'd distributed guidelines about where to go and how to behave in coordination with group leaders from other levels. It had been almost festive—a celebration of like-minded people devoted to the Empire, together and amazed at their own strength.

Then the terrorist threat had come in, and everything had fallen apart.

"It's a fake-out. They want to shut us down."

"Why would Palpatine want—"

"Don't be dense. Organa brought the terrorist here, he's the one who . . ."

They'd regrouped in the dive bar where Chemish had first met the 4040s, after the memorial for Zhuna's killer. The place was full of protesters ousted by the security forces locking down the Federal District, slurping soup and passing around protein pills as they awaited Laevido's return. Every surface was wet with rainwater carried in by the crowd.

Chemish kept their head down. Chemish drank their soup. Chemish wanted to go home and didn't know what they were watching for anymore.

They caught a whiff of deodorant as Fowlitz leaned over them. "You all right? You look wrecked."

Chemish glanced up and forced a smile. "I'm all right. Exhausted. Any news?"

"Laevido's done with the other organizers, heading back this way. Should be word soon."

Chemish nodded and pushed back their chair. "Okay. I'm going to call my mom, make sure everyone's home safe."

"A Separatist terrorist won't last long on Coruscant. He makes any trouble, we'll find him." Fowlitz clapped a hand on Chemish's back. "You need anything, you or your family, let us know."

Chemish thanked him and shouldered their way through the crowd. The conspiracy theories and gossip and news broadcasts all merged into background static. They found a comm booth next to the restrooms and squeezed in, punched in a sequence, and waited for the inevitable buzz of a rejected linkup.

Chemish had tried to contact Haki every day since their ill-fated meeting with Imperial Intelligence—since Chemish's interviewers had shown more interest in Senator Mothma than whatever Laevido was up to and Chemish had been informed that Haki was "out, even if she doesn't know it." Maybe it was careless. Maybe it would incriminate Chemish if Haki really was in trouble. But there were too many questions only Haki could answer.

Besides, Chemish was worried. Haki was difficult and unpredictable, but she'd given Chemish's life meaning after Homish had died. Rightly or not, Chemish thought of her as a friend.

But Chemish had received no word, no indication that their mentor was receiving their transmissions, until now. A mechanical voice asked for a code. Chemish replied with a series of numbers.

"All right, Chemish," Haki's voice said from the speaker. "So we're in a bad way."

"Haki?" Chemish asked.

"If you're hearing this," the voice continued, "I'm past my check-in, and you should assume I'm dead. Might not be, but so far as you're concerned, I'm gone and no help to you. Don't worry why or how. That's for my employers to deal with.

"I'm sorry I couldn't give you the training you deserved. Sorry I wasn't able to bring your brother home. I did what I could, but it wasn't enough. Bit of money's coming your way, but it might take time, and it won't make you rich—just a gesture, really."

Chemish listened, but all they'd really heard was *Assume I'm dead.*

"You're a good kid. You're okay at the work. You want to join Intelligence the proper way, they'll take you. There are worse things you can do in life than serve the Republic. The Empire. Same thing. But if I can offer you one bit of advice . . ."

There was a long pause.

"I'm trying not to get mawkish, trying to stay practical. Here's what I'll tell you, Chemish. Do right by your people. Do right by your employers. Do right by your nation. Do it in that order. And don't forget the galaxy can get by without you. This work . . . it inflates your ego, but none of us are that important in the end."

The transmission ended abruptly. Chemish blinked and thought of Haki, and Zhuna, and Homish.

/ / /

"Senator Mothma and Senator Organa have been released by the security bureau," Laevido declared. "But we have every reason to believe their intentions are treasonous. The terrorist identified as Soujen Vak-Nhalis is at large. The Separatist *representatives* are arriving as we speak, and their allies in the Senate are plotting their next move. This confluence of events is no coincidence." He stood at the front of the bar, and Chemish had to strain to hear him. No one else spoke, but the rain, the squeak of shoes, and the rustle of coats muffled Laevido's voice. Chemish felt too hot in the crowd. Their undershirt was stained with sweat.

"My friends in the administration," Laevido went on, "have not authorized me to share everything that they know. I cannot tell you whether Mothma and her ilk seek to *cause* tragedy or merely benefit from it. But my contacts encourage us to take appropriate action. We won't have access to the Federal District, but we can patrol the city to assist the police and continue protesting away from the Senate. I'll provide a list of senators' residences shortly. If you spot Mothma or Organa, signal me. If you spot Vak-Nhalis, alert local security and signal me after."

As Laevido handed out assignments, Chemish tried to pay attention and not think about Haki, dead somewhere for reasons Chemish would never know. They tried to care about whether Organa and Mothma were *really* plotting treason or whether the 4040s were putting lives in danger unnecessarily. It all seemed unreal. Even the terrorist threat felt distant and intangible. Chemish had friends of friends who'd died in the Siege of Coruscant. They recognized the damage Vak-Nhalis could inflict. But Chemish didn't seem to have enough space in their mind to process it.

"You're with us," Laevido said. He was directly in front of Chemish.

"Where are we going?" Chemish asked.

"Hunting," Laevido said, tapping his umbrella on the floor. "You up for it?"

"Absolutely," Chemish said, and put on the face of the spy, the liar, the 4040 member. Because whatever their feelings, they were stuck in the mission. What other choice was there?

CHAPTER 49
A SUGGESTION
OF MURDER

Mon had made record time from the Federal District to the ports. The protests were still going on, but they'd been driven away from the government center and into adjacent sectors, leaving the security forces free to lock down the district perimeter and patrol it for Soujen Vak-Nhalis. The Separatist agent's image was on every screen imaginable, and even outside the district the trams were nearly empty. The pedestrians looked about nervously and hurried on to their destinations.

Who could blame them? Mon understood that fear wasn't rational. Fear was *felt,* and the people of Coruscant were feeling the terror they'd experienced when Separatist warships had entered orbit, when battle droids had marched through the streets just a few months prior and debris had rained down to pulverize housing blocks. They felt the utter uncertainty of war—the bone-marrow knowledge that death could come at any moment, and that intellect, strength, and wealth couldn't save you when the sky fell.

The shuttle captain frantically waved Mon aboard, and she settled into her seat as the vessel lifted itself on repulsors, then jolted as it engaged thrusters. Her staff had worked miracles, she was sure, to get her a flight. She'd woken up her chief of staff after parting ways with Bail, described exactly what she'd needed, and brushed off questions about her detention. Then she'd disconnected and proceeded to call in half a dozen favors. That would hurt her in the coming days, months, and years. But she had to survive the night first.

For the third time since her release from interrogation, she retrieved her comlink and prepared to call Perrin. She'd yet to speak to him since her return to Coruscant, though surely he'd heard she was onworld. Surely one of her staffers had mentioned it, or he'd called her office or been approached by the security bureau himself? But each of the previous times she'd begun to call, she'd remembered some other, more urgent problem to tackle first—and now she simply didn't know what to say.

She couldn't delay any longer. *Talk to your husband, Mon. It shouldn't be so hard.*

She activated the link and got an audio-only connection.

"Mon?" His voice was thick, and his tone was puzzled. He'd been drinking, perhaps, or sleeping. "Where are you?"

"I'm back," she said. "I'm working. I can't talk long. You're all right?"

"I'm all right," he said.

Her sense of relief surprised her.

"What about you?" he asked. "Where are you? You know there's—"

"I know. I really can't talk." Better if she didn't share her plan, and better if the security bureau couldn't trace the call. "I'm—" *Say you're okay,* she urged herself, but that was a lie she couldn't bring herself to tell. Perrin had seen her joyful and curious, and he'd seen her in despair. He'd accompanied her on that last visit to her mother, when the woman had seemed so frail, arguing about her appetite and refusing her medication as she'd withered away in bed.

There were many things Mon could hide from Perrin—but not everything.

She hoped he hadn't heard about her "affair" with Lud Marroi. She doubted he had.

"I'll tell you someday," she said. "Stay safe. Stay inside. I'll be home as soon as I can."

She ended the call while Perrin fumbled for words, then turned to study the stars beyond the shuttle window.

The tensions unleashed by the protests and the assassin had reached Hesperidium, too, and a full security team surrounded the shuttle as it landed. Mon disembarked, spoke a few words to the officer in charge, and was escorted through the port. There was no ornate carriage this time, just a militarized speeder that dropped her off at the entrance to the Axiom Club. The lights were so dim she could barely see the elegant wood and stone interior, but she could smell springtime and she could smell money. The holographic trophies had been deactivated. A single figure stood inside, near where she'd first met Arvik Cornade, Baron Yew, and Hasalia Prederiko.

"I didn't expect us to meet again so soon," Tychon Nulvolio said.

"Nor did I, until a few hours ago. You arrived safely?"

Nulvolio inclined his head. "I was en route to Coruscant for the reintegration when your message came. We diverted to Hesperidium without incident. You must have impressed Arvik Cornade, for him to arrange this on your behalf."

"Oh, I expect he's furious with me. But he's made his bet, and there's no backing out now." She crossed the room toward Nulvolio and gestured for him to sit. He remained standing, and she didn't blame him. It was all she could do not to pace. "You heard about the Separatist assassin? Soujen Vak-Nhalis?"

"I've seen the feeds."

"He came from Eyo-Dajuritz. You were concerned about something happening there."

Nulvolio watched her, impassive. She hadn't really expected a response.

"I have additional information about Vak-Nhalis's past and his actions on Eyo-Dajuritz. You asked me to share anything I learned, and I'm doing so now. But you clearly know things I do not, things that could be invaluable in resolving this situation before anyone else is hurt."

She again tried to picture the attack on Eyo-Dajuritz and the ruins crumbling into dust. Then she blotted the horror from her mind. She had to stay focused.

"What is it you've heard," Nulvolio asked, "that isn't on the public feeds?"

Tell me what you know so I know how to lie to you.

Still, she answered. "Vak-Nhalis was a Separatist weapon of last resort, given a mission to continue waging war against the Republic if the rest of the Confederacy fell. On Eyo-Dajuritz, he was seeking a Separatist supply cache. The cache was destroyed, and he proceeded here. I don't know what he wants now."

All of that was true, so far as it went.

Nulvolio turned away and strode to the one-way windows, staring out onto the moon's artificial landscape.

"That is correct, per my own understanding," he said. "There were elements inside the Confederacy concerned that our good fortune would not hold, that the series of wonders that had positioned us to win the war could just as easily be undone. A contingency was desired, so Vak-Nhalis and others were created for that purpose."

What was your role? she wanted to ask. But knowing would do her no good, and that wasn't what she needed to press him on.

"What will Vak-Nhalis attempt to do next?" she asked. "Where will he go?"

"It is possible he has some grand scheme. He had a hostage, did he not? But whatever he intended, it can't have been this." Nulvolio looked back to Mon. "He has no resources other than his wits and his augmentations. He will find no allies on Coruscant. That suggests to me he will return to his most basic directives."

"Meaning what?"

"He is a mercenary and assassin by training, yet he is also a man of passion. I think he will look at the targets Coruscant offers and choose based on practicality and ideology. I think he will take special notice of the coming reintegration and the presence of those representing former Separatist worlds. He will view me and my fellow senators-elect as traitors—that much I am certain of—and I suspect he will target us first."

"Why prioritize you and not members of the administration? Or senators like me?"

Nulvolio shrugged. "Kill *you,* and he shows the cause is still alive. Kill *me,* and he does the same—but he also sends a warning that disloyalty will be punished. This is the logic of revolution."

She supposed he was right. That had been the way of the Thulgars of Cheelit, and of the Coruscant Revolutionary Battalion in the Republic's early years. Only the hive minds of the galaxy seemed immune to the urge to rank heresy the highest of crimes, and they simply didn't understand betrayal.

Yet Nulvolio spoke with too much confidence. He did not act like someone working through the logic of a thing, but like someone presenting foregone conclusions.

"It would be in our interests," Mon said, "to address this situation quickly."

"I concur."

"But"—she would need to be careful here, or else she'd lose him—"there are *complexities* that I'm not at liberty to share. It would be best if he were not caught by the security forces."

"Is that so?"

"It is so." She offered a smile, in recognition of the game. "If there was a way for me to meet Vak-Nhalis, I believe I could move matters toward a beneficial resolution."

Nulvolio scowled, and she spoke over him before he could object. "I understand it would entail risk, and I'm willing to shoulder that risk myself. All I ask is your help in arranging a meeting, if you are able. Will you claim this is beyond you?"

He grunted softly. "Even if I were to eliminate my personal risk, *your* death would be a severe inconvenience to me, Senator. Like Arvik Cornade, I have bet a great deal on your continued existence. I do not see what I have to gain by putting you in contact with Vak-Nhalis, even if I were able to do so."

"Perhaps little," Mon said. "But I wonder what you might lose by inaction. You do not want him to succeed at disrupting the reintegration, and I believe you do not want him apprehended by Imperial Security.

You may have other plans, but I tell you this: Vak-Nhalis will speak to me if I can find him. And if you attempt to find him *without* me and deal with him via your own methods—"

Then what? Was it worth threatening him for this? For Bail's mad plan to exonerate the Jedi?

"Then I can promise you that Imperial Intelligence will find reason to dig deeper into your connections to Vak-Nhalis." She let the words settle before adding, "I am not your enemy in this."

Nulvolio understood, she was sure, yet he appeared unfazed. "I do not believe you are. But war was *simpler,* wasn't it?"

"It was. That's what's got us here."

Nulvolio laughed, low and mirthless.

"I can arrange a message to be delivered somewhere Vak-Nhalis may find it. If I ask for a meeting, he may come to the coordinates I provide. After all, I suspect he wants me dead quite badly." He gestured, looping a jagged fingernail through the air. "Under no circumstances will I show my face. He is not a *sentimental* man, and armed with a sniper rifle, he could shoot me from a kilometer away. If he finds you at the coordinates instead, he may shoot you or choose not to approach at all."

"As I said, I'm willing to take the risk. And for whatever it's worth, I have made arrangements for the vote to proceed in case I'm unable to sponsor the Rebirth Act."

Nulvolio smiled for the first time since she'd arrived in the lodge. It wasn't warm, but it seemed like a display of grudging respect.

They sat together, and she proposed a location for the meeting with Soujen. Nulvolio warned her to proceed there as soon as she could but not to be surprised if the assassin showed up late—under the circumstances, the logistics would be challenging. When the business was done and Mon peered through the door of the lodge, hoping her shuttle pilot hadn't abandoned her on Hesperidium, Nulvolio approached her from behind and said, "There is one more thing. Because, as I said, I do not wish you dead."

"What is it?" she asked.

"The agents chosen for augmentation—the ones built to fight on after the war's end—they had fail-safes installed in their systems, hidden in their databanks. A means to trigger their self-destruct devices without their consent."

She tried to hide her distaste. "A means for the handlers to murder their agents?"

"You assume the agents were not trusted, that the fail-safes were a security measure. This is not the case. The agents were outfitted for payload delivery, for targeted assassinations. Their outfitters anticipated one type of mission that would test the limits of the agents' self-preservation instincts, and thus . . ." Nulvolio watched her until she understood.

"You needed a way of turning them into living bombs," she said. "The Confederacy wanted suicide bombers who couldn't possibly back out."

"At least they were volunteers, not bred for the task and given a role they never asked for."

She waved a hand to forestall another argument. She'd only lose her temper. "I take your point. This fail-safe, then . . . ?"

"It relies on audio cuing, face-to-face or over a clear comm. One keyword, spoken aloud, to prime the self-destruct device. Wait five minutes for it to charge, then speak the second keyword, and the agent will detonate."

She had no intention of killing Vak-Nhalis, but the more she knew about him the better. She nodded to show she'd heard.

"I'm afraid I can't speak to the force of the blast," Nulvolio continued, "or what would happen if you mistimed the second keyword. As I said, this sort of situation is not what the fail-safes were built for. Nonetheless, I give you the keywords with my blessing: First, *oubliette*. Second, *sublime*. Repeat them, please."

"Oubliette." She met his gaze. "Sublime."

Nulvolio nodded. He seemed to hesitate, then extended a hand. As when they first met, his fingers were curled into a claw, and it was clear to Mon the gesture was foreign to him. She clasped his hand and shook it before he stepped backward.

"He is dangerous," Nulvolio said. "Do not hesitate to act."

"Thank you," Mon said, and she left the lodge for the warm Hesperidium night.

CHAPTER 50
OLD-FASHIONED POLITICS

With the Federal District on lockdown, they'd relocated to Cantham House, and Bail had been transported back to his first year as a senator: Back to when he'd been seen as a mere accessory to the Queen of Alderaan. To when Breha had laughed at Bail and told him to be glad he didn't have a planet to run. To when Bail and his staff had spent long nights at Cantham writing speeches, eating takeout, napping on cots, and prepping for floor debates no one else had cared about.

Now Cantham's living room was full of Bail's advisers, speechwriters, and junior aides, along with assessment droids and messenger units—and Breha, his salvation, who'd offered all the resources at her disposal for "this ridiculous scheme you've concocted."

He'd embraced her and told her he loved her. He hadn't explained half the complexities of it all, and he could see the questions hidden behind her eyes, the unanswered tension. But they were together once more.

Now both of them were switching from call to call, reassuring Mon's coalition that everything was on track. The terrorist attack on Eyo-

Dajuritz and the presence of the assassin on Coruscant wouldn't disrupt anything. The protests were already factored in—Senator Mothma had expected a degree of backlash but was confident the Rebirth Act would still have broad support. Mothma's absence was nothing to be alarmed by, and Senator Organa had her full confidence. Bail told senators, some of whom he'd never met, precisely what they wanted to hear. He cursed Mon under his breath as he read the bill between crises, a few paragraphs at a time, and saw the rat's nest of promises and sweeteners that ballooned its page count.

But he made amendments only to preserve some fragile alliance on the verge of breaking, or when one of the droids flagged passages unlikely to survive court challenges. He did not rewrite the bill to his own vision. Mon had trusted him, and she was—he reminded himself—very good at what she did. The galaxy would be better off *with* the Rebirth Act than *without*.

Besides, he'd relinquished his chance to improve it when he'd run off with Haki. The bill's imperfections were his fault as much as anyone's.

Accounting for the hundreds of senators who knew nothing about the bill but who were likely to follow their bloc leaders, and accounting as well for last-minute defections and general chaos, the droids gave the Rebirth Act a 58 percent chance of passing. That number was recalculated every fifteen minutes, and Bail saw it as his duty to keep it above 50 percent.

He was kneeling on the floor beside one of his junior staffers, hurriedly dictating a reply to an Outer Rim senator who wanted to tack anti-terrorism measures onto the bill, when he heard a roar from the foyer. Bail straightened and turned to see a Togorian with the bulk of a small mountain push his way past an army of aides, shaking his mane and baring his fangs. A formal black overcoat accentuated the man's musculature and contrasted with his white fur.

"Senator Wajiss?" Bail called, quickly crossing the room. The aides parted, though several stayed close. In the foyer, Bail spotted two house security officers with their hands on holstered weapons. "Good to see you again. We didn't get to talk much at the treaty ceremony, but—"

"Where is Senator Mothma?" Wajiss asked, glowering down at Bail. He was a full head taller than the human.

"Unavailable. What's the trouble?"

"The *trouble*," Wajiss said, "is that this is *not* what I agreed to. I joined your Delegation of Two Thousand, and I was arrested for my efforts. I told Mothma I'd vote for the Rebirth Act only if it contained no power grabs, nothing to complicate the messaging."

"That was the goal," Bail said, "but you've been through this process. The only way—"

"She broke her promise to me! I spoke to Senator DuQuosenne, who says she's been betrayed as well. And now you have the gall to call my staff after midnight, in the midst of a terrorist threat, wanting to know where I stand?"

"No one should've been calling you at this hour," Bail said, though he felt the lie in his chest. He could hear staffers all around him talking into their comlinks. "Look, why don't we speak on the patio? If you've been mistreated, I'll gladly take the blame."

Because as long as Wajiss focused on *him*, there was still a chance to salvage a yes vote on the bill.

"Find me Senator Mothma," Wajiss said.

Bail lowered his voice. "Senator Mothma is unavailable, thanks to the lockdown. I don't know the details, but it's entirely possible she's working with the administration to protect us all—"

It was *entirely possible* but extremely unlikely, and this half lie, too, revolted Bail. These were the easy falsehoods, the ones that he'd learned to deal out habitually years ago, but all it took was a few weeks away from politics to make him aware of how often he dissembled and distorted the truth.

Wajiss saved him from having to continue. The massive Togorian shoved Bail, and Bail tumbled into a lounge table, felt the metal edge of the tabletop strike his spine before his bottom hit the floor. Wajiss was yelling something, and security was hurrying into the room, and Bail waved them all off, calling through the pain, "Stop! Stop!" He picked himself up and, doing his best to stay steady, met Wajiss's gaze. "Are you through?"

The Togorian growled, turned about, and headed back into the foyer.

At least one vote lost. Wajiss was a man with some pull as well. If he and DuQuosenne were *both* abandoning the bill . . .

The thoughts dissolved as he felt himself guided, gently but decisively, out of the madness of the living room and into the primary bedroom. Breha sat him on the bed and said something he didn't hear, and he flinched as she rolled his shirt up his back.

"What happened to you?" she asked, and he heard a shock and dismay in her voice that he hadn't anticipated.

He twisted his neck to try to see. "Am I bleeding?"

"No," she said. "Yes, a little. But you look—what happened?"

He understood then. She hadn't seen his body since Eyo-Dajuritz.

He started to explain, but she was puttering in the bathroom, and a moment later she'd brought out bandages and bacta spray. He smelled the pungent mist as she tended to him, and he tried not to flinch as she touched his injuries.

Eventually she came to sit next to him. "Someone hurt you," she said.

"Yes."

"When you were captured?"

"Yes."

"Do you have time to tell me?"

He knew what she meant—not just *time,* but the strength and wherewithal to revisit the brutality.

"I don't."

"Then we should get back to the others," she said.

He nodded. "Thank you for staying on Coruscant—for everything."

He knew in his heart she wasn't there just for him. She *believed* him when he said that his work could change the galaxy and that the Queen's word might mean the difference between success and failure. Breha was a woman of duty and faith. She trusted in Bail as no one else ever had, and he would forever be grateful for that.

He stood and straightened, flexing to test the bandages and the pain in his back, and before he could return to the living room, Breha stopped him and turned him and embraced him gently. She held him for a long time, stroking his hair, and he felt the memory of what had been done to him at the cache—felt the acute weakness of his body, the violence that had been inflicted and that he'd managed to deny until now. Breha's touch drew forth the pain, and it was too soon—because it would draw forth other pains, too, and he could dwell on his agonies in a month but not today. Not today.

He removed her hands from his body and kissed them. She seemed to understand. She dabbed at his fresh tears. "I'm proud of you," she said.

He laughed softly, but her expression was somber.

"I am," she said. "You look like yourself again, under all the scars. More than you have since Padmé died, or—any of the others."

Since the Jedi.

"I didn't know," he said.

Had he lost himself? Had he found himself again? As Breha trusted in him, he trusted in her. What she saw was *real,* even if he didn't understand.

"Earlier"—she hesitated, seeming to reformulate her words—"you said the journey was all for her, for Leia. But that's not the way we save her, not by running off, grieving and desperate and ignoring who we are."

"If we don't set things right—"

"We *will* set things right," she said, in the voice of the Queen of Alderaan. Then she became Breha again, and her lips pursed. "But if we fail, she'll need both her parents—because both of us carry too many burdens to be a parent alone. She'll need to learn from us, learn by example, and . . . you're good at this." She tilted her head toward the living room. "Not wrangling a bill, not playing hero, but . . . working with people, bringing them together. Don't forget that."

Then she moved past him, and he was left to wonder whether sitting in his living room making calls was somehow more valuable than risking his life. He wondered what the Jedi would have said, and how that notion fit their lives of unmitigated peril.

Think on it later, he told himself. He checked his face for tearstains, then followed his wife back into the crowd of staffers and the pandemonium of Cantham House.

CHAPTER 51
SECRET LAYERS

The underworld police began sealing off the block moments after his departure from the club. If they'd had clone backup, Soujen might never have escaped.

Yet he'd managed to locate a decommissioned water main, a shaft running through the city to a reservoir or an ocean far below. It was fifty meters across, unlit, and lined with sensors, pressure meters, and purification systems. There had been no ladders and few handholds, and he'd nearly fallen three times during his descent. Any mistake would have killed him, implants or no.

Now he didn't know where he was—five hundred levels under the Federal District, at least. He crawled across catwalks spanning generators and heat pumps and more esoteric machinery. And though he saw no living creatures, he watched warily for maintenance drones. When he located a droid's recharging alcove, he tucked himself inside, knees drawn to his chest, and shut the door.

The darkness was broken by green and white status lights, not much like stars but the closest he'd seen since arriving on Coruscant. This world was a place of killers, fools, and hedonists, he thought, a world of metal, without ground or sky or anything natural, anything *true* to bond with.

He wondered whether he could hide forever in the bowels of Coruscant. He could emerge to scavenge food and water before returning to the dark. If someone saw him, he could descend lower, and lower again, until he reached abyssal depths never touched by sunlight. He could survive as the ghosts of Eyo-Dajuritz had survived—until they hadn't.

Those ghosts were gone now. Hiding would be no life. And what difference was there between a meaningless life and the embrace of death?

He felt the walls of the alcove and found a data socket. He plugged into the level's maintenance network, probing gently, checking for alerts and unscheduled changes—turbolifts deactivated, sluice gates sealed, anything that might suggest his pursuers were closing in. He found nothing. He felt his software searching for weaknesses, a way deeper into Coruscant's computer systems—again, nothing.

No. There's something.

He didn't understand his programs, but he knew they sought data in the shadowfeeds, the network established by the Confederacy for covert communications and disruptive propaganda. The Separatist data in Coruscant's network was fragmentary—old, decayed, and overwritten— but there was *something*, and his software knew it even if his mind couldn't identify it.

Then he had it—a computerized dead drop, a sort of mailbox in the shadowfeed. Inside was a second *something*, this data newer—an encrypted message encoded for him, set to auto-delete if unopened after twenty hours. Someone knew he was on Coruscant and was attempting to reach him.

He ran the decryption, and his implant fed him the message: MEETING IN PERSON. COORDINATES ATTACHED. WE HAVE NOT FORGOTTEN.

The coordinates meant nothing, but his programs recognized the authentication codes.

Tychon Nulvolio.

Why was Nulvolio on Coruscant?

As soon as he asked the question, the answer came to him. The mobs were protesting the reintegration of Separatist worlds, and Soujen had seen Nulvolio's servile interviews attempting to endear himself to the Empire. The man had come for his consolation prize, a seat in the Imperial Senate, after failing to win the war.

That meant Nulvolio was probably aiding Imperial Security. Possibly he'd admitted to his role in Soujen's creation and was desperately trying to escape the consequences, trading Soujen's life for his own. Or maybe he intended to present Soujen as a gift to the military without ever acknowledging how he'd lured Soujen in. Either option seemed plausible for a man who'd turned so completely against his cause.

Yet Nulvolio *was on Coruscant,* and he was offering himself as bait. Soujen hadn't known the man well, but he'd never seemed a coward. He might well turn up at the coordinates he'd proposed—protected, but doing what was necessary to bring Soujen close enough for the trap to be sprung.

Soujen had failed at so many things. But assassination was something he understood. He had devoted his body and mind to a purpose, and his mission had always been one of vengeance—vengeance for the Separatists and vengeance for his people, against traitors within and enemies without.

Perhaps killing Nulvolio was only a first step. Perhaps he wasn't trapped behind enemy lines without resources. Perhaps he'd infiltrated enemy territory, and Nulvolio was his chance to begin his mission anew, picking foes off one by one.

It was a trap. It was sure to be a trap. But he'd shown too much mercy and too much fear tonight. He could not refuse a chance to reaffirm his purpose.

CHAPTER 52
THE LIMITS
OF PATRIOTISM

They went by foot and by speeder, along empty skyways and down
boulevards littered with foil wrappers, empty bottles, and the
debris left by the protests. They carried handlights and truncheons
and, in a few cases, blasters. Chemish remembered the time Thrizka's
brother had been bludgeoned by an ex-lover and left to bleed out. The
neighborhood had gone hunting, same as the 4040s were hunting now,
loading into delivery vehicles and shouting from rooftop to rooftop
until justice had been done.

Chemish rode in the rear-facing back seat of a cargo speeder, along
with Dakhmi and Jayu. They passed around a pair of macrobinoculars,
each watching the street from a different angle, while Laevido muttered
into his comlink up front and gestured at the driver. Chemish didn't
know the driver. Chemish didn't know enough about anything going
on, and somehow Haki's death made that fact more overwhelming than
ever. Every voice seemed too loud, the textured metal of the macrobinoculars too abrasive. Chemish wanted to climb, to wear their body
down, but they were trapped in the hunt.

"Down three levels," Laevido called. "She's been spotted."

The vehicle lurched forward. Chemish twisted around to look over the synthleather seats at Laevido. "Senator Mothma?"

"You're damn right," Laevido said. "We're on her trail now."

But they'd been on her trail the better part of an hour—thirty of the 4040s, with the rest assigned to protest at senators' homes or track down the terrorist. They'd started at the docks and followed a round-about route through the Warehouse District and the Upper Arts Sector. Three levels down would take them across Chemish's courier haunts near the Duros Blocks.

"Who spotted her?" Chemish asked.

The vehicle bounced, and the odor of old candy bars rose from between the seats. Laevido looked back at Chemish, fidgeting with the scattergun he held in his lap in place of his umbrella. "Pardon?"

"Who saw Senator Mothma? We didn't send anyone down there."

"We have friends all over," Laevido said.

Chemish was ready to argue. *Friends* didn't explain much. *Friends* couldn't have told them the moment Mothma's shuttle had landed. Did the 4040s have someone in Mothma's office? Were Laevido's connections inside the security bureau?

Laevido seemed to recognize Chemish's frustration. "I'll tell you later," he said, and Chemish nodded.

All the 4040s were on edge, tired from a day of protests and primed for violence. Chemish liked Dakhmi and Jayu, and they seemed to like Chemish. Laevido had shown no reservations about Chemish's loyalty since the night Chemish had been drugged. But this wasn't the time to start raising doubts.

Besides, without Haki and without Imperial Intelligence, the 4040s were all the purpose Chemish had left.

They slowed along Glassbreaker Way, and Laevido told the driver to stop, that he and Chemish would proceed on foot while the others went to the senator's last known position. "In case she doubled back," Laevido explained. Soon he was standing on a wet street corner beside a chandelier shop, tapping his scattergun against the ground while Chemish squeezed out of the cargo speeder. Laevido started walking when the vehicle was out of sight.

"I know what you did," Laevido said.

The streets were nearly deserted, though Chemish could see frightened faces peering out from windows, waiting for the terrorist attack. Chemish doubted witnesses would save them.

"What I did?" Chemish asked.

"You went to Imperial Intelligence to report on the 4040s. You were worried what we might get up to at the reintegration." Laevido flashed a smile. His tone was matter-of-fact. "This was days ago. If you've done worse since, you'll have to update me."

"No," Chemish said. They tried to process this, saw a dozen potential paths forward—Haki would have been proud—and settled on playing the fool. "You had someone follow me?"

Laevido laughed and twirled the scattergun. "If I'd been worried enough to have you followed, I wouldn't have kept inviting you in. No—I'm *not* Imperial Intelligence, Chemish, but my backers felt I should know. You want to say why you did it?"

"Why do you think?"

Laevido swung his weapon in Chemish's direction—only for an instant, but long enough to warn. "I asked first."

A speeder whipped down the road, spraying rainwater over them both. Chemish flinched and blinked away the droplets. "You claim we need to be a step ahead of the administration," they said, "that we need to pave the way forward. But that's how allies trip over one another. I wanted to make sure someone was keeping watch."

"Reasonable. Irritating, but reasonable." Laevido held up a hand, listened to his comlink for a moment, then nodded to Chemish. "You mean well. You're loyal to the Empire. I can't hold those things against you. But I need to know you're on our side and you're willing to take direction."

"Why not just cut me loose?" Chemish asked.

They were pushing their luck. And the question probably didn't matter—not if Chemish was trying to understand how the 4040s fit in with the administration, trying to separate out the violence that had killed Zhuna from the violence of the mob—but Chemish wanted to know.

"There's lots to be said for caution and curiosity," Laevido replied. A web of cables overhead was strung with laundry and blinking lights, and his face flashed green and yellow. "Besides, you've seen who's attending the protests—plenty of old men and precious little fresh blood. Your generation grew up in the Clone Wars. You don't appreciate what peace can be, what order can look like. So when I find a young person craving purpose as much as you do, I don't let go easy." He grabbed Chemish's shoulder, squeezed their wet jacket. "You can't be rid of us. You understand?"

"I do," Chemish said. "I'm grateful. I really am. But what about—"

Laevido gestured for silence, muttered something into his comlink, and picked up his pace as they turned down a side street. "You're not convinced we're legitimate?"

"You say you've got backers, but it's just words. And we're hunting an Imperial senator now."

"You know the sort of person Mothma is."

"I do."

Mothma was an opportunist and a hypocrite, but Zhuna had loved her. She wasn't a monster.

"If she's *that* dangerous," Chemish said, "why aren't the police after her? Why didn't Intelligence arrest her weeks ago?"

They picked their way along an underpass, trying to make decent speed while avoiding plunging ankle-deep into stagnant water. Chemish had to squint against the glare of glittering graffiti, but Laevido seemed unaffected. "The galaxy is more complicated than that, and you know it," he said. "The Emperor isn't served by a dozen single-minded loyalists. Even at the highest levels of the administration, there are thousands of governors, department heads—half of them new recruits and half of them remnants of the Republic. Even if their dedication isn't in doubt, how many agree on anything?"

"Isn't the point of having an Emperor to make us all agree on *something*?"

"On *vision*, yes. Implementation is thornier, especially in these early days. Senator Mothma is writing a bill to reorganize the government, and she's doing it with Separatist support. There are factions who want to see her fail on her own because they're worried about seeming heavy-handed. Then there are those who feel that permitting her actions would send the wrong message to the Emperor's enemies."

The logic made sense, though it made Chemish uneasy. They were processing *why* when Laevido gripped his comlink tighter and started to run. Beyond the underpass, he called out an address, and Chemish sped to grab him, turn him, take the lead. "There's a faster route," Chemish said, and they raced beyond Glassbreaker Way and into the Irons. Thirty meters along a rusting byway under sparking conduits, then out of the neighborhood and down a fire escape onto Zephlin's Chrome.

That platform led them back to a central street, where they spotted a gathering of 4040s under the awning of a hostel. The group members shook their heads as Laevido approached.

"We just missed her," Jayu called. "Spotted her from above, but she was gone when we landed."

Laevido snapped orders, instructing the group to spread out, find witnesses, and chase every possible lead. Chemish joined the others as they knocked on doors, passed out credits, and asked the locals what they'd seen. A woman in a poncho had come through, the neighbors said, but she'd moved on—and was this about the Separatist terrorist? Was the neighborhood under attack? Chemish wanted to stay and reassure them, but Laevido was already waving Chemish on.

"She's close," he said. He stabbed the air with his scattergun. "She's *close.*"

"What do we do if we find her?" Chemish asked.

"We stop her."

"What does that *mean*? Your backers—would they really let . . . ?" Chemish trailed off.

"The 4040s are protected. I've been promised that."

"By Intelligence? By who?"

The two of them turned down a narrow road barely wider than an alley, and they were forced to trek around a series of industrial garbage bins. The rain had drawn out a bouquet of rot, and something inside the containers was slithering.

"Tell me this," Laevido said. "In your heart, do you doubt that our efforts are backed by people inside the administration? And if it's true, does it matter *who* backs us? Ideology aside, what would make one party more legitimate than any other?"

It was a good question.

A shrill whistle cut through the night. Laevido's comlink activated at nearly the same moment. "She's ahead!" he barked. "Fifty-five-oh-one Rishon Street. Go!"

Chemish's muscles tensed. "What do we do if we find her?" they asked again.

Laevido scowled, and his voice was urgent and frustrated. "Take her into custody if she'll let us. Senators ought to be locked down during a terrorist threat anyway. If she doesn't cooperate . . . what happens is her problem."

Chemish bolted. Laevido followed, but Chemish was built to run, to climb, to maneuver through the metal canyons of Coruscant with speed and precision. Laevido could never outrace Chemish. They took controlled breaths of the cold, wet air as they found footing on the metal street and darted around the garbage bins. Their mind was blissfully overtaken by the regulation of their body as they sprinted across a catwalk, then swung down to another road beneath. They ran and they climbed and they felt like *Chemish* again, because there was wind in their face and home was all around.

They scrambled onto a rooftop overlooking a fenced junkyard. A figure in a poncho hurried between the scrapped speeders and power units, frequently glancing back toward the street. Outside the fence were a dozen 4040s, shouting and moving toward the junkyard gate. One fired a blaster into the air. The crimson bolt lit the night like a flare.

Chemish kept running along the rooftop above the yard. They could reach the senator before the others, but then what? Would they tackle Mothma to the ground? Hold her until the others arrived? Trust Laevido and his unseen faction inside the administration, hoping justice was served?

Think. What would Haki do?

The truth was, Chemish had no idea. Haki believed in the Empire, and Haki believed in stability. "*Do right by your people. Do right by your employers. Do right by your nation.*" That's what Haki had said—but it was useless to Chemish, and the Empire had failed Haki.

What would Homish do?

Chemish's brother had died for his nation, but Homish hadn't even told Chemish he'd joined Republic Intelligence. Chemish wasn't afraid of making sacrifices. They were afraid of making *mistakes.*

Homish had loved Chemish and their family. He'd loved birds and synthetic barbecue and high-end audio equipment. None of that helped in the here and now.

What would Zhuna do?

That was an easy one, and likewise unhelpful. But thoughts of Zhuna led to thoughts of Zhuna's grisly death, and Chemish remembered the reports of their cousin beaten and terrified. Chemish didn't know whether Zhuna's killer had acted with the support of the other 4040s— Chemish genuinely believed he hadn't—but they looked at the mob pursuing the senator and could see only violence and madness and murder.

Chemish knew what they would do for Zhuna. Even if it meant helping a senator bent on starting another war.

Even if it meant Imperial Intelligence deciding that Chemish was no better than Mon Mothma.

Act now before you talk yourself out of it. Chemish could figure out the politics and the power of it all later.

Chemish dropped four meters into the junkyard, a stone's throw from the woman in the poncho and between her and the mob. Chemish screamed, "Run!" and didn't wait to see whether the woman obeyed. They didn't try to glimpse the woman's face, to see Mothma in person for the first time since Zhuna's memorial. Instead, they stepped to an outbuilding and pulled open a control panel, panting for breath and grinning as they found a heavy switch.

The gates of the junkyard were open. Chemish figured the owners had gone into hiding without locking the place down. They pulled the switch and heard a hum and the clatter of metal. They smelled the faint odor of debris sizzling off protective fields. Only then did they look toward Mothma, and they were relieved to see her gone, out the back way, with the secured junkyard now between her and the mob.

Chemish looked to the 4040s. They were at the shielded fence, and one of them was prying open the gate controls, attempting to override them. Chemish met Jayu's glare, registered Fowlitz's look of disapproval, and felt cold as the ire of the mob was turned upon them.

Chemish tried to remember if they were carrying ID. The 4040s didn't know their real name, but what would happen if Laevido took Chemish's chain codes off their body? Would the 4040s come for their mother? Their cousins?

A speeder pulled up to the gate. More 4040s poured out. Chemish scurried back toward the roof they'd come from and tried to climb a pipe, but they slid back down, failing to find traction on the wet surface. They heard Fowlitz call for them, and they heard two blaster shots, high-pitched and loud as if coming from close by. When they turned, they were looking into the bulbous eyes of a stranger clutching a rifle in both hands.

The stranger spoke rapidly. Chemish struggled to make sense of it: "He did it to the Jedi. He did it to the Jedi, said they were a threat and killed them all. The commission, Palpatine, the Senate, all liars." Chemish shook their head, but the stranger didn't seem to notice. "They're doing it again! Terrorist threat, my ass. They'll do to the Separatists what they did to the Jedi. Make up a threat and kill them all."

The stranger spun, fired a shot at the gate, then slapped Chemish between the shoulders. "Run. Run. My junkyard. My home. I know trouble when I see it. Run!"

CHAPTER 53
THE RENDEZVOUS

Someone was proclaiming via loudspeaker, "War has come again! Return to your homes and pray for swift victory or swifter defeat— but first visit the Personal Defense Emporium to prepare for the coming conflagration! Arm yourselves! Arm your families! Ready yourselves with generators, food, and water! Every customer will be entered into our interplanetary raffle for tickets to Alsakan, Quermia, and Lianna!"

There was a ghoulishness to it, Mon thought, along with a comforting normalcy—better the sounds of despair and profiteering than the threats of the mob or, worse, the sounds of bombs and turbolasers.

She pulled her hood low and hurried through the underlevels. It had been nearing dawn up above, but the lower she went the thicker the darkness became, until midnight reclaimed its crown. She stayed on foot, avoiding even the trams and turbolifts when possible. They would be monitored, she was sure. And if the security bureau found her, then everything had been in vain.

It had been an hour since the protesters had nearly caught her, and that had been her last close call. She'd been saved by a stranger, for reasons Mon didn't dare question. If she felt a touch of guilt for not turning back, not seeing whether her savior had survived, it was guilt easily buried under the crush of her responsibilities. Now she passed through a cordon—little more than a series of warning signs and toppled barricades—and into the rehabilitation zone she'd last visited weeks before. It looked different on foot and in the dark. She saw no construction droids, and the last of the rescue crews had finally accepted defeat. There were only the buildings torn apart by debris during the Siege of Coruscant.

Only that was wrong. There were *people* hidden in the shadows. They slept exposed, inside skyscrapers without facades and tucked into alleys turned into shelters, appointed with wall plating, carpets, dishes, and chairs. No one was supposed to be living in the zone, but of course there were people doing so—she felt foolish for not knowing. Some would be locals who'd lost their homes during the siege. Others, Mon supposed, might have come in search of a deserted place where they might go unmolested.

Were these people afraid that war would come again? Did they care about the Separatist reintegration or the assassin at large? Did they care whether their Emperor was a figurehead or a tyrant? Maybe, Mon thought, everything she'd been working for meant nothing to them— and rightly so, when basic necessities were denied them.

Then again, maybe a person could care about the galaxy as well as their next meal. *Maybe,* she thought, *you should treat them like people and ask them. Maybe you should stop making assumptions.*

Maybe after all this was over.

She heard shouts and groans and someone crooning a lullaby as she maneuvered deeper into the zone. The damage to the ladders, lifts, and boulevards created a labyrinth of dead ends. She had to turn back repeatedly, changing from an easy pace to close to a run as the night moved on. If she missed the rendezvous, she was confident she wouldn't have another chance.

She was within sight of her destination when she found she could proceed no farther. All that was left was to descend one level and cross a single street. But she stood on a narrow, blackened walkway that fol-

lowed the contours of a spire, and the emergency ladders leading down
had all been burned and shattered. The nearest turbolift wasn't functional, with the lift hanging askew in the shaft. There might have been a
stairwell within the spire itself, but whenever she tentatively stepped
through an open doorway or a broken window, she heard the floor
crack menacingly beneath her.

She followed her walkway to a place where the side of the spire became a slope of rubble. To her untrained eye, it appeared that some
starfighter—or pieces of a starfighter—had hit the building there. Its
remains had intermingled with the supports and mechanisms of the
spire, and all had been engulfed in flames. Mon was nearly out of breath,
but time was running short, and backtracking guaranteed no greater
success. The way ahead was clear.

She started her climb down the slope facing forward, as if it were a
stairway, and regretted it almost immediately. She could probe with her
toe for footholds, but she risked toppling with every step. To compen-
sate, she leaned backward and blindly searched for grips on either
side—piping fused into the mound or duracrete blocks heavy enough to
resist being dislodged. She feared slicing her hands open or plunging
them into decaying remains, but she'd committed to the climb. She no
longer had a choice.

Chunks of scorched matter crumbled beneath her feet, inciting miniature avalanches as she picked her way down. At one point, what she'd
mistaken for a solid metal generator turned out to be an empty chassis.
It failed to hold her weight as she stepped on the thing, and she twisted
her ankle as the chassis tumbled to the street. The pain wasn't great—it
was a sprain at worst—but she found herself aggravating the damage as
she wriggled her leg into nooks and crevices. She took the final meter in
a sort of half jump, half run, ending up on scraped hands and knees. But
she'd made it.

Her destination was the hollowed-out skyscraper that stood opposite
the spire, and she proceeded without bothering to look for the assassin.
If Soujen Vak-Nhalis was watching, there was nothing she could do
about it.

The skyscraper interior was much as she remembered, an enormous open space gutted by the construction crews, like a cathedral honoring some ancient god of dust and durasteel beams. It was where the good-will tour had ended all those weeks before, where the reporter droid had needled her and Lud Marroi had saved her. It was perhaps a bit neater now, with the broken conduits stripped away and the construction equipment removed, but nothing had been repaired. The air smelled of soot.

She wished Lud were there now. She wondered whether he was worrying about her somewhere, or whether word had leaked to him about the affair she'd concocted for them. She wondered what he would think about what she was attempting to accomplish, and whether there was any part of him—politics aside, polling aside—that would want her to succeed. He was a friend to the administration, but he wasn't without a conscience. She pushed aside thoughts of her husband before they could form.

She'd drifted to the center of the floor when a voice came out of the dark. It was a voice without emotion, loud enough to penetrate and soft enough not to echo, with the hint of an accent she couldn't place.

"You came alone," the voice said.

She turned toward the source. Soujen Vak-Nhalis stood ten meters distant, dressed in a red pilgrim's robe like the shroud of a dead man. He looked more dangerous and more worn than the images on the news feeds.

Mon nodded. "I'm alone."

"It wasn't a question," Soujen said. "There are no snipers. No surveillance droids. You haven't brought Tychon Nulvolio."

"No, I haven't," Mon said. "He won't be coming."

"Who are you?"

"My name is Mon Mothma. I'm a member of the Imperial Senate, and I was sent by Bail Organa."

As far as she could tell, he was unarmed. There might have been room to conceal a pistol beneath the robes, but his arms hung at his sides. He did not look like a man who felt threatened. Yet she thought about the things Bail had told her, and she wondered how easily Soujen could kill her if he so desired.

The assassin paced a few steps, seeming to consider what she'd said.

"Go on," he said, and Mon felt an unexpected relief.

"Bail believes the plan can still work—that it may be difficult, but that you can bring your evidence to the chief justice and testify before the Senate if we act with speed and discretion. The administration will try to stop you, but it can be done."

" 'It can be done.' " Soujen smiled mockingly.

"Bail told you of his allies in the judiciary and in the security forces. There are levers I can pull as well. Not everyone on Coruscant accepts the administration's claims without question. Even some of those most trusted by Palpatine are loyal to the Republic—or the Empire—above all else."

"You think they'll risk their lives to bring a Separatist terrorist before the Senate? Because the *truth* about the Jedi must be brought to light?"

"Bravery's more common than we often believe," Mon said.

"No. It isn't."

Soujen looked into darkness at something only he could see. Mon shifted her weight and gasped at the pain in her ankle.

With the pain came a surge of impatience—one without justification, grounded in the frustrations of her own endless night, but real nonetheless. She'd suffered humiliation and injury and countless threats since returning to Coruscant. She'd been imprisoned, interrogated, possibly drugged, and nearly murdered by an angry mob. She'd suffered not because she'd done anything grand or terrible—her assailants didn't even know about the Rebirth Act, a tangled ball of compromises that no one could love and no one could hate—but because her politics were no longer fashionable, because neither the administration nor its imperialist followers believed they should have to suffer her impotent entreaties.

She was tired of it all. She was tired of saying half of what she believed and being vilified for it. She was tired of the game she loved, and she hated everyone who'd driven her to such a place.

She tamped down her feelings. *Get on with it!* she thought at Soujen as he paced. Aloud she said nothing.

"Do you really believe," Soujen asked, in a voice that sounded like an accusation, "that my testimony will do any damage whatsoever to those who control your Empire? Do you believe that proving the innocence of the Jedi would cause more than a passing ripple?"

Mon knew the right answer, but she no longer had the strength for it.

"I don't know," she said. "Do I think there's a chance? Yes, absolutely. Wars have been incited by less. Smaller injustices than what became of the Jedi have spurred dictatorships down the path of reform, when those injustices came to light at the right moment, in the right manner. But do I think the Jedi are the key here, now? Do I think their suffering will ring louder than all the cries of the last war? Probably not, Soujen. Probably not."

She couldn't read his expression. Maybe that was why she went on instead of regrouping, instead of trying to *persuade*. "Here's what Bail was right about. The Jedi were *good*. Like all of us, they failed to secure the peace. They were drawn into the war like everyone else, and their hands were *not* clean. If I can accept the blame for my part, they certainly earned their share, too. *But*"—she spat the word and nearly laughed at her own stridency—"for thousands of years they could have ruled the galaxy, and instead they chose to serve. They had their own vested interests, their own ways of politicking. But they believed their power came with an obligation to live humbly, to do good without asserting authority.

"Maybe they failed to live up to those ideals in the end. I haven't seen your evidence. What do *I* know about the extent of their betrayals? But they were good and they were ordinary and they were fallible, and even the most smug and arrogant were trying to hew to a tradition older than the Republic. They deserved better than to die at the hands of power-hungry old men who saw them as a threat. *We* deserved better than to lose another people, another religion, from the universe. All of us are poorer for their loss."

She thought of Eyo-Dajuritz and the things Soujen and Bail had witnessed. She struggled for speech, her mouth working noiselessly. Then it passed, and she continued, "The universe is full of tragedies, and I was happy to ignore this one until Bail handed me something I could *do* about it. Maybe clearing the Jedi's name won't matter a whit to Palpatine and his people. Maybe we're risking ourselves needlessly, or maybe this is exactly what I require to bring a storm to the Senate. But here we are regardless, and as I see it, acknowledging the truth would be a fine start. The Jedi deserve justice . . . or at least a decent funeral."

Then the fire went out of her, the need to speak plainly and truthfully when plain truth was all she had left. Now she was at the world's mercy.

Soujen had listened. She didn't know how much he'd understood, and his face gave away nothing. Eventually something subtle changed in his eyes, though she couldn't identify what from across the floor.

"But the dead will still be dead," Soujen said.

Mon wasn't sure whether he was talking about the Jedi or all the others who had fallen. Maybe he was thinking of Eyo-Dajuritz, too. "Yes."

Soujen frowned. He stood perfectly still awhile, then for the first time turned his back to Mon, studying the shell of the skyscraper. "What is this place?"

"What was it? A housing block, I think—residents who couldn't afford the upper levels but probably worked there."

"No," Soujen said. He was walking slowly through the room. "How did it get like this?"

The question surprised her. "The Siege of Coruscant," she said, and when he glanced back, she took it as a prompt to continue. "The orbital defenses took care of most of the falling wreckage, but there were areas . . . Well, you can see what happened. The workers left this building intact because the superstructure was sound, even if the interior was a loss."

"The Siege of Coruscant," Soujen repeated. "Where Count Dooku died?"

"And your people kidnapped Chancellor Palpatine. There were battle droids outside the Senate."

Soujen made a sound of comprehension—a small, gruff noise, as if it were a fact he hadn't known but might as well have forgotten. Again, a prolonged silence—he peered out a paneless window, then went to the next.

"You said you accepted the blame for your part when it came to the war," he said.

"I did. I do. I said the same thing to Tychon Nulvolio. I stood up to the warmongers in the Senate. I was part of the back-channel negotia-tions. But I do believe we should've done more to avert disaster decades ago. I didn't take Separatist concerns seriously enough—"

He cut her off with a gesture. "Could you take me to Nulvolio?"

"Why?"

"Could you?"

"Perhaps. Probably not. He thinks you'd try to kill him."

"I would."

She flinched, despite herself. "Even though—"

"I would kill you both. But what would be the point?"

He was no longer at the windows. He approached her slowly, as if each step were a decision.

"Help me," Mon said.

"No. No." Two more steps. "The Jedi are dead. My people are dead. We could trade dead for days, and none of it matters. Do you know why I was made?" He drew nearer, and she could see his face clearly now, though his expression was no easier to interpret. She looked for anger and found it, but it was buried behind cold eyes, behind bone plating that masked whatever was real inside Soujen. It was there, but the anger was a foundation upon which so much else rested.

"Nulvolio called you a contingency," she said.

"I am a ghost raised to haunt the living." He was still three meters away, but his presence felt intimate. "What Organa wants—what you want—will not lay me to rest. But I will finish my mission."

CHAPTER 54
NO WAY OUT

She looked frightened, and that was a small pleasure—a drop of water after a day in the desert. Soujen watched her expression as he stalked one step forward, one step forward, trying to keep his voice steady, trying to be what he claimed to be—not a man but a nightmare, a vow come to life. Because if the guise slipped, then he truly had nothing, not his people or Poan or Karama or anyone from the times he couldn't remember, the years of life sacrificed to the machines inside his body. He stalked the woman, Mon Mothma, because he couldn't make the people of the Empire suffer or even pay attention. But *she* was here, and he would kill her if he had no other way out. He would kill her and find another bureaucrat, another traitor or coward, and kill them, too, and he would be caught long before he made any difference in the galaxy; because what were the lives of a few politicians in a congress of thousands representing a million worlds?

He would kill them anyway, as many as he could, if he had no other solution. But there was one last possibility, and he thought it might be enough. The ruins around him were a promise, unkept yet not forgotten. Mon Mothma held the key.

"I'm going to kill the Emperor," he said.

CHAPTER 55
DÉTENTE

"You're mad," Mon said.

The assassin was close enough that she could smell his soiled robes. He looked down at her, and the gesture resembled a nod.

"I'm going to the Executive Center," he said. "I'm going to kill everyone I find—the advisers, the viziers, anyone present. And I'm going to kill Palpatine. You can help me or not, but it will be done."

"You'll never get close." She was processing the notion, the repulsiveness of it, even as she protested. "The security—under ordinary circumstances, *maybe* someone could infiltrate the building, but they've already locked down because of you. Palpatine hasn't appeared in public at all lately. He may not even be there. He could be in a bunker or halfway across the galaxy—"

"Organa thinks Palpatine is a murderer, a perpetrator of Jedi genocide. Why rush to protect him?"

She wanted to say, *Because murder is an offense beyond any other. Because if we act outside the courts, outside the law, we forfeit any claim to upholding the law's principles. Because no one deserves to die terrified, at blasterpoint. It was wrong during the war, and it's wrong still. Because*

Palpatine aspires to be a dictator, but anything worse is unproven. Because his viziers and his governors will take his place and inherit Palpatine's approval ratings, and nothing will change. Because you can't just slaughter people!

But his declaration had loosed her instincts for bargaining, and she sought more effective pleas. "I'm not *protecting* him," she said. "But if you do this—even if you fail and especially if you succeed—you'll guarantee a backlash against all the worlds of the Confederacy. I can't begin to imagine the punishment a new administration would inflict. The Senate would *demand* retribution—"

"Assuming the Senate survives the crisis. Has the Emperor designated a successor?"

"He has not," Mon snapped. "Not in public, at least. But if you're hoping to start a war for the throne—"

"No," Soujen said, as if she'd taken a joke too seriously. "No. But if the next administration demands retribution, then maybe that will force the Separatist worlds to rise up. Maybe they'll learn to fight without droid armies or corporate sponsors."

"And how many more people will die?"

"All of them. Everyone dies, Senator, and this generation has already known suffering. They can endure a little more."

The idea was an obscenity. "You won't even get close," she said softly.

"I'm more capable than you think," Soujen said. "You would be useful to me, though. Take control after I'm finished, become Supreme Chancellor or Empress if it pleases you. But if you won't help, say so now."

She wondered whether he would kill her if she refused. Certainly he'd have no compunctions about it, but that alone wasn't reason to cooperate. Self-preservation was not the highest of virtues.

"I'll help," she said.

"Can you get me through Federal District security? Into Executive Center airspace?"

"I can't—I don't know. But I have a better chance than most, and if you can get inside, I can guide you. I've been to the Executive Center many times, and I doubt they've renovated since the war's end."

Soujen nodded carefully and stepped past her, walking through the dust. Mon hesitated, turned, and followed.

"Why change your mind?" Soujen asked.

"I want to live. Would you believe that?"

"No," he answered after a pause. "I would not."

He stepped over the remnant of a wall and into the silent street. She hurried to keep up. Her ankle nagged at her.

"I can't *stop* you," she said, "whether I live or die. So if you're going to do this, I might as well help limit the casualties and be around for the aftermath."

He jerked his head to one side, looking back to catch her eye. It was a challenge—a way of saying, *I know you're lying*. He kept walking.

He led them through the rubble and down an alleyway. At the far end, someone had parked an airspeeder—a bright-red number with a tapered body, a tinted dome cockpit, and oversized engines. Perrin would've recognized the model. Bail would have, too. Soujen approached it and tapped the controls, sliding the dome back.

"Sporty," Mon said.

"It's what I found. It was this or a garbage collector, and I wanted something with acceleration."

She nodded and joined him in the speeder. For a moment, she wondered whether she could wrest the controls from him during takeoff.

"One piece of advice up front?" she said.

"I'm listening."

"If anything goes wrong? You won't want them to take you alive. In the best case, they'll throw you in an oubliette for the rest of your life, watch you every hour, and never let you see sunlight. In the worst case . . . I don't know. I don't know what the administration is capable of anymore."

She'd said it. *Oubliette.* And if she'd sounded nervous, well, why wouldn't she sound nervous, given she was the hostage of a man with little regard for her life? She looked ahead as the airspeeder lifted off, trying not to study the assassin's face, to see whether he'd recognized the keyword Nulvolio had given to her.

"One keyword, spoken aloud, to prime the self-destruct device. Speak the second keyword, and the agent will detonate."

But Soujen was silent as the vehicle hummed through the air, slipping between broken buildings and navigating the maze of the city. He flew under the prescribed speed for the sector and—except for a few quick darts through the skeletons of buildings and down pedestrian walkways—kept to designated routes. He descended away from the Federal District, and she realized he must have planned some roundabout course to avoid security cams and checkpoints.

Once they'd left the rehabilitation zone and were sharing the skyways with the late-night and predawn commuters, he asked her questions about the Federal District lockdown and various points of entry, security codes, and the like. She answered honestly and fully. At times the assassin requested she use her credentials to access data and comm channels, to further inform his approach, and she did so. He was so methodical and thorough that Mon began to worry about the time. What would happen if she failed to speak the second keyword before too long? Nulvolio had said the self-destruct charge would be primed after five minutes. Would the charge hold? Would Soujen become aware of what was happening?

She wasn't sure how long it had been already. Five minutes at least.

Soujen completed his series of course changes and finally began to fly back toward the Federal District. Mon shifted in her seat, trying to see any sunlight above and trying not to fidget.

She risked another glance at Soujen. What would he notice if he did become aware?

"May I ask you something?" she said.

The assassin nodded.

"Are you Alvadorjian?"

He looked her way before returning his eyes to the sky. He seemed surprised. "Yes," he said. "Of the Nahasta clan."

"I'm . . . well, *somewhat* familiar with your people," she said. "Did all the clans side with the Separatists?"

"Most."

"May I ask why?"

"We were offered a future."

She nodded, clasped her hands together, unclasped them, adjusted the vents of the air circulators. She was suddenly cold, and the odor of the synthleather seats seemed grossly artificial.

She was speaking to distract him, she told herself, not to persuade him—not any longer—and not out of some desire for absolution. "There was a proposal—this was years ago, under Chancellor Valorum. There was a proposal to solve the *dilemma* of your people that almost made it to the Senate floor. There'd been an activism campaign after what happened to the Yehoulta clan, genuine popular support among youths and academics on Coruscant and Brentaal. There were discussions about not just funding the genetic repair of your people but even setting aside land for the clans on newly colonized worlds."

"But it didn't happen."

"No. I co-sponsored the bill, but it was tabled in committee. That was the year of the Selonian worker scandal, and absolutely nothing was getting to the floor that wasn't pertinent. Then there was the blockade of Naboo, and by the time that business was over, public interest in the Alvadorjian dilemma had faded. I'd moved on to the wrong committees, and no one else wanted to pick up the torch . . ."

"In short, we failed. I failed. The moment passed."

The assassin stared out at the city, steering the speeder with small, deft motions. The skyscrapers had begun to glow as daylight reflected off their panels.

"Senator Organa," he said. "Did he support the bill?"

"He did, for longer than most."

"He didn't mention it," Soujen said, and there was something like respect in his voice—as if Bail's humility meant more than his support.

They passed through the outermost security perimeter into the Federal District. The protesters had been kept out by the lockdown, and the million or more workers who tended the machinery of government had begun trickling in. Mon could see the great dome of the Senate and, beyond it, the smaller dome of the Executive.

Soujen flew low, stopping the speeder outside a data-processing center (affiliated with the Department of Agriculture and Non-sapient Creatures, as Mon recalled). There was no public walkway, but a maintenance platform jutted out from the building's facade.

"Out," Soujen said, retracting the cockpit. Mon cautiously extracted herself from the speeder, not sure what came next.

Soujen checked the speeder's storage compartment before climbing out as well. He passed a comlink to Mon. "I can't stop them from shooting you. You'll stay here and guide me once I'm inside the Executive."

She squeezed the cold metal of the comlink against her palm to stop from shaking. "You're sure you want to go in?" she asked.

"Yes," he said.

"There are so many other ways," she said.

"Not anymore."

There was resignation in his voice, perfectly balanced by determination. But there was no compassion, not for her or the universe or even for himself—and she suddenly wondered whether he knew exactly what she'd done, what she planned. She wondered whether he'd ever intended to reach the Emperor at all.

"Stay on the comm," he said. "If you try to warn them, it will go badly for everyone."

Soujen climbed back into the airspeeder and closed the cockpit. She heard his voice through her comlink as he tested the signal, and she replied to confirm. Then he activated the speeder's repulsors and began a slow vertical ascent. Soon he would rise alongside a pedestrian bridge carrying jumpsuited technicians returning home for the night and bureaucrats arriving for the early shift. A security vehicle floated nearby. Some broad-winged creatures—flitterbats, maybe—clung to the bridge's underside, tucking themselves away for the morning.

If Soujen passed the bridge, he would be out of Mon's sight. She would relinquish all control.

She knew what she had to do. She knew the good, right, and necessary thing. And for the single instant that she imagined the assassination of Emperor Palpatine, she felt only the deepest shame. It was time. It was time.

CHAPTER 56
FEAR

Soujen was not afraid as he left the senator behind. The airspeeder rose, and he ran his self-diagnostics and confirmed that his body was as ready as his mind and soul. And if the dark spot in his mind loomed larger, if his skin seemed hot and sensitized, then so what? He knew his purpose, and whatever the senator did, however she betrayed him, he would see his mission through. He had obtained the secrets of the cache and understood all his body was capable of. There had only ever been one ending for him, anyway, from the moment he'd arrived on Coruscant. It had simply taken time for him to find it.

Her voice came through the comlink as the pedestrian bridge swept toward him in the light of an alien dawn.

"Sublime. Sublime. Sublime."

CHAPTER 57
DEATH

She shouldn't have looked up. She shouldn't have been watching the speeder. It hadn't occurred to her to look away until it was too late, when she heard a sound like the sky cracking and saw a light brighter than the dawn. She recoiled, stumbling in the shock wave, and a moment later she felt herself pelted with a hail of metal—large pieces and small, sharp and dull. She tasted blood on her lips along with the words of death she'd spoken, and she hoped with her final thoughts that she had been swift enough, spoken soon enough, to save the pedestrians on the bridge—and maybe the flitterbats, too.

She was a murderer now, an assassin like Soujen Vak-Nhalis, and her purpose was every bit as pure as his own.

CHAPTER 58
SILENCE

"A bomb," someone said. "There was a bomb in the Federal District," and Bail turned on the vid feeds, and Cantham House went silent, all calls on hold as they watched cam droids magnify the fire twice over, five, ten times, until nothing existed but the flames. Breha stood beside him as they listened to newscasters report on the early morning traffic and potential casualties, the miraculous absence of all vehicles save one. Outside, even the protesters—the imperialist hordes had descended on Cantham House hours earlier—grew quiet. They were listening to the reports, too.

They all watched together, and Bail realized that he, Breha, and his staffers were waiting for the next bomb, the chain of destruction that would wreak devastation across the district the way the Separatists had. But there was no second bomb, no simultaneous attack. When the reporters began speculating that the danger was contained, when the security forces began arriving amid the ashes and ruin, when the first unconfirmed accounts came in regarding the pilot of the vehicle, everyone in Cantham House seemed giddy with relief and leftover fear.

Only Bail slumped as if struck, because he was certain Soujen was dead. Soujen was dead, and he'd taken Bail's hopes with him.

CHAPTER 59
ECHOES

They were shorthanded from the losses on Eyo-Dajuritz, and Saw had already given Karama and Nankry assignments elsewhere. But the deal had been set weeks earlier, so he'd gone to the salt-walled smoke den and brought the casks himself, with only Vorgorath and Rynark for company. He'd shown the buyers the casks, let them taste the red water stolen from Imperial-occupied Po'yin, and asked them what this substance, this benediction from their now-inaccessible homeworld, was worth in credits and armaments. When a newcomer had interrupted them, Saw had assumed the deal was off and all would end in blood.

"Attack on Coruscant," the newcomer said, laughing. "Attack on Coruscant! Pox on those elitist bastards."

The buyers shook their heads as if it were a joke, but Saw asked terse questions until he understood. The newcomer passed a datapad to him, and Saw smiled bitterly when he read the name Soujen Vak-Nhalis.

Like a drop of water in a bonfire, he thought. *But you served your purpose.*

"Prep the *Dalgo* for flight," he told Vorgorath. "Soon as we're done here, we head back to the Ash Worlds. Could be things are in motion."

CHAPTER 60
SENATOR ORGANA
SPONSORS A BILL

Thirty-six hours after the attack on the Executive Center, Bail Organa stood on a floating platform in the Senate Rotunda and called for a vote on the Imperial Rebirth Act.

After the news of the explosion and the death of Soujen Vak-Nhalis, he'd allowed himself five minutes for fury and shock and the realization that his hopes had been dashed—his hopes to expose Palpatine for the manipulator and murderer that he was, and his hopes to exonerate the Jedi and give solace to those in hiding. He'd told his staff to hold his calls, to pause their work, and he'd retreated into the bedroom to process the complete and utter failure of his mission.

He'd set a timer. Five of the hardest minutes of his life had passed. Then he'd returned to work.

The protesters had battered at doors and windows. They'd howled for the arrest of Bail and his staff, demanding their punishment for a litany of crimes that began and ended with "treason against the Empire." House security had lowered blast plates, and the entrances were holding. But Bail and Breha's efforts to reassure the staff—to appear unfazed by the calls for their deaths—had limited effect. Bail had hoped the crowd would disperse at daybreak, but the mob was undeterred, and

Bail's repeated calls to the police went ignored. Sooner or later the protesters would find a way inside.

He'd considered stepping out, luring the mob his way while his staff
fled. But before he'd been able to act, the house had been shaken by the
roar of engines. He'd peered past the blast plates and seen a gunship
take position above the mob. Three clone soldiers perched aboard had
aimed their weapons downward. Behind the soldiers had stood a Tarsunt in the uniform of an Imperial admiral. The admiral had nodded
respectfully toward the house, as if he might meet Bail's gaze and speak
as they had in the Holy City of Jedha.

Then the admiral had ordered his men to open fire.

Most of the mob had managed to flee. They hadn't returned. Bail had
yet to decide whether to thank the admiral who'd saved his life or to
report him for the massacre.

So Bail and the others had pretended to be blind to atrocity and continued prepping for the vote. Over twelve hours, Bail had doubled down
on his efforts to hold Mon's coalition together, making hundreds of
calls to no-name representatives and power brokers alike, insisting
every time that the vote would proceed. He'd based that on absolutely
nothing—the events at Cantham House went unreported, but the attempted terrorist attack on the Executive Center was galaxy-wide news,
and there were rumors that the reintegration of Separatist worlds would
be postponed. The lack of any known victims from the explosion gave
him hope that the attack would be forgotten after a day—but then the
security forces had discovered Mon Mothma dying amid the wreckage,
and everything had gone south again. The senators whose trust Mon
had earned had viewed Bail skeptically, and he'd struggled to fill her
shoes—to be the politician instead of the uncompromising idealist. At
the same time, the regional governors had moved fleets into position
over ex-Separatist planets, preparing for a resurgence of violence or to
initiate one themselves. Bail had wondered if *that* was what Soujen had
hoped for—to reignite the war through a bold and self-destructive act.

He'd shifted tactics then. He'd asked Breha, Streamdrinker, and
Norve-Gloss to focus on maintaining the Senate coalition and keeping
Mon's hidden backers in line. Meanwhile, Bail had spent his own en-

ergy conducting back-channel negotiations with the military to keep
tensions from rising—burning every bit of credibility he had left, knowing his friends in the navy and among the joint chiefs could only *delay*
the governors' orders, not refuse them. At the same time, he'd stormed
the news channels, offering interviews to anyone who'd see him and
declaring the need to move forward with reintegration. He'd used Mon's
name liberally, and even the most antagonistic interviewers seemed re-
luctant to challenge him. Mon was, for a day at least, a martyr. That
made her the perfect shield against criticism.

Maybe none of it made a difference. Maybe the Emperor and his
inner circle had already determined that they would benefit from keeping the peace instead of starting a new war and had begun corralling the
governors behind the scenes. All Bail knew was that no one started
shooting.

Eventually, the reintegration had proceeded. When the ceremony
had ended, the Imperial Senate had welcomed thousands of new members.

That was when he had stepped forward. Mon had set the stage, arranged for the right senators in the right positions to let him bypass the
usual order and bring the bill directly to the floor. One of Arvik Cornade's bootlickers had seconded the call for Bail to speak. Bail had
tapped a few keys and distributed the bill's text to countless viewscreens
throughout the Rotunda. And he'd begun to talk.

He'd rewritten his script ten times over, passed it through Breha, his
speechwriters, and three protocol droids. Now he largely ignored it.

"Gentlepeople of the Imperial Senate," he said, bowing his head to
the tiers of viewing pods that stretched above and below, disappearing
into the dark corners of the vast chamber. "You all know who I am. You
know of the harrowing journey I've experienced these past weeks. But
I tell you, I would have gladly endured far worse to be here today."

He adjusted his stance, made sure to position himself for the benefit
of the cams without *looking* like it was for the benefit of the cams. The
galactic public was his audience. He would win no converts in the Senate, but if he was persuasive, commanding, and relatable—if he made
the correct case in the correct way—he would give his coalition justifi-

cation for voting yes. They needed cover, and he intended to give it to them.

So he began to lie.

"Roughly one week ago, I was taken hostage by Onderonian terrorists while on a goodwill tour of worlds formerly held by the Confederacy. These terrorists were operating from a hideout on the galactic heritage world of Eyo-Dajuritz, and they were committed to halting the reintegration of Separatist worlds into the Senate. They claimed to be working on behalf of the Republic.

"The terrorists treated me with callous brutality, and I will bear the scars for years to come. They saw anyone who sought to reunite the galaxy—no matter what side they served on during the war—as a danger to be eliminated. For them, the war had never ended. For them, the war never *could* end in anything less than the utter decimation of all Separatist worlds."

This, too, had been part of the interviews he'd given. He'd chronicled his captivity—or a fabricated version of it—in elaborate detail. His story contradicted the account he'd given to the Imperial Security Bureau, but that was a problem for another day. If he was fortunate, the sheer brazenness and the publicity around his claims would make an arrest difficult.

"When the brave forces of the clone army came to my rescue, the terrorists unleashed a series of calculated detonations that did irreparable damage to Eyo-Dajuritz's historic sites. They did this to cover their escape, and I was left in the hands of one of their most despicable members—a former mercenary named Soujen Vak-Nhalis, who was drawn to the Onderonians' extremist ideology. Vak-Nhalis threatened my life and the life of my family, forcing me to bring him here, to Coruscant.

"Luckily, I was able to escape. And luckily, Vak-Nhalis had no desire to sow chaos and death across this city. His plan was as straightforward as it was sinister: He wished to carry out a suicide attack on the Emperor himself. The security forces undertook a coordinated search, but it wasn't until our newly inaugurated colleague, Senator Tychon Nulvolio, was able to work in collaboration with Senator Mon Mothma that

Vak-Nhalis was lured from hiding. And as we all now know, Senator Mothma triggered the assassin's bomb herself, preserving our hard-won peace at the price of her own safety."

Nulvolio had offered up himself after Bail's first interview, much to Bail's surprise. He'd gone to the press with his own tale before coming to Bail, and together they'd concocted the scheme to protect Mon's reputation and support the Rebirth Act. Nulvolio had asked nothing in return, and Bail was grateful. Nulvolio would come out of it looking like a hero, but the man would also pay a price by drawing the ire of the administration.

Soujen, Bail knew, would have despised every part of the story—hated his transformation from a Separatist stalwart dedicated to his people to an ex-Separatist mercenary soured on his old masters and motivated by hate. Saw Gerrera came off little better, and now he would be hunted across the galaxy—remembered for centuries and loathed for his involvement in the defacing of Eyo-Dajuritz. Bail felt a twinge of guilt but no remorse. Their reputations were a small sacrifice.

He felt something closer to remorse over the sheer number of lies. But he'd been holding back the truth since Palpatine had proclaimed himself Emperor. It seemed a small sin now.

"We have taken a first step in defiance of the hatred and division that motivated those terrorists." He gestured fiercely, raising his chin to look at the sea of faces arrayed before him. Many watched him closely. More were focused on their screens, hurriedly reviewing the text of the Rebirth Act or checking the response from their constituencies. "By uniting here, in this sacred chamber, by reaffirming our kinship with the noble representatives of worlds we once warred against, we say that we are one"—he forced himself to say the word, for the sake of Mon and the universe—"Empire.

"Each of us is devoted to this great project. We are no longer members of the Galactic Republic or the Confederacy of Independent Systems, but of a Galactic Empire unfettered by the sins of its predecessors, still young and free to determine its own legacy. Indeed, that is why I stand before you—to help us determine *what we shall be*. Unity is not enough. The next step toward rejecting the hateful philosophies, the bloodthirsty vengeance, of terrorists like Soujen Vak-Nhalis is to show that we are *strong*, to show that we are united in purpose as well as heart, and that we will *not be divided again*."

Believe in it, he told himself. *Believe in the Empire because, for the moment, it's all you have. Believe in it as you believe in the Rebirth Act—as a flawed tool, mired in corruption, that can help many people if used properly. If you don't believe it now, they won't believe you, either.*

For a moment, the ghosts of the Jedi and the ghost of Padmé Amidala intruded on his thoughts. They were warning him. But they were dead, and the galaxy had changed.

"The Imperial Rebirth Act is a call for our Empire to take its first steps toward greatness. It will provide money and resources to worlds on both sides of the conflict, rebuilding institutions that were so terribly damaged and helping trillions of innocents caught in the struggle. It will not discriminate between the wreckage here on Coruscant and the destruction in the kelp cities of the Quarren on Mon Cala. It will not divide the Empire into allies and enemies, as the terrorist Saw Gerrera did.

"The Rebirth Act will also strengthen the existing ties between our worlds, making right many troubles neglected by the Republic. We will boost protections for our industries and our workers, ensure that our cultural traditions are preserved for our children. We will take up the challenge given to us by our new Emperor and make the Empire what the Republic could never be!"

There was a smattering of applause from the otherwise silent assembly. *How's that for explaining away slashed tariffs and deregulated droid manufacturing?* Mon would have been proud.

"Lastly"—and this was the delicate part, the part that if he misjudged could get him arrested or stoned in the street, the only part that *mattered*—"the Imperial Rebirth Act will complete the Emperor's institutional reform of our union, guaranteeing that there will be no weaknesses for our enemies to exploit, no hope for those terrorists who would seek to destabilize our government and throw the chain of command into question. This bill merely formalizes the structures and hierarchies already in place, creating additional clarity for the judiciary and the military, making sure the Senate can act without fear of contravening the executive, and—though we hope such guidance is never necessary—ensuring continuity in the event that some future strike on the capital proves more deadly than this last evil effort. We've seen the danger that can arise when the security forces are paralyzed, when the executive lacks the resources it needs to meet a threat. When the Rebirth Act is in place, our government will stand unified with the worlds of the Empire, ready to act and ready to serve."

The real power stays in the Senate. Now and forever.

Someone was shouting in the highest reaches of the chamber. Someone below echoed the cry. But the voices were distant and indistinct. Bail didn't imagine anyone was fooled about the true intent of the bill, but everything he'd said about it had been arguably true, and he'd given the opposition no time to coordinate a counterattack. Most in the chamber understood that to yell *liar* or *traitor* now, at a man who'd nearly died on Eyo-Dajuritz and who was arguing for the completion of the Imperial project, was not a winning move.

No one dared applaud, either, but Bail would take what he could get.

"I urge you to vote without delay," he said. "We must not show weakness. We must not declare to our enemies that we are fractured, uncertain, unable to govern ourselves or to serve the Emperor. This is the moment to band together—all of us, once from Republic and Separatist worlds, now one people again."

There *were* cheers this time, beginning from somewhere among the Mid Rim representatives. He wondered whether someone had put them up to it, whether Mon had orchestrated that as well. His pod began to retreat toward the wall, leaving the center of the Rotunda empty as the cheering echoed, the votes were processed, and the representatives who'd been unprepared for this moment—the ones Mon had never let in on her scheme, who were only now being instructed by their coalition leaders how to act—stared around them in confusion and dismay.

Now let the tyrant fall, Bail thought. And he watched his screen to await an answer.

CHAPTER 61
PREDERIKO AND THE VOTE

Hasalia Prederiko, chief financial officer of General Trade Galactic and one of the Core Worlds' top agents of the Crymorah syndicate, watched the proceedings from a dozen angles on a dozen viewscreens. She was pleased to hear her representatives cheer when the moment arrived. She was pleased to see them stop the opposition from postponing the vote.

For the most part, Prederiko liked the senators she'd acquired through bribery and blackmail. While the grossly corrupt were a minority in the Senate, they were also the *fun* ones. The tougher cases were the senators who stood with Prederiko only as long as their interests were aligned—as long as the Crymorah kept street crime down on their planets, say, or pushed out rival syndicates. Those were the senators Prederiko couldn't control, the ones she could only *influence,* and she waited for their votes with some impatience.

She'd made her arguments to them. She'd hinted to a few who hated her guts that the Crymorah *wanted* to keep the Emperor around, and she'd hinted to senators who saw the Crymorah as a necessary evil that the Emperor was planning a crackdown. She'd done all she could.

She sipped her tea. She listened to her daughter playing in the next room. She fidgeted, knowing her bosses would kill her if the vote failed.

The first notifications came through on her screens:

Senator LoLell: "Nay" on the Imperial Rebirth Act.

Senator Khrobastra: "Nay" on the Imperial Rebirth Act.

Senator Eho: "Nay" on the Imperial Rebirth Act.

"Well, screw you all," she said, and she poured her steaming tea directly onto the floor.

CHAPTER 62
KHLAIDES AND THE GRUDGE

Senator Ta'am Khlaides toyed with her claw rings as the Senate descended into chaos. Pods reshuffled as new coalitions formed and dissolved. Imperialist senators floated within shouting distance of the corporate colonial bloc, then scattered when Senator Ko-No-Rosu voiced his support for Bail Organa. Nulvolio's whips stalked the Rotunda, hunting any ex-Separatist who'd yet to vote for the Rebirth Act. To Ta'am's left, the delegates from Skustell argued over whether Bail had insulted them *deliberately* by not consulting them—and, if so, whether it was too late to demand compensation to vote in favor.

It all galled Ta'am. She'd accused Mon Mothma of being toxic—said her Delegation of 2,000 had destroyed the reputations of everyone involved—and she still believed it. She'd later warned Nulvolio not to ally with Mon, and she'd been roundly ignored.

"I'm too old for nonsense," she muttered.

One of her aides warned her that Nulvolio's whips were on their way, and she guided her pod across the Rotunda, beneath where the representatives from Byss were shouting at one another. She thought she heard one say, "You made him Emperor! It's on you to unmake him!" But she doubted her translation. She tapped at her control pad, hoping that if she procrastinated long enough, a heart attack would spare her the decision that—whichever way she chose—would end her political career.

If only it had been someone else, someone more competent than Mon, more experienced than Nulvolio, who'd put the bill together. She didn't like Palpatine, either, but she didn't need the grief his ire would bring.

Senators were gathering in a pod below hers. Senator DuQuosenne of Yabrenito was yammering about how Mon Mothma had betrayed her, how Organa wasn't to be trusted, how she intended to vote nay and how Palpatine was being stabbed in the back, and on and on . . .

Shut up, you senile fool.

If Ta'am loathed anyone in the Senate more than she loathed Mon, it was DuQuosenne, that awful creature in her fishbowl containment sphere, forever trying to murder people in games of firepath.

Ta'am tapped at her screen, pondering. It had been Bail Organa who'd made the final pitch, not Mon . . .

Now who's acting foolish?

But she really did hate DuQuosenne, and Palpatine, too. And maybe her constituents would laud her bravery.

"Tell Nulvolio we're a *yes* on the bill," she told her aide, "and that he'd damn well better appreciate it."

CHAPTER 63
MARROI AND
THE FUTURE

"What would happen, exactly? If we voted yes?"

"You mean would your constituents kill you *before* setting you on fire? I can have Anra do a flash poll—"

"Don't be glib. What would happen?"

Lud Marroi watched his chief of staff and dear friend Spigh try to suppress the twitch in his forehead. Lud knew the look. Spigh was terrified. Spigh was probably right.

"You'd never survive the next election," Spigh said. "I'd say odds are pretty good there would be an emergency recall ballot within the month to try to oust you. You could fight it, and *maybe* Catadra would make up for the votes you'd lose on Troithe, but best case you'd be delaying the inevitable."

"What about—"

"Let me finish. You're thinking some of your friends on Coruscant would stand by you, right? Tell you how brave you were for doing the right thing, say they wish they'd done the same? No. Once the dust settles and Palpatine reasserts control, and he *will*, your old friends will call you a heretic. They'll launch investigations into your finances, into everything, whether you're still in office or not."

"Don't be so sure Palpatine will survive this."

"You know he will, Lud. He and the grand vizier, they're untouchable, and it's our job—it is *your* job, as a duly elected representative of the Cerberon system—to make the best of it. The administration is fulfilling its promises, and if you don't screw this up, you can do a lot of good with the revitalization funds—"

"Half of which will be eaten up by corruption—"

"While the other half goes to people neglected for fifty years!" Spigh slammed his hand onto the rail of the pod. It was a dramatic affectation, the sort he used to scare junior staffers, but there was nothing less than rage in his voice. "I'm repeating your own argument. You wanted to cozy up to Palpatine, you were right to do it, and I don't understand why you've gotten cold feet."

Lud waited until Spigh's breathing evened out. "There are higher obligations," Lud said at last. "There have to be."

Spigh watched him. The sounds of the Rotunda—the thousand arguments along with the chatter of the press—became white noise.

"Is it true?" Spigh asked. "Are you sleeping with her?"

"No," Lud snapped. "Never."

Spigh shook his head. "It's a hell of a reason to throw everything away, Lud. Hell of a reason."

Spigh left the pod. Lud wondered whether he'd be back, then put the question from his mind and turned to the controls. He stared at the text of the Rebirth Act on the screen without reading it, because it was the only place he could look without meeting the gaze of another senator across the Rotunda, another politician with another agenda and another reason he should do a thing he didn't want to do.

He pictured Mon's face. He pictured the delicate arch of her eyebrows and the pallor of her skin. He pictured her laughing, as she laughed when they discussed anything but politics.

Slowly and deliberately, he pushed that image into the darkness of his mind. When he was staring at the control panel again, he cast his ballot.

CHAPTER 64
THE COUNT

I t was out of his hands now.

Bail watched the tally shift as lone senators and mighty coalitions committed their votes. One moment *yea* was ahead by eight, nine points, the next it trailed by four, as Palpatine's two hundred supporters in the Perlemian Trading Bloc voted *nay*. If Mon had been present, she'd have been watching the bellwethers and noting who'd stayed loyal and who'd turned against her, but Bail was happy to leave the postmortem until after the patient was dead.

For Mon, the *mechanics* of politics were a place of safety—or even joy. Bail preferred to sit out the tense moments with a drink among friends, but that didn't work when the bill was yours to sponsor.

A voice spoke to Bail's right, crisp above the overlapping conversations of staffers: "Two minutes left, with eighty-six percent of votes received. You're doing quite well."

The *yea* vote was half a point ahead.

Bail turned to the gold protocol droid beside him. The unit had once belonged to Padmé, though he'd had its memory wiped. That had been a necessity.

"I appreciate your optimism," Bail said. He glanced back at the gaggle of aides and runners moving in and out of the pod. "Anything I can help with?"

"I don't believe so, sir," the droid said. "It's mostly factual inquiries, plus a few translation requests."

That was to be expected, but he could've used a distraction. Ninety seconds left, *yea* a quarter point behind.

He looked out into the Rotunda. Fewer pods were in motion, and representatives were taking up formal postures, emoting for the cams. Several dozen heads tilted gently upward, and Bail followed their gaze toward the upper levels. He made out the distant figure of the Emperor's grand vizier—once the Senate speaker and vice chair, now possessed of a more amorphous authority. He'd taken to presiding over sessions on a whim.

The protocol droid's servos squeaked softly as the unit began to turn around. Bail gently tapped the droid's shoulder plate. "Stay, Threepio," he said. "Watch the results with me."

In Padmé's honor.

The droid said something about an *enormous privilege,* but Bail was focused on the countdown. Zero seconds left, and the chamber went silent. The tally appeared, and thousands of whispers sounded. Bail looked to the pod of the vizier. The vizier made no pronouncement, only pointed toward Bail with his ceremonial scepter and turned to depart.

That left the formalities to Bail. He touched his pod's controls and floated it to the center of the Rotunda.

"I speak for Senator Mothma," he said, "because this was her project. This was her vision."

The Senate watched him.

"The count is complete. The Imperial Rebirth Act passes."

There was applause. There were shouts. All Bail could think was that through some miracle, against all odds, the galaxy made sense again.

CHAPTER 65
WANTED

The news took the better part of a day to reach the Ash Worlds, bouncing between hyperspace beacons at incomprehensible speeds and then, much more slowly, between the in-system comm relays. By the time Saw received the alert—by the time he finished adjusting dials and realigning the antenna and finally, finally heard a tinny, static-cracked voice announcing the passage of the Rebirth Act—he knew the consequences would already be unfolding on Coruscant. But if he was a few steps behind the rest of the galaxy, that just meant he needed to pick up his pace.

The news feed replayed Organa's full speech, and Saw laughed when he heard the senator's lies. Sometimes the laughter was bitter and know-ing, as from a man who'd expected betrayal and had his cynicism re-warded. Sometimes the laughter was louder, bordering on hysterical. "We're a wanted crew now," he muttered to his console, "the Empire's most wanted."

That would make things difficult. It would make recruiting harder, for one—there wasn't a lot of support for planetary vandals. It might turn a few of the allies he still had against him. It would mean the Empire wouldn't have to be shy about pursuing him—no point pretending he wasn't worth attention when he'd already come into public view.

But it would be all right. Along with challenges, it would bring a certain clarity. Those allies who did not abandon him would have proved their fidelity, and the accusations would filter out recruits who lacked the stomach for the grueling times ahead. Besides, he hadn't left Eyo-Dajuritz empty-handed. The weapons, supplies, and credits salvaged from the flood hadn't added up to much, yet he'd gained one thing that had served him well:

Bail Organa's access codes.

I would've stepped aside, he thought as he reconfigured the transmitter in the dim light of the cave. His hands were filthy, and everything smelled of salt and crushed beetles. *If you hadn't come at me first—if you hadn't hunted me, demanded my weapons, and treated me like a threat—I would've let you have your Empire.*

When the antenna was in its new position, he activated the signal and spoke one word: "Now."

PART IV
NIGHT

CHAPTER 66
AN ACT OF TERROR

Karama had waited almost forty hours, lying under a coarse blanket laced with grass, dirt, and a local flower the color of an old bruise. To stay hydrated, she'd sipped watery paste from a tube and tried not to ruffle her camouflage. She'd allowed a black and amber insect the size of her fist to crawl across her face and mosey down her back into the foliage. She'd smelled the fragrant dew at dawn and the musk of the hunting fields at night.

Through it all, she'd kept watch. She'd peered over the walls of the complex, past the construction cranes, and observed the spot where Nankry had planted the first device. The codes had worked. No one had noticed. But Saw had told them to wait, and they'd waited.

If she'd dozed, it hadn't been long enough to refresh her. Her head ached, and a subtle haze of unreality had descended upon her. She'd had a great deal of time to think about everything she'd been through—not just on Eyo-Dajuritz, not just the bedlam of the flood, and not just the loss of her comrades and Soujen. She thought about the war, about her sister, and about the choices she'd made that had landed her in a Separatist prison camp.

She'd thought about Saw, and how they'd begun as fugitives from an ungrateful government, veterans on the run yet ready to defend themselves. And Saw had turned them gradually, *so gradually,* into scavengers and thieves. And then Soujen had come, and they'd become murderers on Li'eta, when they'd shot clones like they were droids. Then Eyo-Dajuritz, and now . . .

Now they really were terrorists. Now they were what the Empire had wanted them to be all along.

Tell me you didn't plan this, Saw.

One day, if she survived, she would resuscitate her reporter's mind and ask the right questions. She'd assemble the whole story, even if it damned her.

The signal arrived at last. She moved her numb hand to the detonator under her breast and dug her thumb into the trigger. The result was like a nova below the hills, and the sky was full of fire.

CHAPTER 67
THE CENTURY PLAN

Mon Mothma was not dead, though to hear her colleagues speak—the way they praised her accomplishments and anguished over her fate—she might as well have been.

She'd been in the medcenter a week now. The first days she'd spent floating in bacta tanks and lying on surgical cots while droids picked shrapnel from her organs and replaced what needed replacing. She didn't remember that time well, but she could conjure up the sensation of drifting in and out of anesthesia. She could recall the scent of the bacta and the sound of the droids' servos as their knife hands delicately marked, cut, and excised. The first thing she'd done after regaining full awareness had been to pull off her flimsy gown and inspect her body as if it belonged to a stranger.

She'd found no scars. She'd panicked, not understanding why—not understanding that the bacta had erased every trace of her surgeries. A droid had put her back to sleep "for her own safety."

Later she'd learned she no longer had a stomach. She now had a mechanical equivalent, which would take training before it could process anything but prescription nutrient packs. She'd learned that her heart had been pierced by debris and that microscopic traces of metal had been left in place. Her body, in short, was not entirely her own, and this felt *true* to her somehow, as if it had been the case since her first interrogation by the Empire and the medics had merely discovered what was really inside.

///

Once she was allowed visitors, Perrin came to her bedside and stayed there. He said—and the medical staff confirmed—he'd been present the entire time, waiting in the lobby and the observation areas. Mon couldn't quite believe it.

It was good to see him.

He didn't proclaim his love for her, and she didn't lie to him and say, *I was scared I'd never see you again.* She asked him to read her the news, and he obliged awhile before insisting she sleep. When she said she wasn't tired, he threatened to sing lullabies, and she surrendered and closed her eyes. Over the course of several days, they developed a routine along these lines. He didn't attempt to keep her from her work, her *purpose,* but he held her hand while she waded ankle-deep into those waters, and he pulled her out when she grew weary. They spent several hours one afternoon ranking the get-well gifts Perrin assured her were piling up at their old apartment. Taking last place: a packet of storebought jerky from Senator Doroon with a message reading, GET WELL, SENATOR MOTHMA.

She insisted at last that he go home. He'd found new lodgings, he told her—more comfortable than the temporary housing provided by Senate Security. Mon would like the place, he said, and she said she was sure she would and that he could settle in without her, make certain it felt lived-in by the time she got there.

She missed him dearly when he was gone.

///

The next day the droids took her walking down the scrubbed medcenter corridors, testing her balance and coordination before her scheduled discharge that afternoon. She carried a cane, which the droids told her wasn't strictly necessary but would be beneficial for a day or two. She remained in her gown, though Perrin had promised to bring proper clothing when he came to pick her up.

Halfway back to her room, as she shivered from the chilled air blowing across her bare arms, two black-clad military officers intercepted her and said they'd come to escort her out.

"Out to where?" she asked.

"We're not at liberty to say," one of the officers replied.

"Are you at liberty to say who sent you? Give your names and credentials?"

"We're not at liberty to say," the same officer said. The other hadn't spoken since arriving.

Her droid escort *tut-tutted* but backed away, as if recognizing the officers' authority.

So she didn't really have a choice. She asked about clothes and was told they would be provided. She asked whether she could notify her husband and was told he'd be informed of her status. Fleeing was out of the question. If she'd been less tired, she would've been more fearful. She didn't have the capacity for fear anymore.

The officers took her to a speeder, which took her to an unmarked yacht with an Imperial Navy crew and a visible complement of clone troopers. The clones brought Mon to a small but elegantly appointed room where—quite to her surprise—she found clothing laid out. The black suit with its oversized brass buttons wasn't to her taste, and she was tempted to remain in her medical gown as a show of defiance, but the ship was even more frigid than the medcenter. Some battles weren't worth fighting.

She slept in the cabin. She woke when she felt the faint jolt of the ship emerging from hyperspace. A few minutes later, a crew member came to escort her to the viewing deck. When they arrived, Mon entered alone. The turbolift door slid shut behind her.

Standing at a viewport twice as tall as Mon was a man in a ruffled red robe that neatly complemented the blue of his skin. He wore the two tendrils hanging from his skull like a mantle, and his horns rose like a crown. Unbidden, her mind called up images of ancient etchings, of deities of rain, death, and fertility. Maybe it was the way he stared at the stars with a hint of disappointment or disdain. Or maybe it was the lack of the scepter he normally affected, distorting her bludgeoned brain's ability to recognize him for what he was.

Mas Amedda, grand vizier of the Empire and the worm in Palpatine's ear, turned toward her with a twitch of his lips almost like a smile.

"Senator," he said with a voice to command a congregation. "How goes your recovery?"

She still had the cane. She leaned on it deliberately as she stepped forward. "I wouldn't know," she said. "They said I was ready for discharge, but I missed my final appointment."

"Well, I'm pleased you were able to join us, at least. There is medical care on board if you require it."

"That's very generous."

She might have asked, *Why am I here?* But she knew the answer. What she really wanted to know was, *What happens now?*

"Come join me," the vizier said.

Even without exaggerating her reliance on the cane, it was slow going. The vastness of the viewport and the darkness of space seemed to magnify the emptiness inside and outside the vessel. The vizier never turned away while Mon forced her muscles into operation, but nor did he speak or approach. Mon could feel the deck shift beneath her as the yacht engaged its thrusters, and a brighter dot caught her attention in the starscape—their destination, perhaps.

Finally she stood before the vizier, and he nodded to her as if acknowledging an obeisance.

"I want to congratulate you on your bill," the vizier said. "The entire affair was masterfully executed. We knew you were up to *something,* of course, but by the time we knew *what,* you'd bound the Rebirth Act so tightly to the Imperial project that stopping it would have proved politically costly. I even briefly wondered if your martyrdom was part of the plan—if you'd arranged your own injury to make Organa's pleas in your name more compelling."

She felt flushed from the walk and returned a bitter smile. "And what did you conclude?"

The vizier grunted slightly, as if to say it had been a passing fancy, one that had bored him before he'd come to a conclusion.

"The bill can't be allowed to stand, of course," he said, shifting his attention back to the viewport. The bright dot became a green-brown world as the yacht rushed toward it. "The Emperor will have to veto the provisions related to executive authority and the oversight roles of the Senate and judiciary. The rest of it can remain in effect. Some portions are quite popular, and we've no qualms about throwing a bone to Arvik Cornade and his lot."

"The Emperor has no power to *veto* the Rebirth Act. The bill is passed."

"He is the *Emperor*. This is the *Empire*. His power, Senator Mothma, is absolute."

She kept her rage in check. The argument did not surprise her. She'd known Palpatine and his people would attempt to wriggle free.

"The power of any government," she said, "is contingent upon the will of the people. And many influential people stood behind the Rebirth Act. I would not think the Emperor wishes to make them into enemies."

The vizier grunted again. Mon ignored him and continued, "Arvik Cornade *and his lot* can shut down trade, manufacturing, communications— everything that allows the Empire to function. I have hundreds of senators ready to rally their worlds, turn public sentiment into a weapon aimed at the administration's heart. Palpatine has the title *Emperor*, but if the Empire turns against him, what is he then?"

"There will be no popular uprising," the vizier said, sneering. "That much should be obvious. Any attempt to rally support will be viewed, quite rightly, as a power grab enacted by corrupt senators clinging to old Republic ways or to radical Separatist ideologies. You saw the protests on Coruscant. Do you honestly believe that the pampered cosmopolitans of Chandrila outnumber the galaxy's tired and struggling? Outnumber the people grateful to the Emperor, who brought peace? Do you think that even *on Chandrila* your population would vote to reconcile with the Separatists, given their druthers?

"As for the corporations"—he went on before Mon could stop him—"they *are* the greater threat, and I commend you for winning over as many as you did. If they favor your cause as greatly as you believe, they could prove genuinely disruptive.

"Should it come to that, however, the Emperor will simply seize their assets, take control of their operations, and justify it—again, quite rightly—as a matter of galactic security. The clone army is more than up to the task. You may have heard that the corporations' capacity for battle droid production has fallen *precipitously* since the war's end."

"And what if the workers revolt?"

"The *workers* indeed. I see no reason for them to side with their employers in shutting down ten thousand worlds, to embrace chaos and servitude over the Emperor's offer of freedom and order. But for the sake of argument, suppose they are uncharacteristically loyal to corporate management. Suppose as well that private security and mercenaries flock to their cause, seeing a profitable opportunity. Do you truly think that they could stop the clone army? Let alone the volunteer force that is coming. The galaxy would suffer immensely in such a conflict, and it would be highly unpopular. But you and I both know the outcome would never really be in doubt."

There were questions she should've asked, challenges she should've offered, but all she heard herself say was "The volunteer force is still being designed."

The vizier half smiled. "You should join the Military Oversight Committee. Progress is rapid, and the pilot programs have had tremendous success."

The *pilot programs*, she'd been told, were limited in scope—a defensive force, local garrisons to create jobs for veterans and patriots, not a replacement for the clone army. For a thousand years, the Republic had stood without need for a military at all. Now the administration wanted ordinary citizens to offer themselves on the altar of war?

She was aware this was a distraction, thrown out by the vizier to redirect her. Nonetheless, it served its purpose. And before she found her next line of attack, the vizier spoke again, haughty as she'd ever seen him.

"Let me put the matter simply," he said. "You've offered up your threats, your portrait of *resistance* by the corporations, the nobility, the elite of the coddled Core Worlds. I think you're deluded, or at best speaking with unwarranted optimism—but I could be mistaken. So it comes to this: Would you *really* start a war, Mon Mothma? You, the outspoken pacifist? Knowing the cost would inevitably fall on the wretched, the exhausted creatures still limping from the Separatist conflict? Would you go to war against the Emperor? Because if not, there's no threat you can make that we cannot counter with overwhelming force."

She wanted to recoil at the vizier's perverse pleasure in the question. Instead, she met his gaze, looked into his soulless eyes, and asked, "Would *you* start a war? Knowing what would become of your Empire even if you won? Knowing history would call your master a tyrant and you his sycophant?"

Grand Vizier Mas Amedda laughed.

"I want to show you something," he said. "I think it will be instructive."

He turned back to the viewing window. By now the dark of space had been replaced by the mists of a planet's upper atmosphere. Mon watched beside the vizier as the yacht descended through cloud cover and into a gloomy sky the color of wine. She saw, in the distance, lights that were not stars moving slowly across the horizon—satellites, perhaps, or warships.

A rocky plain spotted with slate mesas and sapphire forests rose beneath them, all contained within a great bowl rimmed by mountains. The yacht continued descending, and she saw dimmer lights far below, glimmering amid geometric shadows like the bones of a city.

"You see it?" the vizier asked.

The yacht swept closer to the lights without passing directly above them, presenting a clear view for Mon and the vizier. Mon realized that the brightest lights were *not* glimmering—they were mounted floodlights, entirely steady but refracted by clouds of dust and smoke that occluded parts of the site. Deep within the clouds, she spotted dimmer lights, too: orange and red embers that must have been raging fires on the ground.

Shadows became steel. Mon's eyes focused on a gargantuan compound enclosed by half-finished walls the height of cliffs. The inner buildings—those that weren't in flames—were surrounded by fencing. Construction cranes and industrial load lifters stood beside square pits and ziggurats of scaffolding. The place might have resembled an incomplete military base—one of the largest Mon had ever seen, intended to house hundreds of thousands of troops—but she saw nothing resembling missile batteries, turbolasers, or shield generators. Nor were there hangars for vehicles or landing strips for incoming vessels. There was something, too, about the architecture itself that felt unlike what she'd seen of the Empire's latest designs—something starker than the black and brutal layouts the regime favored. She couldn't yet put a name to it.

A cloud of soot drifted across the face of the yacht, intersecting with the vessel's shielding and generating a crackling aurora. Mon turned away and back to the vizier. "What is this place?"

The vizier waited for the soot to burn off, then shifted his attention to Mon. "We're calling it Center One. It's a reeducation facility, built to house those whose views of the Empire lead to antisocial behavior. Here, a trained staff—an *organic* staff, no more than twelve percent droids—will work to correct the minds of their charges before releasing them back into the general population."

She understood the rhetoric. It echoed older terminology, from worlds beyond and before the Republic. Nonetheless, it took a moment for her mind to accept what she'd heard. "You're talking about political prisoners."

"Not the term I would use," the vizier said, "but if you please. The goal is rehabilitation."

She looked back to the viewport and saw it now, the thing she'd missed: the linearity of the place, the way a person on the ground could move from building to fenced-in field to building to entrance but only in that specific order, progressing through checkpoints and funnels. She saw a layout designed not for ease, accessibility, or spontaneity, but for uniformity and coercion. She couldn't help but imagine herself living out months and years in the cellblocks and cafeterias and classrooms and—how far would the horror go? Would there be interrogation suites? Surgical centers to change minds through brute force?

The vizier was still speaking. "The damage was inflicted by a chain of explosive devices. At this point, it's safer to let the fires burn out than to try to extinguish them, given the temperatures and the toxicity." He paused. "We believe the culprits are from the same Onderonian terror cell that attacked Coruscant, though it's better not to publicize it. The work crews estimate they can make up for lost time and have the facility ready within six months."

"Why are you telling me this?" Mon asked.

"Because I want you to understand the scope of our work," the vizier said. "This is Center One. Four others are under construction, and Center Six is in the design phase, shepherded by an ambitious young engineer from the University of Cato Neimoidia. If six reeducation facilities prove too few, we can triple the number in a year or prefabricate them for airdrop.

"None of this"—he grasped Mon's arm, squeezing tight enough to make her flinch—"is more than a minor effort in the eyes of the administration. The trillions of credits spent on this project are a pittance. The Emperor, the governors, the minds we've brought together have grand plans for the galaxy—not just for the next year, or the next five years, but for the next *century*. We are the architects of the universe our grandchildren will live in, and it will be one where there is no conflict, no dissent, and no *visionaries* who would undo the work of their betters. Today we will maintain order through military might, but in the future every child will learn a superior history, be raised in a superior family. And the concept of defiance will be as antiquated as the spear."

He released her arm, then, though he did not step away. His breath stank of mints and rotten meat.

"You ask me if we would start a war to maintain our grip on power," the vizier said. "This is my answer: We already did. While you were obsessed with the Separatist conflict, we were doing battle on another front, capturing the love of the people of this galaxy. The Emperor *won*.

Now we are securing our victory and reaping the spoils, while *you* seem to believe the fighting never began, let alone ended. I am here to correct your thinking."

Mon pressed the tip of her cane into the deck plating. She felt nauseated and off-balance. And as her mind sought to prove otherwise, her soul knew the vizier was right. She had misread the situation.

She could abandon every principle, rally her allies, blackmail the galaxy, and hold hostage the machinery that kept ten thousand worlds thriving. She'd acquired the power to do so. She could call the administration's bluff, and in response there would be blood and outrage and death—and she would probably lose and the galaxy would lose and the Emperor might be the most hated man in the universe, but he would retain his throne and he *would not care.*

She didn't understand.

She had misread the situation.

"The Emperor's concern is the century plan," the vizier said, and suddenly his voice was almost sympathetic. "Not with tomorrow. Tomorrow is safe. Tomorrow he leaves to people such as myself—and to you, if you wish it. You are free to go home and hold your news conference and call the passage of the Rebirth Act a triumph. You can pick fights with the governors and push back against the executive and earn the admiration of your peers who wish for a return of the Republic. The Emperor understands the value of opposition. You are a fine administrator, so, please, do administrate.

"But you will not attempt to interfere with things that *matter.* The century plan will move forward because there are actions the Emperor will *not* abide. You are a pragmatic woman, Mon Mothma, not an ideologue, and I believe you understand this."

She cast a glance to the compound below. She couldn't help herself.

"Tell me you understand," the vizier said.

"I understand," Mon answered.

"Good. I look forward to your return to the Senate, and seeing you on your best behavior."

He gestured with one hand, and the gesture must have been seen by a cam or a droid, because the yacht responded and rose rapidly away from the compound, back into the wine-dark sky. Mon watched Center 1 dissolve into shadows and light again and the embers of the fire disappear and the whole of the site retreat into the rocky plain within the bowl of the mountains.

Soon they were out of the atmosphere.

"There's one thing I'd like to know," Mon said.

The vizier bowed his head with the graciousness of a man who knew he'd won. "Speak."

"Does the Emperor believe any of it?" she asked. "All the talk about peace and order and reform—is it all just a way for him to dominate, or does he believe even a little?"

The vizier furrowed his brow, apparently thinking this through. After a while he smiled. "The remarkable thing," he said, "is that I never thought to ask."

///

A few days after returning home, Mon had dinner with Lud Marroi. Perrin was out with friends—she'd urged him to stop hovering, told him she was practically fully healed, and persuaded him to go out—and Mon had flown sixty levels to meet Lud at an out-of-the-way bistro specializing in Gordian Reach fusion. She hadn't mentioned it to Perrin. She didn't know whether Perrin had heard the rumors about her affair, and Perrin hadn't said anything. Once she'd arrived, Lud had spent twenty minutes fussing over her before she'd snapped and asked him to stop. "I'm fine," she said, and for a little while they ate in silence.

She'd felt guilty after, and they'd managed a strained conversation about the food and the Interior Leagues and, during an especially awkward stretch, the decor of their childhood homes. Finally, Lud reached across the table, hesitated, withdrew his hand, and said, "I'm sorry about the Rebirth Act. I know how much you put into it."

"It passed, didn't it?" Mon said, refilling their half-full wineglasses.

"Thanks to you," Lud agreed.

She hadn't checked the record to see how he'd voted. It had occurred to her to look, but she'd chosen not to.

"Thanks to Bail," she said, "and to my convenient martyrdom. That's a tip for you, Lud. If you ever need to drum up support for a bill, get yourself killed, or at least maimed. It does wonders for polling."

"That's not funny," he said. She didn't think so, either, but it had been a thing to say. She watched him shift uncomfortably in his seat, then he said, "I may not be worrying about polls much longer anyway."

"Meaning what?"

"Meaning"—he sipped his wine and looked dismayed by the taste—"I'm not planning to run for re-election. In six months, I'll be out, and may we all be better off for it."

Her tension and discomfort were washed away in a flood of anxiety—the dread that foretold an unexpected loss. "Why? I thought you had support, financing—"

"I could win," he said. "That's what my campaign manager tells me. That's not why I'm doing this. Everything's . . . You know I've always admired you? The way you believe in the greasy, noisy machinery of democracy. Even if the Emperor cheated at the game, knocked the board off the table in the end, you stayed true to an ideal."

"Lud. Tell me why you're not running."

He sighed. "Part of it is I feel like I've been shut out these past months. I've got plenty of friends in the administration, but I'm always third to hear anything. They loop me in as a courtesy, not because they care about my opinion. Part of it is the way the Senate is now—not many of the old faces left. And even I don't have a lot of patience for the hard-core imperialists. I appreciate what Palpatine's done, but the way they worship at his feet . . . It's not for me anymore." He paused, seeming to weigh something, then added, "The Imperial Security Bureau has been looking at me lately, poking around in my business. There's nothing to find, but it's one more reason to get out while I'm still a winner. Go off and be a respectable former statesman. Retire to a paradise planet and tune out the news altogether."

"I never thought you'd leave Troithe," she said. It was a foolish thing to say.

"Never thought I would, either. But maybe it's best to make a clean break."

"You make it sound very simple."

"It could be, though, couldn't it?" He sounded suddenly nervous, and he flinched as the remains of his meal—a steak of glittering algae—crawled toward the edge of his plate. "We've both given ourselves to our work over the years. But maybe the work doesn't *need* us. Maybe walking away would be . . . less disruptive than either of us would like to believe."

"Because no one would care once we're gone?"

"Frankly, yes. Who remembers any politician once they've retired?"

She told herself not to say the words and they came out anyway. "I'll notice if you go, Lud."

"All the more reason you should come, too. No one can say you—you, of all people—didn't give it everything you had. And after what just happened—" He cut himself off, shaking his head. "Forget I said that. Even without the attack, you've earned a rest, Mon. You've earned a life that's not about scrambling for the next vote and looking over your shoulder. You deserve people who care about you, people who aren't just allies and partners in a political project."

I deserve someone like you. You may as well have said it out loud. It was a violation of their oldest bargain, the thing they never talked about.

"So, what . . . should I run off with you to your paradise world?" she asked, and now she was doing it, too. There was a tremor in her voice. She reached for the wine bottle, ready to busy her hands, but their glasses were still full. "Teach history and government at a local university, maybe?"

"Or coach smashball. Or both. Tell me it's not time."

She smiled quaveringly at him and said nothing. They resumed their meal, neither of them doing more than picking at their food, and at the end of the night, he walked her outside and made sure there was a speeder waiting and she told him, "I can't. It's a fantasy."

I want to. But I can't.

CHAPTER 68
A CONFERENCE

The Palace of the High Games Masters of Phothrell resembled a burnt and broken cocktail glass, its umber walls curving skyward and ending abruptly in jagged crenellations. Mon had last seen the tower thirty years prior on a visit with her personal tutor, who had not, as she recalled, been enthusiastic about the trip. But Mon's parents had wagered that a tour of obscure ruins on an unpopulated planet would dissuade her from a career in history, that she'd become bored an hour after arriving. Instead, she'd spent days exploring the tower's theaters, imagining the holographic game pieces and the crowds, and asking her tutor a thousand questions he could not answer and had no interest in researching.

This time she'd chosen the palace because of what had happened at Eyo-Dajuritz. Not as a message but for herself—to reclaim something of what she'd once loved as she tossed aside so much else.

She traveled the road out of the fungal desert and entered through the Puzzle Gate, descending into the first theater. Daylight spilled through a hole in the ceiling half a kilometer above, illuminating the mosaic floor and the upside-down stairway. Bail Organa was already waiting, staring quizzically at the paint chips that were all that remained of a forgotten fresco.

He turned at the sound of her arrival. "You look well," he said. "No more cane."

"Not today," she agreed. "You're certain you weren't tracked?"

"I've learned not to be certain of anything. But I did all I was able and had a friend look the ship over."

"A friend. Not one of—"

"No. If there are survivors, I wouldn't try to contact them—not for this."

He might have been lying, but she thought he understood. This was not a matter for Jedi.

"What about our third?" she asked. "Any word?"

Bail shook his head. "If he received the message, he made no reply. I say give him a few hours and don't hope for too much."

"You're becoming a cynic."

"Aren't we all?" Bail asked, but there was no lightness in his tone. Mon had persuaded him to arrange the meeting, but he'd been stubbornly opposed then and he remained resentful now. Not toward *her*, she thought . . . yet there was rare depth to his bitterness. He did not want any of this.

It wasn't long before they heard another set of footsteps. Bail inclined his head toward a side passage, but Mon strode to the pool of daylight in the center of the room. They'd planned no passwords or secret knocks, and if they were ambushed by clones they had no escape plan. Mon figured she might as well look fate in the eye (and perhaps learn a lesson for any future covert councils).

The man who stepped into the playing theater looked not at all like the pictures Mon had seen. Images of Saw Gerrera from the war had shown a young man, grim-faced and with a touch of naïvete, as though the toughness were half performance. This Saw was older, the lines of his cheekbones carved deep, and he moved with the confidence of judges and chancellors, knowing the room was *his*—certain that when he entered a place, everything became part of his story. Whether he'd earned that confidence, Mon did not know, but she recognized its magnetic power.

Her eyes went to the rifle slung across Saw's chest. Its paint was scratched and the synthleather cracked, yet no speck of dirt sullied the metal. This, too, told her something about the man.

Saw's gaze went to Bail, who returned the stare. Then Saw looked at Mon. "You're the one Soujen almost killed?"

"Yes," Mon said.

"You wanted to meet me?" Saw asked.

"I did. I think the three of us have much to talk about."

Saw shrugged off a heavy jacket without removing his rifle. He tossed the jacket onto the floor and spread his arms in the universal gesture: *Well?*

"I was told," Mon said, "that your people were responsible for the explosions at Center One. I need to know if that's true before we go further."

"It is true," Saw said with a smirk.

"Did you know about the facility's purpose? Why choose it as a target?"

"I knew that sooner or later we'd need to go on the offensive. We've been running and hiding from clones long enough. But we needed a good story, and when I came upon certain information . . ." He shrugged. "A prison like that is for people like *us*. And if there are *more* people like us, they'll have a reason to join when they hear what we accomplished."

"You're recruiting, then—" Mon started, but Bail spoke over her.

"I saw reports about an attack on a construction site," Bail said. "The specifics were redacted. The administration implied the facility was a refueling station, but there were holos, images. They wanted us to know that the Onderonian terrorists are an ongoing threat." There was anger in his voice, though his tone was level. Mon wondered whether Saw noticed. "You made a promise to me, and you broke it."

"What promise did I make?" Saw asked.

"You told me *no one would die!*" Bail marched toward Saw until he was a finger's length from the man. "You took my codes, and you used them to murder people!"

"Clones," Saw said. "If I'd warned them, you really think they would have evacuated?"

Bail snarled and swung away from Saw.

Mon replayed the scene in her mind until she understood what had happened. It complicated things, but it didn't change the calculus of the situation. Bail must have known that, too, or he wouldn't have agreed to the meeting.

"I've broken my share of promises," Mon said. "Would you walk away from me, too?"

She said it not to persuade Bail but to endear herself to Saw.

Bail waved a hand, and Mon took it as her cue to move on. "I believe we all agree the regime is dangerous and deeply entrenched," she said. "Palpatine and his allies will not be removed by an act of the Senate or by an act of terror. If the solution was ever that simple, we're past that point now.

"It is also becoming clear that the worst excesses of his administration will not stop now that Palpatine has secured power. The death of the Jedi was a *beginning*. Now he plans mass arrests. He plans—"

"Who is this speech for?" Saw asked. "Is it for my benefit?"

Mon fell silent.

"I have my own speeches," Saw said. "They don't waste as much time, but they come to the same point: If you stand and watch, things get worse."

"There are other ways that *things get worse*," Bail said. The anger was gone, though the intensity remained. "I met your people, Saw. They're dedicated, proud, loyal to you and the man they believe you to be. But if you turn them into tools or weapons—"

"As *you* are tools of the Emperor!" Saw replied. "You debate in the Senate while people are dying. You have the habits of a people at peace, but there is no peace! You talked about treaties with the Separatists, but the Separatists never wanted a treaty. Now you seek to remove the Emperor's power through law, but the Emperor doesn't care about law—"

"We have *all* failed!" Mon's voice cracked. "Not one of us has done anything meaningful to stop the Emperor's rise—not my bill, not Bail's search for truth. And you, Saw Gerrera—you've won more enemies than friends. What happened to Eyo-Dajuritz—"

"We were not to blame for that."

Her voice fell. "It doesn't matter. The whole galaxy could hear about what you did to the prison camp, but they'll remember you for Eyo-Dajuritz."

"Where are you going with this, Mon?" Bail asked. "We wouldn't be here if we weren't ready to listen."

It was a gentle handoff. He was on her side. It didn't make the words any easier to say.

"People *want* this." Mon squared her shoulders. "Our trouble isn't that Palpatine is a dictator or that he has total control of the military. Our trouble is that, by and large—all exceptions aside—the citizens of our nation are willing to believe his lies, ignore his purges, and accept his rule in return for stability. They may not want *him,* but they don't want war. They want anything *but* war, and Palpatine has boxed us in so that war appears to be the only way out.

"So if we believe in democracy—if we believe the will and wisdom of the people is sacred and that they have a right to determine their destiny—how do we square that with what we're trying to accomplish? The Emperor is a threat to democracy. Opposing him is also antidemocratic. That comes with implications. A friend tried to tell me that once."

"If people understood—" Bail began, but Mon shook her head.

"They understand. They understand enough. If they hadn't been willing to trade the Jedi for stability, they wouldn't have accepted the Emperor's lies so easily."

"Democracy is a principle," Saw said, "and people don't fight for principles, no matter what they say. They fight for land, for resources, for their lives. Besides"—he grinned, corpse-like—"the Separatists were democratic. A democratic genocide isn't any more agreeable to its victims."

"I believe in my oath to democracy. Still, Saw has a point." Bail swept air aside. "Let people who want Palpatine have him, but I've no qualms about standing against the Empire to defend the targets of his administration."

"Then we need to answer *how*," Mon said. "All of us are willing to risk ourselves to stop what's coming, but so far all we've done is get in one another's way. If we don't have popular support then we need—" She drew a long breath, forcing herself to look from Bail to Saw. "We need to work together. Or at least stop working at cross-purposes."

Bail paced across the mosaic. "Work together to perfect our 'antidemocratic' strategy. Are you suggesting . . . what, a coup?"

Saw laughed. "She doesn't have it in her."

Mon wheeled on Saw. "Don't I? I *killed a man* just days ago because I thought it was expedient." She'd tried not to think about it, yet it was always just below the surface—the memory of the words, knowing that Soujen would never find joy or redemption or family because of her, knowing she had made the galaxy a darker place and she could never reclaim that speck of innocence. "I didn't order it done or watch from a distance. I might as well have strangled him, and I violated every principle I can imagine."

I would do it again. She couldn't say the words, but she trusted Saw would hear them.

"Now tell me," she said, "what I have the stomach for."

Saw's eyes were still laughing. "How do we work together?" he asked.

She felt Bail watching her, with . . . was it disappointment? Fear? But he said nothing, and the three of them began the experiment, dissecting their lives and their beliefs to find the heart of the problem.

///

Saw second-guessed them at every turn. He questioned their ideas around public support and their assumptions of what the Empire would tolerate. He scorned the notion that they shared the same goals. He thought he was in control, and Mon marveled at how he'd fallen into her trap. As long as he was arguing, he was *participating*. He was working with them without agreeing to work with them. And he knew he needed Mon and Bail, because his band had limits to what it could accomplish alone.

Bail was the most vocal and the most ideological. Mon gladly ceded that ground. She no longer trusted her instincts for pacifism, purity, and justice, and if Bail wanted to talk about what it meant to end the Empire on moral grounds, she was willing to listen. For Bail, bringing Palpatine and his cronies to account was key—he would accept no compromise in which the grand vizier assumed the throne, no grand bargain allowing the governors to maintain their positions. Any victory that required accepting the lies the Empire was built upon was no victory at all.

"We tried it the *clever* way," Bail said. "We tried hiding everything good and decent under a cloak of self-interest, and we failed because we never gave people a reason to do what was hardest, to fight for what really mattered."

"There may be times," Mon countered, "that deception is necessary. There may be situations where we can't avoid playing to others' self-interests."

"But it's not how we *win*," Bail said.

Mon had gathered them hoping to forge a plan, as she'd done with Bail and Padmé Amidala in the Delegation of 2,000 or with Doroon, Streamdrinker, and the others at Lud Marroi's estate. But as the three of them spoke, as hours passed and they squatted on the mosaic long after nightfall, they discussed less and less what they could do *together* and focused instead on what they were capable of individually. Saw talked about recruiting lost soldiers and those disgruntled with Imperial rule. "There will be more," he said. "Every day there will be more."

Mon imagined his guerrilla cell becoming an army.

"There is precedent," she said. "Social movements often succeed by combining militant tactics with nonviolent approaches."

"Is that what we are?" Saw gestured and sent shadows lapping at the walls. "A *social movement*?"

Bail looked somber. "Too early to say. What we are—a political or a social or a military cause—may depend on which of us see success. The others will fall in line or fade away."

It was, Mon thought, the most realistic thing any of them had said.

"If you had an army," she asked Saw, "what would you do with it?"

That started a new argument. Saw tried to laugh the question off. Then he said he would tell them nothing the security bureau could use against him. Bail accused Saw of having no strategy at all—of fumbling his way through the war and now doing the same with the Empire—and that seemed to unlock the floodgates. Saw spoke of modest plans and grand ambitions, telling them stories of how he had hit Separatist military installations, droid factories, and prison camps. He'd stolen equipment and credits and forged ties with smugglers and arms dealers, and he was prepared to do it all again.

But even Mon could see the flaw in his designs. Saw was clever, pragmatic, and more attuned to public opinion than she'd guessed. His experience rallying the people of Onderon, of building a reputation as a planetary hero instead of as a Republic-backed militant, would serve him well. Yet nothing he said suggested a vision beyond a single-sector conflict, and when Mon asked him questions about the scale of his operations, she came away unsatisfied. Bail asked him about the laws of war and what rules he would set for himself and his followers, and this only frustrated Saw. "Tell the Emperor to send only droids to fight, and I will destroy only droids," Saw said. "Until then, I guarantee nothing." The more they pressed him, the more he resisted, until he snapped: "I am not your hound! I will not be sicced on whatever targets you deem worthy!" And that was the end of that conversation.

Bail ushered them onward. "Whatever else happens, we will need more allies. People with the resources to take advantage of any opportunity that arises. People as committed to the cause as we are, willing to risk themselves without payment or hesitation."

"People who won't be eager to be discovered," Saw said.

Bail nodded. "It will take time and discretion and new methods of communication. I've given some of this thought already."

"You want to find the Jedi."

"If there are Jedi left to be found. But there may also be people in the military who still believe in the Republic, people unknown to Mon and myself. People in local government, too, where Palpatine's reach has never fully extended. People outside government, in academia or relief organizations . . . any of them could prove invaluable at the right moment."

Saw's voice echoed weirdly through the darkness. "Giving you control of the purse strings when it comes to our little conspiracy? If your friends have the resources, everyone else has to beg you for access?"

"Giving me veto power," Bail said dryly. "And a reason for you two to stay on my good side."

He went on to speak of Alderaan and its potential as a symbol of hope, a place where the ideals of the Republic could live on in the age of the Emperor. The Queen would have her own opinions, but Bail was confident she would embrace the general principle. He talked about welcoming refugees from worlds suffering under Imperial policies and sheltering thinkers who could write about hypothetical reforms. "If we're to convince people that the Empire must change, we need to show them a real alternative. They lost faith in Republic governance. We'll prove to them that Palpatine's vision is not the only way."

"It's a good idea," Mon said. "It's a virtuous idea. But you will draw attention. Your governor may tighten control over Alderaan, and more serious repercussions—"

"I know what the Emperor is capable of," Bail said. "And while I may be loud, I will not be bold. These recent weeks, I've shed all the protection I once had. He will be watching me now, and I must move so slowly that the Empire forgets I ever could have been a true threat—for our endeavor's sake, and for my family's sake."

Mon never had told him she'd given his name to the intelligence services. Maybe that was for the best. He understood the need for caution now, and that truth would only hurt him.

The three of them sat in silence awhile.

Eventually it became clear how little Mon had proposed herself, and Bail and Saw both asked what she intended to do. She hesitated. Her answer, when she offered it, sounded weak. She told them she would continue doing what she'd already done, that she would oppose the administration in the Senate and build coalitions to resist Palpatine. She would cleave to allies whom Bail mistrusted and Saw disdained.

"You may be right," she told them, "that the movement requires fire and a willingness to sacrifice. It may need an ideological center to hold together. But we can't win with only true believers. The coalition we built for the Rebirth Act is a model worth pursuing."

"You've learned nothing," Saw said.

Bail spoke more kindly. "Is this what you want to do, or is it the only thing you know *how* to do? You can't fight evil with compromise."

"Perhaps not," Mon said. "But you can't build anything lasting without it."

She didn't try to convince them. She didn't need to. Saw could fight his unwinnable battles and become a hero and a martyr, inspiring followers who'd throw themselves against the Emperor's army of death. Bail could keep the flame of purity alive, to remind them all—and remind the galaxy—of what another way could look like. And Mon could levy a tax on arms production here, organize the megacorporations to oust a governor there. She would compromise and walk away tainted, and she would change lives.

She *would* change lives—maybe not many, maybe in the least efficient way imaginable. But whether or not she believed in the art of politics anymore, it was still the art she loved.

She said nothing about her encounter with the grand vizier. She did not say that she'd promised never to oppose the Emperor's century plan. They would only have doubted her resolve.

❙❙❙

They came to no conclusions. They made no formal alliance. But by the end, they had an understanding of the scale and depth of the threat they faced—its malignant heart and its trillions of willing servants. They had an understanding of the impossibility of thwarting the Imperial project in a month or a year, and an appreciation of the fact that none of them could succeed alone. And if they had no binding plan, no promise of mutual aid, they at least recognized the possibility of something more.

Toward the end, Saw asked Mon, "How shall I contact you? When I need to know the schedule of an imperialist senator or the security codes to a military base?"

"You will not contact me," Mon said. "Not ever. Not unless the galaxy is at stake."

Saw nodded and, to her surprise, looked satisfied.

Saw was the first to leave the Palace of the High Games Masters. Mon stayed with Bail, vaguely intending to use the time to discuss anything best kept between themselves. But neither she nor Bail spoke much. They'd exhausted themselves and exhausted their thoughts of revolution and assassination and the changing of an era. When Mon heard a vessel streak through the atmosphere, she looked to Bail and said softly, "You're a good man. I do admire you for that."

"You shouldn't," he told her, and he clasped her hand before climbing the stairwell.

She waited for Bail, too, to leave the planet. She tried to keep everything that had happened in her memory. She'd taken no notes, of course, made no recordings, and already the conference was taking on the qualities of a dream. In a week she'd be so wrapped up in the affairs of the moment that it might seem as if the meeting had never happened. In a month, she might be fighting against Bail on the Senate floor or signing an anti-terrorism bill to better secure Onderon. She wanted to lock everything the others had said in her mind, somewhere dark and deep where nothing could escape. She wondered what she would retain.

Before she left the palace, she took time to walk through its theaters, studying the games, the tiles, and the etchings abandoned to history. She could not have said why.

CHAPTER 69
HOME

Bail was home. Eastwind Manor was only half-familiar—a country-side retreat he'd summered in as a child—but the style of the columns and the flowering scrollwork were of Alderaan's neo-classical period. The flagstones were carved from Alderaanian ranges, and the floor's pale surface hinted at rose and lilac. The forest scent of pines and blackwoods drifted in on breezes that rustled the balcony curtains.

He couldn't remember the last time he'd been to the manor. Breha often struggled to leave the Royal Palace. Visits to Coruscant were one thing, carrying their own expectations, but on her own planet, she could rarely escape the gravity of her cabinet and her courtiers—and Bail ordinarily stayed with Breha. Yet anywhere on Alderaan was *home,* and Bail needed serenity after the events of the past month. Breha had given him her blessing and promised to join him that night, assuming no new crisis arose.

He stepped into Eastwind Manor's upper gardens, where the soil beds bore jackflowers and rysanthines that stretched skyward like rock-ets, or—and as he thought of it, he preferred this second image—like ladders into the clouds, as in a fable. He passed holograms and statues arrayed in tribute to House Prestor, the house of his ancestors, and arrived at the balustrade overlooking the lake.

He leaned against the stone parapet, and as he did he recalled another balcony, one overlooking the infinite city of Coruscant. He saw himself at a table with friends, with Senator Padmé Amidala and the Jedi Master Obi-Wan Kenobi.

Padmé looked gaunt in his memory, her doom already evident in her slender, frail form. That portent hadn't existed in reality, but it was nonetheless what he saw now. Poor Padmé, who had wielded Bail's ideological fire and Mon's mastery of politics. Padmé, barely more than a child herself, who'd given birth to Leia—the child who, day by day, was redefining Bail's existence. Padmé, who had been a monarch in her youth and, once she had matured, relinquished that power to participate in the subtler processes of democratic governance. If Leia inherited even half her virtues, Bail would be proud.

Obi-Wan, like Padmé, appeared grave in Bail's memory. The war had chiseled at his spirit and turned a thoughtful and joyous young knight into a casualty—*reducing* him, as war reduced everyone into heroes and villains.

For all its vividness, the memory carried with it little specificity. Bail couldn't recall when exactly the three of them had met, or what they'd discussed. The loss hurt in his chest, because it meant the day really was gone forever. Padmé was dead, Obi-Wan gone, and Bail had failed to preserve the moment. Like so much else, the memories of his friends were slipping away, and they would never be reclaimed.

But there was *something more* than the image itself: There had been an instant in the conversation when Bail had felt, painfully strongly, that the three of them had been equals—equally devoted to their cause, equally able to give of themselves. Obi-Wan's mystical connection to the universe, his Jedi wisdom, had balanced Padmé's grounded idealism and Bail's years of experience. They'd confronted the troubles of the galaxy together, and what should have been frightening—the understanding that there was no one out there who knew more, who was more capable, who might save them—had in fact been comforting.

None of them had possessed answers, yet they were proud seekers together.

Bail had craved that certainty with Mon and Saw. It was a luxury he did not expect to reclaim.

Another memory: Bail was back in Eastwind Manor, but now he was a child, peering through the crack of a door at Thraymus Argent, the Jedi Knight he'd known so briefly. Thraymus was squatting on the ground, legs folded and eyes closed, while a censer in front of him unlidded itself. A pouch of herbs and oils floated over, delicately shaking its contents into the basin before the censer ignited. Thraymus turned his head toward the door and, without ever opening his eyes, wiggled his brow and smiled mischievously.

Bail had loved Thraymus as only a child loves. In later years, he'd sifted through the family records to learn why a Jedi had stayed with House Prestor, and he'd learned about the feuds, the assassination attempts, and the Jedi's investigation. But as a child? It felt as if he'd been given a gift. It felt as if he'd found the perfect friend, the perfect model for what he wanted to be: calm and centered; dashing, strong, and virtuous; mysterious and possessed of secret truths the galaxy could never fully appreciate.

Bail had understood even then that he couldn't hope to become a Jedi. But over the years, he'd endeavored to reflect their finest attributes, as a moon reflects sunlight.

The memories passed. He walked on through the garden and found, among the statues, the abstract metal rendering his great-uncle had commissioned upon Thraymus's departure. Beneath it a plaque read, Argent Dawn.

Bail liked the sculpture, with its odd blocks and silver spokes. He liked what it represented and liked showing it to visitors. Looking at it now, however, he imagined the sector governor coming to Eastwind Manor and asking, *What about this one?* He imagined children, friends of Leia's, playing in the garden and becoming curious.

Bail loved the Jedi. If he was haunted by them, it was because he cried out to their ghosts, because he strived to emulate their clarity and endurance—their faith that one brave soul, guided by the Force, could set the galaxy right. It was the wish of a child, carried with him since childhood, and it would shackle him forever if he didn't act.

He heard gurgling from the comlink at his belt—the baby monitor, piping in Leia's soft sounds and the cooing of her nurse droid.

Breha might be home soon. She needed Bail, and Leia needed Bail, and the ghosts would linger forever if he allowed it. The ghosts he'd given himself over to, and nearly died for. The ghosts he'd feared would come for Leia—but she was his daughter, not theirs.

"Forgive me, my friends," he said, running a finger down one of the statue's spokes. Each word tasted like dust. "Let her define her own legacy. Neither of us can carry yours."

Jedi might not have attachments, but *he* did. He hoped those attachments would offer strength enough.

Tomorrow he'd order the statue warehoused. Tomorrow he'd begin forgetting the Jedi and attempt to unbury the parts of himself he'd lost in his grief—the forgotten joys, the hope and kindness that Breha had adored. Tonight, if the ghosts were with him, he prayed that they would look upon his daughter and love her without expectation.

He left the balcony and made his way to Leia, who awaited him.

CHAPTER 70
SHANTYTOWN

The *Dalgo* filled the shantytown square, dwarfing the squat tents and the repurposed cargo containers. Karama had asked whether they should land at a distance, but Saw had insisted they go directly to the settlement. Anything else would've wasted time and put the ship at risk. Karama wondered if Saw just wanted to make an entrance.

They started moving out supplies as soon as the ramp was down, and though the locals were mistrustful, they didn't turn away when Saw explained that the *Dalgo* was on a relief mission. Karama had never met an Alvadorjian other than Soujen, and she felt at once curious and ashamed seeing this clan, the Houramis clan, with Soujen's features and Soujen's plating and Soujen's eyespots. Part of her wanted them to act like Soujen, too, to mirror his gestures and way of speaking.

They did not. Soujen was dead. These people were no more like him than Saw was like her. Yet she hoped Soujen would've seen the job as a tribute, the best they could offer under the circumstances.

She still wasn't sure why Saw had agreed when she'd proposed the operation. The guerrillas were shorthanded, and the supplies they were giving away—ration packs, power converters, third-tier medkits—were more than they could easily replace. Some of the supplies had come from the cache on Eyo-Dajuritz, while the rest they'd purchased or stolen along the way. As she looked around, it was clear to Karama that the Houramis clan would benefit. The Alvadorjians had reportedly been driven out of the nearest spaceport city during a planetwide drought, and they'd brought little but their shelters and their instruments.

"Should we ask them?" Karama murmured to Saw as they pulled hoversleds out of the ship.

"Ask them what?" he said.

"About the Nahasta clan. Where to find them, what they'd want done—"

"Soujen's name was reported by every news feed in the galaxy," Saw said. "There's nothing we know that his clan does not. If we found them, we'd bring them no insight."

This was almost certainly true. Karama felt discomfited by it nonetheless.

"You didn't like him, did you?" she asked.

"He was utterly dedicated to his cause." Saw spoke as if proud, as if Soujen's dedication were his own. "He had no illusions as to what he might accomplish, and he didn't hesitate to pay the price. His only dilemmas were dilemmas of strategy, and that I admired. He was useful to our movement."

"But you didn't like him," she repeated.

Saw shook his head and grunted, adjusting the sled controls. "He was a Separatist. He chose his side, and I chose mine."

"And these people?" she asked. "The Alvadorjians were Separatists, too."

"Only five of the seven clans," Saw said. "The others maintained neutrality."

Karama frowned at him, uncertain what to say.

As the Alvadorjians gathered around the sleds and young boys and old men grasped at the packages (first hesitant, then eager), Saw strode into the crowd, raising his voice as he said, "Good clanspeople of Houramis—will you listen to my story?"

He told them he was Saw Gerrera of Onderon, a proud world that had become embroiled in the war when the Separatists had overthrown its king. Karama recognized his recruiting speech, and she saw the Alvadorjians watching him as the desperate always watched Saw, and she knew why Saw had agreed to come to the shantytown.

She wondered whether she had betrayed Soujen. She wondered whether somewhere along the line, all soldiers lost their souls, and how long she would cling to hers.

CHAPTER 71
FUGITIVES

Chemish had waited in the safe house without knowing what they'd waited for. They'd checked the news feeds every hour, looking for their name or face and hoping to determine whether Laevido had ruined their life—whether he'd told his contacts that Chemish had aided Senator Mothma and, if he had, whether the security bureau or Imperial Intelligence had uncovered Chemish's real identity and decided they were a traitor.

They watched a lot of speeches, a lot of talk from Bail Organa and others about Mothma and the Imperial Rebirth Act. Chemish didn't follow the details, but it certainly didn't seem like the Empire was going to fall apart, which was good. Laevido had been wrong on that point and presumably others. Chemish wondered for the first time whether Zhuna had seen something real in Mothma that Chemish had missed. Maybe, maybe not. But either way, Chemish decided to do some reading on the topic when they got the chance, study a political science text or two between Anzellan mystery novels.

There was no mention of Chemish on the feeds. As the days went by and Chemish ate through their supplies and listened longingly to the noises of the street—the cries of vendors, the snap of wet blankets on clotheslines, the hum of heavy vehicles on garbage day—they began to wonder whether answers would ever reach them in the safe house. Maybe, Chemish grudgingly reasoned, they needed to exit into the world and seek enlightenment there. It was a world without Zhuna, Homish, or Haki—a world without evident purpose—but it was the only one Chemish knew.

So Chemish decided to ease back into existence. They walked around the block late one evening, half expecting to be ambushed. They bought cheese blossoms from a street cart. And when they returned to the safe house, they found Haki waiting at the kitchen table. She was scratched and limping, she seemed unable to move one arm, and overall she gave Chemish the impression of a lost pet that had finally found its way home. She greeted Chemish with strained cheer and peppered Chemish with questions and answered none. They sat together and ate Cook'em Cakes until Haki finally seemed satisfied by Chemish's story.

"I couldn't find your brother," Haki said after a silence. It was late at night now, and they could hear the flitterbats' mating calls. "I am truly sorry."

"It's all right," Chemish said. "I knew he was dead."

"Could've told me. Would've saved a lot of trouble." Haki rose from the table, struggling to push her chair back with only one arm, and went to the sink to fill a cup of water. When she returned, she said, "Now we're both fugitives, like it or not."

Chemish tilted their head curiously and waited.

"You made some terrible choices," Haki said.

"Seems that way."

"The Empire tried to kill me," Haki said.

The statement lingered. Chemish didn't know how to respond.

Haki sipped her water. "Had me dead to rights, too," she muttered into the cup. She didn't seem to be talking to Chemish. "Let that be another lesson: Sometimes a moment is all the distraction you need. Tell a lie, any lie, and make them listen so you can run. Run where they can't follow.

"Maybe—" Haki kept going and swiveled to face the window. Her shoulders slumped, and Chemish recognized the exhaustion in her voice. "Maybe I'd have done the same in your position, looking into the 4040s and that rot. I don't know. I don't know much of anything."

Chemish had never seen Haki uncertain before.

"What happened to you?" Chemish asked.

"I got old," Haki said. She lifted her limp arm with her good one and rested it on the table, still not looking Chemish's way. "That's the real problem. I'm smart, but I'm slow. And I got sloppy.

"And you—you're quick, but your generation hasn't seen what mine has, seen the price of *getting involved,* seen what dark times really look like. I'm old enough to know better but too old to suffer the consequences.

"I really hoped you'd be well, Chemish. I only came to say goodbye."

Haki seemed to shrink into her chair as she closed her eyes.

"Sorry my treason's a disappointment," Chemish said. They tried to sound sardonic, but it came out self-pitying.

"Saving a senator's not treason," Haki muttered. "Poor judgment under the circumstances, but not *treason*."

"I'll be all right."

"Oh, will you?" Haki's eyes flashed open. "I should pretend I'm not responsible for your plight? You've got real decisions to make, real troubles, and I'd like to set them right, but—I'm old." She laughed, and it went on until she drank her water and looked back to Chemish and seemed focused and alert again.

"I can try to figure out whether you're really a fugitive, see if I've got any back doors into Intelligence that haven't been nailed shut," Haki said. "Always a chance you're in the clear and we can get you back to your family. But then the people who tried to kill me might come looking for my sources, and that could cause trouble of its own. Even if you sell me out, I don't imagine they'll trust you for a while—though that'd be your best shot at building a career."

"I'm not going to sell you out."

"Well, don't write it off like that. There's still good work to be done with Imperial Intelligence, if everything lines up—for you, not me." She shrugged. "Then there's the worst case, where we go on the run together."

Chemish spent a while trying to imagine this. Where would they go? How would they survive? What would they do? Haki and their brother had saved them from a life of odd jobs and family dinners—but both seemed precious to Chemish now.

"I've never been off Coruscant," Chemish said.

"Any interest?

"Some. Maybe."

Haki nodded.

"We both tried to do right by our Empire," she said after a while. "We both screwed it up, and here we are."

"Here we are," Chemish agreed.

Haki pushed the packet of sweets to Chemish's side of the table. "So, given the trouble we're both in . . . maybe the best thing I can do is finish up your training, make a clever spy out of you before anything else."

Chemish frowned. The notion was tempting—the idea of having purpose and structure again, if only for a while.

"What's the catch?" they asked.

"You'll have to figure out what to *do* with the skills. I'm retiring, and we're both short a sponsor." Haki winked. "So pick a mystery to unravel, pick a question, and let's see if we can find the answer. Once you know how to find your way around, we can worry about how to earn a living."

Homish had told Chemish, "You have the mind of a philosopher." And the questions that came to Chemish seemed proof enough of this—questions about purpose, about family, about why it felt wrong not to help their aunt Clejo fix the neighbor's airspeeder and why it felt equally wrong to miss Fowlitz's next show with his band. What had happened to Haki seemed less important than these questions that spycraft could not answer.

Still, they got Chemish thinking about the Duros Blocks and the 4040s. And if the next set of questions that came to mind—about the terrorist attack, about Mon Mothma's goals, about Laevido's plans— weren't as close to Chemish's heart, they *did* stimulate Chemish's intellect. And gradually, Chemish realized that one question remained unanswered, a question they'd asked long ago: *Why had Zhuna died?*

That was a philosophical question but also a practical one. "I want to know," Chemish said, "what connection the 4040s have to Imperial Intelligence. If that's all right?"

Haki grunted. "I apprenticed you because you struck me as cautious, sensible. You had to wait till now to show me your true face?"

"I picked up bad habits while you were gone," Chemish said. "Stick around this time."

Haki took the last cake from the packet, lifted it to her lips, and murmured a prayer for peace and patience as Chemish smiled.

CHAPTER 72
INTIMACY

She kissed him as he slept, knowing he wouldn't wake. Or if he did wake, Mon supposed, he would pretend he hadn't and lie still until she left the bed. Perrin wouldn't ask questions she didn't want to answer, and that, in its way, was what held their relationship together.

She slipped out from under the covers, feeling their thousand-credit caress on her bare skin. She couldn't explain to herself what had driven her to intimacy with her husband that night. She couldn't remember the last time *that* had happened. His watchfulness in the medcenter, her rejection of Lud, her fear for her life, and her absolute vulnerability to the galaxy had probably all played a part.

Stop it. Stop overthinking it. Let it be.

Let all of it be.

The apartment was still unfamiliar, and she struggled to maneuver through the bedroom in the dark. She kicked over Perrin's boots, flinched, laughed, and managed at last to reach the bathroom. After she washed up, she splashed water onto her face and crawled up onto the windowsill beside the tub, looking into the Coruscant night and all the buildings she failed to recognize. She wasn't even sure what direction to look in to find the Senate.

Let all of it be.

There would be no security bureau agents watching through the spy-proof windows. No one looking to break in, either—if she barely knew where she lived, surely her stalkers hadn't found her yet. She should have found this comforting, but it only intensified her loneliness. Perrin loved her, in his way, but she hadn't told him about the vizier or about Bail and Saw Gerrera. She could cling to her husband awhile, but he didn't live in her world, and he would never know all her secrets. The things she'd done and the things done to her blurred together and became a weight in her body like the shrapnel in her heart.

Let all of it be. Please.

She couldn't stop the thoughts. In the morning, her anxiety medication might help, but for now her stressors stabbed her brain. She thought about Lud and what he'd said about her unwavering dedication to democracy, and she anguished over how much of a hypocrite she'd become. She craved the certainty, the *clarity* of knowing that whatever she did, whatever mistakes she made, the foundations of the Republic were strong beneath her. She missed knowing that decades and centuries into the future, her decisions would be judged by scholars who saw the good times, saw the bad, and weighed them with the understanding that it had all come out okay in the end.

It was all right for her to fail if it would be okay in the end.

What future could she believe in now? What certainty was there that anything would get *better*?

Maybe it hadn't ever been true that the Republic was *good*. Maybe the flaws in the foundation had always been present, and the systems of democracy had never guaranteed justice. But she had *believed*, and belief had given her hope, and now . . .

Now there was only darkness and uncertainty. Now things might not ever be right again, and no one would even tell her if her actions mattered—whether fighting back was noble or foolish, whether everyone would be better off if she really did take up teaching somewhere and helped people in small ways rather than grand ones.

It was terrifying.

It was what she had to live with.

Maybe accepting the truth was the start.

Her fear was her only source of reassurance. Her fear told her she hadn't yet become numb to atrocity and injustice. So she wrapped her fear around her, clung to it like hope, and watched the city in the night.

And she told herself that in the morning, when the sun rose and it came time to work, she would let it all go—her fears, her dreams, and her love for the Republic she'd believed in. She would leave it behind, and the galaxy would be different, and she would remain unbowed, unyielding, indomitable, a creature of politics and pacifism who had murdered a man and kept secrets from the people she'd sworn to serve. She would remain a hypocrite, and she would remain committed to her cause, no matter the risk to her body and soul.

In the morning, she would remain Senator Mon Mothma of Chandrila. That would have to suffice to save them all, for it was all she had to give.

ACKNOWLEDGMENTS

Where to begin? Let's start with Tom Hoeler and Gabriella Muñoz at Random House Worlds, whose unflagging patience and thoughtful feedback allowed this book to take flight (despite some problems in the blueprint and on the factory line). I didn't make this one easy on you, and I'm extraordinarily grateful for all the assistance. Truly, thank you for all of it—including approaching me in the first place.

Everyone over on the Lucasfilm team likewise deserves praise for providing insightful notes, cogent guidance, and quite a lot of rope. You put enormous trust in me, and I can only hope that decision still seems wise.

For those clients who put up with my divided attention—you know who you are, and I can't sufficiently express my appreciation. Friends, too, have put up with long periods of radio silence broken up by occasional bellyaching. Most of you are used to it, but that doesn't mean you're not owed acknowledgment.

Given this novel's subject matter, I could cite a nearly endless list of journalists, historians, and political memoirists whose work provided fodder and food for thought. Rather than picking only a few, I'll simply note that concocting political fiction is surely easier than studying political fact. Your work is invaluable to the functioning of any democracy, whether real or in galaxies far, far away.

Last but certainly not least: thanks to Rebecca Roanhorse and Fran Wilde, whose involvement with this project is a wonder that can only make me look good by association. Excuse the mess and have fun with the toys. I'm looking forward to what comes next.

ABOUT THE AUTHOR

ALEXANDER FREED is the author of the *Star Wars: Alphabet Squadron* trilogy, *Star Wars: Battlefront: Twilight Company*, and the novelization of *Rogue One: A Star Wars Story* and has written many short stories, comic books, and video games. Born near Philadelphia, Pennsylvania, he endeavors to bring the city's dour charm with him to his current home of Austin, Texas.

ABOUT THE TYPE

This book was set in Minion, a 1990 Adobe Originals typeface by Robert Slimbach (b. 1956). Minion is inspired by classical, old-style typefaces of the late Renaissance, a period of elegant, beautiful, and highly readable type designs. Created primarily for text setting, Minion combines the aesthetic and functional qualities that make text type highly readable with the versatility of digital technology.

A long time ago in a galaxy far, far away. . . .

STAR WARS

Join up! Subscribe to our newsletter
at ReadStarWars.com or find us on social.

𝕏 @StarWarsByRHW

⬜ @StarWarsByRHW

f StarWarsByRHW